Praise for *Just As I Am*

"In *Just As I Am*, Harris—a truly gifted writer—has taken on a Herculean task. Aside from dealing with homosexuality and homophobia, he also tries to tackle a long list of complex problems: racism based on skin color among blacks; the church's reaction to gays; conservative Southern values vs. modern urban life. *Just As I Am* is a powerful and poignant piece, like a passionate letter from a close friend who has seen the best and worst this world has to offer."

—Tallahassee Democrat

"*Just As I Am* is a potpourri of political complexities related to sex: sexual confusion, bi-straight relationships, interracial relationships, interfaith marriages, etc. Harris has much to say about bisexual eroticism, and his honesty and apparent lack of any political agenda serve the novel well."

—Lambda Book Report

"*Just As I Am* answers the essential question all black gay men must eventually ask themselves: how can I be black and homosexual and remain a part of my family and community? Harris has given us a book on survial and a glimpse at the wonderful possibilities that await us when we decide to love ourselves without compromise. This book is about courage and the necessary journey to examine and reexamine our lives. Every day."

—Southern Voice

"This eagerly awaited follow-up to Harris's first novel, *Invisible Life*, is a stirring plea to accept people as they are."

—shade magazine

"Harris's characters and their milieu are tellingly unexplored in much of contemporary fiction. His books therefore do double duty as mind-opening and heartwarming."

—Genre

"Harris's work exemplifies a command of the language and a skill at describing physical settings and mental states that elevate storytelling into the realm of literature."

—Austin American Statesman

"*Just As I Am* is a worthy sequel and a fascinating read in its own right. Together, *Invisible Life* and *Just As I Am* form a major contribution to both African American and gay literature."

—The Gazette (Tampa, Florida)

"*Just As I Am* is a romantic, old-school fairy tale. Harris's triumph is that he allows the audience to grow, struggle, and learn with his hero and she-ro. Both Raymond and Nicole find the men of their dreams because they refuse to let anybody bullshit them into believing that they don't deserve love and respect. When honesty rises and converges with love, how can there be anything but perfection?"

—SBC

"Harris confronts several important issues head-on in this novel of a black American's coming out. . . . Superb character development and insight make this a powerful sequel to *Invisible Life*."

—Library Journal

Just
As I
Am

Also by E. Lynn Harris

INVISIBLE LIFE

Just As I Am

a novel by

E. Lynn Harris

Anchor Books ⚓ Doubleday
New York London Toronto Sydney Auckland

AN ANCHOR BOOK
PUBLISHED BY DOUBLEDAY
a division of Bantam Doubleday Dell Publishing Group, Inc.
1540 Broadway, New York, New York 10036

ANCHOR BOOKS, DOUBLEDAY, and the portrayal of an anchor are trademarks of
Doubleday, a division of Bantam Doubleday Dell Publishing Group, Inc.

Just As I Am was originally published in hardcover by Doubleday, a division of
Bantam Doubleday Dell Publishing Group, Inc., in 1994. The Anchor Books
edition published by arrangement with Doubleday.

Book design by Terry Karydes

ISBN 0-7394-0219-0
Copyright © 1994 by E. Lynn Harris

For

Jules and those who fight the battle against AIDS

each and every day

and

The Huntleys

Tracey, David, and Calhoun

for a friendship supreme

Acknowledgments

*F*irst and foremost I thank my savior Jesus Christ for His blessings in my life daily. I am blessed to have the most wonderful group of family and friends, especially my mother Etta Harris and my aunt Jessie Phillips, who always give me their unconditional love. Much love and thanks to Tina and Jonee Ansa for their love and friendship, and for teaching me the true meaning of being an artist.

Special thanks to Timothy Douglas and Ellis Smith for providing me with wonderful friendships and a home away from home. Steve B., Jerry Jackson, Ray and Darice Ellis for friendship and financial support. My sweet inspirations and sheroes, Valerie Boyd, Loretha Jones, Vanessa Gilmore, Lencola Sullivan, Linda Chatman, and Regina Brown. My friends and heroes, Carney Carroll, Keith Thomas, Troy Donato, and Carlton Brown. I must thank Sallye Leventhal for coming out of retirement to edit this book and helping me to become a much better writer. My test readers, Tracey Nash-Huntley, Kelvin Pillow, and Cindy Barnes for their time and valuable input. Thanks to Bill Britton for great lines. My agent John Hawkins for just being there to listen to me bitch and moan, and Warren Frazier for putting up with my calls. I am also grateful to Martha Levin, my friend and mentor, for her belief in my talents and welcoming me with open arms into the Doubleday family. Shout outs and thanks to her able assistants Deborah Ackerman and Delia Kurland for their help and understanding. Deborah, I will miss you much. Good luck with school.

Finally I must thank all of you who buy my books and have taken the time to write and share your thoughts with me. It means so much to me and it's the reason that I get up every day and think what can I write today?

Just

As I

Am

There are always
two sides to
every story . . .

Raymond Jr.

I imagine the world was created beneath a canopy of silence. Perfect silence. While in my own personal silence I would create the world I dreamed of. A world full of love and absent of life's harsh realities. A world where all dreams would come true. A place called Perfect. But I've come to realize that some dreams you have to give up. I live in a world that promises to protect me but will not catch me when I fall. In this life I have fallen many times. From these falls I have learned many lessons. Lessons involving lust, loss, love, and life. Lessons that hit as hard as an unannounced summer thunderstorm, sudden and sometimes destructive.

One of my life's unexpected lessons occurred during my senior year in college. It was on the first Friday in October that my brain released a secret it had struggled to protect throughout my adolescence. I learned on that day that my sexual orientation was not a belief or choice, but a fact of my birth. And just like the color of my skin and eyes, these things could not be changed, at least not permanently.

My name is Raymond Winston Tyler, Jr., and I am a thirty-two-soon-to-be-thirty-three-year-old, second-generation attorney. The son of attorney Raymond Winston Tyler and Marlee Allen Tyler, an elementary school teacher, and big brother to fourteen-year-old Kirby. I had a happy childhood, growing up deeply ensconced in the black middle class. A child of the integrated New South, born and raised in Birmingham, Alabama, a city that in the past was known more for church bombing than being the bedrock of college football.

I returned home after law school and several years of successful practice in a large New York firm. About a year ago I moved two hours south to Atlanta, after a two-year stint of running my pops's law firm while he followed his lifelong dream and became a member of the Alabama State Senate.

Atlanta struck me as a vibrant city. A cross between country and cosmopolitan, a city where popular eateries still took personal checks, that is with a valid driver's license. A city consumed with sports and the dream of becoming the Motown of the nineties. Atlanta was a city on the move and even though it didn't have the flash and energy of New York City, it was more conducive to my life than Birmingham. Now don't get me wrong, I love my family and my birthplace, but I knew it was time to move on and continue my search for Perfect.

I was living in a trendy Buckhead condo and working for Battle, Carroll & Myers, a black, female-owned law firm specializing in entertainment and sports law. I had originally moved to Atlanta with the understanding that I would go to work for the city government, but a few days before I was to start, I received word that a hiring freeze had been put into effect. I later found out from a friend of my father that the reason for the freeze was because someone in the mayor's office wanted the position promised to me to go to an openly gay, black attorney. Now wasn't that just the shit. My Columbia Law School education and major New York firm experience didn't amount to anything. Just my sexual orientation and then only if I was willing to make it public, which I wasn't. So with the help of my good friend Jared Stovall, I went to work for Battle, Carroll & Myers. My position created an ironic dilemma. I was hired in part because of my love and knowledge of college sports. The firm was actively seeking college athletes about to turn professional and it was my job to convince these young men, mostly black and from black colleges, that the firm would be looking out for their best interests. I had just entered a period in my life when I was practicing celibacy and trying very hard to put the male body out of my mind, but now I was constantly in steamy locker rooms with some of the most beautiful bodies in the world.

Our firm also represented a number of rappers and singers, but Gilliam Battle, the founder and only remaining partner, handled the majority of them along with the recording executives. Though an extremely smart woman, Gilliam didn't know jack about sports, other than the fact that pro athletes made a great deal of money and didn't have the slightest idea of what to do with it. Gilliam not only assembled a top team of attorneys but also a staff of investment counselors, speech coaches, doctors, and whatever it took to make sure our clients represented us as well as we represented them.

My social life in Atlanta was in a lot of respects similar to life in Birmingham, back in the closet. Atlanta did have a visible gay community but it was visibly white. I wasn't forced into the closet, it was just a choice I'd made out of respect for my family, especially my pops. My parents knew about and tried to accept my sexuality, but the fact that they knew didn't mean they wanted to discuss it around the dinner table or with my little brother. So like my parents, I too decided to ignore my sexuality and went back to my old straight act the minute I left New York. Talk about your safe sex. Besides, men were basically dogs—couldn't tell the truth if their life depended on it. And now your life does depend on it. Trust me I know. In my past I too have been guilty of not being totally truthful, either with men or women. But men never expect honesty. Women, on the other hand, say that they want the truth, but then they act like they don't hear you when you try to tell it like it is. Sometimes in the heat of passion men are not the only ones who let their sex do the thinking.

Currently there is not a female in my life besides my mother and Gilliam, but there was a man, a good man. I'd met Jared Taylor Stovall in Birmingham when he'd come to run my pops's political campaign. Jared was a political consultant who had been highly recommended when Pops's victory was in doubt. Jared became a member of our family, practically moving into my parents' home during the race. Jared actually convinced me to move to Atlanta by offering me a place to stay and remarking with a devilish smile, "I want my niggah around me all the time."

Jared was quite handsome in a rugged sort of way. His looks inspired confidence—tall and strapping, six foot three and two hundred and ten pounds of slightly bowlegged, biscuit-brown masculinity. Large bittersweet brown eyes, and a smile that would have lit up the Atlanta skyline. He was as smart as he was good-looking, finishing at the top of his class at Morris Brown College and later getting an MBA at Clark-Atlanta University. He was the oldest child and the only son of a devoted mother who had raised him and his two sisters alone in southwest Atlanta. Jared never mentioned his father.

I hadn't shared my sexuality with Jared mainly because it had never come up. I hadn't determined if Jared himself was gay or straight, just as I couldn't tell if his closely cropped hair was naturally curly or mildly relaxed. Only when I felt lonely did Jared's sexuality cross my mind. Sleeping alone with just my pillows for comfort created an insatiable void in my life. Our relationship wavered between brotherly love and romantic love, though it was a romance without sex. A romance in my mind only, at least as far as I knew.

I'm what you would call a romantic, a severe romantic, yet lasting romance has eluded me. I grew up believing that you really fell in love only once and that that love would last forever, like in the movies. I now know that most people consider themselves lucky if they fall in love once and have that love returned. But I wasn't even that lucky; the truth of my present situation was a love life that consisted only of daydreams about Jared and listening to R&B songs about love dreamed but never attained. I longed for a love that would make me feel like the soothing love songs that caused an involuntary smile to linger not only on my face but in my heart. A love life that was an eternal "quiet storm."

My love life had included a quartet of lovers—two men, Kelvin and Quinn, sandwiched between my first love, Sela, and Nicole, the woman who had broken my heart because I hadn't told the truth. A lie that sent me packing back to Birmingham, back into the closet, and into my present celibate state.

Now even though I hate labels, I still consider myself bisexual. A sexual mulatto. I mean how else could I explain how members of the singing group En Vogue and certain members of the Atlanta Braves aroused my sexual desires with equal measure?

I didn't feel comfortable in a totally gay environment or in a totally straight environment. I often wondered where the term gay came from. Lonely would better describe the life for me. There was absolutely nothing gay about being a black man and living life attracted to members of your own sex in this imperfect world I called home. For now a place called Perfect remained a dream.

Nicole

W*hen* I was in the fourth grade, the boy who sat behind me would always pull my hair any time he thought no one was looking. He would really get on my nerves. One day instead of pulling my braids he slipped a note in my hand. It read, "Will you go with me? Yes . . . No . . . Maybe. Please circle one."

Since I didn't know where he wanted me to go, I placed the note in my knee socks and took it home to my daddy, asking him what I should do. He gave me some advice I've always tried to live by. "Listen to your heart," he said.

From my daddy's words of wisdom I realized that my heart has a voice. It speaks to me with each beat. My heart protects me, shielding me from the things I can't see or lack the courage to face. My heart knows who I am and who I'll turn out to be.

My name is Nicole Marie Springer, former beauty queen, Broadway actress, and sometime word processor. Thirty years of age, but that's twenty-five in show biz years. Born and raised in Sweet Home, Arkansas, right outside of Little Rock, population five hundred and eighty-five, and one stoplight. Daughter of cotton farmers James and Idella Springer, older sister of Michael. A small-town girl with big-city goals.

They say in every life some rain must fall, but I've just come through a couple of years dominated by thunderstorms. Right now my life is cloudy and overcast, anxiously awaiting the sun.

In the last three years I lost my beloved father to a sudden heart attack, my best friend Candance to AIDS, and Raymond, the brief love of my life, to another man.

The death of my daddy, though sudden, was not quite a surprise. He was seventy-seven years old and had spent his twilight years defying his doctor by not taking his high blood pressure medication. But the loss of my college sorority sister and closest confidante was devastating.

Candance, the first person I had met at Spelman College, was not only beautiful and brilliant, but was just months away from her dream of becoming a physician. Her sudden illness hit like a ton of bricks. Candance, who told me hours after our initial meeting that she was going to become a doctor, marry, and have two children. She lived to see only one of those dreams come true, marrying Kelvin on her deathbed. Kelvin Ellis, the suspected culprit of Candance's demise. Kelvin, the same man who introduced me to Raymond who I fell quickly and deeply in love with, the love I thought my heart had led me to. I never found out if Kelvin was in fact the man in Raymond's secret life. I was too distraught to even think about it.

After the breakup with Raymond, I began to doubt my own sexuality. Had I not been enough woman to satisfy him, or had I been too much? I spent night after night crying myself to sleep, praying that my daddy and Candance would send down some advice, since I could no longer count on my heart.

I questioned how Candance and I could have fallen in love with men who were so incapable of loving us completely. Men who would never give the one thing they could give for free. Honesty.

My relationship with Raymond did slap me into reality. I realized that things were not always what they seemed. I now questioned any man I was interested in dating, asking if he was gay or bisexual or if he planned either in the future. Though I couldn't always detect the truth, I got a lot of interesting responses, including one guy who threw wine in my face and then stormed out of the restaurant we were in. The wine tasted like a "yes" to me. There was also the guy who when I posed the question to him, politely excused himself from the dinner table, went into his bedroom, and returned minutes later, standing before me butterball, butt-naked with a certain part of his anatomy at attention. "Does this answer your question?" he smiled. I wanted to respond with a song I loved, "Is That All There Is?" But I know how men are about their . . . well, you know.

These dates from hell led me to my current beau, Dr. Pierce Gessler. In a decade where everybody was looking for safe sex, I was searching for safe love. With Pierce, I was able to maintain my self-imposed celibacy vow and still have a suitable escort when needed. Oh yes, Pierce is white and Jewish. So much for my dreams of marrying a BMW (*Black Man Working*) or a BMS (*Black Man Straight*). But Pierce was wonderful, supportive, and loving, without a lot of luggage. He helped me out in the lean times when I was getting more calls from temp agencies than my agent. An agent whom I later fired when I heard him tell a casting person at a soap opera that I was a dark-skinned Robin Givens.

Pierce was always telling me how beautiful I was. It made me feel good. No man besides my daddy had ever constantly told me I was beautiful. Raymond told me a couple of times but his honesty was in question. And even though I had won several beauty pageants and was third runner-up to Miss America, I never considered myself beautiful. When I looked in the mirror I saw a face enhanced by *Fashion Fair* makeup, and hair, even though it was my own, permed with the help of a colorful box of chemicals.

In addition to Pierce, I was also blessed with two wonderful friends, Delaney and Kyle. I first met Delaney at an audition and again later when she was doing hair and makeup for a show I was appearing in. My big Broadway starring role that closed after thirty-one performances. Delaney was very beautiful, a talented dancer and a just a little bit crazy. She made me smile and take a look at life from a more upbeat view. Kyle, Raymond's best friend, had become a friend through default and, in a selfish way, our friendship allowed me to keep in contact with Raymond without really being in contact. Kyle was handsome in a cute little boy sorta way. Cornbread brown skin, deep-set brown eyes, thin black curly hair that was starting to recede, and a smile that could dilute darkness. Kyle was openly gay and didn't pull any punches. You knew where he stood. I could deal with that. He was my first openly gay friend, and he kept me in stitches with his quick wit.

My career in New York, similar to my love life, had been one of highs and lows. Moments when I didn't feel very successful, times when I would have given anything to be sitting on the porch back home watching my dad eating sardines and crackers while I munched on strawberry Now 'n' Laters. After signing with another agent, I was constantly being told that I was talented but they were looking for a different type. But I wasn't going to complain because I was back on Broadway, waiting in the wings, again, as the understudy for the female lead in *Jelly's Last Jam*. I have been in the show for six months but I've never gone on. Renee Kelly, the lady I'm understudying, once commented in her Chatty Cathy doll–fashion, "I think it's so unprofessional to miss a performance at any time. I mean these poor people pay their hard-earned money to see me." I took this to mean, don't even think about going on, Miss Thang, not now, not ever.

So in this life that offered more rainstorms than rainbows, I relied on my faith, my trio of friends, and a great therapist. I was learning to count and enjoy my blessings. I realized that luck ran out, but blessings never did. I was constantly employed on stage or in a steno pool, I had my name on a lease in a rent-controlled building and a little money in the bank. And even though Pierce was not the man I'd dreamed of as a little girl, he treated me like royalty. The choice I had to make was whether or not I wanted to wear this crown. For now my response was similar to that note from the first suitor of my youth; like then, I think I'll circle *maybe*.

Part One

*L*ust

Lust the
One You're With

One

The ringing phone seemed to shake the darkened hotel room. I quickly reached for the phone, knocking over a glass and sending my watch to the floor.

"Good morning, Mr. Tyler. This is your 8:30 A.M. wake-up call. Thank you for staying at the Capitol Hill Hyatt Regency. Have a great day," the computerized voice said.

I noticed a shaft of light coming through the thick curtains as I pulled myself up from the bed and headed toward the bathroom. I picked up the green folder that included the charges for our three-day stay. Reading material for the plane, I thought.

I relieved myself and stumbled back into the still dim room.

"Kyle," I whispered.

"Yeah," Kyle mumbled.

"You up?"

"What do you think?"

"Well, I'll take my shower first. What time does your train leave?"

"Ten-thirty. What time is it?"

"Eight-thirty."

I returned to the small bathroom, started the shower, and turned on the hot water in the sink. I rummaged through my shaving bag to locate my razor and toothbrush. The large mirror forced a glimpse of my red eyes and the haggard look on my face. Boy, what a weekend! I couldn't believe it was over. When I got back to Atlanta the first thing I was going to do was sleep—for days.

Kyle and I were in Washington, D.C., for the annual Memorial Day weekend, when thousands upon thousands of black gay men convened in the nation's capital in sort of a silent fraternity convention. The parties had been nonstop meetin' and greetin'. During the day there were brunches and in the evening barbecues and numerous house parties. The Sunday preceding Memorial Day, the attendees had waited hours just to get inside a packed bar called Rails, a massive warehouse located near the Navy yard that could not accommodate the men who had simply taken over the city. Kyle went to Rails and said it took him three hours to get in but it was worth the wait. I opted for a more elegant affair given by a group called The Men. I'd told Kyle, "I am going to a party where the men may be a little older, but the majority of them are homeowners and not simply owners of Metro cards."

Since I didn't go to gay bars in Atlanta, this weekend played an important part in my social life. It was exciting seeing so many good-looking black men in one place. The only sad part was that the three-day holiday was so short and since I was not engaging in sex, I could only look and lust. Still, I met some interesting men—one in particular, an attractive sports lawyer from Philadelphia named Errol, who when I repeated his name replied, "Yes, Errol, like in Flynn."

Errol was interesting but we both faced the you're-too-nice-for-me syndrome—a common syndrome in the black gay community, where nice, good-looking, educated, black gay or bisexual men didn't mind being friendly, but would never date each other. The funny thing was most men would say they didn't like the syndrome but no one did anything about it. Some traditions were hard to break, thus making it difficult to establish long-lasting relationships that weren't based on sex and penis size. And black women thought they had it tough finding a suitable mate.

I quickly showered and threw my clothes into my leather garment bag. I had taken great pains packing for the trip and now all of my clothes were wrinkled and stained, and smelled of my various colognes.

My flight to Atlanta was due to leave at nine forty-five so I was cutting things close.

"Well, buddy, I'm outta here. I'll call you later tonight when I get home," I said.

"Have a safe flight, baby. It's been fun. Real fun," Kyle said as he positioned himself on the edge of the bed.

"Yeah, it has been fun. I don't know why we do this to each other."

"Yeah, me either. You get on outta here before I get emotional. I'll see you the next time you're in the city. Now seriously think about meeting me in L.A. for the Fourth of July weekend."

"I will. Hey, you know I love you. Have a safe trip home. Tell Nicole I send my best and to get rid of that white boy," I joked as I gave Kyle a hug.

"I'll make sure I tell her just that," he responded.

As I headed out the door I heard Kyle call my name again.

"Ray."

"Yeah, Kyle?"

"Tell Jared."

I nodded in wordless agreement and then moved quickly down the hotel hallway to the elevator and rushed through the lobby. The doorman, whose face I had grown accustomed to during the weekend, gave me a broad smile and signaled a taxi as I came through the automatic door. "Have a safe trip and come back and see us again," he instructed.

"Thanks. I will," I replied and firmly placed two crumpled dollar bills into his large hands.

As he slammed the door to the taxi, he leaned through the front window and told the driver, "National Airport."

As the taxi sped away from the hotel and down Fourteenth Street I enjoyed one last glimpse of the nation's capital. It had been a great weekend, but I was excited about my return home. I hoped Jared would be waiting at the gate when my flight arrived. Knowing him, I was sure he'd be right there.

We arrived at the busy National Airport, and after paying the taxi driver, I stopped briefly to enjoy the honey-sweet morning air. It was a clear day, the sky was a cloudless, piercing blue, and I perceived that spring was making its retreat as summer approached.

At the gate I detected trouble; the line was nearly a mile long—at least it looked like a mile. I checked the monitors and saw that my flight was now leaving almost an hour behind schedule. I overheard people in line talking about weather problems in Cincinnati. I thought about Jared and hoped he'd call the airline before heading out. While I pondered my next move, my eyes began to travel around to the various news and food stands, but I decided to get my shoes shined instead. There were a lot of familiar faces roaming around the airport from the weekend. The place had the look of a large meeting of African-American men, but the majority of these men were members of the silent frat.

There were three chairs at the shoeshine stand. Two elderly black men were shining the shoes of customers as though it was their last shine and one young, attractive black female was just finishing up a client. She looked my way and gently tapped her empty chair. I quickly jumped into the well-worn chair and she began rolling up the legs of my black linen pants with one hand and offering me a copy of the *Washington Post* with the other.

"Where you going?" she inquired.

"Atlanta."

"Atlanta. That's where you from?"

"Yes. That's where I'm living for the time being."

"How do you like it?" she questioned.

"Oh, I love Atlanta. A great city," I said with pride.

"I heard there are a lot of jobs down there with the Olympics and all," she commented.

"Well, it's a little bit better than the rest of the country, but the jobs are still pretty scarce."

"I heard there are a lot of good-looking men down there. I mean with all the colleges and stuff."

"Well, I wouldn't know about that," I lied, suppressing a smile. Of course Atlanta was full of good-looking black men.

"I know this, if you're an example of how the men look, then I'm getting my ass in that bag of yours," she joked with a girlish giggle.

"Now stop teasing me," I laughed.

We were both enjoying the exchange when suddenly her laughter stopped. While busy shining my shoes she spotted an attractive, well-built black man, who from his outward mannerisms led you to believe he was gay. Actually I knew he was gay, since I had seen him at one of the weekend parties. He noticed my gaze and gave me a broad smile, revealing beautiful teeth, and I returned a polite, chilly nod.

"You know that's a damn shame," the shine lady muttered.

"What?"

"A motherfuckin' shame. Here he is all that man and he wants to be a woman. You know I don't understand why all our brothers got to be sissies. I guess that's some more shit the white man has laid on our brothers. If they ain't in jail then they're punks."

By now I had turned my eyes back to the newspaper, not looking at her or the guy under attack. I just wanted her to finish so that I could get down and head to my gate.

"What do you think about that?" she asked, interrupting my thoughts.

"Excuse me?" I asked with concealed resentment.

"How do you feel about all these black sissies? It seems like a whole army of them have invaded the district this weekend. Just a damn shame. A damn shame," she repeated.

This lady was burning. Her cheerful face of moments ago was now painted with a sour look. I could envision smoke coming from her ears as she rolled down my pants leg and tapped the toe of my shoes. She gazed around the airport with a laser stare and the expertise of an air traffic controller about to direct the landing of a troubled plane. She didn't look in my direction until I placed a five-dollar bill in her hand.

"Keep the change," I suggested dryly.

"Thank you, sir. You have a safe flight now," she said in a preoccupied tone.

I grabbed my bags and started toward my gate. About five steps into my walk, I turned and for a moment became frozen like a frame in a comic strip. The hatred in her face and voice bothered me deeply. The fact that she was black made my feelings more intense. I released myself from my freeze frame and slowly reapproached the shine stand and the angry young lady.

"Miss," I called out.

"You back already," she grinned.

"You know you should really be careful what you say. You never know who you're talking to," I said.

She gave me a puzzled look, obviously unaware of what my statement meant. I walked away feeling a little bit better about myself but still saddened by her outburst. I didn't look back at her nor did she respond verbally as I walked at an accelerated pace toward the gate. Now I was ready to go home.

The large leather plane seat provided a warm sanctuary from which to think and map out a game plan. A friendly ticket agent had upgraded my economy ticket to first class. My smile never failed me. The upgrade was a welcome relief because I could see that coach was packed with what could only be former Greyhound Bus frequent travelers.

I thought of Kyle's parting words, that I must tell Jared how I truly felt about him and my sexuality. For the most part I thought Kyle, as usual, was right, but a remote fear kept doubts lingering. What if Jared responded the way the lady in the airport had to black gay men? No, he wouldn't do that. But what would happen to our now near perfect relationship? If Jared was in fact gay and was simply uncertain about me, then it could be the start of a truly perfect relationship. But if he wasn't gay and he distanced himself from me? How I would mourn the loss of his friendship. And if what goes around comes around then I was due for payback because of all the pain I brought on Nicole and Quinn. The last time I was truthful with someone I loved about my sexuality the relationship ended abruptly.

I waited for so long because I strongly believed the best romantic relationships were those solidly based on friendship. I didn't, however, believe that every special friendship would turn romantic. Kyle and I had been friends for over a decade and there had never been a trace of romance. Yes, he was very smart and attractive and one of the most self-assured black men, gay or straight, I had ever met. He was gay, make no bones about it. He relished being gay—the lifestyle—and enjoyed everything it had to offer.

Kyle had overcome alcohol and drug abuse and was now the owner of a small but successful costume design and fashion firm, Picture This. It was great seeing him enjoy the weekend of parties without drinking or doing drugs. I was not certain, however, if he had conquered his addiction for strong, well-built, and of course well-hung black men, but I was still quite proud of him. Kyle was one of the reasons that I missed New York. We still talked almost every day on the phone, but it wasn't like the old days when he would phone and minutes later we would be on the subway headed toward the Village or catching a taxi to the now closed Nickel Bar.

Kyle felt strongly that honesty was the best policy when it came to Jared. A few years back he hadn't felt that way when I was dating Nicole and decided to come clean with her. He'd felt that what she didn't know wouldn't hurt her. I guess that proved that even the gayest of men could still be chauvinistic in their attitudes about females and the truth.

In the case of Nicole, Kyle had been right. My being truthful cost me a chance at happiness. But how long would that happiness have lasted before my sexuality would have caused her more pain than my early admission? Maybe my timing had a lot to do with it. I did reveal myself to her during a very difficult period in a hospital just doors away from her dying best friend and shortly after we'd made love for the first time without protection.

I'd decided I had to tell her at that exact moment rather than risk the chance that somebody else might tell her to protect himself, the somebody being my first male lover, Kelvin, husband to Nicole's best friend Candance. I still secretly hoped that one day Nicole and I would sit down and talk, face to face, about our relationship and what future, if any, we had. I wanted the chance to explain my life in more detail, so she would understand that it wasn't something she did or something I planned. I believed very strongly that my chances for a long-term relationship were greater with a woman than with a man, but I thought Nicole deserved something better and maybe Jared offered me something I hadn't dreamed possible. He was, like Nicole, one of the most extraordinary human beings I had ever met.

Jared's infectious smile was a welcome sight. He was all decked out in a crayon-red polo shirt, tight and outlining the muscled contours of his chest. I could see this despite the fact that he was wearing a cotton T-shirt under the polo. Jared was one of those guys who always wore a T-shirt no matter what, an undershirt that I was certain was tucked tightly into his jockey underwear. It could be the dead of summer and there was always that T-shirt and Jared looking cool, calm, and collected. The T-shirt and Jared's smile caused a big grin to break out across my face.

"What up?" Jared asked as he gave me a big bear hug.

"You the man," I replied.

"How was the trip? Did you miss me? Of course you missed me," Jared asked and answered confidently.

"Didn't think about you one second," I teased.

"Yeah, right. Cool. So did your business go as planned?"

"Business? Oh yeah. Business was great." I quickly recovered.

Jared and I stood by the steel-gray carousels, just looking and grinning at each other as assorted luggage rolled by. In this enormous airport it seemed as though we were the only ones there. There was an unnatural stillness surrounding us—the two of us acting very bashful.

"How much luggage did you take?" Jared asked, breaking the silence.

"Luggage?" I quizzed, suddenly realizing that all my luggage was on my shoulders. "Oh shit," I laughed. "I forgot I didn't check my luggage."

"Niggah, pleeze. What are we standing up here looking stupid for? Let's drive," Jared said.

"Whose car did you drive?"

"Yours, of course. It's much nicer and the females notice me more when I drive it," Jared observed.

I didn't respond as I walked side by side with Jared through the airport, out the sliding glass doors, and toward the parking lot. Jared picked up the pace, allowing me to catch a glimpse of his backside in clinging white jeans. His rapid steps made it clear that he wanted to get to the car before me. I thought about Jared's comments regarding women and my car. Yes, I had to admit that my royal blue BMW 535 attracted a certain amount of female and male attention, but did Jared say female to throw me off or was that the real deal? It wasn't that Jared had never mentioned females before. He had a great admiration for the female form, but so did I. He never spoke of women in a derogatory fashion or by body parts. Jared was always very respectful as though he were speaking of his mother. I appreciated that. I had spent enough time to last a lifetime with men who always referred to women by names usually reserved for female dogs.

As we approached my car, I could tell that it had been waxed. I mean the car was shining so brightly that I could see my reflection even while I was several feet away from the door. I couldn't recall the last time the car looked so good, with the exception of the day I purchased it.

"Jared, what did you do to my car?" I asked.

"What do you think I did? I gave it the cleaning it so desperately needed."

"Oh shit. Man, it looks great. Thanks a million."

"No problem. Get in. Since I cleaned it I'm going to drive it."

"You don't have to say it twice," I said as I reached for the door handle on the passenger side.

Just as I was preparing to sit down I saw a little gift box, neatly wrapped. Two plastic champagne glasses were lying over the glove compartment.

"What's this?" I asked, trying to conceal my smile.

"Welcome back, my niggah," Jared smiled.

"Man, you're something else."

"Go ahead, open the box."

I threw my luggage in the backseat, quickly snapped my seat belt on, and started to rip open the small box. Moments later I saw there was nothing but tissue paper in the box and I looked over at Jared, who was picking up speed to enter the freeway heading toward downtown Atlanta.

"There's nothing in here, Jared," I said.

"Hold up. Look under the seat first."

I felt under the seat and with my slight touch out rolled a bottle of Cristal champagne.

"Open it. Let's celebrate you getting back safe and the end of the holiday."

"Okay, but what about the box? Wasn't something supposed to be in there?" I asked greedily.

"Yes, I got tickets to the Braves game tonight, but I didn't pick them up. They're at the will-call window. That's the second part of the surprise."

"Jared, that's the shit. You know this will be my first Braves game. In fact this will be my first professional baseball game ever."

"I know that. Pops told me."

"But my birthday is weeks away. How are you going to top this?"

"Don't worry about it. Just pop the cork and let's do this."

I quickly popped the cork of the champagne bottle. I was as excited as a kid going on his first ferris wheel ride at the fair. The Braves were the hottest thing in Atlanta; only Braves tickets were hotter. I love all sports, but only started to appreciate baseball after moving to Atlanta. It was impossible to live in Atlanta and not get caught up with the Braves and here I was going to a game. I balanced the plastic glasses and slowly poured the golden-colored beverage.

"Maybe you shouldn't drink and drive," I said in a protective tone.

"I know, but just a tiny sip to celebrate. We can finish it at your place before the game."

"Cool," I responded.

I inhaled the champagne's sweet aroma and began to sip it slowly, rolling it in my mouth and letting it glide over the surface of my tongue and then down my throat. I couldn't ever remember champagne tasting so wonderful and exhilarating. I smiled at the fact that Jared had called my father Pops.

Jared, with a warm gleam in his eyes, sped down Highway 85 North as I relaxed and observed Atlanta's phallic skyline and enjoyed my pleasant laziness. I began to hum along with Vanessa Williams's "Save the Best for Last," as the song blasted over the car stereo. Atlanta was enjoying a bright warm day and the air seemed startlingly clear and pure. I rolled down the window so that I could smell the brisk air and continue to savor the moment.

Two

Seconds after I first opened my eyes in the morning, the phone rang. I quickly grabbed it before the answering machine came on.

"Praise the Lord, Nicole girl," Sheila exclaimed.

"Praise Him, Sheila," I replied.

"How you doing?" Sheila asked.

"I'm blessed. How about you?"

"I'm blessed too, girl. Let's get started."

"Okay."

"You got anything special you want to pray for today?"

"No, not really. I have an audition later on this afternoon, but I'm not that excited about it. What about you?"

"No, nothing special. Let's just thank Him and send one up for those who need it."

"Okay. Why don't you start."

Sheila's voice went from its light tone into a very serious and reverent pitch. As she prayed over the telephone line, I stood and pulled myself up from my queen-sized bed and reached for my lilac robe. I closed my eyes and felt a slight chill over my body from Sheila's words as she rapidly thanked Christ for the many blessings He had granted. I thought about all the things I wanted to say when it was my turn to pray over the phone lines.

Sheila and I had been prayer partners for about two years. There were only a few days since we'd started praying that we'd missed. I met Sheila in the SAG (Screen Actors Guild) office one day when she was posting a notice for a prayer partner. I had no idea what a prayer partner was, but I was going through a difficult time and when she explained it to me I was instantly sold.

"Nicole?"

"Yes."

"What do you want to thank the Lord for?"

Without responding, I went into prayer, thanking Christ for waking me up and thanking Him for the positive day I was about to have. A few minutes into the prayer I forgot that I was standing in my bedroom in my nightgown and robe. I felt as though I was in church. Sheila responded regularly with, "Yes, Lord . . . thank you, Lord . . . yes, Lord . . . thank you."

As I brought my prayer to a close I opened my eyes and glanced out my bedroom window. A light rain was falling. "Wrap yourself up, girl. It's raining cats and dogs out there," Sheila instructed with the tone of a mother.

"I will. You have a blessed day," I responded.

"I will. I'll talk with you in the morning."

As important as Sheila was in my life, we hardly saw each other. She was married and lived in Brooklyn with her husband and little boy. We went to different churches but it was hard to imagine my life without her despite her tendency to be quite self-righteous at times.

I went into the kitchen of my small one-bedroom apartment and put up the kettle for my morning tea. I walked back into my bedroom and watched the rain run down the window of my Upper East Side apartment.

Outside, Manhattan rushed, bumped, and shoved toward a new day. I saw taxis splashing through the street and listened to horns blaring loudly with impatience. I pressed my nose against the condensation-covered window and watched people scurrying along the sidewalks under umbrellas, women in soaked tennis shoes, men with damp folded newspapers and briefcases bravely facing the rain bareheaded. The pace and energy of the city were that of the previous sun-soaked day.

The phone and the teakettle seemed to shriek at the same time. I rushed back into the kitchen, grabbed my cordless phone, and clicked it on.

"Hello."

"Hey, girl."

"Delaney. What's going on, girl?"

"You know, the same ole same ole."

"What time are you leaving your apartment?"

"In about thirty minutes. Are you going on that audition?"

"What audition?" I quizzed.

"You know. The douche commercial. I understand it's a national."

"I just know my agent isn't sending me on a douche commercial."

"You better work grand Broadway, diva. I'm scared of you. It must be nice to be able to pass up shit," Delaney laughed.

"Naw, girl. You know what I mean. Is this one of those commercials where they're going to shoot two? One with a white girl and the other with one of us?"

"You know I don't know and I don't give a damn."

"Well, I think I'm going to pass. Sam probably didn't send me up for it. I've got to read a sitcom script she sent over."

"That's cool with me. Less competition. Lord knows I ain't got no problem with people knowing that my pussy is fresh and clean," Delaney giggled.

"Girl, you're crazy!"

"And hopefully about twenty thousand dollars richer when I get this commercial."

"Good luck. Call me when you get back."

"I will, darling. Talk to ya."

"Oh, Delaney."

"Yeah."

"What about step class?"

"I'll be there."

"I'll see you there if I don't hear from you."

"Okay, girl. See ya."

My hot water was now lukewarm. I placed the tea bag into my favorite pink coffee mug and popped it into the microwave. I started the shower and thought about my conversation with Delaney. Who did I think I was passing up a shot at a national commercial and why hadn't Sam told me about it? I mean I was constantly getting on her about sending me out on more commercial calls. Lord knows, years ago I would have jumped at the chance at any product. It wasn't as though I would be competing against Delaney. We had completely different looks and the casting agents probably already knew what look they were going for. I had lost track and didn't know if this was the dark-skinned Naomi Campbell–look or the light-skinned Troy Beyer–look week. If Sam called at the last minute and insisted I go on this audition that would clue me in that they were looking for my type. With the rain still coming down, I would have to contend with my hair. The hot tea and a hot shower sounded so much better—besides I didn't feel like rejection so early in the week.

After my shower, I pulled my hair up, rolled it into a ball, and curled up on my sofa, teacup and script in hand. I smiled at the thought of

Delaney telling the casting agent that she didn't care if the world knew her stuff was clean and fresh. They would hire her on the spot. That is if the casting agent had a sense of humor. A realistic question in my business.

It was great having a close friend in the business whom I didn't feel I had to compete with. Delaney was very talented, but she had a different niche from me. She was constantly being booked for rap and R&B videos and often referred to herself as a "video ho." She was an excellent dancer, classically trained, and an expert with hip hop steps, a dance style I never was able to learn. She'd left the Dance Theater of Harlem over a year ago when cutbacks had forced them to cut out a major part of their season. And since Delaney couldn't depend on commercials and videos, she, like me, knew the major word processing packages, just in case. She was also an excellent makeup artist and had worked as a dresser in several Broadway shows. Her brownish-yellow skin tone, rail-thin body—with a black girl's behind—and short curly haircut made her a favorite among video casting agents and rap artists. The ironic thing was Delaney held a strong aversion to rap music and the men who sang it; said they treated women like crap, although that wasn't the word she used. Delaney had a colorful vocabulary. She was more at home with Dianne Reeves, Patti LaBelle, or Patti Austin, but those divas rarely used women as attractive as Delaney in their videos.

Aside from the both of us being in the business, Delaney and I had little else in common, that is if you overlooked the fact that we couldn't live without each other. Delaney was from the greater Northwest, having been raised in Seattle before moving to New York at eighteen to study at Julliard and later to dance full time with DTH. She said she wasn't college material and deplored beauty pageants with the same antipathy she felt for rap music. Faith wasn't high on her list of priorities and she constantly kidded me about my morning prayer calls with Sheila. Delaney once said, "Many people attend church but very few understand." Made a lot of sense when you thought about it.

She didn't appear to be preoccupied with getting married either. She had dated several guys, but none of the relationships seemed serious. Maybe the wanting to be married was a Southern girl trait. When I advised her to make sure she asked them the gay questions and their HIV status, she instructed me to lighten up. "That nigger, Weymon, Raymond, or whatever his name was, really fucked you up! Not every good-looking black man is a sissy."

The use of words like sissy made me wonder if Delaney was

homophobic but then I would think about how tight she and Kyle were and dismiss the thought. But then again, everybody loved Kyle. Also some of the guys she hung out with from the shows were definitely gay. But she had a point, I needed to lighten up. I couldn't let my failed relationship with Raymond shape the rest of my love life, something I was working on with the help of Dr. Huntley. I realized I had mixed feelings when it came to gay men, especially black gay men.

I'd started seeing Dr. Vanessa Huntley shortly after Candance died. The first year we worked on my grief about Candance's death, but then slowly turned to my relationships with men, my shaky relationship with my mother, and my own lack of self-confidence.

Initially I saw Dr. Huntley twice a week but I had recently cut back to once a week. I hadn't told anyone I was seeing a psychiatrist. It was the one secret I kept to myself. My daddy used to always tell me to keep a secret for myself. It wasn't that I was embarrassed about seeing a doctor. Anyone could understand the need for professional help after what I had been through, but I felt needing professional care said something about my religious beliefs. I had been taught and for the most part believed that prayer and faith could solve any problems I faced. But in the early weeks following Candance's death and my breakup with Raymond I felt I needed to talk to someone I could see.

The rain had stopped and the sun drenched the city when I finally finished the silly sitcom script. I glanced at the mute television and realized from the soap opera on the screen that it was close to three o'clock. I had less than an hour to get over to the West Side for step class, my appointment, and dinner before heading to the theater and another night of wishing that Renee wouldn't show up and I'd finally get the chance to once again do what I loved and was being paid to do.

I debated on my mode of transportation and decided to catch a taxi, since I was wearing my workout clothes. I placed a change of clothes in a garment bag and headed downstairs.

Even though I taxied to the health spa on Seventy-sixth and Broadway, Delaney had gotten there before me and was right in the front row. She saw me come in and signaled me to join her up front. I hesitated because I didn't want anyone tripping. I guess Delaney could sense my reservations so she yelled, "Nicole, come on up. I saved this spot for you."

I meekly moved from the back of the crowded gym to the front, trying not to notice the stares and looks as I got closer to Delaney.

"Excuse me. Excuse me," I said as I moved through the crowd.

"Girl, why are you moving so slow? These children ain't hardly paying you no mind. Besides all my good, good girlfriends are up here."

Before I could respond, the music started and the only sounds besides the blasting pop music were the slapping of hands and thighs and heavy breathing. Minutes later sweat was popping from every pore of my body, but I was beginning to feel good.

After a quick shower, Delaney and I bounced out of the club and onto busy Broadway. "Where do you want to eat?" I asked Delaney.

"Eat?"

"Yes, I've got some time before I'm due at the theater. Let's do Chinese," I said, momentarily forgetting my appointment.

"Nic, I'm going to the Broadway Dance Center. They have a guest instructor teaching a master's tap class and I can't miss that."

"A tap class after that workout. Are you crazy?" I asked as I silently breathed a sigh of relief. I didn't have time for a sit-down dinner.

"Chile, you never know when they bring another one of those colored tap shows back to Broadway. A diva must be prepared."

"What are you going to do after that?"

"I'm supposed to hook up with Kyle. He's due back from D.C. this afternoon. You know he'll have plenty of stories," Delaney laughed.

"Why don't you two come by the theater?" I suggested.

"Okay, we'll see. Maybe you can come by my place or meet us up at Kyle's."

"Not at Kyle's," I interjected quickly.

"Oh yeah, I forgot your ban on that apartment. Chile, you really need to get professional help," Delaney chided.

"Delaney, don't tease me. Kyle understands."

"I'm sure Kyle has changed that apartment so much that you wouldn't recognize it."

"You think so?"

"Nicole, come on now. I don't have time to discuss this craziness, I've got to run."

"How are you getting down there?"

"I'm walking. Got to keep the blood pumping!"

"Okay, girl, see ya later," I said as I kissed Delaney on her lightly made-up cheek. As she started down Broadway I called out, "Delaney, how did the audition go?"

"It didn't," she yelled back. "They were looking for high yeller with long hair and I ain't buying no hair this week," she laughed as she walked swiftly down Broadway.

"Next time, girl, next time," I murmured to myself.

As Delaney vanished into the crowded street I hailed a taxi heading uptown and to my secret meeting place.

The black wrought-iron security gate leading to Dr. Huntley's office was slightly ajar. I rang the loud buzzer and Dr. Huntley greeted me seconds later.

"Good afternoon, Nicole. Come in," Dr. Huntley said as she led me into her office located in the basement of her fashionable brownstone on Harlem's famed Strivers Row.

"Hi, Dr. Huntley. How are you doing today?"

"I'm doing fine," she smiled.

I walked into the dimly lit dark-paneled room and took my regular position sitting upright on the large black leather sofa. Dr. Huntley moved behind her cluttered glass-topped desk and sat in the oil-colored recliner.

Dr. Vanessa G. Huntley was a regal brown-skinned woman, plump, broad-faced, serene with sleepy brown eyes and short gray-black hair. She was wearing dangling earrings that were bigger than the island of Manhattan. Pretty earrings, but big. Dr. Huntley gave me a smile as she arranged herself in the chair. Her grandmotherly smile was soft and reassuring.

"Is there anything you want to discuss today? It's been a couple of weeks since I've seen you," Dr. Huntley said.

"No, not really. Delaney was joking with me moments ago that I needed to seek professional help because I won't go up to Kyle's apartment."

"Refresh my memory, Nicole, why won't you go to Kyle's apartment?"

"Well, that's where Raymond used to live. The place where I risked my life."

"How so?"

"Oh, don't you remember? I made love with him without using a condom. I felt he betrayed me because he went ahead without telling me he was bisexual."

"Did he force you?"

"Oh no!"

"But you still blame him?"

"Why are we discussing this? We've been over this countless times. I know I have to take some of the responsibility. He did look for a condom, but I don't want to talk about that," I said, lifting my voice slightly.

"There is still some anger there, Nicole. I think we need to talk about it."

"Well, I'm ready to go to the apartment, I've gotten over it. I've forgiven myself and I've forgiven Raymond."

"Are you sure?"

"Yes."

"You still sound upset. What's bothering you?"

"I got fired from a recording session."

"What happened?"

"I don't know."

"You don't know?"

"I think the singer got upset because she felt I was upstaging her," I said.

"Upstaging her?"

"Yes, the producer kept telling me how great I was sounding and she kept rolling her eyes at me."

"Were you?"

"Was I what?"

"Upstaging her?"

"No! I didn't think I was. The chile couldn't sing."

"And so what happened?"

"About an hour later she ripped off her headphones, stormed into the area where I was singing, and told the producer to fire me."

"Is that what she said?"

"No!"

"What did she say?"

"Get rid of that black bitch."

"Was she white?"

"No. She was black but . . ."

"But?"

"She was high yeller."

"Did that bother you?"

"Nobody likes being fired. I wanted that job. It could help me break into the recording industry."

"Is that it?"

"Is what it?"

"Did it bother you that the singer was fair-skinned?"

"No."

"Are you sure?"

"I'm sure," I said as I looked at my watch.

"Why are you looking at your watch?"

"Well, I need to make a stop before I get to the theater."

"Well, you still have plenty of time," Dr. Huntley said.

"But I need to go."

"Why, Nicole?"

"I just do."

"Is there something else bothering you?"

"No."

"Okay, Nicole, but I'd like to see you again next week. I think this firing is bothering you more than you'd like to admit."

"Okay. Same time next week."

"Fine," Dr. Huntley said.

I flagged a gypsy taxi from Dr. Huntley's office back to midtown instead of going directly to the theater. Once I was out of the taxi I could hear the sounds of a spring New York City evening. All the people walking along the sidewalks were giving me the extra energy I needed. I could tell that spring had started its struggle to leave the island to make room for another sweltering summer. I stopped at a nondescript Chinese restaurant and ordered a pint of shrimp fried rice and some shrimp toast. I decided to take the food to the theater and eat after the curtain went up. I knew Renee would be there. Although she was married she never seemed to spend time with her husband, even on holidays. I was starting to think that the show would close before I got to go on. Well, at least I would have time to prepare for Wednesday's Bible study. The thought of Bible class brought me a little solace; it took my mind off thinking about how desperately I wanted to do this role and my session with Dr. Huntley.

Although this show belonged to the male leads, the role of Anita was pivotal. She was the female lead and had one of the showstopping numbers at the end of the first act. It was a glamorous role with a lot of sexual overtones and completely different from the roles I'd played previously.

I stopped at a newsstand a few blocks from the theater to get some additional reading matter in case I finished my Bible study material early. I should have brought the sitcom script just in case I got called in for an early audition. The producers were doing a call in the city before heading back to L.A. for the final auditions. The prospect of going to Los Angeles didn't excite me but a chance at a recurring role in a sitcom would be too attractive to turn down. Besides a trip to the Coast might be fun.

I arrived at the theater and went backstage. I was greeting various cast members when I noticed a pink note slip on the bulletin board with my name on it. I pulled the note down and saw that it was from my service—a call from Pierce saying he was sending a car for me after the show and a call from my agent, Samantha, saying the casting agent from the sitcom wanted me to fly to L.A. instead of auditioning in New York. Now that was great news to end an otherwise uneventful day.

Three

Jared Stovall was the only man I knew who could make me get up at 5:30 A.M. daily. He had that type of power. Each morning at 5:15 my phone would ring and I would hear, "This is your niggah with your wake-up call. Get your yellow ass up."

We would meet at the Sports Time Health Spa in Buckhead every morning at six sharp. Free weights on Monday, Wednesday, and Friday and exercise class on Tuesday and Thursday. After a strenuous workout, we'd swim a few laps and then sit in the steam room before starting out for work. We chose early morning because it was less congested than the evenings. Also the evening traffic at the gym included many distractions of both sexes. This was my reasoning and not necessarily Jared's.

Jared beat me swimming and was lying nude in the steam room when I walked in. His body was glistening with baby oil and sweat that had formed into tiny droplets of water. The droplets appeared on every inch of his body with the exception of the dark brown fig-shaped birthmark that accented his left buttock.

"Get in here, slow poke," Jared said.

"Hey, man, thanks again for last night. I had a great time," I said, looking for a spot in the steam room close to Jared.

"I was glad to do it. I got a big kick watching you doing the chop."

"Yeah, buddy, it was big fun."

I lay on the ceramic tile slab and began to rub my body with baby oil and aloe vera. The steam increased and Jared was no longer visible. I couldn't tell if we were in the room alone or if someone could be eavesdropping.

The previous night had been quite magical. Box seats a few rows behind Ted Turner and the mayor. The Braves won in the bottom of the ninth inning and we had two of the best seats in the stadium. Jared and I went to a bar named Tuesday's in the popular Underground Atlanta mall after the game and drank Mexican coffee before Jared dropped me off. During the ride home he quizzed me about the weekend, but when I became evasive he simply changed the subject back to the thrilling game we had just witnessed. Jared did inquire about Kyle and asked when he was going to get the chance to meet him. I knew that I would have to tell Jared before he met Kyle but it was a long time to Labor Day and Kyle's first visit to Atlanta.

In a way it was sad that I couldn't share everything with Jared, especially my friendship with Kyle. I wasn't ashamed of Kyle—I was certain that they would love each other when they met—but Kyle's bold confidence regarding his sexuality sometimes caught people off guard and this was something that could wait until I knew more about Jared's sexuality or his feelings toward gay men.

"How does your work week look?" Jared asked.

"I don't really know. What about yours?"

"It's pretty slow. You know this race for the Congress is all wrapped up. Congressman Thomas doesn't really have any serious competition. I don't know if I like races like this," Jared lamented.

"What? Don't feel like you're earning your money, big boy?"

"No, it's not that. You know me. I like putting out fires."

Jared made no secret about his own political plans. He was going to head Congressman Thomas's Atlanta office for about two years before running for a state senate seat of his own. Maybe these were two reasons we got along so well, sports and politics. Jared said that if the incumbent ran again in two years he would either move to another district or consider going to law school, skipping the state senate race, and going straight for the congressional race. There was talk of creating another black majority district in the Atlanta area and Jared hadn't ruled out challenging Congressman Thomas if he became too complacent in Washington.

"I'm outta here, Ray-Ray. I'll call you later on this afternoon," Jared said as he walked sleekly from the steam room.

"Okay, dude. Peace out."

During the drive to my office I became consumed with ways of breaking the news to Jared. I practiced what I would say to him, mouthing the words, reacting with my face and causing strange looks from other motorists at the many stoplights that lined Peachtree Street. Would I tell Jared about my sexuality and then break the news that I was in love with him? What if he was gay or bisexual, but not interested in me? I would be crushed. What would become of our friendship? Maybe I would tell him and then lead him to believe that Kyle and I were lovers, trying to incite a jealous reaction. Why was I planning scenarios that danced around the truth?

I also had to consider my professional and social standing in Atlanta. If my confession ended my friendship with Jared, then I had to consider the effect that might have on all the people I had met through him, including my employer, Gilliam Battle.

I grabbed the stack of messages from my box as I walked through the lobby of my office, located on the sixteenth floor of the large midtown Union Bank Building. Before I could escape to my office, I heard Mico, Gilliam's legal assistant, call out, "Ray, Gilliam wants me to put you on her schedule today. Morning or afternoon?"

"Did she say what she needed?" I questioned.

"Nope," Mico replied.

"Okay. Let's do it first thing."

"Great. I'll check to see if that's all right with Gilliam."

I asked my assistant, Melanie, to bring me a cup of coffee and the correspondence that had come during my absence. I wondered what Gilliam wanted. Did she expect details about my trip? I'd lied and told her that I had several leads on players at Howard and Georgetown whom I was going to meet with. Well, I had seen a lot of basketball and football players last weekend, but not in places where I normally met potential new clients.

I looked through my messages and mail; nothing important except a handwritten note from a football player at the University of North Carolina expressing his interest in the firm's representing him. He was a top draft prospect; here was some good news that I could give to Gilliam when we met.

Gilliam was on the phone, standing in front of her window, when I walked into her office. She gave me a smile and waved while she continued her conversation, motioning me to a seat in one of the burgundy leather wing chairs that faced her large glass desk. The walls of her office were painted a soft green with pink borders, the same colors in the Persian rug that covered the hardwood floor. An expensive collection of African art was stationed throughout the office and Gilliam's various degrees and citations hung directly behind her.

Gilliam Battle was a blend of sass and class. A thirtysomething, cinnamon-brown beauty with auburn-tinted hair, usually styled in a Dutch boy cut, which always seemed to be perfect. It was as though she went to the beauty shop every morning before coming to the office. She was the type of woman who as a young girl probably wouldn't have captured my attention but who developed into a beauty as an adult—the type who at a high school reunion got a lot of "You were in my high school class?" from incredulous male classmates.

Gilliam took a seat in her black leather chair and held up an index finger toward me as she leaned back and let out a brilliant laugh. I enjoyed working for Gilliam; she was a powerful and respected lawyer in Atlanta. A graduate of Hampton Institute and Tulane Law School, she'd started the firm more than a decade ago with a college sorority sister and a white male classmate. Her sorority sister had died of breast cancer about two years ago and the other partner had decided to sell his share of the firm and move to the Caribbean so he could sail every day. Gilliam employed eight lawyers, including myself, and often talked about adding a senior partner very soon. This was one of the reasons I'd jumped at the offer of a position with her firm in spite of some reservations. I'd heard the horror stories about black men working for black women. But the job market was tight in large cities and most big law firms were laying off instead of hiring.

I didn't know what Gilliam would think if she found out about the secret I was harboring. Black women in the South held pretty strong feelings about gay men, not all of them positive. I thought this was because a lot of black Southern women didn't realize how many gay men they already knew. The majority of black gay and bisexual men lived their lives in the closet. Present company included.

To Gilliam's credit she did have Mico as her legal assistant and close confidant and I could tell Mico was gay from day one. Mico really ran the office and protected Gilliam like a hawk. If he knew my secret, he never let on and treated me with the utmost respect. I didn't know if he would have treated me differently if he'd guessed I was a member of the silent frat, although not an active card-carrying member. Most black gay men were not subscribers of "outing."

"Ray, welcome back," Gilliam said as she extended her fine-boned hands with tastefully polished fingernails.

"Glad to be back. How was your weekend?"

"Great. I went bungie jumping."

"No shit. How was it?"

"Oh it was too wild. Just too much fun. You have to come with me sometime," Gilliam said. "How was the Chocolate City?"

"It was all right. I'm glad to be back in Atlanta."

"How's your schedule in the evening?"

"In the evening?" I questioned.

"Yes. Let me tell you why I asked. A real good friend of mine called me this weekend inquiring about your interest and availability for teaching a class over at AU center."

"The AU center? I didn't realize they had a law school."

"First class enters this fall. I think it will be great for the community."

"What class would I be teaching?"

"Sports and Entertainment Law. You and I could share the load."

"Hey, this sounds like a great opportunity for the firm and me," I said excitedly.

"Yeah, it would be. Should be an excellent experience," Gilliam said.

"When do you need to know?"

"The middle of June."

"Okay—let me make sure I don't have any commitments I can't get out of."

"Okay. How were the prospects?"

"Prospects?"

"Yes. Didn't you see some players in D.C.?"

"Oh yeah. Don't think we should put a lot of energy there. The prospects don't look good that either one of them will be drafted. Smart kids though."

"Okay. You know I trust your judgment."

"Is that all?"

"Yes—unless you have something."

As I started out of the office Gilliam called out, "Ray, what are you doing next Sunday?"

"No big plans."

"Well, I want to invite you to my church. Would you be interested?"

"Church?"

"Yeah, we just moved into a new building. I was on the building fund and I'm really quite proud of our new church."

"What church do you attend?"

"First Birth. It's in Decatur."

"Sure, Gilliam. Thanks for asking. I'm embarrassed to tell you that I haven't been to church since I moved to Atlanta."

"You really shouldn't be embarrassed. I'm just sorry I didn't ask you earlier."

When I got back into my office I thought about Gilliam's invitation. I wondered if this was a date and if so if it was a wise decision to date the boss. I guess I'd forgotten that Gilliam wasn't married and I'd never seen her with a man, not that we socialized a lot outside the office. I mean Gilliam was beautiful, smart, and rich. Why didn't she have a man?

Four

I was almost out the door on my way to Newark Airport when the phone rang. I paused as the answering machine clicked on. It was Samantha, my agent. I quickly dropped my luggage and grabbed the phone as Samantha started a panic-stricken message.

"Hold on, Sam, I'm here," I said.

"Nicole, I'm glad I caught you before you left for the airport. I'm afraid I have some bad news."

"What?"

"Just got a call from the producers of the sitcom. They've already cast the role. They're still interested in you for a one-shot guest appearance, though," Sam said.

"Dang, Sam, I really wanted that role," I sighed.

"Yes, I know it would have been a great opportunity. Are you interested in the guest spot?"

"Do you know who got the job? Please don't say Halle Berry or Jasmine Guy," I pleaded.

"I'm not certain but I think the Ralph girl."

"That doesn't make me feel much better. Let me get back to you, Sam, on the guest spot. I need to digest this first."

"Okay, but don't wait too long. A lot of actresses will be lined up for this shot," Sam suggested.

"Don't worry. I'll let you know this afternoon. Bye, Sam."

"I'll talk to you, Nicole. I know this is a bad way to start your day."

"Don't worry, I'll be fine. This is one of the hazards of the business, right?"

"Yes, you're absolutely right."

I stood in the middle of my living room with my luggage at my side and contemplated what to do. A part of me wanted to cry but a part of me was relieved. I mean I wasn't completely sold on moving to the

West Coast even for the four to six months' shooting a series would require. But the part would have been a big break. A role on a television series would finally let the people in Sweet Home know that I had made it. It was funny how, despite the fact that I had three Broadway shows under my belt, most of my townspeople and even my mother kept asking me when was I going to be on a television show or have a song on the radio and if I wasn't on television soon then why didn't I move back home and start a family? They thought of Broadway as a type of high school play thing, and didn't consider me a "real" actress like Diahann Carroll or Whoopi Goldberg. I think they were more excited when I was chosen for Up with People than when I secured the lead in a Broadway show. They could relate to that. Broadway theater, like New York City, was as foreign as China. They didn't quite understand that Broadway was a long way from Up with People.

I was happy that my daddy got the chance to see me on the Broadway stage before he died. I don't think that he or my mother understood how important opening night was, but I knew they were both proud and that's what really counted. This wasn't the first time my parents had shown support for something they didn't quite understand. They'd never understood why I'd kept entering beauty pageants and why I was usually the only black girl. My mother's pride seemed to be even greater if another black girl was in the pageant and she happened to be light-skinned and I finished higher than she did. It didn't matter to her that a white girl usually beat the both of us. In the South as a dark-skinned black girl I'd had to compete not only against white women but with women of my own race with lighter-hued skin. At least in my mother's eyes.

When I finished as third runner-up and then first runner-up for Miss Arkansas in consecutive years my mother suggested I try Miss Black Arkansas or give up pageants altogether. The one year I represented Spelman College in the Miss Georgia Pageant my daddy made the trip alone. I tried to explain to them that the scholarships were better in the Miss America program and what a great stepping-stone it would be for my career in show business. Despite their misgivings, I don't think anyone yelled any louder when I finally won on my fourth try at a trip to Atlantic City.

My parents usually offered one voice when it came to dealing with Michael, my brother, and me, but this changed when it came to my current beau, Dr. Pierce Gessler. My daddy was okay about it. I'm sure he wanted me to marry a black man, but he also wanted me to be happy. He was his usual compassionate self when he met Pierce in New York. My mother was icy cold toward him and when Daddy died she was adamant about my not bringing Pierce anywhere near Arkansas and my daddy's funeral. I didn't press the issue and returned home alone. I didn't know if my mother would ever accept my relationship with Pierce. I don't think that my mother was prejudiced. Well, maybe she was just a little bit, but she had grown up in the Old South and I knew that there were certain things that she found hard to forget or accept. But she never talked with me about those things and Daddy would always say, "That's your mother. God bless her. She's been through a lot."

When I would question my mother on why she felt this way about white people she simply replied, "If you're lucky enough to live as long as I have, you will learn how they are."

Her comment had a familiar ring. White people often expressed the same sentiment—about blacks.

Since my travel plans had been changed I now had a free day and evening and I decided to take Pierce to lunch and meet Kyle and Delaney that evening. My busy schedule allowed little time to do things with my friends outside the theater and for Pierce. Pierce was constantly surprising me with gifts and small acts of kindness and I wanted to show him that his kindness didn't go unnoticed. When he couldn't pick me up at the theater he would send a car for me because he didn't want me on the subway late at night. He insisted that I carry a can of mace with me at all times and that I never, ever, catch a gypsy cab. Not a day passed without his telling me how much he loved me and how special I was. There were times when I felt a bit smothered with all his attention and I didn't always welcome feeling like a prized possession. During the times I felt this way I could just hear my mother admonishing me to be careful what you pray for.

I'd met Pierce during my audition for my last Broadway show. He was one of the primary financial backers for the show and when the director had kept me late one night going over lyrics Pierce had offered me a ride home when he saw me outside the theater hailing a taxi. At first we were just friends. I was still grieving over Candance's death and the end of my relationship with Raymond, and Pierce was going through a messy divorce. My therapy helped a great deal but Dr. Huntley was not available twenty-four seven. I thought of Candance and how much I missed her every day. I guess three years was not a long time to grieve for someone so important to you. As far as I was concerned there would never be enough time.

Pierce and I would console each other on bad days and I think we were enjoying learning about our differences. I was very interested in the Jewish religion and Pierce was interested in my Southern upbringing. There was not a single Jewish person in Sweet Home. Although I did have Jewish classmates in my large Little Rock high school, I couldn't detect any differences between them and my other white classmates. My daddy told me stories of how Jewish people had helped during the civil rights movement and how they were different from regular white folks. I wanted to learn more about those differences. After a few years of living in New York I became pretty good at spotting Jewish people without asking dumb questions. They had a certain pride about their heritage that was sadly missing from a lot of the African-Americans I came in contact with.

Pierce was a native New Yorker, and had taken over his father's successful East Side obstetrical/gynecological practice. His love for the theater had led him to investing in Broadway shows. I didn't know how wealthy he was but it was plain as day that he never wanted for anything.

Pierce was tall and straight and he was pronouncedly pigeon-toed. He had a bony handsome look about him marred only by his slightly large nose and thin lips. His onyx rich black hair brought attention to his olive complexion and brown-green eyes. Those eyes, big eyes, lively and intelligent with nary a trace of pretense. I was a sucker for a man's eyes; Raymond had beautiful sleepy green eyes. Bedroom eyes. When I looked into Pierce's eyes it was like looking deep into his soul and sometimes I remembered Raymond Tyler.

Pierce understood my reluctance about sex when I shared my relationship with Raymond and what happened with Candance. He offered to take an HIV test when I felt I was ready to pursue a physical relationship. He gave me valuable insight on why Candance had died so quickly from AIDS, explaining how women were often wrongly diagnosed because the diseases affecting women were different from those men experienced.

I hadn't determined if I was going to take my relationship with Pierce to the next level—a sexual relationship. There were times when I felt I loved him but I couldn't distinguish if it was friendship love or romantic love. I admitted I had not felt a spasm of sexual attraction toward him, but this could be because of my focus on celibacy or the fact I had never slept with a white man, Jewish or otherwise.

Pierce was already at the restaurant on Eighty-sixth and Broadway when I arrived a few minutes late. Well, it was more like a half-hour late but as usual Pierce seemed happy to see me. He looked at his watch and let out a big grin.

"Sorry I'm running a little bit late," I said as I kissed him on his clean-shaven face and he pulled back my chair.

"No, you're not, but I've been keeping myself busy," Pierce said as he closed up his black portable phone and took the seat to my immediate left instead of the one facing me.

"What are you drinking?" I asked.

"Chardonnay. Is that what you want?"

"No, I think I'll just have iced tea."

"So how are you doing?" Pierce asked.

"I'm doing okay. How about you?"

"I'm doing great now!"

Pierce caught the attention of our waiter, who was standing at the door leading to the outdoor café looking bored.

"I need an iced tea for this beautiful lady," Pierce shouted.

"What do you suggest?" I inquired as I looked over the colorful and busy menu.

"All the food is great here. Especially the seafood."

"Why don't you order for me," I said.

Pierce ordered blackened catfish with baked potatoes for the both of us and we decided to share a basket of chili cheese fries before our entrées were served.

I told Pierce about the sitcom disappointment. He was very understanding and supportive, telling me my day was going to come soon.

"I called you late last night. Where were you?" Pierce asked. His supportive tone had changed.

"What time?"

"It was way past midnight. You should have been home from the theater. Wasn't the car on time?"

"Yes, it was on time but you know I turn my phone and answering machine off when I go to sleep," I said.

"Maybe I should get you a beeper," Pierce said in a slightly annoyed tone.

"A beeper! You've got to be kidding."

"No, I'm serious."

This was one of the things about Pierce that didn't sit too well with me. What did he think? That I was out with someone else?

"We'll talk about this later," Pierce said.

"Suit yourself," I said, shaking my head in dismay.

The waiter appeared and served our fish and potatoes. The food was substantial but tasteless; maybe I had eaten too many chili cheese fries. As I toyed with my fish, Pierce's voice suddenly became very animated.

"Well, I've got some news that will brighten your day," Pierce said as he moved the glass of wine from his lips and placed it next to his half-full plate.

"Oh yeah," I said dryly, still annoyed about the beeper suggestion.

"One of my good friends called me a couple weeks ago with an opportunity to invest in another Broadway show. It's bound to be a hit because the Shuberts are the primary investors," he said in a cool voice.

"Oh, that's great. What's the show?" I asked, knowing full well that it had to be a white show. Why else wouldn't I have heard about it?

"You'll never guess," Pierce laughed with his boyish giggle.

"What—Jerome Robbins Two?" I said sarcastically.

"No, a musical about the Anita Hill–Clarence Thomas debacle," Pierce explained.

"You're kidding," I responded, dropping my fork. "They're going to make a musical about that mess?"

"Calm down, Nicole," Pierce said as he backed away from me and the checkered-cloth-covered table.

"Pierce, that hearing was an embarrassment for this nation. Especially black people and women."

"Wait until you see the script before you pass judgment," Pierce said.

"See the script?"

"Yes. It could be a great role for you. I think you should look at it."

"You think so?"

"Yes, at least go to an audition."

"Well, maybe you're right. I am tired of just sitting behind stage every night. I wonder if Sam is setting up an audition."

"Don't worry about Samantha."

Smiling at me, Pierce reached for his portable phone and dialed a number. While he was punching the buttons I changed my attitude about the musical. This could be a great opportunity for me. Moments later I heard him say, "I was right, she is interested," and then he gently closed up the phone.

"It's all set. Be at Astoria rehearsal hall Friday at four," Pierce instructed.

"You're kidding . . . right? I have to tell my agent."

"No, that's also set. Have a ballad and an up-tempo number, sing like I know you can sing, and I think we'll have our Anita."

"Oh, Pierce, this is wonderful, you're wonderful," I said with excitement as I reached over and kissed him on his dry lips. I looked into his eyes and saw the surprise in them and the reflection of my own eyes that mirrored Pierce's dazed look. The warm light in his eyes made something intimate out of the moment.

I wanted to stay and enjoy the good news with Pierce, but there was so much work to do. I needed to pick out a couple of songs and decide what to wear, plus I couldn't wait to tell Kyle and Delaney. Pierce said he understood as he gave me another kiss and hailed a cab for me.

Kyle and Delaney seemed even more excited about my prospects for the new Broadway show than I was. We met later that evening at my apartment opting for pizza delivery so that they could help me get ready for my audition on Friday.

Kyle was going through my closet laying different outfits for me to wear on the bed. Delaney was going through *Billboard* magazine for song suggestions and I was going through my sheet music collection of old standards.

"Why don't you sing 'Save the Best for Last'?" Delaney suggested.

"The Vanessa Williams song. Oh, I love that song," I said.

"Yeah, sing that," Kyle yelled from my bedroom. "You know, next to you two, Miss Vanessa is my girl."

Kyle walked into the living room carrying my tight black spandex dress. He had a broad smile on his face.

"Here it is, Miss Honey. This is the dress," he boasted.

"Yes! Yes! You better work, girl," Delaney chirped in agreement.

"You think so?" I asked.

"Oh yeah, Nicole. Even I think about changing my religion when I see you in this dress. It will wear the kids out," Kyle said.

"I think he's right, Nic. Go and try it on."

While I changed into the dress I heard Vanessa Williams's voice floating in the air of my apartment. Someone was switching the CD tracks until the player arrived on "Save the Best for Last." Yes this was the dress and that was the ballad, I thought. Now all I needed was an up-tempo number and an easy hairstyle. Maybe I would wear it down or maybe up in a tight chignon. I'd ask Delaney and see if she could come and help me. I brushed out my hair, put on my diamond studs, and prepared to walk back into my living room. Kyle and Delaney's reaction would tell me if this was right.

Before I could leave the bedroom, my phone rang.

"Hello."

"Nickey. You know who this is?"

"Of course. Nobody calls me Nickey but my baby brother," I said.

"How you doing, sweetheart?"

"I'm good. What about you?"

"Well, I've been better," Michael said in a distressed tone.

"What's the matter, Michael?"

"I need to ask a favor. I've run into some hard times and I need to borrow some money before I get evicted."

"What about your job? Mama told me you had a great job."

"Don't tell Mama, but I got laid off."

"Why not tell her?"

"You know her, she'll worry about nothing."

"Is it nothing, Michael?"

"Yes, Nickey, I'll be fine if you help me out this time."

"How much do you need?"

"Fifteen hundred."

"Fifteen hundred. Michael, that's a lot of money."

"I know, Nickey, but I promise to pay you back once I get back on my feet."

"Well, let me see what I can do. Let me make sure I have your address. I'll send it next-day mail."

"Can you send it Western Union first thing in the morning?"

"Western Union. Well, okay sure. You have ID, don't you?"

"Yes. If you got a major credit card you can do it right now," Michael suggested.

"You need it that quickly?"

"Yes, big sis. I do," Michael said sadly.

"Okay, give me a couple of hours. If you don't hear from me then, you'll know I did it. Is your phone number still the same?"

"Yes. Thanks, baby. Now, please, promise me you won't say anything to Mama."

"I won't. You take care of yourself."

"I will. I love you, Nickey," Michael said.

"Yes, I love you too, baby."

When I hung up the phone I grabbed my purse, pulled my Visa from my wallet, and called information to get the number for Western Union. While I was waiting for an answer I wondered if Michael was telling me the truth and what had happened to all the money he'd got from Daddy's insurance policy and why he didn't want me to mention this to Mama. Lord knows she had spent her life spoiling Michael. Their relationship was always much closer than the one I shared with her. I was just happy he wasn't in any kind of trouble. Or at least I prayed he wasn't in any kind of trouble.

I finished the transaction for Michael. The moment I walked into the living room, Kyle started squealing with delight as he waved both hands in the air and pranced a little jig. Delaney put her long fingers to her chin and walked around me, nodding with approval.

"You go, girl," Kyle said.

"Girl, they can tell the rest of those divas to stay at home. Here is our Miss Anita," Delaney said. "What took you so long? I guess it takes extra time to get in a dress like that."

"No, girl. It takes no time. I had an important phone call."

"Who? Pierce?" Delaney asked.

"No, my little brother. Needed to borrow some money," I said.

"Is he all right?" Kyle asked.

"I think so."

"Oh, Nicole. This is going to be it," Kyle said, changing the subject. "I can see your name on the marquee right above the title. I wonder who they're going to get to play Clarence?" Kyle questioned.

"I love your faith in me. But I haven't got the part yet. What if they've already cast it?" I muttered.

"Oh, don't worry about that," Delaney said.

"Yes, Miss Thing, no man in his right mind would turn you down if he sees you in this dress," Kyle said.

"You two are so crazy. Thanks a million for being my friends," I said as my eyes began to mist. Kyle and Delaney came over and the three of us hugged each other. I briefly closed my eyes to keep the tears of joy inside. As I opened them I spotted a thin slice of streetlight that entered the living room from the open window. I felt Kyle's and Delaney's hands gently massage my neck and I thought how blessed I truly was. Silently, I mouthed a prayer of thanks.

Five

"*Free* Leona Helmsley headquarters," the familiar voice on the other end of the phone said.

"Kyle?" I quizzed.

"Ray, what's going on, chile?"

"What did you say when you answered the phone?"

"Free Leona," he laughed.

"You're one sick puppy," I said.

"But that's why you love me so."

"Where have you been? I've been calling all night."

"Can I please have a life? I've been up at Nicole's place."

"How is she doing? Did you give her my message?"

"Gorgeous as ever and no I didn't because this white man is helping her career. She'd be a fool to let him go when she doesn't have to fuck him," Kyle admonished.

"What are you talking about?"

"Well, he's loaded. Nicole has an audition for a Broadway musical he's backing. She's gonna play Anita Hill."

"Anita Hill? You're shitting me. They're making a musical out of that?"

"And you know it. White folks ain't gonna never let us forget that mess."

Kyle and I talked about Nicole for a few more minutes and how this might really be her big break. The last time I had any direct contact with Nicole was on her opening night a couple of years ago. I was going to show up and surprise her but I chickened out at the last minute and just sent one hundred roses, something I'd done often during our courtship. She called me late that night when I was asleep to thank me. At least I think she called. It could have been a dream.

———

When I talked to Kyle, I could sometimes hear the faint sounds of the city in the background. I pictured him sitting on the windowsill or floor of my old New York apartment. It was during these conversations that I so missed New York.

"So what have you been up to since you got back?"

"Same old stuff. Out there beating the pavement," Kyle said.

"Any good leads?"

"Yes, everything is fine. Actually I've got more work than I can handle."

"How's your love life? Any new men?"

"What love life? What men?"

"Now don't tell me you haven't been meeting some new men," I said.

"Ray, I'm so sick and tired of being sick and tired of niggers and all their shit. I long for a date where I don't have to hide my wallet and watch. What about you? How's Jared?"

"I didn't tell him, Kyle."

"What are you waiting on?" Kyle asked.

"I don't know. I'm really scared Jared is either going to be upset or that he already has a lover."

"Well, you won't know until you confront the issue, Ray. Act like you're in court and he's under cross-examination. Besides, if he has a lover, don't you think you'd know?"

"Yeah, I guess you're right," I said.

"What else is new?" Kyle joked.

I shared with Kyle Jared's welcome home surprise and what a magical evening it had been. I also told him about Gilliam's invitation and asked him what I should do if she came on to me.

"Well, you might have to fuck her," Kyle said. "But I think that's sexual harassment," he teased.

"Come on, Kyle, this is serious. Maybe it's all innocent."

"Ray, you need to get some. I don't care from who, male or female. I think all that semen has backed up in your brain."

"Now I release myself, by myself," I defended.

"Ray, listen to me. This is what you do. Invite Jared to your place. Cook a fabulous dinner for two, have lots and lots of champagne, and then look him in the eyes with those killer eyes of yours and say, 'Jared, I'm a punk.' He'll understand that," Kyle laid out.

"Why did I call you?"

" 'Cause you knew I'd tell you the truth."

"Oh, before I forget, I got a card and picture of JJ, Bernard, and Christopher," I said.

"I got one too. Doesn't she look wonderfully happy? Christopher is going to be a killer," Kyle said.

"Yep. It seems like only yesterday when the three of us were in my apartment and JJ told us she was pregnant," I recalled.

Janelle, or JJ as she preferred, was the female member of my New York trio. She'd played an important part in the development of my feeling totally comfortable around a woman who was aware of my sexuality. But things had changed drastically in Janelle's life. She'd married a former New York City bus driver and moved to Charlotte, North Carolina, with her husband Bernard. Her son Christopher was born shortly after.

"See? That's what a good man will do for you. Miss Thing isn't a fag hag anymore," Kyle laughed.

"Hey, you want to call her? I've got three-way calling," I said.

"Yeah, let's surprise her."

"Hold on," I said as I clicked my phone line over. I dialed JJ's number and a few seconds later I heard the phone ringing. I then clicked back over to Kyle.

"Kyle, you there? It's ringing," I said.

"I'm here," Kyle said.

"Hello," the deep male voice said.

"Bernard?" I quizzed.

"Yes?"

"How you doing? This is Raymond Tyler and Kyle Benton," I said.

"Hey, Bernard," Kyle said.

"Hey, guys. What a nice surprise. How you two doing? How's New York City? You guys keeping it safe for the rest of the world?"

"That's Kyle's job. I live in Atlanta," I said.

"Oh yeah. I forgot, Ray. Janelle told me that. Why haven't you visited us living so close by?"

"I'm going to do that real soon, Bernard, I promise. Where's your wife?"

"Downstairs in the laundry room. I'll get her. Good talking to you two," Bernard said.

"Same here, Bernard," I said.

"Yeah, me too," Kyle added.

While we were waiting for JJ to come to the phone Kyle commented on how sexy Bernard's voice sounded.

"Chile, Bernard's voice got my juices flowing. Can you imagine Miss JJ washing dirty diapers?" he joked.

"Hello, you two divas from hell," JJ's sweet-sounding voice said.

"Divas you're the one!" Kyle said.

"Hey, Janelle. How's it going?" I asked.

"I'm doing great. What about you two?"

"Can't complain," I said.

"I can, but Ray's paying for this call and we don't have enough time," Kyle said.

Janelle told us about her busy life in North Carolina, informing us that she was now working on her master's in child psychology at Johnson C. Smith University. She spoke proudly of Christopher and what a great and gifted child he was and of how she and Bernard were talking about having another child when Christopher reached four. Bernard was running his father's garage and their sex life was better than ever.

"It doesn't get much better than this," JJ said.

"Bitch, I hate you," Kyle said. "You are evil and must be destroyed," he joked.

"JJ, I'm really happy for you," I said.

"So you two still single?" JJ asked.

"Yes," I said.

"Me too," Kyle said. "But I haven't given up. I ride the bus every chance I get looking for my Bernard. Now that was the 190 wasn't it?"

"Queen, please be quiet. It was the 103. Ray, when are you coming to visit?" Janelle asked.

"Well, Kyle says he's coming to Atlanta Labor Day. Maybe we'll drive up then," I said.

"Yes, we should do that," Kyle said.

"That would be great. We're adding a room to the house and it will be finished by then," JJ said.

"That sounds great," I said.

"So you sure you two are doing all right?" JJ quizzed.

"I'm doing okay," I said.

"Yeah, me too, but sometimes I don't know if I should shoot myself or go bowling," Kyle joked.

"Well, kids, my other child is calling. This has been fun. I can't tell you how much I miss you two," JJ said.

"Yeah, I miss you too," I said.

"Me too," Kyle said.

"I love you, Raymond. I love you, Kyle," JJ said.

"I love you, JJ. Give Christopher a hug," I said.

"What is this, the colored Waltons?" Kyle said.

"I see he hasn't changed a bit," JJ said. "You guys take care."

"We will. Kyle, hang on the line. Bye, JJ," I said.

"I love you, JJ," Kyle said.

"You better. Bye, stay sweet and be safe," JJ said as she disconnected from our three-way conversation. When she hung up the sound of Kyle's voice changed to a depressed tone. "Ray, you still there?" he asked.

"Yes, buddy. I'm still here. Janelle sounds so happy."

"Yeah." Kyle sighed.

"What's wrong?" I asked.

"Ray, do you think our lives will ever be that happy?" Kyle asked with a melancholy edge in his voice.

"Yeah, buddy. One day. One day very soon," I assured him.

"You promise?" Kyle asked with the innocent voice of a child.

"I promise."

Six

I was nervous about my audition and upset with Pierce's beeper suggestion. The combination led me to Dr. Huntley's office for the second time during the week. Thank God she'd had a cancellation.

"He wants me to wear a beeper."

"A beeper? Who, Nicole?"

"Pierce and he is dead serious," I said.

"How does that make you feel?" Dr. Huntley asked.

"Like a possession."

"A possession?"

"Yes, like the time he paraded me in front of his family and friends and kept commenting on how much I looked like Diahann Carroll."

"That bothered you?"

"At first I was flattered but then . . ."

"Then?"

"Well, a couple of days later I was talking to my mother, telling her about meeting Pierce's parents, and I told her what he said. My mother pointed out I was darker than her."

"But that was your mother," Dr. Huntley observed.

"Yes, I don't think Pierce means anything by it. Maybe it's a white thing."

"A white thing. How so?"

"You know, being in control."

"How does saying you look like Diahann Carroll mean he's looking for control?"

"Well, sometimes he makes strong suggestions on what I should wear when I'm meeting friends of his."

"What about what your mother said?"

"Oh, that's just the way she is."

Dr. Huntley didn't respond. This was one of those times when her eyes spoke for her. It was so quiet I heard someone running upstairs in Dr. Huntley's brownstone. I wondered if it was one of her children.

"Doesn't that sound racist?" I asked.

"What?"

"Pierce and control. How a lot of people think white men always have to be in control no matter what," I said.

"Does it?"

"I don't know. What do you think?"

"Well, you haven't brought the race issue up when it comes to your relationship with Pierce. You only seem to bring it up when talking about other black people," Dr. Huntley observed.

"I don't understand, Dr. Huntley. What are you talking about?"

"Well, you always mention the color of your black friends, using terms like light, black, brown . . ."

"Yes, I guess I do."

"Do you have any idea why?"

"No."

Dr. Huntley didn't say anything. She started to move from side to side in her chair, looking directly at me with an unreadable expression.

"Maybe it goes back to my childhood. I don't know if I told you but my brother is very light-skinned. I'm sorry, there I go again. Well, anyhow, whenever my brother really wanted to make me mad he would call me *black thing* and when he *really* wanted to get me he would say *blue black*."

"What would you do?"

"I'd cry."

"Why?"

"Because sometimes words hurt."

"It still doesn't explain why you never bring up race when talking or dealing with Pierce."

"Well, we both know it's there. *It* being the difference in our color and religion but I think ignoring it means it will never be an issue in our relationship."

"How would you respond if a black man suggested you carry a beeper? What if Raymond had asked you?"

"Raymond would never do that."

"You're sure?"

"I'm sure. If he asked me, I'd ask why and we would discuss it."

"Did you ask Pierce?"

"No, not really."

"I think you should, but I still don't think it will answer why you both seem to be avoiding the race issue. It's something to think about."

"Well, why bring it up if it hasn't been a problem?"

"That's one way of dealing with it," Dr. Huntley said as she picked her watch up from the desk.

My time was up.

The cool air conditioning in the empty theater caused a bit of concern for me. What if it affects my voice? I tried to take my mind off the cool air while going over the lyrics for the ballad I'd prepared for the audition. I should have scheduled Dr. Huntley for after the audition. All that talking was not good for the vocal cords.

This wasn't a typical audition. With the exception of a few stage-hands, backstage was totally empty. Most auditions I'd attended in the past included every black actress who was a member of SAG. Samantha had told me the producers had held open auditions for SAG and non-SAG actors for two days prior.

One of the rituals of auditions in the past was psyching out the competition with your voice, dance movements, or your attire. When that didn't work, divas would start to verbalize their résumés. I went against the advice of Kyle and Delaney and chose to wear a blue silk suit with a black leotard top instead of the black spandex dress. I was going for the role of Anita Hill and I doubted very seriously that Anita owned a spandex dress of any color. I wore very little makeup and had pulled my hair back into a tight chignon that brought attention to my diamond stud earrings, a gift from Raymond, and to the pendant that my daddy had given me before my first pageant. I was looking in a mirror tucking tiny strands of hair back into place when I suddenly heard my name called.

"Nicole Springer," the deep baritone voice said.

I quickly grabbed my sheet music from my bag and darted toward the empty stage.

"What are you going to sing for us?" the voice asked from the darkened orchestra section.

" 'Save the Best for Last,' " I responded.

"Great. Have at it," the faceless voice said.

I walked over to the heavy-set blonde sitting at the piano, gave her a smile, handed her the sheet music, and then walked to the center of the stage. I looked at the pianist and signaled that I was ready.

Just thirty seconds into the song I heard the voice again.

"Thank you. That was great. Do you have an up-tempo number?"

"Yes," I said, realizing that I'd left my other sheet music at home. I walked over to the piano and asked the accompanist if she knew the Diana Ross version of "Why Do Fools Fall in Love?" She smiled and directed her head toward center stage, giving me the signal to return to my designated spot. When she began to play I started snapping my fingers to add a beat to the single instrument. Again just as I was getting into the song, I heard the voice once more.

"Thanks. Samantha Walker is your agent, right?"

"Yes."

"Great, thank you. We'll be in touch."

I walked to the piano and mouthed a thank-you to the lady and started toward backstage. I noticed several male dancers going through stretch motions as I looked for my bag. I overheard one of the guys say that Robin Givens was up for the leading female role. I didn't realize Robin sang or danced, but she was Robin Givens so what difference did that make?

We'll be in touch, I thought, that couldn't be a good sign. They didn't ask me to dance or read and why did I choose that dreadful Diana Ross song? I was used to sealing the deal with my up-tempo numbers. Oh well, I sighed, as I pushed the heavy steel door, at least I have a job. I wasn't performing but I was getting a paycheck.

I stepped out onto Forty-third Street and headed toward Broadway. I was going to meet Delaney at JR's. She was taping a rap video at Radio City Music Hall. It was times like this when I envied Delaney. She would audition one day and shoot the next. The turnaround would be swift and stress-free or so it seemed. It might be weeks before I heard the bad news about this job.

As I walked down Broadway I convinced myself that I didn't want the part. The show was bound to be controversial. It would mean twelve-hour rehearsal days and then the possibility of out-of-town try-outs only to return and close in a night if the *New York Times* critic didn't like the show. Besides, I didn't want to be away from the city this summer. I didn't know why but I knew I had to be here.

Jelly's Last Jam was settling in for a long run and there was sure to be a national tour. All I needed was one chance to go on, sing, and hit my marks and the rest would be history. Renee was bound to get bored.

Maybe I would talk to the director about a role as one of the Hunnies, part of the female Greek chorus very important to the show.

I walked into JR's and saw that the popular bar was empty with the exception of Billy, the regular bartender.

"Hi, Nicole. How's the show?"

"The show is going great. Sold out every night."

"What can I get you?"

"Give me a cranberry and orange juice," I said, lifting myself onto a stool at the end of the bar. While Billy was mixing up my favorite juices I stepped down from the bar stool and went to the ladies' room to see how well my makeup was holding up. On the way back to my stool I called and checked my messages.

"Yes, Ms. Springer, you have two messages. One from Sam, you got the part, and another one from Dr. Gessler, saying congratulations and I love you and wear the black dress." I hung up the phone and took a deep breath and then let out a loud squeal. I quickly dialed Sam's number to confirm her message. She said the director called right after my audition. Sam's voice was filled with excitement. She said she had never got a director to call back so soon after her client auditioned. I didn't tell her about Pierce's intervention. When I hung up from Samantha I called Pierce's office but his secretary told me he was with a patient. I dropped my remaining quarters in my purse and headed back to the bar.

"Good news?" Billy questioned.

"The best. Great news," I said gleefully as I walked briskly to the stool, took a long sip of the drink, and grabbed my bag and headed out the door. I stopped long enough to ask Billy to put it on my tab or make Delaney pay for it when she showed up.

"It's on me," Billy yelled as I walked out the door.

As I headed toward Eighth Avenue to hail a taxi, I was so happy that I was literally skipping. I would give my mother a call to share the good news and then prepare my farewell to the cast of *Jelly's*. I knew my mother would be happy but I could also count on her saying, "When are you going to get in a show that lasts as long as that *Dreamgirls* show?" Was there any way to satisfy my mother?

Seven

The things you do for love. Jared not only got me up each and every morning to exercise but he also got me to do something that I'd never envisioned doing in this life. Bowling. We would meet Friday evenings after work at a bowling alley near Lennox Mall and then head to a restaurant called Mick's in Buckhead or to the popular bar Mr. V's Peachtree for drinks. On this Friday all the time we were bowling Jared seemed preoccupied and in deep thought. So preoccupied that I came close to beating him, which would have been something of a miracle. I too was preoccupied, thinking about the dinner I would use to reveal my feelings and myself to Jared. After bowling we decided against going to Mick's or Mr. V's but went to my condo instead. We were drinking a couple of Rolling Rocks when Jared walked quietly toward the sliding glass door that led to the patio looking out over north Buckhead.

"What's on your mind, buddy?" I asked Jared. "You seem to be out there with the stars."

"Oh, just something I've got to clear up," Jared answered.

"Anything I can help with?"

"Well, you know this guy from my old neighborhood is running against Congressman Thomas," Jared said.

"I've only heard you mention it. He's not serious competition is he?"

"No, not really. There's just some information I know and I can't decide whether or not to share it with the congressman," Jared lamented.

"What kind of information?"

"Well, Jimmy Dee is gay," Jared said with a trace of disappointment in his voice.

"Gay?" I repeated, trying not to change my facial expression.

"Yeah, and a couple of guys working on the campaign found out about it and want to use it to get him to drop out of the race," Jared said.

"Well, how do you feel about that?" I asked.

"That's the problem. I don't know how I feel," Jared said as he took a long gulp of his beer.

I took a sip of my warm beer and saw the disturbed look on Jared's face. This was really a big concern for him. In the two-plus years that we had known each other this was the first time the word "gay" had been uttered by either of us. I thought maybe now would be the perfect time to tell Jared, when he suddenly started to think out loud.

"I mean I don't have anything against a person if that's what they choose to be and I really don't like to start throwing dirt in political races, especially since there are two black men against a white candidate. But he could split the black vote and force a runoff."

Choose, I thought. So Jared thought someone chose to be gay. Should I correct him or let him continue to voice his feelings? The expression in his eyes was hard to read.

"How real a possibility is that?" I asked anxiously.

"Well, you never know," Jared said. "I mean Jimmy has been on the City Council for years and people in the community love him. He's done a lot for them. I've heard some people, even my mother, say that Congressman Thomas has gotten too uppity since he's been to Washington."

"Shouldn't the people decide? Do you think it's right to use something like that? And how do you know for certain he's gay?" I quizzed, playing devil's advocate.

"Yes, the people will decide, and trust me on being certain about Jimmy," Jared said.

Well, I wasn't going to touch that. I mean, it could only be one thing —this guy had come on to Jared at some point. If he had made a pass, I wondered why Jared didn't share that with me. Maybe the pass had turned into something more. Jared leaned on the steel banister, swallowed the rest of his beer, and stared aimlessly.

"So what's on the agenda for the rest of the weekend?" Jared asked after a brief period of silence and obvious deep thought.

"Well, I'm going to church with Gilliam."

"Oh, that should be fun. Didn't you say something about a special dinner?"

"Yeah, but that can wait till later. I mean it looks like you've got a lot on your mind," I said.

"Yeah, but you know I can make time for you," Jared said.

"Let me give you a call tomorrow. You doing your big brother thing?"

"Yeah, first thing in the morning. Give me a call and let me know what you want to do," Jared said as he grabbed his briefcase and gym bag and walked slowly toward the front door.

"Okay, buddy, don't think too hard about that situation. You'll make the right decision," I assured him.

"You think so?"

"I know so."

"Okay," Jared said as he gave me a hug with his powerful arms.

After Jared left I got another beer from the refrigerator and walked back outside to the patio. I watched dusk descend with orange and purple streaks as the sun blended with the clouds. I tried to interpret my conversation with Jared and wondered if his current dilemma was caused by his disgust or his own insecurities. I was beginning to feel a strange sense of betrayal. I wanted to believe that in Jared I had the most difficult of all things in this world to find. A friend and lover in the true sense of the words. Someone with whom I could share my deepest confidences and completely bare my soul. Just hours before it had all seemed possible. Now, with a single conversation, I was not so certain.

I heard a knock at my door and since my doorman hadn't buzzed me I assumed that it was Jared. I quickly opened the door without even looking through the peephole and realized that it was Trey, the evening doorman.

"Got this package for you, Mr. Tyler," Trey said as he handed me a box wrapped in my mother's familiar brown paper.

"Thanks, Trey. Looks like a care package from home," I said as I reached in my pocket to retrieve a tip for Trey.

"Don't worry about it, Mr. Tyler," Trey said when he saw my hands come out of my pockets empty.

"I'll take care of you later on this evening," I said.

"No problem."

I was right, it was a package from my mom. I ripped open the box and from the escaping scent I realized what it was. There in a tin box were my favorite chocolate chip butterfinger cookies that only my mother could make. There was a little note from Mom stating that she would love to hear from her number-one son.

I bit into one of the tasty cookies and headed for the phone to call home. Friday evening was the one night Mom didn't cook and demanded that, like it or not, Pops take her and Kirby out to dinner. I looked at my watch and was certain they wouldn't be there, but I could leave a nice message. Much to my surprise, my mom picked up after two rings.

"What's going on, lady?" I quizzed.

"Ray-Ray," my mother said with a slightly startled voice.

"Who else?"

"How you doing, baby?"

"I'm doing great now that I have my care-package cookies," I said as I took a bite from my second cookie.

"Oh, you got them already. That was quick," Mama said.

"Yeah, how is everybody and why aren't you out on your Friday night date?" I asked.

"I'm here waiting on your father now. He's out looking for Kirby."

"How are Pops and Knucklehead?" I asked.

"Oh, your father is fine, but your little brother, well, that's another story," my mother said, concern in her voice.

"What's wrong with Kirby?"

"Too long a story to go into right now, baby. But I will tell you this. Your father is thinking about shipping his lanky butt off to military school very soon," Mama said.

"No shittin'," I replied.

"You'd better watch your language, mister," my mother laughed. "I might have to tell your father to send you too."

"Is there anything I can do? Do you want me to talk with Kirby?"

"I don't know right now. Let's see what Ray Senior can do."

Mom went on to explain that Kirby was staying out past his curfew and hanging out with a bad group at school. She said his grades were dropping and all he had on his mind were girls, basketball, rap music, and pressuring her to allow him to get a hole in his ear. She told me that Kirby's peers constantly kidded him about making good grades and being from a rich family. "A rich family," my mother laughed. "If these children only knew how hard we struggled to get here."

"But you're a schoolteacher, Mrs. Tyler. You've got to be rich," I joked.

We talked about how kids had changed since I was a youth growing up in Birmingham and how there was even talk of L.A.-type gangs moving into our hometown. I assured my mother that Pops would take care of it and if she wanted me to I would allow Kirby to come to Atlanta for an extended visit this summer. She said she would talk with Pops about it and give me a call next week. My mother also assured me that Pops, as always, had everything under control when it came to Kirby.

After hanging up, I started to undress, put on a Whitney Houston CD, and debated how to spend the rest of the evening and my weekend. I thought about my conversation with Jared and tried to decipher his concerns. There he was on one hand condemning the gay lifestyle and subtly flirting with me on the other. I mean he was sending out mixed signals but so was I. I had to come face to face with the looming possibility that my friendship with Jared would not lead to romantic love.

I also thought about my little brother and how he was growing up so fast. Since I didn't really have a social life I thought it might be good to have him here with me. Thinking about that made me realize that the day when I would have to share my sexuality with my little brother was close at hand. I knew he was growing up fast and that I would have to sit down with him soon, but I was going to clear it with my parents first. I took a long hot shower and sat nude in the darkness of my living room, sipping a warm, stale beer on the sofa as the sounds of pre-summer played a haunting symphony outside my sliding glass door and a soulful female voice floated throughout my condo.

Eight

During the taxi ride to meet Pierce I became excited all over. I had just got the lead role in a new Broadway show. Maybe this one would last longer than thirty-plus performances. When I spoke with Pierce he sounded excited about seeing me and celebrating my new role. He also said he had another big surprise for me. As the taxi moved through the busy city streets I wondered what the surprise could be.

Pierce chose Jezebel's for dinner. It was one of my favorite places to eat in midtown Manhattan and was just blocks away from most of the major theaters. It was one of Pierce's favorites too. Jezebel's was an alluring establishment with large palms and assorted delicate shades of green foliage towering overhead. The furnishings were antiques that looked like they came straight from a New Orleans brothel, with the exception of a large mahogany bar facing the eating area and Ninth Avenue in the background. Hanging from the ceiling were beautiful, multicolored shawls and antique chandeliers, glittering in the night, giving the room a romantic effect. Some of the tables had old-fashioned swings around them, instead of the regular wrought-iron chairs. The swings were reminiscent of the old swing on my grandma's porch back in Arkansas. How I adored that swing.

As soon as I walked into the restaurant I spotted Pierce sitting at a table located next to the large picture window. He stood up to greet me as I walked past a crowd of people waiting for tables.

"Don't you look beautiful. You're wearing my favorite dress. How is Broadway's newest star feeling?" Pierce asked.

"Yes, and I'm feeling great. What about you?" I asked as I gave Pierce a gentle kiss on the lips.

"I'm doing just great. So how was the rest of your day?"

"It was great, thanks to you," I said.

"Don't thank me. The bottom line has always been your talent," Pierce said.

"But still I really appreciate all your help."

"I know you do. Are you excited?"

"Yes, I am. I'm starving too. Where is our waiter?"

Pierce motioned toward an attractive-looking black man who quickly came to our table with a sly grin on his face.

"Would you like an aperitif?" the waiter asked.

"Sure, two Dubonnets," Pierce said.

"No, I think I'd like a Campari instead," I inserted.

"Fine, one Dubonnet and one Campari," the waiter said as he handed the two of us menus.

"So when are you giving *Jelly's* your two-week notice?" Pierce asked.

"Well, I haven't decided. I don't have a contract for the new show yet and I haven't seen a completed script. Giving my resignation might be a bit premature," I responded as I scrutinized the menu.

"Well, I'm certain everything is going to work out. There is even talk of BeBe Winans doing the music," Pierce said.

"You mean they don't have the music yet? That's odd."

"I think they have some of the music. They're still waiting on the final word from BeBe's agent."

"Oh, I hadn't heard that or much of anything else yet," I said with excitement. "That would be great!"

"Yes, I think everything is going to be just fine," Pierce said crisply, as he sipped his drink.

When our entrées arrived I settled back to enjoy the evening. As I began to relax I felt a lot of the eyes in the restaurant were on Pierce and myself. This was something that despite our racial difference rarely happened, especially in places like Jezebel's. I mean everyone from the wine steward to the bus boys was either staring or just overly attentive. The last time I had gotten this much attention was at the opening-night party of my last Broadway show.

Pierce and I discussed the pros and cons of my taking the new show. He assured me that he was not about to invest money in another bomb. The producers were going after the top in every field from lighting design to costumes. I thought about Kyle and the possibility of his putting in a bid to do some of the costumes for the show. It would be a great boost for his business and nice to have him around for moral support.

As our dinner came close to completion, Pierce became very nervous. I had never seen him like this. He was gazing around the restaurant as though he was expecting someone.

"Is everything all right, Pierce? You seem a bit preoccupied," I said.

"I'm fine but I have something very important I need to discuss with you," Pierce said.

"Sure, what?" I asked.

"Let's order dessert and brandy first," Pierce suggested.

"Just coffee for me. I'll have some of your dessert," I said.

Pierce motioned for the waiter once again and ordered dessert, coffee, and brandy. He gave the waiter such a strange look I was beginning to believe that Pierce's surprise was close by. But what was it?

Minutes later another waiter showed up and served us coffee, Pierce's brandy, and deep-dish peach cobbler. The waiter looked awfully familiar. I was certain that I knew him but I couldn't recall from where. His knowing smile led me to believe that he recognized me too.

"Nicole, how long have we been going out?" Pierce asked as he swirled the gold-colored brandy around the bottom of the snifter.

"Oh, what has it been—almost two years?" I replied as I sipped the warm coffee and dipped into the cobbler resting in front of Pierce.

"Well, I guess it's no secret how much I love you and how I want to spend the rest of my life with you," Pierce said, his voice unsteady and his eyes centered directly on mine.

"Pierce, that's so sweet of you to say," I said.

"Well—" Pierce paused as his eyes motioned to something or someone behind me.

I turned around and there was the familiar-looking waiter now accompanied by two more men, one with a violin and the other with a flute; a fourth man was standing next to them holding a silver platter with a glass top protecting a small black box.

"Pierce, what—" I stammered, but before I could complete my sentence or thought, the waiter started to sing, "When I First Saw You," from *Dreamgirls*. That's where I knew him from, he had taken over the role of Curtis right before *Dreamgirls* closed.

By now *every* eye in the restaurant was on Pierce and myself as the waiter sang beautifully one of my favorite songs. His rich tenor voice caused my naked arms to feel chilled and his voice filled every space in the restaurant. It was like a scene out of a movie, only this wasn't a movie. As he came to the last note, the man holding the platter walked over to Pierce and lifted the glass cover. Pierce reached for the black box, stood up and moved closer to me, and then gently lowered himself to his knees.

I could feel my stomach turning and my eyes filling with tears. But were these tears of joy or embarrassment as the large restaurant was now deadly silent.

"Nicole Marie Springer," Pierce said with a loud and clear voice, "will you marry me?" Four words I thought I'd never hear, especially in front of a room full of strangers. What could I do, what could I say? I felt my emotions ricocheting all over the packed restaurant. I looked into Pierce's face as he opened the small black box revealing a stunning diamond. I couldn't ever recall being so close to a diamond that big.

"Well, are you going to make me wait all night?" Pierce whispered. I had to say yes. I couldn't embarrass him.

"Yes," I stammered. "Yes, I'll marry you."

The room broke out into thunderous applause. Pierce lifted himself from the floor after gently slipping the large ring on my finger and kissing me softly on the lips. "She said yes!" he yelled at the top of his lungs. "Champagne for everyone," he added.

Waiters and busboys alike began to scurry around the room placing champagne flutes in the patrons' hands. I was in a semi-daze, make that haze, my eyes fixed on the exquisite ring. I couldn't move. I sat motionless as a statue. I was scared and delighted. But my fear battled the excitement. This had caught me completely off guard and I had said yes. Had I done the right thing? I did care a great deal for Pierce, might even love him, but marriage . . . and was what I felt romantic love? What had I gotten myself into?

The rush of strangers and well-wishers to our table brought me out of my self-induced trance. Men and women both came over to our table and offered congratulations. I felt like I was in a beauty pageant again, but I'd won a title I hadn't expected to win.

Nine

A substantial traffic jam led me to believe I was going to a concert or sporting event instead of a church. Gilliam had called me early Sunday morning with directions and the suggestion that I leave early to avoid traffic.

Several uniformed policemen directed cars into a large parking lot that showed no signs of the First Birth Baptist Church in suburban Decatur. I followed nattily attired churchgoers as they parked their cars and then hopped on a bus that took us to a structure that resembled a mini-version of the Georgia Dome. I had never seen a church as large as First Birth, nor had I ever seen so many black people—or white people for that matter—gathered together to worship something other than a sports team or popular entertainer. I entered the sanctuary and was greeted by everyone that I made eye contact with. I mean these people seemed happy to be here. How was I ever going to find Gilliam? After a few minutes of looking around the circular lobby of the massive church I suddenly heard Gilliam call my name.

"Ray, you made it," Gilliam said as she turned her neatly made up cheek to my lips. Gilliam was dressed in a beautiful peach silk dress very different from the tailored suits she wore to the office.

"Gilliam, this is a big church," I said.

"Isn't it beautiful?" Gilliam said proudly. "Let's get inside before we have to sit in the choir stands."

"Okay, let's do that. I don't want to turn this church out with my wonderful singing," I teased.

The interior of the sanctuary was even more beautiful than the exterior. It brought to mind the kinds of churches you see on television, which had, unfortunately, been the extent of my worship experience since moving to Atlanta.

Gilliam and I found seats close to the back since the church was already filled almost to capacity. I could feel the warmth in the church as I took my seat in the crowded pew. Everyone smiled and had an air of inner peace about them.

Soon after we sat down, a large youth choir marched in singing at the top of their lungs. Worshipers in the church jumped to their feet, clapping and swaying to the voices of the choir and the musicians. The feeling was more like a pep rally than like any church service I had ever attended. The sound of all of the clapping hands and shouts was as thunderous as any football crowd I'd been a part of.

I thought some of the people seated close to me were going to take off at any moment and fly out of the church into the heavens and that included Gilliam.

As I watched Gilliam immerse herself in the service, I thought of Nicole and how she used to take me to church with her in Harlem. I thought Gilliam and Nicole would probably really like each other if they ever had the opportunity to meet.

After about fifteen minutes of loud clapping, stomping, and cries throughout the church we finally were instructed to take our seats. A well-dressed young lady with great diction invited visitors to stand and be properly greeted. Gilliam gave me a sweet smile when I remained in my seat. Somehow I didn't feel like a visitor. I felt at home. Like I was back in the church I'd grown up in, in Birmingham. The youth choir sang wonderfully. Not only did they sing well but they moved with choreographed movements like a precision high school drill team. At times I got a bit nervous watching them, because it looked like instead of singing praise they were going to start a soul train line and break out into the latest dances. But at least these young people were doing their moves in church and not at a local nightspot and they appeared to be having the time of their lives. It made me feel good to see so many young black men in the choir singing as if their lives depended on it.

An undeniable excitement permeated every inch of the church, from the ushers to the youthful minister. His sermon was more like teaching a lesson rather than the fire and brimstone tone I was used to hearing from black preachers, especially Southern black preachers. Yes, there was something splendid and unconventional about First Birth, but at the same time there was something basic and down to earth about it.

Enjoying the service, I began to look around the packed sanctuary, making eye contact with several men and an occasional woman. There seemed to be a large contingent of gay men attending this church, but wasn't that always the case?

I brought a halt to my scanning to enjoy a young man with an exceptional voice singing a solo. His voice soared from deep baritone to falsetto. Every time he hit one of his glass-breaking high notes the church would erupt with shouts, applause, and worshipers leaping to their feet. I wondered why it was the high notes that caused such demonstrations and if the many gay men in the choir stands were open about their sexuality.

My speculation allowed a mischievous thought to cross my mind: I tried to imagine the church minus its gay men and women. I was certain more than the soloist and musicians would disappear, not only in this church but in black churches all across the country. How many choir members, ushers, deacons, and ministers would no longer take their appointed positions on this day of absence? Would there ever be a day when gay people would be accepted with open arms in a place that advertised miracles, love, and forgiveness?

After church, I felt exhilarated. The time had passed at a pace as rapid as a thoroughbred horse race. Gilliam's face was blanketed with a broad smile as we walked toward the outside of the church and the bus stand to return me to the remote parking lot and my car.

Once we got outside, Gilliam suggested that she give me a ride to my car and that I follow her to her home for a light brunch. Since I didn't have big plans for this beautiful Sunday afternoon I quickly agreed.

After she dropped me at my car I followed Gilliam's silver Jaguar X26 down a narrow two-lane street behind the large church. A few minutes later we pulled into a fashionable housing subdivision with a sign advertising homes beginning in the low three hundred thousands. Gilliam's street was a treeless cluster of new homes that resembled mini-castles. Her salmon and gray two-story home sat at the apex of a cul-de-sac, demanding attention and respect, like its owner. Inside, the house was beautiful and tastefully decorated in a way that would make HG magazine proud. Gilliam steered me to a big glass-enclosed deck off the dining room that faced a large golf course.

As I watched golfers study the tiny golf balls, I remembered Jared and how he loved to golf just as much as he loved to bowl. As my thoughts were going toward Jared and my impending problem, Gilliam appeared in a beautiful black silk pantsuit carrying two piping hot mugs of coffee.

"You drink your coffee black, don't you, Ray?" Gilliam inquired.

"Yes, thank you," I said as I took the mug from Gilliam.

"It's a beautiful day, isn't it?" Gilliam exclaimed.

"Yes, it is. Gilliam, your home is beautiful and this view is superb."

"Thank you. It's home," she said.

"Do you golf?"

"Yes, I do. What about you?" Gilliam asked.

"I've been out a couple of times with Jared," I said.

"How is Jared? I haven't talked with him in a while."

"Oh, he's fine—busy trying to get Congressman Thomas reelected," I shared.

"Oh, that shouldn't be a problem. Provided he can keep his libido in check," Gilliam said confidently.

"Is that a problem for the congressman?"

"It used to be but I haven't heard any rumors lately. It should be an easy race for him."

"I think you're right."

Just as I was about to comment on how much I'd enjoyed church, a middle-aged black man came out with dishes of food that smelled appetizing.

"Ray, this is Mr. Nevels. He takes good care of me," Gilliam boasted.

"How are you doing, Mr. Nevels? Something sure smells good," I said.

"I'm fine, young man. Pleased to make your acquaintance," Mr. Nevels said. "I hope you like chicken and waffles."

"I'm from Birmingham, Mr. Nevels, so you know I do," I joked. "I hope you have some grits too."

"I'll see what I can do," Mr. Nevels said.

Gilliam and I sat at the black lacquered table and enjoyed a feast of pecan waffles, fried chicken, link sausage, and cheese grits that Mr. Nevels prepared. The food was some of the best I had eaten since moving to Atlanta. We traded our coffee for mimosas and appreciated a day that was made for relaxing and sipping champagne. We talked about upcoming prospects for business at the firm and then went on to more personal issues. Gilliam shared with me the fact that she was dating someone who was very powerful in local politics and was also dating a younger attorney who practiced in Philadelphia. She laughed loudly as she explained that, "The gentleman in Atlanta was good for her future and the younger attorney was good for *fulfillment.*" I was pleased and surprised how open and comfortable I felt with Gilliam.

Maybe it was because I now realized that she was not remotely interested in me sexually and she was just regular folk.

I shared with her my past relationships with Sela and Nicole and explained that I was taking a break from relationships. I did not mention Kelvin and Quinn. I pondered how Gilliam felt about gay people and if she had even been held suspect because of her powerful demeanor.

"Maybe that's best," Gilliam said. "We women can be God-awful distractions."

As Mr. Nevels cleared the plates from the table Gilliam and I strolled out toward the golf course. She explained to me that she'd invited me to church and her home because she wanted to tell me about how pleased she was with my work and that she was strongly considering expanding the firm with more attorneys and perhaps a senior partner. Just when she was about to elaborate further, Mr. Nevels called out from the house that she had an important phone call. Gilliam excused herself and I planted myself in the hammock I had been eyeing since my arrival. I lay back and watched the sun peek through the clouds and find its place against the silver blue sky. My body swayed the fishnet hammock side to side and my nose inhaled the sweet-smelling air. It was hard to believe that a bustling urban city was only a few miles away. I became very comfortable and a wave of sleepiness crept through my body like the warm syrup that covered the waffles Mr. Nevels had prepared. I smiled at the stereotype that most black folks go to sleep after stuffing themselves. The sleep and stereotype won out as I fell deep into dreamland. In the dream I was just about to tell Jared my secret when I was awakened by Gilliam's voice.

"Well, I guess that's what I get for passing out my cards," Gilliam said.

"What . . . ?" I asked as I wiped embarrassing wet dribble from my face.

"Looks like we have another client. Or should I say you have a new one," Gilliam said.

"Huh?" I slurred, not fully understanding her.

Gilliam explained that her lawyer friend in Philadelphia had a pro-football-player client who had been arrested in a popular Atlanta nightclub for punching out a patron for an unwanted stare. "I've arranged to have him released on his own recognizance," Gilliam said. "He'll be in our office first thing in the morning."

"Is this going to be a criminal action?"

"It is now, but I'm sure we're talking civil lawsuit when the victim finds out his assailant is a pro-football player who has a sizable income but sounds like a flaming asshole."

"Well, I guess I better head home to get myself ready. Thanks for a wonderful afternoon, Gilliam," I said, hoisting myself from the hammock and looking for my suit jacket.

"Mr. Nevels put your jacket in the hall closet. Let me walk you to your car," Gilliam offered.

"Does this guy play for the Atlanta Falcons?" I asked Gilliam.

"I don't think so. The attorney who asked us to help out is from Philadelphia so it's probably an East Coast team."

"What's he doing in Atlanta?"

"I didn't get all that information. That's why I'm so glad I have a talented attorney like yourself to deal with these jokers," Gilliam declared.

"Yeah, flattery will get you everywhere," I laughed.

"I'll call Mico and have him come in early to take his statement," Gilliam said.

"Great. Again, thanks a million," I said as I kissed Gilliam on the cheek.

As I drove down Highway 20 I toyed with the idea of stopping by Jared's. It being Sunday meant he was probably at his mother's house greasing down. Going without seeing Jared two days in a row with both of us being in town was a rare occurrence. A situation that I had the strangest feeling was going to become more frequent.

Ten

My favorite day arrived. It started off as one of those rare Sundays when I didn't go to early morning church service. I'd made up my mind to go to afternoon service when Delaney and Kyle phoned on a three-way call and convinced me to meet them at the Shark Bar on Amsterdam Avenue for brunch. When I explained to them I'd promised to meet Sheila, they kindly offered to include her provided she didn't try to save them over brunch.

They told me to make sure I wore my new engagement ring, but to wear gloves or keep it in my purse if I took the subway. I got up from bed and went to the small market located in my building and bought a copy of the *New York Times* and a buttered pumpernickel bagel. I climbed back into my bed the moment I reached my apartment and went straight to the Arts and Leisure section. As I skimmed the advertising for Broadway shows, I pictured a full-page ad with my name above the title in a new musical, but what was the name of this musical and whose name would be right beside mine playing Clarence Thomas?

I spent a great deal of the morning daydreaming about the possibilities for leading men when it entered my mind that just days before I had accepted a proposal from a man I was not so certain I loved the way I should. The realization led me to get on my knees beside my bed and pray for direction on what to do. Praying usually helped, but it was on days like this that I really missed Candance and my daddy. While alone in my apartment I would pretend they were both here with me and we would discuss what I should do. I wondered what Dr. Huntley would think of this?

My daddy would just want to be sure that Pierce treated me with love and respect and never lifted a heavy hand toward me, while Candance would speculate on what our children would look like. She would remind me that they would be mixed race and Pierce and I would have to decide what religion to bring them up in. She would also joke that they would probably have good hair and pretty eyes.

Pierce and I had talked around religion. I took him to church with me once and he twitched every time the minister said Jesus, and then fell asleep. He never invited me to temple.

The phone interrupted my thoughts. It was Pierce. He wanted to get together for brunch, but I told him of my plans and promised to call him when I got back. He mentioned that his mother wanted to give us an engagement party at their home in Connecticut as soon as we set the date or location for the wedding.

Well, of course, it would be in Little Rock. I had always dreamed of getting married at the Old State House. It was a beautiful Civil War mansion set on the Arkansas River and was available to dignitaries for weddings and receptions. Being a former Miss Arkansas made me a dignitary. I smiled at the thought that winning a beauty pageant put me on the level of government officials and real important people. Beauty pageant winners were still held in high regard in the South. My pending nuptials were still pretty much hush-hush since I had shared them only with Delaney, Kyle, and Sheila. I'd talked with my mother the previous evening but failed to mention it. It was not a conversation I was looking forward to. I just hoped she wouldn't decide to boycott the ceremony and me too for that matter!

Kyle and Delaney were already finishing up their first cup of coffee when I arrived at the Shark Bar, the current Upper West Side quintessential buppie restaurant-bar. Before I could sit down Kyle grabbed my hand and said, "Let me see it, Miss Girl."

"Hold on a second, Kyle," I protested.

"Come on, Nicole," Delaney encouraged.

I pulled the ring from my purse, still in its tiny black box.

"Oh, it's so big!" Kyle said.

"How many carats is it?" Delaney asked.

"Looks like ten to me," Kyle answered.

"I don't know. It doesn't matter to me," I said.

"You better work, bitch," Kyle said. "This is fabulous. When do you want me to start on the gown?" he asked.

"Wait a minute, we haven't set a date yet. I've got to see how everything is going to turn out."

"How what is going to turn out?" Delaney asked.

"Well, this took me completely off guard. Pierce and I still have some things to work out."

"But you've already taken the ring," Kyle said.

"Yes, I have. You know I'm not getting any younger and this could be my first and last proposal."

"So that's reason to take it? Chile, you need to get a grip," Delaney chided.

"So tell me about the show," Kyle said.

"What show?"

"The new one."

"I'm having my doubts about that too."

"Doubts about what?" Delaney asked.

"You know. Suppose it's controversial. You know it's only been lately I even decided Anita was telling the truth," I said.

"Oh, I knew she was telling the truth," Kyle said as he motioned for the waiter.

"How do you know that?" Delaney asked.

Kyle laughed. "Miss Girl, please, you can look at Clarence and tell he's blessed down there. Trust me, I know these things," he said confidently.

"I'm so glad you got that out before Sheila gets here," I said, reminding them of our expected guest.

"Where is Miss Jesus?" Delaney asked.

"Delaney, y'all please be nice," I pleaded.

"I'll be fine as long as she doesn't start laying hands on me," Delaney declared.

"You've got that right," Kyle added.

We ordered appetizers and munched on strawberry muffins while we talked and waited for Sheila's arrival. Kyle seemed really excited about the goings-on in my life. He turned to Delaney and asked, "So what's happening in your miserable little life, darling?" Delaney informed us she'd gotten the lead in a major rap video that she was really excited about.

"Have you fucked Pierce yet?" Kyle asked right out of the blue. The waiter had a shocked look on his face as he refilled our water glasses. He was shaking his head as he walked away.

"Kyle, please," I laughed.

"Chirl, you better test it out before you marry," he advised.

Delaney was laughing so hard that she had to clap her hand over her mouth to keep the piece of muffin she had just bitten off from falling out. She put the cloth napkin over her lips and playfully hit Kyle on the shoulders with a balled fist.

"We should order," I said, trying to change the subject. "It looks like Sheila is going to be late." While we were waiting for our food, I noticed an attractive black couple at the table directly in front of us. They had two children who looked around five or six years old. They seemed so happy. The man and woman both observed me staring and smiled politely. The little boy noticed us and walked over to our table and handed me a portion of his roll. He was so adorable.

"What's your name?" I asked.

"Tyler," he said proudly.

"Tyler, what a nice name for such a handsome young man," I said.

"Thank you," he said shyly. "You so pretty," he smiled.

"He's starting early," Kyle said.

"Tyler, these are my friends Kyle and Delaney," I said.

"Hi," he said with a half wave in their direction.

"Tyler, let the nice people enjoy their meal," the man said in a deep baritone voice.

"Oh, he's not bothering us," I offered.

Tyler jumped up on the empty seat next to me and began to finish the rest of his roll. He was such a handsome little boy, golden toast-brown skin and beautiful brown eyes, warm and bright as candles. Tyler looked at my ring, touched it softly, and then pulled his hands back playfully, like it was hurting him.

When Sheila arrived Tyler's mother came to the table to get him and thanked us for being so nice to him.

"No problem," I said. "I only wish he was about twenty-five years older," I joked.

Tyler's mother introduced herself to the four of us and motioned to her husband and daughter to come over and meet us too. Tyler's little sister was named Tori, and she was pretty but a little bit shy. As they prepared to leave I gave Tyler a kiss and became sad that my new little friend was leaving. So sad that tears formed in my eyes and I could feel my makeup beginning to run.

"What's wrong with you?" Kyle asked, noticing my tears.

"Oh nothing," I said, grabbing my purse. "I'll be right back."

My tears surprised and confused me. I guess I realized that I didn't really know how I felt about Pierce's proposal.

In the ladies' room I pulled myself together, freshened my makeup, and went back upstairs to rejoin my friends. Kyle, Delaney, and Sheila seemed to be enjoying each other's company and that made me smile.

My waffles and sausage were now cold and the waiter offered to reheat them for me. I agreed because Sheila had just ordered and Delaney and Kyle were preparing to head to Lincoln Center for a violin concert.

The two of them told Sheila it was nice seeing her and promised to call me later that evening. I told them I had plans with Pierce. Sheila exchanged pleasantries with them and promised to pray for them.

"Yeah, you do that, chirl," Kyle said as he gave me a sour look.

Kyle and Delaney gave me a kiss on the cheek and darted out of the restaurant. When they were out of sight Sheila turned to me with a very serious look on her face and asked, "Nicole, what is a chirl?"

I started laughing at Sheila's serious tone. "Oh, it's nothing bad, girl. It's just a combination of chile and girl. Chirl."

"Oh," Sheila responded as she poured sugar on her teaspoon and dipped it into her coffee cup.

Eleven

He was the last man in the world I expected to see in my conference room or any place this side of the Mason-Dixon line. I arrived at my office early Monday morning, skipping my workout session with Jared to meet with my new client. He was facing the picture window that overlooked Peachtree Street, hands in his pants pockets revealing a backside that I would never forget. As I closed the large door to our conference room, Basil Henderson turned around to meet me. For just a moment we stared at each other, mutually surprised but playing it very cool. It hadn't registered with me when I saw the file marked Mr. John B. Henderson.

"John Henderson?" I said with a startled voice.

"Raymond Tyler, long time no see. What up?" Basil smirked.

"About four years, Basil. I had no idea your name was John," I said.

"Never use it, unless I'm in trouble," he said.

"Like now," I said, trying not to look into his beautiful steel-gray eyes.

Basil Henderson, star wide receiver for the NFL New Jersey Warriors, was one of those people you would never forget. Maybe it was because he was so damn good-looking or maybe it was his abrasive and cocky personality. Whatever the reason, he was unforgettable. He had not lost his ability to exude sex under any circumstance. John Basil Henderson was without a doubt a legitimate example of the male body in its most polished perfection.

Basil and I had met when I lived in New York. He had been a client —a sexual client—of my best friend Kyle when he was working for an exclusive male escort service in New York. This was during a difficult period in Kyle's life when he'd been trying to support a drug habit and not let anyone know the financial problems he was facing. Basil had told me he used the service because of his high-profile career as a professional football player and because he really didn't consider himself gay or bisexual; he just kicked it occasionally, as he so aptly put it. So I guess he and Kyle helped each other out.

Basil and I had never engaged in any type of sex, but it wasn't because he didn't want to and to be honest it wasn't because I didn't either. I mean there was no denying Basil's body or attractiveness. If you did, Basil was the type who would let you know, quickly. But I'd been in serious relationships with both a man and a woman at the time I met Basil.

"I didn't know you lived in Atlanta. I didn't think anything about it when the guy outside said Mr. Tyler would be my attorney," Basil said.

"Well, it's a small world," I said. "Here, why don't you take this seat," I instructed as I pulled out one of the leather chairs.

"Don't we shake hands or something?" Basil questioned.

"I'm sorry," I said as I extended a damp palm into Basil's powerful grip.

"When did you move to Atlanta?"

"About two years ago."

"Oh."

I admired Basil, immaculately dressed in a navy blue suit, white cotton shirt, and red and blue striped silk tie. His doughnut-brown face appeared relaxed, almost friendly, and when he smiled, his teeth were sparkling white and his eyes flickered like a sequined jacket in the night.

"So tell me what happened?" I inquired, breaking an awkward silence.

"Some faggot stared me down in the club," Basil said, lifting his voice as if to defend his honor.

"What's the matter, Basil, too much testosterone?" I said. "You really shouldn't use that word and didn't we have this conversation before?"

"What word?" he asked incredulously.

"Faggot."

"Well, faggot, punk, whatever, that's what he was," he said.

Basil went on to explain that he and a football player friend of his had been at a local nightspot owned by one of Atlanta's top sports heroes, as his guests. All night long a guy at the opposite end of the bar stared at Basil. When his friend left to use the men's room, the patron sent Basil a drink, which Basil accepted. When his friend returned and Basil told him what happened, his friend started to tease him, saying the guy must be a faggot and was sweet on Basil. At first Basil said he tried to ignore the admirer, but it seemed the more the man drank the closer he moved down to the end of the bar where Basil was standing. When Basil's friend left for the night, the gentleman, according to Basil, introduced himself as a friend of one of Basil's former acquaintances and then promptly asked Basil if it was true that he had a big dick.

Basil's response was two quick punches that sent the unwanted admirer to the emergency room at Crawford Long Hospital and Basil to the city jail for an overnight stay.

"Had you ever seen the guy?" I asked.

"Fuck no," Basil responded quickly.

"Why did you accept the drink?"

"Fans always send me drinks when I'm out. I didn't think anything about it."

"Well, I hope you have insurance to cover this or a bank account that will. The first thing we've got to do is to get this guy to drop the criminal charges, and if he won't, then we'll have to go to the prosecuting attorney."

"So you'll take my case? Don't worry about the money," Basil stated.

"Well, I think Gilliam is doing this as a favor for your regular attorney," I said.

"I hear Gilliam's some kinda female. That she's dope." Basil smirked.

"Look, Basil, the first thing we need to be clear about is that we operate in a professional manner around here. I'll ask that you keep comments of a personal nature to yourself."

"Does that mean I can't say how good you look?" Basil asked in a soft boyish tone.

"I'll have my secretary call you later in the week to set up a meeting after I've talked with the plaintiff's attorney," I said, purposely ignoring Basil's comment but wanting to smile.

"Can I ask you something?" Basil said.

"If it has to do with your case," I said.

"Think we can keep this out of the papers?"

"I'll see what I can do. It wasn't in the papers today, so it will probably go unnoticed. Believe it or not Basil, Atlanta has a lot more problems than your homophobia."

"Great. I don't want the Warriors to find out about this."

When Basil stood up, he slowly picked up the blue suit coat from the table. His chest, silhouetted by his white cotton shirt appeared bigger than it had been years before but I tried not to notice. He folded the jacket, laid it over his huge left biceps, and gave me a cocky smile. Silently he mouthed, "See ya, handsome," and walked from the conference room leaving his strong scent lingering like a sexual mist. The man had it going on.

Twelve

*A*n early summer had quickened the pulse of the city. I didn't know if that was a good sign or not. I mean the last thing New York City needed in the summer was a faster pace. The subways were packed and sweltering. Monday afternoon the principals of *To Tell the Truth, A Musical* met for the first time at a rehearsal hall in midtown Manhattan. The make-up of the cast surprised me, it was 70 percent white. I don't know why but I hadn't stopped to think in detail about the real Thomas-Hill hearing. I had watched the hearing but remembered only Clarence and Anita.

Several veteran Broadway actors had been cast as members of the Senate Judiciary Committee and Megan Gordon, a well-known movie actress, was to play Virginia Thomas, Judge Thomas's wife. The only blacks in the cast were myself and two actors whom I didn't recognize when I walked into the rehearsal hall. They both smiled when I came in and we migrated toward each other at the first break. This was the first Broadway show for both of them. We searched for a soda machine and a place to sit and learn more about each other.

The guy playing Judge Thomas was a tall, medium-built guy with skin the rich color of bittersweet chocolate and large facial features. Devere Mabry was from Greenwood, Mississippi, and had recently finished filming Spike Lee's *Malcolm X*. He was a Shakespearean-trained actor with a booming baritone voice, one with a deep resonance that forced you to listen.

Timothy Britton was the type of guy I now avoided like visits to the dentist. He was tall and great-looking with green eyes just like Raymond Tyler's. He was playing John Doggett, the arrogant lawyer who'd claimed that Anita secretly pined for him. His yellow skin glowed under the dark black beard that covered his face. Timothy had graduated from Yale Drama School. He'd understudied all the roles in

Five Guys Named Moe and had been the first black actor cast in *Phantom of the Opera*, also as an understudy. He'd never performed in either show.

When he introduced himself to me, I smiled and tried to avoid his eyes. I looked for mannerisms that might give me a clue as to his sexuality. I guessed I'd have to get Kyle to run him through the computer. It was funny but it didn't matter to me if Devere was gay or not, which made me realize I shouldn't be concerned with Timothy either. I mean I was an engaged woman.

I hadn't given my notice to *Jelly's* yet. We weren't going into full rehearsals for almost a month and I wanted to make sure that I wanted to do this. My first take on the script was that it needed work, serious work, and there was no music for us to start looking over. For me this was not a good sign.

We located a row of vending machines and Devere, Timothy, and I drank colas in the hallway, talked about the make-up of the cast, and laughed when we all confessed that we'd thought this was going to be a black musical. We also laughed when we decided that we'd better disperse before the rest of the cast thought we were starting some type of trouble. Even on Broadway, white people became concerned when they saw black people grouped together, especially if black men were involved. It didn't matter that none of the white cast members made an effort to come and join our conversation.

This would be my fourth Broadway show and it was the first time that the cast was majority white. All of the shows that I'd been in previously contained no more than three white cast members. It's not that I wasn't used to working with white people; all my high school productions were majority white and every pageant that I was ever in contained no more than three black women. It would be interesting to see how the cast would interact once the musical went into full production.

After the read-through I met Delaney at the Paramount Hotel for a drink before heading to the theater. Delaney was already sipping some tea and reading a copy of *Backstage* when I walked into the dimly lit room. She had a glass of white wine already waiting for me.

"Hey, girl. How did it go?" Delaney asked as she gave me a kiss on both my cheeks.

"Oh, it was okay, but I don't know, girl," I said as I motioned for the waitress.

"What's the problem?" Delaney asked.

"Well, the script is weak, which means the music is bound to be," I said while looking over the small bar menu.

"So when are you going to give your notice?"

"Not until I see the music," I said, waving my menu toward the waitress.

"Don't tell me you're going to eat?" Delaney asked in an unbelieving tone.

"Oh, come on—just a few chicken wings," I said.

I pointed to the wings on the menu and the waitress smiled and took the menu from my hands.

"Girl, I wish I could eat like you and still stay thin."

"Oh, chile, look at you. You weigh less than me," I protested.

"Yes, but I don't eat shit and I take at least two dance classes a day," Delaney defended.

"I've got enough problems. I guess the good Lord didn't put the extra burden of weight on me," I said.

"Tell that to Nell Carter, and what kind of problems do you have, girlfriend?"

"You know. Oh, before I forget, do you know a guy named Timothy Britton?"

"Timothy Britton—no. Who is he?"

"He's in *To Tell the Truth* and, Delaney girl, he is so fine."

"Black or white?" Delaney asked.

"Black, but what difference does that make?"

"To me all the difference in the world." Delaney shrugged.

"I can't tell if he's gay or straight," I said.

"Assume he's gay but who knows. He could be bi," Delaney laughed.

"So when are you going to tell me how you feel about my engagement?"

"So we go from some fine black guy to Pierce?"

"No, honey, I just wanted to know if you knew this guy. But what I really want to know is how you feel about me getting married."

"Chile, that's your business. I like Pierce, but I'm not the one marrying him! Even more so, do you more than like him?"

"What do you mean?"

"Do you love him?"

"Well, sorta." I paused and sipped some of the wine.

"Sorta?" Delaney asked.

"Aren't you the one who is always saying you should go out with someone who cares more about you than you do him?"

"Yes, but I didn't say marry him."

"Well, at least I have Kyle's support," I said.

"Kyle? Why do you say that?"

"He's so excited. He called me late last night saying he wanted to start on my gown right away and that he has all these designs he wants me to see."

"Where is he going to find the time? I think he's spreading himself too thin," Delaney suggested. "Maybe that's why we don't see him as much," she added.

"Yeah, you might be right, but he seems happy," I said as I moved my wineglass to make room for the wings the busboy placed on the small table. Delaney didn't touch them. She just sat there and sipped her tea. She looked like a European model with her high cheekbones and short haircut, which she'd recently started to let grow out. I was devouring the chicken wings when abruptly Delaney started laughing so hard that everyone in the bar gazed at our table.

"Did you say *To Tell the Truth?*" Delaney laughed as she set the cup down on the saucer.

"Yes," I said, wondering what Delaney found so funny.

"Girlfriend, the title alone will sell tickets," she giggled.

"Girl, I thought the exact same thing," I said, joining in her laughter.

After the flurry of laughter died down, Delaney carefully steered the conversation to Pierce and my acceptance of his proposal. Delaney shared with me that she thought I was in too big a hurry to get married and although she felt that you should marry someone who loved you more, she felt that I admired and respected Pierce—and perhaps even cared for him, but not enough to marry. When I protested she pointed out that my religious beliefs alone were reasons to reconsider. I hadn't thought about it until Delaney posed a question that Pierce had not: "Would you convert to Judaism?"

"I haven't really thought about it but I seriously doubt it." I told Delaney that she had given me something to think about and added that I planned on a long engagement so I couldn't be in that big a hurry to get married.

As Delaney and I prepared to leave, she said, "Don't forget about this weekend."

"This weekend?"

"Yeah, the group up in Harlem."

"Oh, of course. I'll be there. I'm looking forward to it."

Delaney and some of her friends had started teaching dance at a community center in Harlem and they came up with the idea of having self-esteem workshops for the teenage girls. She asked me to come and give some beauty pageant pointers and I agreed. She convinced Kyle to volunteer his services to make party dresses for the girls, who ranged from age twelve to fifteen. Kyle was scouting thrift shops around the city looking for old ball gowns that could be transformed to fit these teenage girls' tastes. This, despite the fact that Delaney said they all dressed like the female rap group TLC. A group I never heard of. I must be getting old.

Delaney was the type of person who couldn't say no when it came to helping those less fortunate than herself, especially if it involved a group of young black kids. It was one of the things I admired most about her.

We said our good-byes and Delaney headed toward the Forty-second Street subway station and another dance class in the Village and I headed up Eighth Avenue to the Virginia Theater. Before I reached the theater I stopped at a pay phone to check my answering service. Much to my surprise there were no messages. I was expecting a call from Kyle and there was always a message from Pierce. Kyle and I were planning a shopping trip for Delaney's project and I needed to talk with Pierce. I didn't have my watch on so I didn't have a clue as to the time. I knew it was getting close to half-hour. The sun had lowered, leaving streaks of red and magenta in the sky while bathing the city with its warmth. It was on evenings like this that I wouldn't trade places with anyone in the world.

Thirteen

Basil had managed to get himself in a shitload of trouble. I received a police report and pictures of his victim, Charles Marshall, whose left eye was multicolored and puffy from contact with Basil's fists. The victim's attorney immediately filed a lawsuit asking for two million dollars and appeared in no mood to settle out of court. Basil had been lucky in some respects; the district attorney had elected not to press charges because of the lack of cooperation from the witnesses and the name of John Henderson didn't mean anything to her or reporters on the police station beat so the story fortunately escaped media attention.

I decided to hire a private investigator to find out any information that might assist in the case. The report caused mixed emotions for me. It turned out that Marshall was a twenty-nine-year-old unemployed schoolteacher with a police record who was HIV positive and currently taking AZT. The investigator found this out by following him to the drugstore and then bribing the clerk at the pharmacy. Marshall had served a six-month term for credit-card fraud when he was twenty-five years old and had only come off probation within the last few months. He lived in a midtown Atlanta duplex with two male roommates. The places he frequented sounded like some of the gay bars Kyle told me to check out for his visit.

Basil instructed me to do whatever it took to keep the case from going to trial so we made an offer of fifty thousand dollars, which was promptly rejected by Marshall's counsel. I informed Basil of Marshall's HIV status and suggested that he strongly consider being tested in view of the condition of Marshall's face. Basil said he didn't remember seeing any blood on his hands but agreed to be tested anyway.

The case was taking up a great deal of time and provided a very good excuse for me to not spend time with Jared without having to give the real reason. In the past two weeks I'd seen him only once and that had been one morning at the health club. He called my secretary to remind me that my birthday was coming up in a few days and to advise me not to make any plans.

While working for Basil solved one dilemma it was creating a different type of problem. He was constantly making sexual innuendos and whenever he came to my office he always wore clothing that accented his body. When I reminded him that he wasn't gay or bisexual he remarked, "I know but I wouldn't mind kicking it with you." Every time he came into the office all of the secretaries and Mico would find some reason either to walk by or come into my office.

It was hard to ignore Basil's sexual presence and I tried to conduct most of my conversations with him over the phone. During the times we had to meet in person I avoided his eyes and always tried to have some type of legal document close at hand to take my attention from Basil. He didn't have any idea that the papers in my hands didn't have a thing to do with his case.

I called Basil early one morning and suggested that we up our initial offer. His insurance company was cooperating and I felt that if we doubled our offer then at least I would be able to get Marshall and his attorney to meet with us. Basil agreed and I was able to schedule a meeting for the following afternoon. I asked Basil to meet me that evening at my health club. I wanted to go over strategy and give him pointers on his conduct for the meeting.

Suggesting the health club wasn't such a great idea. Everywhere we went in the club people recognized Basil and came over to talk or just stare. It was then that I saw another side of Basil. He took the time to speak with everyone who wanted to talk to him about football, the Warriors' upcoming season, and their chances against the Atlanta Falcons. The arrogance that was usually so apparent vanished. It didn't matter if it was a male or female, Basil listened intently to their questions and smiled, flashing his immaculate teeth. Once I realized we weren't going to accomplish anything at the gym I headed to the locker room and walked right into Jared.

"Say, buddy, what are you doing here?" Jared asked.

"Jared, uh . . . oh, I'm here with a client. What are you doing here in the evening?" I said unsteadily.

"I lost my workout partner," he said mournfully. "You got time to grab something to eat?"

"I don't think so. I'm going back to the office."

"Aw, come on now, I've missed you," Jared said.

Just as I was getting ready to agree, from the corner of my eye I caught Basil walking into the locker room. Jared was wearing tight black biker shorts and his chest was covered only with his sweat. I could feel Basil's eyes on me but I didn't turn around to acknowledge him immediately. Jared saw Basil staring at me and his eyebrows arched as Basil suddenly moved and positioned himself directly in front of me while purposely ignoring Jared.

"Hey, Ray, I'm sorry about all the distractions. Let me take you to dinner to make it up," Basil said.

Jared looked puzzled, and I searched for a response. Jared politely positioned himself in front of Basil, extended his hand, and said, "Excuse me, I'm Jared Stovall, I don't think we've met."

"Yeah, I'm Basil Henderson," Basil said rudely, and then turned to face me. "So what about it, Ray? Can we do dinner?"

So much for a kinder, gentler Basil Henderson.

"Yeah, Basil, we definitely need to talk. Let me talk with Jared and I'll meet you out front in about fifteen minutes," I said.

"Okay, I'm going to shower," Basil said, removing his sweatshirt as if to show Jared that his barrel chest was equally impressive.

Jared stood there silently for a moment just looking at me as if he were looking at a total stranger. It was the first time anything like this had happened between the two of us. Finally breaking the silence that had descended upon us, Jared said, "Okay, Ray, call me when you have the time."

"Yeah, I will call real soon, buddy. I will."

Jared walked to another section of the locker room very slowly, stopping to look back at me and then continuing out of sight. Suddenly Basil appeared from nowhere with a towel wrapped around him and came over to me, smiling. He whispered in my ear, "Is that your boyfriend?" I wanted to smack the fuck out of him but I resisted the urge and instead grabbed my bag from the locker and headed out of the gym still dressed in my workout clothes. "Forget about dinner, Basil," I yelled back.

As I drove home I thought about what a jerk Basil was and how he had deliberately fucked with Jared and me. Was he jealous of Jared? Jared hadn't seemed to notice and only appeared intent on finding out what was wrong with me.

———

Instead of dinner with Basil, I found myself making a ham and turkey sandwich on rye bread and pouring myself a tall glass of cranberry juice, readying myself for an evening alone, when my phone rang.

"Hello."

"Is this the Raymond Tyler?"

"Speaking. Who am I speaking with?"

"Don't tell me you don't recognize my voice," the deep baritone said.

"Look, I don't have time to play games. Who is this?" I demanded.

"Man, I'd love to see you mad. Guess I better tell you before you hang up on me. This is your number-one client," he said.

Suddenly I recognized the voice. It was Basil.

"Basil, how did you get my home number?" I asked with slight irritation in my voice.

"Calm down. I went by your office and that guy Mico gave it to me," Basil said.

I wondered if Basil was lying. What would Mico be doing in the office so late, and why would he give Basil my number? Then again, it wouldn't be the first time Basil's masculine charm had disconcerted an otherwise unflappable person. But I was going to make sure that I wouldn't fall prey to his act.

"What can I do for you?" I asked sternly.

"I just wanted to say I'm sorry for this evening. I was just being an asshole," Basil said.

"No problem. I'm getting used to your behavior," I said.

"Do you want me to come by your place to discuss the meeting tomorrow? I could be there in fifteen minutes," Basil said.

"No, Basil, I have my game plan. You just follow my lead and don't answer any questions or say anything unless I instruct you. Understood?"

"Yeah, cool," Basil replied.

"Okay. Have a good night," I said and gently placed the receiver in the cradle on my kitchen counter.

I took about three big bites from my sandwich and pondered what tomorrow's meeting would be like. I wanted to know what this guy looked like without the markings and if he already was suffering from AIDS or if he was just HIV positive. I hadn't been in the same room with somebody with AIDS since Kelvin's wife Candance died from the disease. I didn't tell Gilliam about this guy being HIV positive. Come to think of it, I had failed to tell Gilliam that I'd known Basil prior to meeting him in our office. Gilliam had mentioned she knew the opposing counsel and that if this went to trial I would eat his lunch. She concurred with me that Basil's ass was lucky not to be facing criminal charges and that we should try and settle out of court.

Right before I went to bed, I took a warm shower. While in the pulsating shower I started to think of Jared and how he'd looked this evening in the gym. He was smiling but I could tell there was a sadness surrounding him and I was sad too. Maybe I was wrong to try and pull away from him without giving him an explanation. I really needed to determine if I, in fact, was in love with Jared or if this was just a case of lust caused by my celibacy vow.

As I dried off and prepared myself for bed, I found my thoughts shifting to Basil and the view I'd caught of him in the gym. He had been bending over putting foot spray in his tennis shoes. His backside was covered with hair and his butt seemed to have a life of its own.

Standing there drying off I felt my sex begin to take on a magical weight encouraged by nude pictures of both Jared and Basil in my mind. Instead of rubbing the creamy, sweet-smelling lotion over my body as I normally did, I put it in the palm of my hand and then placed my hand on my sex, gently moving it up and down with the picture of Basil's butt and Jared's face in my mind.

Moments later with a great deal of tension released, I couldn't tell the difference between the lotion and my own body fluids. I took the towel and wiped my sex muscle, ignored the white jockey underwear I had laid out, and crawled between the white cotton sheets of my bed. I'd reached up to turn off the lamp near my bed when the phone rang.

"Hello."

"Ray, whatcha doing?" Kyle asked.

"Kyle, just got through jerking off. You know, safe sex," I laughed.

"You got that right. Need I ask who you were thinking about? Jared right?" Kyle said.

"Well, yes and no."

"Oh."

I realized that I hadn't told Kyle about running into Basil and that I was defending him in a case.

"You'll never guess who I'm representing."

"Who, somebody famous and fine?"

"Well, you could say that. Basil Henderson."

"No shit. What did that fool do?"

"Beat up some guy for making a pass at him."

"That flaming asshole. He is such a fucking jerk. I hope you're not going to do it."

"Do what?"

"Defend him," Kyle said.

"Well, Kyle, I sorta have to. I mean Gilliam assigned the case to me. I do handle all the football players," I defended.

"But, Ray, do you think that's right?"

"What?"

"Now don't be so stupid. Do you realize how many of the children are beat up daily by assholes like Basil? If anything you should be helping the guy he beat up."

There was a period of silence while I contemplated what Kyle was saying. To be honest I never thought about the true implications of Basil's actions.

"But if I refused to represent him I would have to explain why to Gilliam. I don't think I'm ready for her to know why I shouldn't represent Basil."

"Well, you should really think about it. What if Basil had beaten me up? Would you still defend him?"

"Of course not!" I shouted.

"Well, it's the same thing. You know how I like to flirt with confused boys. It could have just as easily been me that Basil beat up. You really should check yourself, Ray. I'm not saying you have to be out at work. But you're actually promoting gay bashing when you defend people like Basil," Kyle stated.

"I really hadn't thought about it, Kyle, but it might be too late. Tomorrow I meet with the guy and his attorney. It's really too late to pull out."

"Why didn't you tell me this before?"

"I don't know. It just never came up."

"Yeah, right," Kyle mumbled.

"I'm serious, Kyle."

"Well, maybe you should get Basil to confess to being gay. Make a public statement. Go on the 'Oprah Winfrey Show.' When people realize that people like him are living a life in the closet it might stop some of the hate."

"He would never do that. He's still in denial."

"Like somebody else I know," Kyle snapped.

"Who me?"

"I didn't say it. You did, mister."

"Oh, come on, Kyle, let's not start fighting over this shit. It's not worth it."

"Well, it might not be worth it to you, but it's definitely worth it to all those kids being beaten and killed every day by people just like your client."

"Yeah, you're probably right," I murmured.

"You know I'm right."

"So let's change the subject. When you called you sounded like you had some news," I said.

"I forgot. I've got to get some sleep. I'll talk to you later in the week but think about what I said."

"I will. Be safe."

"You too."

"Kyle."

"Yes?"

"Will you still love me if I go ahead and defend Basil?"

"What do you think?"

"I'll take that as a yes."

"Good night, Ray. Go back to jerking your dick."

"Good night, Kyle."

When I hung up the phone I sat up in my bed, folded my arms around my knees, and lowered my chin to them. Kyle's arguments lingered in my thoughts like the darkness that covered my silent bedroom.

Basil sat in a chair at the end of the long walnut conference table and doodled absently on the yellow legal pad as we waited for Marshall and his attorney. Basil appeared nervous but was trying desperately not to let on.

"How long do you think this is going to take?" Basil asked.

"What? The meeting or us getting this mess cleared up?" I asked.

"The meeting," Basil replied.

"Oh, probably about two hours."

"Aw," Basil said softly.

"Basil, can I ask you something?"

"Sure!"

"Do you feel any remorse for what you did?"

"Yeah, sure I do," Basil said, lifting himself from his slumped position in the chair.

"Why did you do it?"

"You know," Basil said.

"I'm sorry, I don't. Why don't you explain it to me?" I suggested.

Just as Basil was about to respond, Melanie walked in with Marshall and his attorney, who was a slightly overweight young black woman, not the man I'd expected. Basil's intense gray eyes got bigger and there was a spooked softness to them.

"I'm Sherrod Jones," the young woman said as she extended her hand toward me. "I've taken over Mr. Marshall's case."

"Raymond Tyler, Jr.," I said. "And you must be Mr. Marshall."

"Yes, I am, but you can call me Charles," the tall, thin gentleman said.

"Ms. Jones, this is my client, John B. Henderson," I said, motioning my hand toward Basil.

Basil got up from his chair and shook Ms. Jones's hand but ignored Charles, who was attired in a horrible-looking burnt-orange suit. His large head of hair didn't know if it wanted to be a Jheri Curl or natural and was combed back into a short ponytail. He looked as if he were a client of Reverend Al Sharpton's House of Hair. Marshall's elfin features didn't look nearly as bad as the pictures and I thought I could see signs of makeup. If it hadn't been for his hair, I guess you could have called him nice-looking.

Charles took the seat closest to me and his scent clashed with whatever Ms. Jones was wearing. He crossed his legs and arms so tightly that he looked like a human pretzel. I took note of his long fingernails, which were covered with gloss polish.

Our clients posed quite a contrast—Basil dressed like a corporate executive rather than a jock, and Marshall looking as though he were on his way to a tent revival meeting.

Ms. Jones started the meeting by stating that they'd received our new offer but that it was not nearly enough considering her client's pain and suffering, not to mention his embarrassment. She expressed her interest in not having to go through a lengthy trial but let it be known that she and Mr. Marshall ultimately had no problem with that possibility.

I asked Ms. Jones if I could question her client and she nodded her head in agreement and said, "If Mr. Marshall doesn't have any objections."

My first questions were regarding Marshall's place of residence, his age, and other information that was a matter of public record. He bristled slightly when I questioned his employment record and his brief period of incarceration.

When I asked him if Basil's understanding of his question had been correct, Ms. Jones interrupted and told him he didn't have to answer that. Marshall didn't answer my question but volunteered, "I was just trying to be nice to the asshole."

I asked Marshall if the bar in question was the type of establishment that he normally frequented and if not, what other places he went to in Atlanta.

"You don't have to answer that," Ms. Jones said as she jumped from her seat. Her client ignored her, looked me directly in the eyes, and said, "I go all over. I'm that type of person. Versatile," he added.

All during my questioning Basil remained silent, looking around the conference room, doodling, and occasionally raising his eyebrows at some of Charles Marshall's responses. When I realized that I wasn't going to get Marshall to admit what I already knew, I took a piece of paper, wrote $150,000 on it, and pushed it in front of Ms. Jones and Charles Marshall.

"Is this your final offer?" Ms. Jones asked.

"Yes, it is," I replied, looking at Basil out of the corner of my eye.

"Well, I guess we'll see you in court, Mr. Tyler. Nice meeting you," Ms. Jones said as she grabbed her briefcase and purse and motioned for her client to get up.

Just as they were preparing to leave the room, Marshall turned around and faced Basil. "Hey you," he called out in a whisper.

"Me?" Basil said with a confounded look on his face.

"Yes, you. You picked the wrong one to fuck with, Mr. Man. I know your T and when I'm finished everyone in the world is going to know," he said as he snapped his fingers in the air and turned with the dramatic flair of a runway model and followed Ms. Jones out of the room. Basil's face appeared to turn scarlet as he struggled to remain seated at the opposite end of the table and to keep his volatile temper under control.

After the meeting I calmed Basil down and told him my reservations about handling his case. I explained that the only way I would stay on the case was if we could settle it out of court. I also informed him that his actions could be classified as a hate crime, which was a federal offense. I realized after my conversation with Kyle that defending Basil would mean attacking Charles Marshall and that would be just as low as Basil's beating. And even though I was a little put off by Marshall's demeanor and his threat to out Basil, I did realize that no one deserved to be beaten up just because of who he was.

Fourteen

"Do you think you're ready, Nicole?"

"I think so," I said.

"Well . . ." Dr. Huntley said as she removed her glasses.

"I think if I'm going to marry Pierce I should have sex with him beforehand."

"Oh."

"You don't think I should?"

"Nicole, that's not my decision. So you've decided to marry Pierce?"

"I think so."

"Think. What about your reservations?"

"The part about me accepting because I didn't want to embarrass him in the restaurant?"

"That's a start."

"Well, since I haven't broke off the engagement it must mean that I do love him and should marry him."

"Really? Do you think it's fair to Pierce? What about your religious beliefs?"

"My religious beliefs?"

"Yes."

"Sometimes I think I use religion as a crutch."

"That's a pretty powerful statement. Why do you feel that way?"

"I use my religion to keep from making decisions. I miss sex. My religious teaching says no sex without marriage, but I'm not so sure. Of course, I'll have safe sex, but I have to admit to myself that I long to be held and . . . you know . . ."

"You know?"

"Yes, real sex."

"Real sex? I don't quite understand what you're saying, Nicole."

"Having a man make love to my entire body."
"Okay. That's clear."
"Is my time up, Dr. Huntley?"
"Yes, Nicole. It's up."

Dr. Huntley made some good points. I was trying to justify in my mind why I should go ahead and sleep with Pierce, despite the fact that it went against my religious teaching, although that hadn't, unfortunately, stopped me with Raymond. I didn't feel bad after the fact either. But Pierce wasn't Raymond Tyler. I mean sex with Raymond was wonderful and I felt like a complete woman afterward and my religion didn't enter my mind. I only felt regret when I found out Raymond was bisexual.

A part of me thought that if I had sex with Pierce it would damage our friendship; having a strong friendship with my future mate was still at the top of my list of husband requirements. As much as I treasured the friendship we had, though, I also wanted to be kissed, held, and touched in places that I now allowed only my own hands to touch.

When I talked with Sheila about my lustful thinking she, of course, advised me to pray for strength. That was easy for her to say; she was married to a handsome man and talked freely about how wonderful their sex life was. When she reminded me that sex was blessed only in marriage I wanted to inform her that if you went strictly by the word, then sex was really only for procreation. Delaney, on the other hand, agreed with Kyle that I should sleep with Pierce before marrying him. That way, they suggested, I could still back out if the sex wasn't right. Once we were married, bad sex would then become an issue for a marriage counselor. I knew that at times my Ms. Polly Purebred routine was wearing thin on Pierce. To be honest it was getting on *my* nerves.

The starting date for rehearsals for *To Tell the Truth* had been put off until late July while the producers finished casting the chorus and understudies. I was really interested in whom they would choose to understudy me—I wondered if they would choose someone with my skin tone—and anxious to be in the company of Timothy. Timothy Britton really aroused my interest. I saw him a couple of times after our first rehearsal and he stopped me once when I almost stepped in front of a taxi while we walked down Eighth Avenue. When he touched me I felt excited over my entire body. But Timothy wasn't really an option for me. I still didn't know what his sexual preference was and love affairs with cast members in shows I'd been in always spelled disaster.

Kyle had done some checking and hadn't found a thing, but upon meeting Timothy said, "Anybody that pretty was bound to have a key." (Kyle and I had this little game we played when we were out in mixed company and Delaney and I wanted to know if a certain guy was gay. If the guy in question was gay or bisexual, Kyle would ask one of us for his keys. "It's time to open the door so I need my keys," he would say.) When I chastised him for thinking everyone was gay he assured me that wasn't the case. "It takes two heterosexual people to create one of us," Kyle said. "Why on earth would we want everyone to be gay?" he questioned.

Kyle remained my only constant support in regard to my upcoming wedding. He brought over sketches of gowns he wanted to make for me. Every time I tried to put it off, he said, "If you don't marry Pierce you're going to eventually marry someone and this way you won't have to worry in case I'm not available. You know I'm going to be really major one day." I didn't know if he was really anxious for me to marry Pierce or just wanted to brush up on his wedding dress sewing skills.

Wednesday afternoon between shows I went up to Kyle's apartment on Ninety-sixth and Broadway to look at some fabrics he was really excited about. This would be the first time I had been to his apartment since I'd dated Raymond. Dr. Huntley would definitely consider this a major breakthrough.

Kyle was very understanding about my not coming to visit him, but he assured me I would feel nothing. When I arrived at the building lobby I started to feel a wee bit strange. That was probably because the same elderly black guy who was the doorman when Ray lived there was still on duty. He gave me a knowing smile and told me that Kyle and Delaney were expecting me and to go on up. Once I arrived on the floor I expected to see *Tyler* on the door but instead there was Kyle's business card and a black metal plate with Picture This on the heavy steel door. When I walked into the apartment I realized that I had nothing to worry about. Kyle had turned the entire living and dining room into an office showroom. There were sewing dummies everywhere and a large black desk that faced the picture window overlooking Broadway. It was a lot more crowded and messier than the way Raymond had kept it.

"I don't believe it," Kyle said.

"Believe what?" I asked.

"You finally made it. Now, you're not going to pass out, are you?" Kyle joked.

"Oh, pleeze," I said as I gave Delaney a hug.

"Hey, girl," Delaney said in a depressed tone.

"What's wrong with you?" I asked.

"Please don't ask her!" Kyle suggested.

"My life is a mess," Delaney said.

"What are you talking about?" I asked.

"Girl, you wouldn't understand," Delaney sighed.

"What do you mean, I don't understand? Aw, come here and let me give you another hug," I offered.

"That's my problem. I spend too much time with you two," Delaney said.

"Well, excuse me, Miss Thing. I know what you need," Kyle said.

"Please, Kyle, don't say a stiff dick. That's the last thing I need."

"Now see, there you go jumping to the wrong conclusions. I was going to suggest a nice glass of wine. Maybe you need a woman," Kyle joked.

"Do you have some wine?" Delaney asked as she rolled her eyes at Kyle.

Before Kyle responded he looked over at me. I knew that Kyle was a recovering alcoholic and my face had that *what are you doing with alcohol in your apartment* look.

"And before you ask what I'm doing with wine, Ms. Raymonette, no, I'm not drinking," Kyle said as he looked me directly in the face.

"What are you talking about?" I defended.

"So do you want a glass too?" Kyle asked.

"Now you know I have to go back to the theater," I said.

"So what. Like Miss Thing is going to let you go on," Kyle laughed.

While Kyle was in the small kitchen, Delaney walked very slowly over to the window and then back over to Kyle's sound system. I had never seen her look so sad. She grabbed a stack of Kyle's CD's and looked swiftly through them, then grabbed his cassettes and did the same. Just as I was going to go over and ask Delaney what the problem was, Kyle returned with a glass of wine in one hand and a glass of water in the other.

"Now take this and go over there and sit down. You are wearing me out with all this depression and drama," Kyle said as he led Delaney by the hand to a chair that faced the window. Delaney complied and sat staring at the sun as it burst through the windows. I looked at Kyle and he just waved his hands in the air in disgust, then motioned for me to come into his bedroom.

Once we were in Kyle's bedroom I noticed piles of beautiful lace fabric on his bed. I was getting ready to pick up the fabric when I realized Kyle was trying to get my attention without using his voice. Kyle mouthed, "Get that bitch outta here."

"What's the matter with her?" I whispered.

Kyle motioned I don't know with his hands and then mouthed again, "Maybe it's that time of the month."

"Okay, I'll take her with me," I mouthed back. I thought, why do men always think it's that time of the month when women are depressed or moody?

Instead of looking at the fabric I went back into the living room, went over to the chair, and knelt down beside Delaney. She had one hand inside her ivory silk blouse and her other hand holding the now half-filled wineglass. Her brown eyes looked weighed down in sadness. I gently removed the glass from her hand and set it on the floor.

"Delaney, are you all right, baby?" I asked.

Delaney just shook her head slowly and removed her hand from the inside of her blouse.

"Come on then, baby. I'm going to take you home," I said.

Kyle walked back into the living room and came over to Delaney and me. We glanced at each other and when I looked back at Delaney her eyes were filled with tears and I felt tears beginning to form in mine. Large tears fell down her cheeks, but she did nothing to stop their flow.

Kyle looked at the both of us and started to scream, "What's the matter, girls? Please, I can't take all this drama."

"Kyle, calm down," I instructed.

I reached down and hugged Delaney as her tears turned to sobs. Kyle came over and put his arms around the both of us. "Now come on, girlfriends. Whatever it is, we'll get over it," he said.

After a few minutes of silence and tears, Delaney removed herself from our embrace, wiped her face with her hands, and stood up in front of Kyle and me.

"Nicole, Kyle. I was attacked by somebody I was working for," Delaney said sadly.

Delaney's announcement left even Kyle speechless. I mean what could we say? I went over to Delaney and put my arms around her.

"What happened, Delaney?" I asked. "When?"

"A couple of nights ago at KG studios right after a taping. I was the principal and he said he needed some additional shots," Delaney said.

"Who? Who was the motherfucker?" Kyle questioned.

"Papa Kee," Delaney said softly.

"Papa Kee. Who is that?" I asked.

"He's a rap star," Kyle said.

"Do you want to talk about it, Delaney?"

"You don't have to," Kyle said.

Delaney remained silent.

"Did you report it?" I asked.

"Report it to who?" Delaney asked.

"The police," Kyle said.

"No," Delaney said as she lowered her head toward the floor.

"Delaney, baby, you have to report it," I said.

"I don't know. He's a really popular singer and I want to keep working," Delaney said.

"A popular singer? Chile, fuck that shit," Kyle said. "You can't let him get away with it. What did he do?"

"Kyle's right, Delaney. Did you have any clue that he was like that?" I asked.

"Well, I knew he was a big flirt. He had been flirting with me since the audition. When he came on to me by touching me and I removed his hands, he pinned me against the wall and reached under my skirt and ripped off my panties," Delaney said.

"Was there anyone there?" I asked as I continued to rub Delaney's hands. Kyle's arms were wrapped around her shoulders.

"No."

"Delaney, you don't have to talk about this if you don't want to, but we want to help," Kyle said.

Delaney wiped her tears with the corner of her blouse and Kyle jumped up and went into the bathroom and brought back a damp face cloth. Delaney took the cloth and wiped the corners of her eyes, which were smeared with makeup.

"Is there anything you want us to do? If you report it, we'll go with you," I said.

"Yes, Delaney, I think you have to report it. Did he penetrate you?"

"No!" Delaney said in a loud, cracked voice.

"So what happened?" Kyle asked.

"He stuck his finger inside me and then did oral sex on me," Delaney said as she started to cry again.

I pulled her back to me and just rocked her gently and shook my head in disbelief.

"Don't worry, darling. It will be all right," I said.

"Come on, Delaney. It *will* be all right. What do you want us to do?" Kyle asked.

"Let me work this out. I haven't told anyone because I didn't want to be pressured. I feel better telling you guys, but I need to call my mother," Delaney said.

"Here, girl, take the phone and go in my bedroom and call her," Kyle said.

Delaney took the portable phone and walked slowly into Kyle's bedroom. Kyle and I just looked at each other. He walked over to the large picture window and stared out. "What should we do?" he asked.

"Just be supportive. We have to respect Delaney's wishes. She'll make the right decision."

"Okay. I hope you're right. I just hope she doesn't let the motherfucker get away with it."

While Delaney talked to her mother, Kyle went into the kitchen and started to make some tea. All sorts of thoughts raced through my head. How could this happen to someone like Delaney? She was so strongwilled. You heard rumors all the time about some of the stars using heavy-handed tricks to get sexual favors from aspiring actresses, but this was rape. I had to convince Delaney to press charges without pressuring her. This jerk couldn't get away with hurting my friend.

Delaney came back into the living room and I gave her another hug. Minutes later Kyle brought out three mugs of tea on a tray. We drank in silence. I suggested Delaney come and spend the night with me and she agreed.

Later that evening Delaney seemed back to her old self. She didn't want to talk about the attack, but said she would think about what we'd said. Her mother wanted her to come home, but Delaney declined.

Right before we went to bed, Delaney said she needed to call her mother again to let her know where she was and that she was doing fine.

I went into my bathroom to get ready for bed. I removed my makeup and placed my earrings in a tiny dish resting on the face bowl. When I walked into my bedroom, Delaney was still on the phone but at least she was smiling. When she hung up she said her mother told her everything would be fine and she would fly to New York Friday morning.

Delaney seemed to enjoy a great relationship with her mother and I envied her for this. As Delaney prepared for bed I reached for the portable phone and called Sheila as I walked into the living room.

"Praise the Lord," Sheila said when she answered the phone.

"Sheila, this is Nicole. I'm sorry to bother you so late but I wondered if you would say a special prayer for a friend of mine."

"Now, Nicole, it's morning anyhow. Let's get started," Sheila said.

The prayer session with Sheila made me feel a lot better. After I hung up, Kyle called wondering if he'd been too insensitive earlier this afternoon and to make sure everything was okay. I told him everything was fine and joked by telling him he didn't know any better. "I think we should go out and take care of the motherfucker ourselves. We should hold a big press conference and see how that helps his record sales," Kyle said.

"You've got a good point there, Kyle," I said. "I think I hear Delaney. We'll give you a call tomorrow."

"Okay, darling. Tell Delaney to hang in there," he said.

"Consider it taken care off. Good night, Kyle."

Delaney came out of the bedroom wearing one of my old cotton nightshirts. She gently removed the gold earrings from her ears and laid them on the coffee table silently. Delaney picked up a brush, which had been lying on the top of her bag, and started to slowly brush her hair.

I walked over to the wall unit and looked through my music selection.

"You feel like some Patti LaBelle?" I called out to Delaney.

"Naw, not Patti tonight," Delaney said.

"But she's your favorite," I said.

"And she'll be my favorite tomorrow, but tonight I want to hear some gospel music. You got some of that, don't you?"

"Are you okay? I mean really okay?"

"I'm starting to feel much better. I'm so glad you talked me into spending the night."

I smiled at Delaney and put in the first religious disc I saw. Powerful gospel voices quickly filled my apartment as I turned off the lights and checked the locks. Delaney and I held each other tightly by the waist and walked slowly into the bedroom. I jumped on my bed and Delaney joined me and playfully hit me with the pillow. She pushed my dolls to the floor. "These girls got to go," she joked. We were like two teenage girls at their first slumber party.

She gave me a hug and thanked me for the support and I looked at her, pulled her close to me, and said, "That's what good girlfriends are for!"

Fifteen

It was my birthday and Sherrod Jones gave me one of the best gifts I'd received in several years. Over lunch she accepted my final offer of two hundred thousand dollars and a private apology to Charles Marshall from Basil. I also suggested and Sherrod agreed that Basil make a contribution from his own pocket to the Gay and Lesbian Alliance Against Defamation or the Minority AIDS project. Basil would decide on the charity but the amount was a non-negotiable ten thousand dollars. In return we received a gag agreement and avoided a lengthy trial. Basil was due back in the New York area for summer training camp in about a month and wanted to get this mess resolved. I wanted to get rid of him. The summer was usually a slow period for me and I wanted to relax before the college football season started. Maybe I would go to New York and hang out with Kyle. I needed to make sure he wasn't still upset with me. It was really strange not talking with him every day.

I'd had several meetings with Sherrod before we finally reached an agreement. She was a great attorney and Gilliam had warned me she wouldn't be as easy as the lawyer originally assigned to the case. When Sherrod discovered it was my birthday she suggested we meet at a small French-African restaurant in the Little Five Points area. During lunch with Sherrod, I experienced something out of the ordinary for me. I found myself sexually attracted to her. Maybe it was the way she carried herself—a sort of Oprah Winfrey–like confidence that gave her an overwhelming sexuality. I mean she carried herself as if she weighed a hundred and ten pounds. She wore clothes that made no concession to her weight. Her ebony face sparkled, her mysterious, docile brown eyes enhanced by a hint of makeup. She was not like any of the women I'd ever been with or found myself attracted to.

"Everything here is great," Sherrod said as she looked over the menu, which had been printed on a brown paper bag.

"It smells great. How did you find this place?" I asked as I looked around the restaurant, its walls covered with beautiful African art.

"One of my clients turned me on to it."

"Sherrod, how did you come to represent Marshall?"

"Oh, he was a referral. I do a lot of pro bono work for people who are HIV positive and have been fired from their jobs."

"Is there a lot of that going on in Atlanta?"

"You'd be surprised. I mean it's really sad having to deal with the disease and not having an income to support yourself," Sherrod said.

"Maybe I'll talk to Gilliam about our firm helping out."

"That would be a great help."

"Well, on to the agreement. I think everything is in order," Sherrod said as she handed me the legal-sized pages.

"I'll make sure Mr. Henderson signs this immediately and I'll messenger the check over to your office."

"Great. Now that we've gotten that out of the way, tell me about Raymond Tyler. I mean Raymond Tyler, Jr., correct?"

"Yes, I'm a junior. How did you know that?"

"I've met your father. Worked on a few national and local campaigns with him. I must say good looks must run in your family," Sherrod said with a sly smile.

"Don't make me blush."

"Aw, come on, I'd like to see that."

"Let me put the shoe on the other foot. Tell me about Sherrod Jones. Married, divorced, or otherwise engaged?"

"None of the above. Very happily single and loving it," she laughed.

The waitress came and took our orders and I became more intrigued and captivated by Sherrod's lively manner.

"So what do you do in your spare time, Sherrod?"

"Oh, I bowl and I sew, but going to sporting events—all types—is my passion."

"No kidding. Me too. I love sports. Especially college football. That's one of the reasons I went to work for Gilliam."

"Then you'll have to go to *the* game with me," Sherrod said.

"The game. Which one is that?"

"Florida A&M versus Tennessee State. Every year they play in Fulton County Stadium."

"When is it?"

"Always the third weekend in September. There are tons of parties."

"Sounds like a lot of fun. I love FAMU's band," I said.

"So will you?"

"Will I what?"

"Will you be my date?" Sherrod asked.

"Sure I'd love that, but do we have to wait until September? I'm a pretty good bowler."

"Oh no, we don't have to wait. Here is my home number. Call me anytime," Sherrod said as she scribbled down a phone number on the back of one of her business cards.

"Great!" I said as I slipped the card in my suit pocket.

There were times when I thought she reminded me of Janelle, but then she would do something to dispel those similarities. I surprised myself when I caught myself daydreaming about making love with Sherrod. I got the feeling she was attracted to me and I also sensed she felt that if she really wanted me, she could have me.

Our lunch was served and Sherrod and I exchanged flirtatious glances as we devoured the delicious food. We were finishing our coffee when Sherrod looked me dead in the eyes and asked, "So, Raymond, tell me why some lady hasn't snagged you off the market yet?"

"Haven't met the right one," I fibbed. "Haven't met the right one."

Sherrod lowered the coffee cup from her lips and placed it in the saucer and smiled. It was a smile that left me wanting more.

When I got back to the office, I burst into Gilliam's office to share the great news. She had just gotten off the phone and was putting an earring back on when I came in.

"Ray, what's that big smile about?" Gilliam asked.

"Well, Sherrod and her client accepted our offer and Basil's insurance company will foot the majority of the costs," I said. "But he's going to have to make the donation we discussed from his own pocket."

"Oh, that's great. I just got some good news too. Well, it's semi-good news," she said.

"What?"

"Just got off the phone with my friend, you know the one that I told you was high up in state politics."

"Yeah."

"Well, he just told me my name is on the short list for a federal judgeship, the next time there is an opening," Gilliam said.

"That's great. Congratulations!" I said.

"Yeah, thanks, but you know I don't know if I'm ready to reduce my standard of living. I mean I would have to give up some things," she mused. "Being a public servant isn't that lucrative."

"Oh, I didn't think about that. But it's an honor not many of us will ever get."

"You know, Ray, you're right. This buppie mentality can get out of hand. Here I am worried about making over one hundred thousand dollars for the rest of my life. Do you know how ridiculous that sounds?" Gilliam quizzed.

"I guess our generation takes a lot for granted," I said.

"You got that right! Our parents never had these opportunities," Gilliam said.

"Well maybe now is a good time to ask you something."

"What, Ray?"

"How would you feel about the firm doing some pro bono work for AIDS patients?"

"Sounds like a great idea. What made you think of that?"

"Sherrod. She does a lot of work and mentioned they could always use the extra help."

"Fine, get the information and get back with me. Ms. Jones is quite impressive, isn't she?"

"Quite. So when will you find out about the judgeship?"

Gilliam went on to explain that nothing was certain, her name was just on a list along with several other attorneys in the state. I did find out that she was the only black female on the list. The current court only had one minority member and that was an older Hispanic judge who was close to retirement.

She said this was going to speed up her decision to add a partner and for the first time she asked directly if I was interested. I tried to contain my excitement and said I would be willing to discuss it. It had always been a dream of mine to make partner in a firm other than my pops's before age thirty-five.

I returned to my office and phoned Basil and gave him the good news. I could tell from his voice over the phone that he was pleased. I told him I would messenger over the agreement, but he suggested I drop it by his place because he had something he wanted to give me. When I asked what, he said, "It's a surprise." Despite my better judgment and since it was my birthday, I agreed. I was supposed to meet

Jared that evening at a place called Intermezzo, a classy piano bar located at the entrance of Buckhead. Maybe this would be the perfect place and night to broach the subject of feelings.

Basil gave me directions to his townhouse which, it turned out, was close to my place, just a bit further north, near Lennox Mall. He told me it was a place he'd leased for the summer from one of the Atlanta Falcons who lived in California during the off-season.

A minor traffic jam caused me to get to Basil's place a little later than I expected. I stood in front of the red brick two-story townhouse and looked at my watch as I rang the bell. I would call Jared when I got inside and tell him I was running late. Making sure everything was in order had taken longer than I expected. The day had gone so swiftly.

Basil opened the door with a glass in his hand and a big smile on his face. "Ray, come on in. I'm glad to see you," he smiled.

"Basil. You gave great directions," I said as I walked through the sparsely furnished living room noticing a bone-colored leather sofa and a red ten-speed bike lying against the wall. Basil was wearing a white tank top and lime green neon shorts. They looked great against his bronze body.

"Let's go out by the pool and look over this agreement. I talked to my insurance agent and he told me everything will be taken care of when I sign this," Basil said as he stopped at the bar and grabbed a beer stein.

"Yeah, that's right, but I can leave this and you can look it over," I said hurriedly.

"What's the rush? I may never get you over here again before I leave," Basil said.

"Now you're aware that the contribution must come from your personal account. You decide between the two charities," I said.

"Yeah, yeah, I'll have my accountant take care of it," Basil said.

"Do you have Marshall's number to arrange the apology?"

"Yes, your secretary gave it to me."

"Basil, please handle him with kid gloves. The apology is important to him. Leave your arrogance home," I instructed.

"Don't worry, Ray. I'll be the perfect gentleman," Basil said.

"Basil, are you really sorry about hitting him?"

"How many times are you going to ask me that?"

"Until I get an answer."

"What do you think?"

"I don't know. Tell me."

"Well, I still don't think it was right for him to confront me like that. But I know you're right about black folks beating on each other."

"I hope you mean that."

"I do."

I followed Basil through a set of french doors off the small kitchen and into the backyard that included a small pool and a brilliant landscape scorched by the heat of the June sun. Basil offered me a seat at a wrought-iron table with beach chairs. He walked back into the kitchen and returned with a six-pack of Rolling Rock beer.

"Here, let me pour you a brew," Basil offered.

"Well, I don't think I should. You are a client and this is business," I protested.

"Not after I sign this. As soon as I do, you're fired." He smiled.

Basil walked back into his townhouse and emerged minutes later with a ballpoint pen. While inside he'd activated his sound system and the mellow sounds of Oleta Adams surrounded the backyard.

He skimmed over the document and was getting ready to sign, when I stopped him.

"Basil, you should really read that," I said.

"You think it's right, don't you?"

"Yes, but . . ." Before I could finish my sentence Basil quickly signed the document, handed it to me, and said, "You're now officially out of my employ." He smiled. "Drink up."

I smiled back at him and was about to take a sip of the beer when Basil reached over and stopped me.

"Wait a minute. Toast," he said.

"Toast. How did you know it was my birthday?"

"It's your birthday? I didn't know that. I was going to toast to your being such a great lawyer. Now I'll have to break out the good stuff."

"Basil, don't, I have to meet someone," I said.

"Oh, come on, Ray. Just one," Basil pleaded.

I didn't object. The beautiful scenery was having a seductive effect on me and the pool looked inviting.

Basil returned with two long-stemmed glasses and a bottle that looked like Dom Pérignon.

"Loosen up your tie. Call your friend and tell him or her you're running a little late," Basil said.

"Yeah, I'll do that. But just one glass and I'm history. Can I use your phone?"

"What, you got to call your boyfriend?"

"What?"

"I'm just messing with you. There is a phone on the kitchen wall. Knock yourself out," Basil smiled.

"Thanks," I said as I walked toward the kitchen. Once inside I dialed Jared's number, pausing to watch Basil bending over and dipping his hands in the pool. *My God, was this boy fine!* I reached up and loosened my tie as Jared's answering machine prompted me to turn around and face the dining room. At the end of the recording, the automated voice announced the machine was full and no longer accepting messages. I hung up the phone and walked back to the patio. Basil smiled and handed me a glass of champagne.

While we drank the wonderful-tasting champagne, Basil volunteered information about his background. He'd grown up in Jacksonville, Florida. His mother had died when he was young, and he was extremely close to his father. I was surprised to find out he had a Chemistry degree from the University of Miami. He said as a kid he'd wanted to be a mortician and he always dreamed of one day having a chain of funeral homes. How strange, I thought.

Our conversation somehow ventured off into our sexuality, well, at least my sexuality. Basil stood by his story of being seduced by a rich alumni and he still didn't consider himself gay or bi. When I asked him what he and Kyle did, he replied, "We just jacked off. Kyle might be a sissy but he has a beautiful body."

I asked Basil why he used those terms and he softly said, "I don't know. I just do. I'm trying to change."

"Why did you feel you had to pay for sex while you were in New York? You're a nice-looking brother but, of course, you know that."

Basil smiled and said, "Well, to protect myself and maybe because of guilt."

"Guilt?"

"Yeah. I earned a lot of money while I was in college by having sex with men. Maybe it's a way of paying back. But I also didn't want my business out in the streets and New York has many big streets."

"I guess I understand your logic. I don't agree, but I understand."

Basil must have owned a CD player with an automatic changer, because instead of Oleta I now heard Anita Baker's sweet voice fill the air. We had finished the bottle of Dom and I was feeling its effects.

I realized that the chair I was sitting in was a recliner so I leaned back and noticed that dusk had arrived; a full moon was forming as immense and orange as the sun it replaced. It was also quite humid and I pulled off my tie and unbuttoned the top buttons of my white cotton shirt.

I closed my eyes and suddenly, I heard a loud splash and felt drops of water on my face and neck. Basil had removed his tank top and had dived into the pool. With clean, rhythmic strokes, he swam the length of the pool, touched the railing, and then pulled himself up and out of the pool. It was when he stood up straight that I realized trouble was close at hand. So much for the big body–small penis theory.

His neon green shorts were actually swimming trunks and now that they were soaking wet I could see right through them and even though Basil was wearing a jockstrap, it hardly proved up to its task.

Basil wiped his face with a multicolored towel and smiled. "You should come in, Ray. The water will cool you off."

"Who said I was hot?" I muttered.

Basil jumped back into the pool and started splashing water up on the deck and me. I leaped from the chair but my gray suit pants were already damp. I unbuttoned my shirt and removed it and my pants quickly, stripping down to my boxers with the jockey fly front. The peacock blue water in the pool looked inviting and I could smell the scent of chlorine in the night air. Basil came up to the railing again but I could now see his green shorts floating around the pool alone. I found myself captivated by the evening and various lights that streamed over the pool with a splendid luminosity and Basil's superb body swimming naked in all that gorgeous water. I had to feel the water and Basil—I had to feel his touch. Maybe being so close to Basil's body would give me something for my masturbation memory. I immediately jumped into the water and was surprised at its coolness.

"Come here. I want to show you something," Basil said with something provocative in his voice, his beautiful eyes challenging me.

I swam slowly toward Basil, using my hands as oars to control my motion.

Seconds later we were face to face. I looked him straight in the eye and said, "What do you want to show me?"

Basil put his hands under the water and came closer to me, taking my hands and placing them on his long and hard sex. I quickly pulled back, determined that this time I would do the seducing. I removed my underwear and threw it to the wooden deck, smiled at Basil and then quickly pulled him toward me. He looked faintly surprised. Maybe he thought he had lost control of his planned seduction. I leaned forward and gently kissed his hard neck and then playfully bit it as he lifted his head toward the star-filled sky. I swayed back and forth against him, feeling the solidness of his body along mine, the warmth of his arms folding around me, the sensation of his lips exploring my neck, the sensual warmth of the water.

Basil started to kiss my body, from the neck down to my chest and then softly kissing my arms and even my elbows. In fact he kissed almost every part of my body except my lips. When he got close to them he would kiss my nose instead or my forehead. Everywhere but my lips—and while his tongue was sending me into ecstasy I wondered why he was avoiding my lips. When I tried to force my lips on his he would quickly jerk his head. Did I have bad breath or something? Maybe the combination of the beer and the champagne created a sour taste, but he had been drinking the same thing.

"What's the matter, Basil?" I asked.

"What? Everything is fine. Your body feels so good," Basil moaned.

"Then kiss me," I demanded.

"I don't kiss men," he said with his usual attractive arrogance.

I instantly pulled back and felt my sex go down, my face grow hot. Basil's warm smile faded and he gazed at me in astonishment. His expression softened.

"I'm sorry, Basil—if you can't kiss these, then you can't kiss that," I said pointing first to my lips and then downward toward the water.

"Okay, Ray, if that's the way it is," Basil said as he waded toward the pool edge and went up the steps to the deck. His nude backside was facing me as I stood in the water alone. I looked around the pool area for a towel or my underwear. I then followed Basil up the steps and suddenly I was standing inches away from him, both of us nude, and I could feel my adrenaline and sex race. I was furious at myself for allowing this raging asshole to get me so worked up. Abruptly Basil enveloped me, putting his brawny arms around me and pulling me against him as if there was something in me that he needed, something that only I could provide. I could feel his erection pulsating against my navel. My body began to sway against him in a subtle motion. He took my hands and made soft circular strokes on my palm and then brought my hands to his lips and kissed my fingertips. And then he kissed me.

The first thing I saw the morning after my birthday was navy blue and white. Navy blue sheets and pillowcases in which I found my head buried and white jockey underwear that Basil wore as he walked into the bedroom with a glass of juice in his hand.

"I hope you like cranberry juice," Basil said softly. "It's usually good for hangovers."

"Yeah, that's fine. What time is it?"

"Six-thirty."

"Wow, my head is hurting a little bit," I said as I looked around the large bedroom for my clothes.

"Your clothes are downstairs," Basil said, noticing my silent search.

"Okay. Do you have a robe I can put on?"

"Sure," Basil said. He walked into a large closet and returned with a light blue striped robe. Basil threw the robe at me without a smile. His face had a look that was hard to read. He was drinking something from a mug that he set down on his dresser. He put on a pair of bleached jeans and a cotton T-shirt.

"I'll get you a couple of towels in case you want to take a shower before you leave," Basil said dryly.

"Sure, I'd like that," I said, wondering what the deal was with Basil's tone.

I slowly removed myself from the king-sized bed and walked toward the adjacent bathroom. While taking a warm shower, I thought back on the night before. Had I done something that I would live to regret? Not only was Basil a client, even though technically he wasn't, he was someone whom I wasn't even certain I liked. The sex was stupendous, but a deep sense of guilt shrouded me. Guilt because I'd given up my vow of celibacy for lust and in a strange way I felt I had betrayed Jared. It was as though I had committed adultery.

My feelings were familiar. This was usually the way I felt after sex with men. After all these years the uncomfortable feeling always managed to creep in. Even if it was somebody I was really interested in, it didn't matter. I always felt dirty and empty. With women, lovemaking, not sex, was always filled with a lot of warmth and caressing before and after the actual sexual act. Maybe it was because of the extra caring that it didn't leave me with an empty feeling. I wondered if all guys felt this way after sex with each other and if so, why? Maybe it was just me not dealing with my reality, though Basil's cool reception wasn't helping matters. The night before he had been so warm, so giving of himself. After he'd kissed me the first time, he'd kissed me over and over again, as if he was experiencing something for the first time. His lips were surprising and strong.

The lovemaking, or sex, had been feverish and substantial. Basil had screamed out obscenities as we both reached a climax, seconds apart from each other. The last thing I remembered was Basil positioning himself so that he could lay his head on my chest; he'd taken his hands and gently rubbed them through my hair. His body smelled like a combination of masculine funk and scented roll-on deodorant. I woke up in the middle of the night and just gazed at his wonderful body. I studied the contrast of Basil's hairy chest and his baby smooth legs and butt and the tiny strings of black and blond hair coming from his toes. Basil suddenly changed his sleeping position without opening his eyes, avoiding my hypnotic gaze at his body. He now lay flat on his stomach and I rested my head on his beautiful ass and gently rubbed the back of his thighs until I fell asleep.

When I walked back into Basil's bedroom from my shower he threw me a pair of black boxers.

"I think we're about the same size," he said.

"Thanks. I'll get these back to you," I said.

"No hurry. I put your underwear in a bag downstairs," Basil said.

As I put on the underwear I realized that it was new and I gently tore off the tag. I noticed the gold condom wrappers on Basil's nightstand and another two on the ivory-colored carpet below. How many condoms had we used? There was an empty champagne bottle and a potato chip bag sitting alongside the lamp and digital clock that now displayed seven o'clock.

"Well, I guess I better get outta here before your neighbors leave," I offered.

"Okay," Basil said without looking in my direction.

"Basil?"

"Yeah."

"Is there a problem? Are you sorry about last night?" I asked.

"Naw, no, Ray. It was great, but . . ." Basil paused. "Well, you know I'm not gay . . . right? I have a girlfriend."

"Sure, I know you're not gay," I lied.

"You know I love pussy. In fact I've had so much pussy I could give you some," he laughed.

"I know." What was this fool talking about?

"And this will be just between you and me. No strings."

"Who am I going to tell? Of course no strings."

Basil walked downstairs with me and led me through the dining room, out the back french doors, past the pool area, pointing out a shortcut to my car. Absent was the warmth of the night before, the warmth of the pool's water, and Basil's constant flirting. There was a definite chill in the air and it was the middle of June.

Sixteen

*J*une 20th turned out to be a red-letter day. I met Delaney and her mother at the Lincoln Center Café for lunch after Delaney's second doctor's appointment. The preceding days had been tension-filled for me so I could just imagine what they were like for Delaney and her mother, who had packed their days with shopping trips to New Jersey and the Pier area.

Delaney followed her mother's advice and got a complete physical examination to make sure her attacker hadn't given her some STD. She still hadn't made a police report. Today was the day she would get her test results.

When I walked in and saw the look on Delaney's face I knew she had good news. She and her mother were engaged in happy conversation, clicking champagne flutes together. Delaney told me about her complete physical exam including an HIV test and how she had gotten a clean bill of health, with a small warning to gain a little weight. Maybe it was the worry that had caused Delaney to drop below her normal hundred and five pounds.

When I met Dellanor Morris, Delaney's mom, I quickly recognized where Delaney got her zest for life and all-around wackiness. Although she was over sixty-five, Dellanor, as she insisted we call her, was a spitfire, taking on New York as if she had lived here all her life. Small-boned with beautiful, gray hair streaked with black, Delaney's mom was into reading tarot cards and had predicted that Delaney would be just fine. One night she told me I was going to be very big in the recording industry, which took us all a bit by surprise, since I had just mentioned weeks before that my secret dream was to have a successful recording career and family life similar to Vanessa Williams's. Kyle had looked at me and then at Dellanor and said, "Quick, Miss Mother, read my cards. Miss Dellanor here can put Ms. Dionne Warwick and her psychic friends out of business," he joked.

After lunch, the three of us took in a movie and window-shopped along Columbus Avenue. When it was getting close to the time for me to depart for the theater, Dellanor suggested to Delaney they get tickets to *Jelly's* for the evening because she wanted to see her other daughter, me, perform.

Delaney and I explained to her I was just a standby, but told her it was a great show and she should try and get tickets for this evening. Then she could brag to all her friends in Seattle that she had "done" Broadway! I promised to get her an introduction to Gregory Hines, whom, it happened, she had seen as a little boy when he was performing with his brother, Maurice, and his father.

Just when I was getting ready to walk over to the Seventy-second Street subway stop, Dellanor told me she was going to get the chance to hear me sing before she left town. "Yes, Delaney, Kyle, and myself will do a show for you at the airport when you leave," I joked.

"Whatever, just so I get to hear that lovely voice Delaney always tells me about," Dellanor said.

On the subway headed to the Virginia Theater, I thought about the wonderful relationship Delaney and her mom had and wished that I shared the same type of relationship with my mother. I guess since I had been a daddy's girl all my life it was a little hard. Not that my mother didn't love me, I knew she did. It was just at times she didn't understand my ambition or my dreams. She didn't understand that I wanted more out of life than being a wife. I often worried about my mother being alone since Daddy's death, but she had moved into a retirement home in Little Rock and seemed to have a very full social life with all the activities she wrote to me about. My mother didn't like to talk on the phone that much, but she could write some long letters that bordered on mini-novels.

I arrived at the theater and Deborah Brown, one of the Hunnies in the cast, gave me a big smile and said, "I heard Renee's husband is sick and she might not be here."

"What? You're kidding," I said in a shocked voice.

"No, girl, that's what I heard the stage manager say a few minutes ago," Deborah said.

Suddenly my palms became moist with sweat. Could this be possible? Was I going to get the opportunity to go on? I started going over the lines and lyrics to the songs in my head. I balled both of my fists and walked around in circles looking upward at the ceiling backstage.

Every time the stage door opened, I quickly looked to see who it was and breathed a sigh of relief when it was someone other than Renee.

I wondered if the director and producers were in the theater. They usually made a point of being there whenever an understudy or standby went on for the first time. I also began to wonder if this was some type of invisible audition for the national tour that was going to be starting in Chicago in about six months. Sometimes producers and directors would set up a performance to see how one performed under real life circumstances. I was so happy I hadn't yet turned in my two-week notice; I was still waiting to see the final script and the music for *To Tell the Truth*, never mind the contract.

Minutes later the stage door opened and in walked Renee; my fast-beating heart suddenly sank.

"Where's Reggie?" Renee called out as she walked right past me.

"He's in his office," a familiar voice called out.

I looked at Deborah and we gave each other a what's-going-on? look.

A few minutes later Renee and Reggie emerged from the wings.

"Nicole," Reggie said.

"Yes, Reggie," I said breathlessly.

"Renee has a family emergency and I need you to go on. Are you ready?"

"Of course I'm ready," I replied.

I wanted to say, "What do you think, stupid? I've been waiting on this chance for months." Renee came close to me and grabbed my now cold hands.

"I know you're going to turn it out, but save something for me," she said. "I do have a family to support," she joked.

"Thanks, Renee. I'll keep the bed warm," I said, referring to the hot bedroom scene the character of Anita had with Gregory.

"Here, I want you to wear these for good luck," Renee said as she placed a pair of gold hoop earrings in my hands.

"Oh, Renee, these are beautiful. You're going to make me cry," I said, fighting back tears.

"Don't do it," Renee said. "Just go out there and make them forget about me for one night."

I gave Renee a hug and glanced over my shoulder, giving Deborah the okay sign. I looked in my purse for change for the phone booth. I needed to call Delaney, Kyle, Pierce, and my agent to let them know that I was going on.

I made four calls and got three answering machines and one answering service. That brought down my adrenaline for a moment. I redialed Delaney's number and she answered, telling me they already had tickets and promising that she would keep trying to reach Kyle. Again I became excited.

I said a silent prayer, praying for guidance on stage this evening, and that my friends, fiancé, and agent would get the chance to see me tonight. I smiled to myself when I thought about Dellanor and her cards and wondered if she had anything to do with this change of events. Maybe she put some kind of bad luck root on Renee's husband, but that was a Southern thing and Dellanor was not Southern by any stretch of the imagination.

If I wasn't already nervous enough, my first appearance on stage was not until the end of the first act, which was different for a leading female role. The part of Anita was the fiery role of the girlfriend of Jelly Roll Morton. She was a jazz singer and a very strong-willed lady who helped Jelly to face the prejudices that he felt about his own race. Jelly Roll Morton was a Creole black, who, in the time period in which the musical takes place, was considered a higher-class citizen than regular black folks. It was not much different from the way some light-skinned blacks still treat their own kind today. I saw the class system at work day after day in the theater and recording industry. I mean what else could explain Paula Abdul's selling more records than Jennifer Holliday? Jennifer would blow that girl off the stage when it came to real singing. The musical, in many ways, was a frightening history lesson for black people of all different hues.

I thought it was funny that both of the roles that I might end up choosing between were characters named Anita and both were based on real-life people. Both were dark-skinned women, which made me feel even better, who'd stood up for their beliefs.

Right before the curtain went up, several cast members came by and grabbed my hands and wished me good luck, many telling me to "knock 'em dead."

After changing into my first costume, a flimsy slip-like dress, I was coming out of Renee's dressing room when I bumped into Reggie.

"You nervous?" Reggie asked, and flashed a hundred-watt smile.

"Just a little bit," I said.

"Don't worry, you'll do just fine. If you get lost just take a deep breath," Reggie instructed.

"Thanks, Reggie. I'll do that."

"I'll see you in the big time," Reggie said as he gave me a small kiss on the cheek.

As I listened to the orchestra warm up, I went over my lines in my head. I wasn't so much worried about my first song as I was my first lines. Mess up on the first lines and it could be a long night. I kept pacing behind stage, going over my first lines. I hadn't been this nervous on my own opening night! But that had been different since I'd known I was going on and I'd felt at home on stage with a cast I had been with from workshop to opening night. Although I felt like a part of this cast it was different; I had never performed with them and even my rehearsals were lone affairs with the director. I thought back to my sophomore year in high school the one year I made alternate majorette instead of the regular squad. Even though I practiced with the squad every day, I'd felt left out when I didn't have the chance to perform at halftime. My senior year when I made captain of the squad I went out of my way to make the alternate feel like a part of the squad, even convincing the rest of the squad to allow her to perform during Homecoming.

I purposely went back to the dressing room right before the curtain went up to avoid hearing the moaning sound that usually accompanied the announcement that a standby was going on. But I couldn't sit down so I went back downstairs. I was standing near the corner of the stage and from the sound of the applause when Gregory made his entrance I could tell that we had another full house and this was one that wasn't sitting on its hands. I was about fifteen minutes away from showdown and I went back up to the dressing room one more time to make sure that my costume and wig fit right. Renee's tiny dressing room looked more like the vanity section of a large bathroom with everything done in light pink and green. Magazine articles and clippings of reviews were pasted on the edge of her mirror. Pictures of her husband and kids held the center stage of her dressing table. I picked up the picture in a gold frame and looked at the blue-eyed blond man and two beautiful copper-colored little girls. They looked like twins. It was the first time I realized Renee's husband was white. I don't know why this surprised me, but Renee hadn't struck me as the type of girl who would be married to a white man. I mean she struck me as a real sistah. Whatever that meant. But what type of black woman would be married to a white man? Was there a type? What did that make me? I wasn't married to a white man but I was pretty close. Was I not a real sistah? Were my thoughts racist?

My heart was racing as I took my first steps toward the stage of the Virginia Theater. The heat of the stage lights swept my face. I was concentrating on the last word to leave Gregory's mouth and the first one to leave mine. For a brief second I drew a blank until I looked into Gregory's eyes and then at his lips as he was beginning to mouth my first word, but before he formed his lips, the words rushed from my mouth and I began to smile inside.

The rest of my performance went without a hitch. I hit all my marks and I could feel the prolonged applause after "Play the Music for Me," my big number in scene six of the first act. The audience gave freely with their applause and I gave them back everything I had. It felt fantastic to be on the stage doing what I loved doing. I became so immersed in the role of Anita, that I wanted the night to last forever.

I had watched Renee countless nights from behind the curtains and I wanted to bring my own to the role. I held certain notes a little longer than she did and I worked the crowd and Gregory. I could tell from the glint in his eyes that he was pleased with my performance. This was confirmed when at the end, he led the applause when I took my bow.

After the show, the first person I saw was Reggie. He came running to me, grabbed both of my arms, and then hugged me tightly.

"Wonderful, just wonderful, Nicole! I've never seen Anita played so beautifully. Just fabulous," said Reggie. "I'm going to make sure you get to go on that stage more often," he added.

"Thank you," I said, beginning to be overcome with emotion as I saw Delaney and her mom walk up behind Reggie with roses in their hands.

"Nicole, girlfriend. You go, girl! You were fierce! Just wonderful," Delaney said as she hugged me tightly.

"See I told you," Dellanor said. "I knew I was going to get to hear that wonderful voice. You were beautiful, baby."

"Thank you, Ms. Morris, I mean Dellanor. I'm just glad it's over."

"I tried to reach Kyle but I kept getting his answering machine," Delaney said.

"Where is he?" I asked.

"I don't have a clue," Delaney said.

"Should we give him a call now?"

"You go meet your fans. I'll give him a call and let him know where we're going to be," Delaney said.

Just as I was getting ready to accept congratulations from members of the cast, I saw Pierce standing near the door with a bouquet of white roses.

"I'm so glad you got my message," I said as I gave Pierce a kiss on his lips.

"I have some people awfully mad at me," Pierce said, "but I wouldn't have missed this for the world. You were great!"

"Thank you," I said. "Let me go change. Why don't I meet you at the Whiskey in about twenty minutes with Delaney and Dellanor?"

"I've got a better idea," Pierce said with a mischievous look in his eyes. "Why don't I send a car for you at the bar in about two hours and you come to my house so that we can have a private celebration?"

"Oh, Pierce, that sounds great, but I warn you I'm tired," I said.

"I promise to let you get some rest," Pierce said.

"Well, okay," I agreed reluctantly.

"Great. Let me go and say hello to Delaney and her mother," Pierce said as he gave me another kiss and walked toward Delaney and Dellanor, who were holding court with Gregory and some other members of the cast.

I went up the stairs to Renee's dressing room, stopping almost every step of the way to accept the compliments of the many cast members. I felt so great. It had been a long time since I'd experienced the high I was currently on.

I looked in my purse and pulled out my own makeup and did my face all over. The wig had caused my hair to frizz on the ends. I would make an appointment first thing in the morning to get it fixed. Maybe I would make an appointment at an all-day spa and get a facial and massage too. I would have a little extra in my paycheck for this performance and I deserved it.

After I'd placed another call to Kyle's answering machine, Delaney, Dellanor, and I walked four blocks down Eighth Avenue to the bar located in the Paramount Hotel. It was packed with people carrying *Playbill*s from various shows. We spotted a table of people leaving and dashed to get it.

"Let's order champagne," Dellanor said. "I'm buying."

The three of us went through a bottle of Moët in about twenty minutes and the champagne began making me light-headed. I remembered agreeing to go to Pierce's later that evening and thought about calling him and offering a rain check but I wanted to see him. He would be honest about my performance.

It was so much fun just sitting and relaxing with Delaney and her mother. Like three good girlfriends out on the town for an evening. I had never enjoyed such an evening with my own mother. First, my mother didn't drink and second, she wouldn't be caught dead in a place filled with so many white people. It was during times like these that I wished my mother could become my friend if only for an evening as special as this one. But my mother was from the old school and felt mothers should be mothers and nothing else.

Dellanor was trying to convince us we should order another bottle when the driver paged me in the bar. When I first heard the page I figured it was Kyle with whom neither Delaney nor I had talked in many days. Delaney said he had mentioned he was really behind on a big project. Good, I thought to myself, maybe that would get him off the wedding dress kick.

I insisted that Delaney and her mom let the driver drop them at home, but they decided they'd stop somewhere close to Delaney's apartment and have Mexican coffee. While we were riding uptown, Dellanor commented to Delaney, "See, you need to get you a white man. Look how good he treats Nicole."

"Woman, pleeze," Delaney said as she rolled her eyes at me and then at her mother.

The elderly doorman at Pierce's building didn't bother to call up and announce me.

"Dr. Gessler is expecting you, Ms. Springer," he said.

A sudden wave of sleepiness came over me as I walked into Pierce's spacious East Side co-op apartment. Pierce greeted me at the door with a glass of champagne . . . the absolute last thing I needed.

Pierce was wearing navy blue silk pajamas and his face was relaxed and still mischievous.

"I don't need this," I said as I took the slender flute from Pierce.

"Yes, you do. You've earned it. Nicole, you were great tonight. Diahann Carroll would have been envious," Pierce said.

"You think so?"

"Yes. Let's go out on the terrace," Pierce suggested.

I laid my bag on the bar and followed Pierce to the terrace that had a breathtaking view of Manhattan. Millions of different-colored lights of the city sparkled in the night. There was a full moon covering the city and classical music surged from the speakers from within Pierce's apartment. It sounded as if there was a speaker right under the chair I was sitting in. A single candle on the patio table threw a shadow on the door leading back into Pierce's apartment.

"It's a beautiful night," I observed.

"A beautiful morning," Pierce corrected.

We sat in silence for a short period of time and then Pierce suggested that I go into his bedroom, that there was something waiting for me there. I walked into Pierce's bedroom and saw a beautiful pair of wine-colored silk pajamas lying on his large bed, covered with a single red rose and a white linen note card that read, *"To my one and only. These are for my eyes only. Love, Pierce.*

The pajamas were exquisite and I couldn't wait to feel them against my skin. I quickly removed my clothes and slipped into them. I went into Pierce's vanity area and took a look at my makeup and hair. First thing in the morning, I thought, make that hair appointment.

The sleepwear felt seductively sleek against my body. I glided back to the patio where Pierce had removed his pajama top to expose an extremely hairy chest.

"I was getting warm," he smiled.

I moved next to him and looked out at the majestic view and enjoyed the cool night air. Suddenly Pierce grabbed my chin, slowly turned it toward his lips, and kissed me softly and then hungrily. Our lips parted and our tongues came into play.

Pierce's lips felt different tonight . . . disarming, disturbing, mesmerizing. Lips designed solely for romance. The feel of his body was exciting, his scent clean and masculine.

Pierce's strong hand started to move slowly to the top of my pajama top and when his finger touched the first button he looked into my eyes and said, "I have to know if these feel and taste as wonderful as they look." His eyes were placed firmly on my breasts. I didn't say anything, but I guess my answer was a yes; Pierce slowly opened two buttons and with his large hands, gently cupped my left breast, lowered his lips, and kissed it softly. He then parted the silk top and repeated the action with my right breast.

Pierce's hard, wet tongue slowly left my breast and started downward toward my navel. I felt my body and face grow hot and my vaginal muscles tighten as Pierce's hand went down my back and his lips moved faster toward my mid-section. I briefly thought to push his face away from my body as I felt Pierce's hand on my back, but I didn't. The silk pajama bottom left my hips and legs and fell gently around my ankles.

"No, Pierce," I moaned as I felt Pierce's tongue over my pubic hair. Pierce didn't stop. I leaned my head back and admired the starlit night and enjoyed the exquisite pleasure of Pierce's tongue. I heard the tape deck click and a silence ensued over the patio.

Minutes later Pierce led me through the sliding glass doors. I made a quick stop in the bathroom and then met him in the bedroom. We converged on the bed, eagerly, and for the rest of the night we experienced lively and intense pleasure from each other. A marvelous sexual feeling overtook my body like warm waves to a rock-filled shore. Something I hadn't experienced in a time period too lengthy to recall.

Seventeen

They say there's a thin line between love and hate, but had anyone considered the line between lust and love? I was convinced that lust dominated my relationship with Basil Henderson. He was still not admitting to being gay or bisexual, so I never brought it up. If he wanted to live in a sexual Disneyland, then that was cool with me. I was just enjoying one of the most passion-filled relationships I had ever known. My celibacy vow was a mere memory. I figured if my celibacy was going out of business it might as well go out in style. Boy, what style. Besides, it was nice to know there was someone more confused than me when it came to his sexuality.

In the midst of all this passion with Basil, my relationships with Jared and Kyle suffered. When I mentioned to Kyle about remotely being interested in Basil he stated simply, "Don't do it, Ray." The summer was almost over before I confessed.

After standing up Jared on my birthday, everything went downhill. When I returned home the morning after my first night with Basil there were thirteen messages on my machine. Birthday wishes from Mom and Pops, one from Kirby, one from Kyle, and ten messages from Jared, the last one saying, "Don't worry about returning this call this evening or ever." The tone of the message was pure anger. I didn't return his call, not because I didn't want to, but because I wanted to avoid a confrontation. I wanted to give him time to cool off and give myself time to come up with a believable story. I ran into him weeks later at the health club and we chatted as though we were just acquaintances as opposed to friends. He mentioned he had gotten an offer to join the Clinton presidential campaign and was strongly considering it, even though it would mean moving to Little Rock, Arkansas.

I still loved Jared and missed him desperately, but Basil had me in such a sexual stupor it was hard to think of much else, including my family, friends, and sometimes my job. I even turned down a couple of dinner invitations from Sherrod. My family was planning a big family reunion at the end of the summer and I wasn't providing the support I'd promised my mother earlier. My pops had personally invited Jared and I knew he would be there. The only reason my alliance with Basil wasn't causing a big problem at work was because Basil was turning me on to a lot of business contacts in the Florida and New York areas.

Despite Basil's strong presence in my life I was determined I would not fall in love with him. The relationship was based purely on sex— fabulous, erotic sex—and I had to remain clear on that fact. We shared a sexual intensity I had not dreamed possible. An intensity that sometimes scared me. It was a rare occasion when we went to a movie or out to dinner, this despite the fact that we spent almost every night in each other's bed, alternating weeks at his place and mine. When we talked it was always about his career and what he was going to do once it was over.

Basil continued a relationship with a black soap opera actress, Dyanna Watson, who divided her time between Atlanta, New York, and Los Angeles. I met Dyanna on a couple of her visits to Atlanta. She was a nice, naive, cocoa-brown-skinned beauty, whose career was beginning to heat up. I was introduced as Basil's attorney. I was also expected to stay out of the way during Dyanna's overnight or weekend visits to Atlanta, even though I got the impression Dyanna didn't mind having me around.

Basil was extremely uptight about public appearances. When we went to the same functions we took separate cars and barely spoke. The first time we went to the movies, I plopped down in the seat next to him after getting colas and popcorn but he quickly jumped to the next seat, leaving an empty one between us. If we went to the grocery store or video rental place and guys cruised us Basil would whisper, "Look at him cruising us. He must be a punk." If it was a female, Basil's reaction was totally different. He flirted, talked, and even took numbers, although he would tear up the number in my presence when we got home. One night he suggested we both call an attractive young lady we met to see who could bone her first while the other one looked on from the closet. "She's a freak I can tell. She would do both of us," Basil said. I declined.

But, in private, when the lights went out, Basil became a totally different person. Passionate, giving, and affectionate beyond belief. He also had a sense of humor that loosened even me up. One morning when I was on my way to the office, all decked out in my blue Brooks

Brothers suit, cotton shirt, silk tie, I paused in the bathroom where Basil was showering. "Basil, I'm getting ready to leave. I'll see you later on tonight," I yelled.

Basil pulled back the shower curtain with that million-dollar smile and asked, "Don't I get a kiss?" Basil was really into kissing now. When I obliged the next thing I knew I was in the shower with Basil, suit and all, kissing like crazy under the thrust of warm water. Minutes later, my expensive suit lay on the floor like a throw rug as Basil and I made love under the rush of the warm water. I called in sick and we spent the day watching his game footage, ESPN, and old Bette Davis movies he had delivered by the local video store.

During that summer, I saw many different sides of Basil. At times he could be the most arrogant man on earth and then, within seconds, he would question his every ability. He talked with the excitement of a little kid at the prospect of making the Pro Bowl and breaking Warrior receiving records and then looked at me and questioned, "Do you really think I can do it, Ray? Do you really?"

It was during these times that I wanted just to hold him in my arms and assure him everything would be perfect. He gave me what I missed so much from Jared. The feeling that I could do anything I dreamed and have someone to share it with. Sometimes Basil would look at me with his bedroom eyes and say, "You know if I didn't know better I would say I'm getting used to this."

When I talked with Kyle I barely mentioned Basil and when he brought up Jared, I told him we were giving each other *brakes*, a term Kyle used all the time when he got tired of the man he was seeing at a given time.

I justified the amount of time I spent with Basil by the fact that he would soon be leaving to go back to New Jersey for football season. It was only when we talked about his pending departure that our future would come up for discussion.

"Would you come to New York if I asked you?" Basil asked one night after our lovemaking.

"If you sent for me," I replied smugly.

"What if we split the cost of the ticket?"

"Then I'd have to think about it."

I thought about inviting Basil to my family reunion. I wanted to see what type of reaction I would get from my family. I mean at times I didn't know if my pops was so fond of Jared because he thought he would be a good partner for me or if he realized that Jared was straight and secretly wished he could straighten me out. There were times I would become jealous watching my pops and Jared enjoying conversations regarding politics and sports.

One evening I got a call from my pops. It became obvious that Jared had called him concerning Congressman Thomas's opponent.

"So I hear this guy Dee is one of your boys," my pops said.

"One of my boys?" I questioned.

"Yeah," Pops responded.

One of my boys? What was Pops talking about? Did he mean my fraternity and what did that have to do with the election? I repeated my question.

"One of my boys, huh. What do you mean, Pops?"

"Aw, come on, you know. One of your boys."

"Do you mean he's a member of KAΩ? I don't think he is."

"Come on, Ray-Ray. You know what I'm talking about. One of your boys."

That's when it hit me what my pops was talking about. I could just imagine him back at home in his office moving his big hands side to side in the air while he talked to me on the phone.

"Do you mean he's gay, Pops?" I asked, trying not to laugh.

"Yeah, that's it," my pops responded with relief in his voice.

"Then just say it, Pops. Jimmy Dee is gay," I demanded.

"Aw, come on, I don't need to say it."

"Okay, Pops, suit yourself. Kiss Mom and Kirby for me," I said as I hung up the phone.

As hard as my father tried, I knew that it was difficult for him to deal with my sexuality. I guess he thought somehow I'd changed or that he had to change to stay close and important in my life. Maybe he thought we couldn't talk about man-to-man things without sexual identity becoming a part of the discussion. When he talked about gay issues, his voice changed—he sounded more animated. At first, I would become angry because sometimes he seemed patronizing, but I realized he was trying to be supportive. Trying to understand.

It turned out Basil was going to be back in New Jersey during the reunion. I knew I was going to miss the sex and maybe even miss Basil, but I was looking forward to the fall. Kyle was coming to Atlanta for Labor Day and I was going back to AU for a fraternity reunion.

I still hadn't checked out the gay bars in Atlanta for Kyle. I did know there were three black bars and Kyle said there would be a lot of parties in Atlanta during the Labor Day holiday.

I thought of asking Mico about where I should take Kyle but decided against it. What if he cracked my face and demanded to know why I was asking him? One night, late, Basil and I went over to the Varsity Drive Inn near Georgia Tech University for greasy hot dogs and onion rings; we passed a big barn-type building with a large crowd of black men in front and on the side street.

"You know what that is?" Basil asked.

"No, I don't," I said.

"It's a black punk bar and I don't want to ever catch you in there," Basil instructed.

"Why? You afraid I'll see you in there?" I joked.

"Fuck off," Basil said with a slight smile.

"Why should I? I've got you," I said.

This time Basil smiled broadly.

Eighteen

"**Why** do you think I feel so guilty, Dr. Huntley?"

"Guilty?"

"I enjoyed making love with Pierce but the next day I suffered a tremendous amount of guilt."

"Is it because of your faith?"

"That's part of it. The other part is that I know now it's really just lust when it comes to Pierce. He brings my body pleasure but I don't love him like he loves me."

"Is it because he's white?"

"No."

"Jewish?"

"No," I said quickly.

"Then what is it, Nicole?"

"I just think maybe I should . . ."

Dr. Huntley didn't complete my thought or ask another question. She just stared at me with her knowing eyes.

"I should have kept the relationship on a friendship basis. Maybe I think I *should* be in love with him because of the way he treats me. But wouldn't that be sympathy love?"

"Sympathy love?"

"Yes—being in love with somebody because you feel sorry for him."

"Is there some reason I don't know about why you should feel sorry for Pierce?"

"No. He's very attractive, smart, wealthy, and very good in bed," I said.

Again no response from Dr. Huntley, just the look.

"Maybe I want the stars and bells we think we should have. It's times like these that I doubt if I really know what love is."

"Why do you feel that way?"

"I was just thinking about the first time, when I lost my virginity."

"The first time?"

"I almost didn't go to the prom. No one asked me until a week before. In a way I was relieved because I knew that it was an understanding that whomever you went to the prom with was the person who you would give up your virginity to, that is unless you had already given in to the pressures of hormonal high school boys. Since I think everybody knew I was a virgin I was surprised when he asked me."

"Who, Nicole?"

"Thorpe."

"Thorpe?"

"Yes, Thorpe Preston Douglas. Everybody called him TP. He was one of the best-looking guys in the entire school. Tall, muscular, fair-skinned, with dreamy brown eyes. He was the first black president of the student body and a star football player. I had secretly had a crush on him since ninth grade. The age my hormones kicked in. He was the kind of boy who I knew would make pretty children."

"So what happened?"

"Well, it was a magical moment. A nice spring night. Thorpe picked me up in his father's new burgundy Monte Carlo. His father was the first black principal at Little Rock Hall High, so his family was well off."

I paused and my thoughts drifted back to the decorated field house at Central High. Black and gold streamers everywhere, a racially mixed rock band. I could see the look of awe on all my girlfriends' faces when I walked into the gym with Thorpe. I smiled broadly at the remembrance.

"You're smiling," Dr. Huntley said, interrupting my memories.

"I was just remembering."

"So you were fond of him?"

"Yes."

"Did you have a good time?"

"I did until I went into the girls' rest room and one of my friends, who was a cheerleader, informed me that Thorpe was secretly dating Nina Porter. Nina was captain of the cheerleaders, a beautiful blue-eyed blonde. I always disliked cheerleaders. No, I'm kidding. She said Thorpe had invited me because Nina's parents didn't know that they had been dating since tenth grade."

"You didn't know that he was dating her?"

"No, I didn't know. I don't think very many did."

"So that bothered you?"

"No!" I shouted in anger.

"Why are you shouting, Nicole?"

"What bothers me is not that he didn't tell me why he asked me to the prom. I would have been a cover for him; I liked Nina. What bothers me is that my insecurities took over and I allowed him to take me to the Red Carpet Inn and make love to me. It was painful, but I thought it was okay because he thought I was beautiful. At least that's what he said when he picked me up. When he finished he took me home, didn't kiss me, and didn't call me ever again."

I felt tears rising in my eyes and I quickly blinked them back.

"Did you ever see him again?"

"Only in passing. At graduation and years later after I had won Miss Arkansas. He had married Nina. Their son was beautiful. You know, the only person who ever knew about Thorpe and me was Candance."

"Why is that?"

"Because she understood."

"So that was your first time?"

"Yes."

"And it wasn't a good experience?"

"No. Can we talk about something else?"

"Do you want to?"

"Yes," I said.

"Why?"

"Because I should be happy instead of having these confused feelings of pleasure and guilt. Guilt about things I can't change. I can't believe I'm spending my time talking about this when so many other people have bigger problems. When I talk about my first time it sounds like a sitcom episode. Let's talk about other people."

"Other people. Are you talking about your friend Delaney?"

"Yes. Delaney seems to be handling things pretty good. She still hasn't filed a police report, but she's doing volunteer work at a Rape Crisis Center. I'm thinking about volunteering some time there too."

"That would be great. Have you made mention of her going to the police?"

"No, I just try and let her know I'll be there to support her in any way I can."

"That's good."

"I am a little worried about her. What if she needs me while I'm in Arkansas? I tried to get her to come home with me but she declined. Kyle said he'd pick up the support slack."

"So you're going back home?"

"Yes."

"Aren't you excited?"

"Yes, it will be great seeing old friends. Maybe I'll see Thorpe and Nina," I laughed.

"Are you going to see your mother?"

"Yeah," I said mournfully.

"Aren't you excited about seeing your mother?"

"Should I be?"

The guilt regarding my now active sexual life with Pierce continued to weigh heavily on me. Every morning when Sheila and I had our prayer calls, I ended my prayer asking for strength. When I tried to talk with Sheila about it she would simply say, "Lust is a part of the body. The body is weak."

I was still with *Jelly's* and had gone on for Renee again when she took a week's vacation. I really loved the role and the producers asked if I would be interested in starring in the national tour. Of course I said yes. There was still no music or start date for *To Tell the Truth* and for me that spelled trouble. The fact that Pierce didn't talk about it as much was reason enough for alarm.

A recording career was also becoming a possibility. While I was subbing for Renee, a talent scout for LaFace Records out of Atlanta saw the show and offered to help me with a demo, or at least some backup work for some of their major artists.

The summer went by so fast and it seemed like Kyle, Delaney, and I had never been busier. So busy in fact, that we'd seen very little of each other. We talked on the phone a lot but very little face to face. Delaney completed two national commercials and took a week's vacation to go back to Seattle and San Francisco. She still didn't want to talk about her attack anymore and proceeded to go on calls for other rap artists. When I expressed my concern, she told me she never allowed herself to be alone with any of them.

Kyle was busy making multiple wedding dresses, one, he joked, that was suitable for marriage into a rich white family and one perfect for a high-class colored family.

In July I traveled back to Arkansas to sing on the final evening of the Miss Arkansas pageant. I couldn't do the entire pageant because it was a two-week job and I couldn't be out of New York that long. The pay was okay but it wasn't New York–scale money. So I agreed to come on the final night and help with the crowning of the new Miss Arkansas. It gave me a free trip home and a chance to break the news of my pending marriage to my mother and brother. It was great being back in Arkansas. The state was bursting with pride because the governor, Bill Clinton, was running for president of the United States and it appeared that he had a good chance of winning. The state hadn't received this much attention since the Central High incident. I just prayed he would win, not only for the country but for this small state that I loved.

It was always funny to me the reaction I got from people in New York when I told them I was from Arkansas. They were even more perplexed when I told them I was a former Miss Arkansas. "I didn't even know they had black people in Arkansas," would be the response of many.

My mother didn't come down to Hot Springs for the pageant. She said she wasn't up to the fifty-mile trip from Little Rock. I told her that was fine. We could get together for brunch in Little Rock before I left for New York City. My mother was staying in a high-rise retirement home near downtown and the airport. We decided to meet for brunch at the Excelsior Hotel right next to the Old State House, the place where I wanted to have my wedding. I was really excited about seeing my mother and having an enjoyable visit with her.

Mother was already at the hotel when I arrived. She looked beautiful in a kelly green silk dress I had sent from New York. She still had that schoolgirl figure and her gray hair was done nicely, but it still looked like she was using a pressing comb. The thought of the pressing comb made me smile when I thought about how I used to think I couldn't live without one when I was growing up. It wasn't until a couple of white gay guys got ahold of my hair and permed it on my third trip to the Miss Arkansas pageant that I got rid of my two pressing combs forever.

"Mother, you look great," I said as I hugged my mother tightly. "Where did you get that beautiful dress?" I asked.

"My fairy godmother," my mother said and smiled as she twirled around in the lobby of the huge hotel. She caught a glimpse of my ring but she didn't say anything.

"What do you feel like eating?" I asked.

"I don't care, baby. You should have come over to the home. Me and Bessie would have cooked for you. But I suppose you're too high and mighty for my eggs and grits," she said.

"Now, Mother. I'm just trying to make it easier on you. How's Michael?"

"Fine the last time I talked with him. I had to wire him some money to help him get a new apartment. He's trying to move into a better area," Mother said.

"Mama, are you sure Michael is doing okay? He's not on drugs or something like that, is he?"

"Drugs? Heavens no, child. Why would you ask something crazy like that? Michael is fine."

"Okay. I hope you're right."

We found a cute little breakfast place in the hotel and really had an enjoyable time. I told Mother about getting to go on for Renee and about the new musical and the possible record deal. She only showed a great deal of concern when I told her about Delaney's attack.

"That's why I worry about you all the time in that big city with all those crazy men. Was it a white man?"

"No, Mother, he was black," I said.

"Oh."

"Why are you concerned about what color he was, Mother?"

"No reason. You girls ought to be more careful where you go and wearing all those tight clothes."

"So blame the victim," I muttered.

"What?"

"Nothing."

My mother took a few long sips from her coffee and then began to stare at my ring. I tried unsuccessfully to turn the ring around so that the diamond would be facing the side of my palm.

"Girl, don't try and hide the ring now. Where did you get that from?"

"From Pierce," I said proudly.

"Is that the white boy?"

"Yes, Mother, Pierce is white and Jewish," I defended.

"Lordy Jesus. I don't care if he's Jewish, he's still white. Don't tell me you're going to marry him."

"Well, it looks that way," I said quietly.

"Nicole, baby, why you got to do that?"

"Do what, Mother?"

"Marry a white man. Ain't there no good-looking colored boys in New York? Chile, I know your daddy is rolling over in his grave," she lamented.

"Daddy liked Pierce," I said.

"Your daddy liked anything you drug into the house," said Mother.

"Well, are you going to give me your blessing?"

"Blessing? Chile, I'm going to pray for you. You don't know what you're getting yourself into," my mother preached.

"Mother, you should really try and get to know Pierce. He's really a special man," I said.

"I don't need to know him. I know his type. You're the one who better be sure you know him."

"Yes, Mother. I know you're right. I'm praying that the Lord will guide me to the right decision," I said. I sipped my tea and looked around the hotel. I didn't look at my mother out of fear that I would start to cry. I tried to understand my mother's feelings. She had in fact grown up in a different era. She didn't have the opportunities I enjoyed. But she had one thing I wanted more than anything in the world, a wonderful, long, and happy marriage to a man who adored her, who worshiped the ground she walked on.

Right before I started getting ready to leave for the airport, I looked up at my mother, who was now silent. I thought back to New York City and how much fun I'd had with Delaney and her mom—what good friends they were and how much they liked each other.

"Mother, can I ask you something?"

"Sure, chile," my mother said as she pulled a lipstick from her purse and inspected her lips with a small compact. It looked like the one I had given her when I was a little girl.

"Do you like me, Mother?"

"Like you? What kinda fool question is that? You're my little girl—of course, I love you," my mother said.

"I didn't say love, Mother. I know you love me. I want to know if you like me," I said again.

"Girl, it's time for you to get on back up to New York with all these fool questions. Are you all right?" she asked as she reached across the table to touch my forehead.

"I'm fine, Mother, just fine," I said as I wiped a single tear from my left eye.

My mother was right about one thing. It was time for me to get back to New York.

Nineteen

F*unny* things happen when you fall in lust. Your libido takes over your brain. You do stupid things, things like forgetting what's important—like family and friends. Basil had returned to New Jersey for football season in the fall and I was trying to figure out what to do about the sexual floodgate he had opened for me. Thank God for memories and masturbation.

The first two weeks Basil was gone I didn't hear a peep from him. I dialed his long distance beeper number and left countless messages with his service, all with no response. I guess I wanted to find out if I should continue monogamy and masturbation. Which now was not a simple task.

We never really talked about a relationship in the true sense of the word. There were times during the summer when I thought I could have a lasting relationship with Basil, no matter how nonconventional, and despite the fact that we were two men, two black men.

One Thursday evening while I was packing to go to Birmingham for my family reunion the phone rang.

"Hey, boy. What's shaking?"

"Basil," I said with a ring of excitement in my voice.

"Who else?" Basil said.

"Man, I was beginning to think I wasn't gonna ever hear from you again," I said.

"Oh, so you've been thinking about me," Basil stated matter-of-factly.

"Didn't you get my page or my messages?" I questioned.

"Yeah, but you know I've been in *two-a-days*. Practicing twice a day is tough shit. Plus Dyanna's been hanging around a lot," Basil said.

"Oh. So how is it going?"

"Great. We've got a good team. I really think this is the year I could make the Pro Bowl and the team could make the playoffs," Basil boasted.

"That would be great," I said.

"Yeah, we've got a good crop of rookies."

"Any of them good-looking?"

"What? I wouldn't know."

"Now come on, Basil. Can you honestly say you don't check some of your teammates out when you're in the locker room?"

"No," Basil snapped.

"Okay, if you say so."

Basil and I continued our small talk about what was going on in our lives. I told him about my upcoming family reunion and he asked me if my boyfriend was going to be there. Of course he was talking about Jared. One night before Basil had left, I'd opened up about Jared, sharing with Basil how I felt about him, but that I was now certain he was straight. Basil didn't agree, saying he saw the way Jared had looked at me in the gym. "He wants you, Ray, but now I got you so he can forget it," Basil gloated.

During the period of Basil's absence I thought about calling Jared, but I felt that would be selfish, so I resisted. I asked Basil what he was doing for sex and he said Dyanna usually came and spent the weekends with him but for the most part he just jerked off. He mentioned that a leading New York sportswriter whom he was convinced was gay kept trying to get him to come to his apartment promising him major coverage in the sports pages. When I asked him what paper, Basil wouldn't say.

"You should go," I joked. "You may have to give it up for your career."

"I don't think so. I'll do my talking on the field. What time are you leaving for Birmingham?" Basil asked.

"Tomorrow night or early Saturday. The main stuff isn't happening until Saturday night and Sunday," I said.

"I sent you something and you'll get it first thing in the morning. You'll have to decide what to do with it," Basil said mysteriously.

"What?" I asked.

"You'll see. What do you have on?"

"What?"

"You heard me, what do you have on?" Basil demanded.

"Just my underwear," I said.

"What kind?"

"You know the kind I wear," I said.

"What color?"

"Basil, what up? Black with gold bands," I offered.

"The ones with the fly or without the fly?"

"Without the fly."

"Pull it out," Basil said, his voice lower and more seductive.

"Pull what out?" I teased.

"You know, pull my piece out."

"Your piece?"

"Yes, my dick, pull it out. You got it in your hands?"

I didn't answer but I complied. I suggested Basil do the same and we talked each other into a moment of self-induced pleasure.

"Is it there yet?" Basil asked breathlessly.

"What?"

"The mayonnaise."

"Mayonnaise?"

"Yeah. The man mayonnaise." He laughed.

"Yeah. It's here," I sighed. "A whole cup full."

"Same here," Basil said. "Good night, and thanks."

"Is that it? Boy, that was a cheap date," I joked.

"But you loved it. Didn't you?"

"Good night, Basil," I said as I hung up the phone with a smile on my face and a need to wash my hands.

The next morning as I was preparing to leave for the office, the doorman buzzed and said a Federal Express carrier was on his way up to my apartment. Just as I hung up there was a knock at the door and the delivery man stood waiting with an overnight envelope.

I wasn't expecting anything. I wondered if this was something from the office.

After signing for the envelope, I looked at the sender's address and saw the name J. B. Henderson and a Jersey City return address. So this was Basil's surprise.

I quickly ripped open the package and out fell an eight by eleven-color photo of Basil's perfect body flexing underneath a one-piece gray flannel bodysuit. On the back Basil had scribbled, *"Got your attention. Steaks are on at seven."*

I was wondering what the note meant when I noticed something had fallen from the package to the carpet. I bent down and picked up an

American Airlines travel folder. I opened it up and realized it was a first-class round trip ticket in my name. I looked at the ticket closer and saw that my flight left at three-thirty today.

I couldn't go to New York, my family was expecting me. I walked into my kitchen to call Basil to thank him and to try to get him to reschedule, but I got his answering machine. While I was waiting for his message to complete I picked up the picture of Basil and felt my sex beginning to grow inside my underwear. When the little beep went off on Basil's machine I said, "I like my steaks medium well. I'll see you at seven."

I pressed the speed dial on my phone and asked the switchboard operator to put me through to my assistant, Melanie.

"Melanie," I said.

"Ray. Where are you?"

"I'm still at home. Look, I've got a client emergency in New York. Please clear my calendar until Tuesday," I instructed Melanie.

"Sure. Is there a number where I can reach you?"

"I'll call you once I reach New York, but you can always call my home and leave a message if there are any emergencies."

"Okay. Have a safe trip," Melanie said in her cheery voice.

"Oh, Melanie, do me a favor. Please call my father's office and tell him I've run into a problem and I might be late getting to Birmingham," I lied.

"Consider it done, Ray," Melanie said.

I threw a few items in my garment bag, grabbed my briefcase, and I was off to Hartsfield International Airport headed for Newark, New Jersey.

During the plane ride to Newark, I enjoyed the first-class treatment and mapped out my plans for the weekend. I would call Kyle early Saturday morning and arrange to meet him in the Village. It would be great seeing him and just going by some of the places we used to frequent. I would see about changing my flight to first thing Sunday morning and going directly to Birmingham. That way I would still make the major activity, the family picnic on Sunday afternoon. I was sure I would be able to come up with a good excuse before I reached Birmingham.

I was really getting excited about being back on the East Coast. There were times when I thought about moving back and then I would think about the cost of living and how Atlanta was such a nice, peaceful place to be. Plus I really loved working with Gilliam and all the people in our office. I was also pretty certain Gilliam would offer me a partner position when she decided to expand. With the boost in my salary I could fly to New York anytime I wanted. As I sipped a tasty California wine, I smiled at Basil's kind gesture. A big-time NFL football player sending for me. Now this was the shit. This was the kind of stuff a lot of gay men dreamed of and it was happening to me. I wondered what Kyle was going to think of this. He really thought I had lost my mind. I tried to explain to him how different Basil was once you got to know him and he simply replied, "He's trouble, Ray. Please be careful."

Basil had sent a limo to pick me up. As I walked off the escalator, a short, chubby guy with a cardboard sign reading Ray Tyler took my garment bag and whisked me off to Jersey City, New Jersey, and Basil's condominium.

His condo was located right in the heart of Jersey City, about fifteen minutes from midtown Manhattan. The complex was large and the area looked like a rail yard with a number of huge red brick buildings close together. I pushed the buzzer with Basil's name on it and his voice came over the intercom telling me to come to 402B.

Basil was standing with the door open as I wandered down the long hallway looking at the numbers on the burnt-orange doors. He was wearing a Warriors sweatshirt and gray running shorts without support.

"Hey, handsome. Looking for somebody?" Basil laughed.

"Yeah, I'm looking for trade," I said.

"Well, I think you found the place," Basil said as he grabbed my briefcase.

Once I got inside the condo, Basil gave me a gentle hug and a simple kiss on the lips.

"I'm glad you came," Basil said. There was tenderness in his voice.

"Thanks for inviting me," I said as I looked around the enormous place with red brick exposed walls and a black spiral staircase leading upstairs.

"Let me take your stuff upstairs. I don't think you're going to need all these clothes," Basil said.

While Basil took my bag upstairs I looked around his place. It had a sunken living room with polished parquet floors and a beautiful NFL round rug in the center. A black leather sofa and black lacquer furnishings rounded off the room. It definitely had a masculine look. There was another room located off the living room and I walked in and realized it was a study-den arrangement. It was filled with pictures and trophies with Basil's name on them. Several pictures of Basil with beautiful women and several photos with celebrities and other famous athletes graced the walls. Just as I picked up a picture for closer inspection Basil walked in.

"See anybody you know?" he asked.

"Just one handsome jock," I smiled.

Basil took my hand and led me up the spiral staircase to his bedroom. Basil's bedroom was huge with a big walk-in closet and a large deck right off the north wall. I looked toward the deck and thought about Basil's rented place in Atlanta with the pool off the kitchen. A pool that had led to seduction. This place was different but just as nice. The deck looked comfortable and well used with its patio table with four chairs and an umbrella, gas grill, stereo speakers, golf clubs, and several tennis rackets lying against the wall with pairs of dirty tennis and football shoes.

"I'm going to the store and over to the stadium. You want anything?"

"No. You didn't ask me if I'd like to go," I said.

"You can go, but I thought you'd like to take a shower or bath and get ready for dinner. I'm not going to be that long," Basil said.

"Okay, I'll see you when you get back."

While Basil was gone I found an open bottle of wine downstairs and poured myself a glass as I walked back upstairs and drew a hot bath.

Sitting in the tub, I thought about calling Kyle but realized if I called him now he would want me to come over to the city tonight. It would be fun but nothing was going to top the night I had planned with Basil.

Basil returned and started a fire for the steaks. He informed me the meat had been marinating all day in anticipation of my visit.

"What meat?" I joked.

He gave me a sexy smile as we sipped a rich-tasting cabernet sauvignon and the scent of the steak cooking filled the air.

Evening was approaching and the sun crested and began a downward arc; the sky was a clear blue, unbroken by clouds. A sultry September day was turning into a cool autumn night. In the distance I could see a bridge leading into an inviting neon New York City; the Statue of Liberty was just visible. It was a spectacular view.

Basil and I sat at the patio table and ate our steaks, baked potatoes, and salads off black plates. Luther Vandross's romantic voice filled the deck. The music vibrated through me, stirring my thoughts toward a night of passion with Basil.

"Do you know how handsome you are?" Basil asked. "Of course, you do."

I felt the hair on my arms rise. "Is that a question or statement?" I smiled.

"Both."

"Thank you, I think."

"So what do you want to do while you're here? Besides the obvious?"

"Oh, I don't care. Maybe we can go to the Village," I suggested.

"Fuck no," Basil said with a half-startled look. "I can't go down there."

"No problem," I said quietly.

Basil's abrupt response made me notice how his eyes could turn icy with displeasure as easily as they could radiate warmth and charm. He was quiet now, just slowly picking at his food.

"Oh, I forgot something," Basil said as he burst through the door to his bedroom. Minutes later he emerged with two lit candles in gold holders. The effect was pure elegance. "So how's this?" Basil asked, his voice low and sexy.

"Fine," I said as I sipped my wine.

The flickering candlelight played over Basil's face like the notes in Luther's voice.

"You know, sometimes I don't know what you're doing to me," Basil said.

"Same here," I said softly, looking at the candle wax slide down onto the gold holders.

"Let's go in," Basil said as he stood up and blew out the candles. The bulge in his white walking shorts suggested a night of lovemaking was close by.

He grabbed the dirty plates and I picked up the half-filled bottle and we went inside.

"Why don't you get more comfortable while I take these downstairs?" he suggested.

I undressed slowly, folding my clothes into a neat stack close to my luggage. Basil walked back into the bedroom wearing only black low-cut briefs. He fell on the large bed, ending up on his back. His stomach was so flat you could put a delicate china table setting on it. I lay next to him on the bed looking up at the vaulted ceiling in the diluted darkness. I leaned over and gently kissed him on the lips; his eyes were closed but when our lips touched he quickly opened them. They glinted with something between admiration and amusement. Basil smiled and was moving closer to me when we suddenly heard a voice from downstairs.

"Basil, honey-bunny. Where are you?" a female voice called out.

"Oh shit," Basil whispered urgently, "it's Dyanna."

"Dyanna?" I said in a shocked low voice.

Basil's smile faded and he stared at me in astonishment. He jumped quickly from the bed and yelled out, "Dyanna, is that you, baby? What are you doing back in town?"

"Does she live here?" I whispered. Basil nodded his head in the affirmative and then stopped his motion and mouthed, "Sometimes."

"I wanted to surprise you," she yelled back. "I'll be upstairs in a minute. I just want to get something to drink first."

"Hold on, I'm coming down," Basil said as he scurried around the bedroom looking for his clothing. He forcibly grabbed me and my luggage and led me to the huge walk-in closet.

"Basil, what are you doing?" I mouthed silently.

"Please, Ray, don't give me a hassle. I'll get rid of her. Just sit in the closet until I do," Basil pleaded.

"What?"

"Please."

I couldn't believe what was happening as I was pushed into the closet in my underwear and with my garment bag. Once I was inside the closet and heard the door slam shut, I was suddenly in total darkness among Basil's wardrobe.

For a moment, in my shocked silence, I was convinced this was a bad dream. I just knew I would wake up any moment but then I suddenly heard Basil's and Dyanna's voices outside in what sounded like friendly conversation. What were they doing and why didn't Basil get her out so I could get out of the closet? As I sat there I could just hear Kyle saying I told you so. I had never felt like such a jackass in all my life.

I don't remember at what point I finally fell asleep amid Basil's suits, slacks, shirts, and shoes, but I can recall just how angry I was as I sat in the dark listening to Basil and Dyanna's lively conversation and later their loud lovemaking.

I woke up hunched in a corner with morning slob and sleep in the corner of my eye. I had no clue as to what time it was until I saw light come into the darkened closet. Basil, fully dressed, was standing there with a placid look on his face as he held up a hand exposing five fingers. No words just his fingers as he slowly closed the door. I assumed he meant five minutes. That was about how long I had before my bladder burst.

I waited about ten minutes and then pulled myself up and peeked out the closet into the bedroom. No Basil or Dyanna and the bed was made up. I boldly walked out of the closet into the room and stood silently for a minute to make sure that there was no one in the house. The house was silent.

I went into the bathroom, relieved myself, and splashed some water on my face. I couldn't look at myself out of embarrassment. I wanted to shower but decided I wouldn't take a chance. I was going to get my shit and get the fuck out of here.

I located my bag, threw in the clothes that Basil had pushed in the closet, and put on my jeans and a clean white shirt. I walked swiftly down the narrow stairwell, hurried out the front door and onto the streets of Jersey City where I hailed a taxi to Newark Airport.

When I got to the airport I decided to head back to Atlanta instead of going to Birmingham. I needed to shower and regroup before making a final decision about going home and my family reunion. I was so mortified and angry with myself I didn't want to face anyone. How stupid could I have been? I tried to call Kyle and while I was dialing his number I decided not to tell him, but his number had been temporarily disconnected. What was that about?

The incident the prior night would have never happened if I hadn't put myself in another one of those crazy relationships with a man who didn't know which way he wanted to go. But I had to take the blame for always taking up with men who were not available to me totally. Maybe it was my way of protecting myself from a completely gay lifestyle. These types of problems never occurred with women, or at least not the women I chose to be with. Maybe it served me right for trying to be truthful and honest with men and lying to the women I was interested in. Why did I think men could deal with truth and honesty when I didn't know how to myself? I had to face the fact that I chose good women and bad men to share my love with. I had run into the same problems with both Kelvin and later with a married man, Quinn. But Basil was not married. I was older and supposedly wiser, but still making the same dumb-assed mistakes. The saga of the tragic sexual mulatto continued.

Twenty

The Miss Self-Esteem Pageant was conceived to give the young ladies of Harlem a head start on a successful school year. I had talked Delaney into following up her Saturday self-esteem workshops with a pageant so the young ladies could put into practice what they'd learned. I figured they needed to be exposed to the spirit of competition at a very young age. Lord knows they would be competing for the rest of their lives.

Twelve young ladies from the ages of ten through thirteen competed in essay writing, party dresses, poise, and personality categories. The pageant plan to give back to the community was a rousing success. Local Harlem merchants and several of Delaney's friends chipped in to put on quite a production not only for the young girls participating but also for many members of the Harlem community, who supported the show by the bus load at matinee performances. The pageant was held at the Harlem YWCA and although we didn't charge, we asked people to give whatever they could to a local AIDS charity.

A Harlem beauty shop donated makeup and two makeup artists for the young ladies. Kyle had bought secondhand dresses from thrift shops and made them into beautiful party dresses for each contestant. He wasn't able to attend because he'd been involved in a fender bender while in a taxi and his back was still giving him serious trouble. He said he had problems sitting anywhere for more than an hour. It was bothering him enough that he had to put a piece of plywood under his mattress. Of course, he was going to sue. Delaney and I had offered to come over and help sew buttons on the dresses but he said he already had friends helping out. Delaney was convinced, however, that he had a new boyfriend and that was why we hadn't seen much of him.

After the pageant, Sylvia's, a popular soul food restaurant and Harlem landmark, reserved a party room and provided food for the contestants and volunteers. Pierce and I shared a table with two young ladies from the pageant, Lashondra and Darice. Lashondra was first runner-up in the pageant and was admiring her trophy when out of the blue she turned to me and asked, "Do you have any kids?"

"No, not yet," I answered.

"Why not?" she asked.

"Well, I'm not married, Lashondra," I answered, catching Pierce smiling out of the corner of my eye.

"You gon marry him?" Lashondra asked, using her spoon to point to Pierce.

"You mean am I going to marry Dr. Gessler?" I corrected Lashondra. "Yes, I think so," I said, smiling at Pierce.

"Oh," she said as she put a spoonful of sweet potatoes in her mouth.

After Lashondra and Darice finished their dinner they politely excused themselves to go over to a table full of their friends.

"I think so," Pierce repeated after the girls had left the table. His eyebrows arched high.

"Was there something wrong with my answer?"

"I think so doesn't sound confident," Pierce said.

"Oh, I didn't mean anything by that," I said.

"I hope not," Pierce said as he lifted his coffee cup to his lips.

"Pierce, do you think when we have children that they will have problems in school?" I asked.

"Not if they go to Hebrew school," Pierce said.

"Hebrew school?" I repeated.

"Yes, Nicole. Haven't we talked about this? I'm sure we've talked about this. It's important. I want my kids to go to Hebrew school until they are old enough to say they want to go elsewhere," Pierce said.

"So you're saying you don't want *your* kids raised as Christians? What about what I want?" I asked.

"Nicole, let's talk about this later. Why don't you continue to enjoy the wonderful program you and Delaney put on," Pierce advised.

Just as I was preparing to respond, Delaney came over and gave me a hug. Her face was radiating happiness.

"Thanks, Nic! This was a great idea," Delaney said.

"You worked it, girl. This was wonderful," I said.

"I tried to call Kyle. I'm a little worried," Delaney said.

"Why?" I asked.

"All I get is a recording saying that the phone is disconnected. I was trying to call to tell him what a tremendous success the pageant was and to see if he needs anything," Delaney said.

"Maybe we should stop by his place on the way home," I suggested.

"I don't know," Delaney said. "You know how he is with people coming over unannounced."

"Yes, but with him having been in an accident I think we can forget about his rules. He might need us," I said.

"Yeah, maybe you're right. I'll call you later this evening and we'll go over," Delaney said.

"Okay, that's a good idea."

After leaving the restaurant, I asked Pierce to take me home. I was so busy thinking about the Hebrew school issue that I wasn't paying attention as Pierce made a U-turn in the middle of Amsterdam Avenue when suddenly a truck slammed into the passenger side of Pierce's powder blue sports car.

"What the fuck!" Pierce yelled as he stopped his car. "Are you all right?" he asked.

"I think so."

An elderly black man jumped from the truck and rushed toward Pierce's car.

"What are you doing?" he asked. "You can't make a turn like that on this street."

Pierce jumped from the car. "You saw me turning. Why didn't you stop, you old black motherfucker! Fucking moron!" he shouted.

Suddenly, I felt a chill. Had I heard him correctly? Had Pierce called this man a black motherfucker? I looked out of the rearview mirror and could tell that Pierce and the old man were engaged in heated conversation. The man got into his truck and drove off, his wheels screeching. The next words out of Pierce's mouth came out loud and clear as he got back into the car.

"Can you believe that black motherfucker? He took off without giving me his insurance information," Pierce said. "The asshole probably doesn't have insurance."

"Pierce, what did you call that old man?"

"What? An asshole?"

"No, Pierce, before that," I demanded.

Suddenly, Pierce's face turned beet red. Maybe it was the anger in my eyes that caused the color change. It dawned on me that he didn't realize that he was up in Harlem calling a black man a black motherfucker with a black woman in his car. A disturbing silence covered the car after Pierce's outburst.

"I'm sorry, Nicole. I didn't mean to call him that," Pierce said.

"You said it twice, Pierce. I heard you!"

"But he hit my car. He saw me turning," Pierce said.

"But you were wrong, Pierce, and then you add insult to injury by calling him that terrible name. Trying to make a wrong a right. How could you?"

"I'm sorry, it just slipped," Pierce offered.

"Slipped! Let me out of this car. I'm catching a taxi home."

"Come on, Nicole, let's talk about this," Pierce said as he reached for my arm. I pulled back.

"Right now I'm too upset to talk about this," I said as I got out of Pierce's car and started to look for a taxi heading downtown.

The wind was blowing cool, but my body was burning from anger. Pierce was calling out my name as I jumped into a rare yellow taxi in Harlem and headed home.

When I entered my building my doorman handed me a package in a pink bag. One of my good girlfriends, Kym, had left an order of skin care products that I used in my beauty regimen. I thanked Stuart and headed upstairs. I wanted to call Kyle to check on him and tell him what happened with Pierce and to see how he was doing. Kyle would give me some advice on what to do. But when I called his phone was still disconnected. I called Delaney, and left a message on her answering machine. I started to call Sheila but decided against it. While I was pondering my next move the phone rang but I let the answering machine pick up and I heard Pierce's voice after the beep sounded. "Nicole, I know you're there. Please pick up. I'm sorry. Please let's talk about this," he pleaded. When the machine clicked off I unplugged the phone and answering machine and climbed into my bed.

The next morning I plugged my phone back in and it rang immediately. I assumed it was Sheila, so I answered the phone with my regular praise the Lord greeting, but I heard Kyle's voice.

"Nicole?" Kyle said.

"Kyle, what's going on, darling? Your phone back on?"

"No, not yet. That's why I'm calling," Kyle said with the sounds of the busy city traffic in the background.

"Yes, what do you need, Kyle?"

"Nicole, I need to borrow some money. This pain medication the doctor has me on is more expensive than I expected, but my lawyer said I'm going to get it all back," Kyle assured me.

"How much do you need?"

"Five hundred dollars," Kyle said.

"Five hundred?" I said with a slightly startled voice.

"Yeah, I know it's a lot, but I'll give it back in a couple of weeks," Kyle promised.

"Okay, no problem. Do you want me to go pay your phone bill?"

"No, my phone will be on in about an hour. I wrote them a hot check," Kyle explained.

"Then what do you want me to do?"

"Can you get the cash, put it in an envelope, and leave it with Grady?" Kyle asked.

"Cash? You want me to leave cash? Why not a check?"

" 'Cause not everybody is as stupid as the phone company when it comes to my checks," Kyle joked. "My drugstore uses a check approval service."

"Okay, I'll run to the bank in a couple of hours and I'll have it there by noon."

"Thanks, Nicole, you're a sweetheart," Kyle said softly.

"No problem. You would be there for me," I said.

I hung up and thought about our conversation. Because it was one sure way to damage relationships, I had an unwritten rule that I never loaned money to family or friends—a rule I could never follow. It never failed you would be the one ending up feeling bad about the loan, not because the majority of the time you didn't get the money back, but because the people you loaned the money to would start to avoid you. I hadn't heard a word from my brother since I loaned him the fifteen hundred dollars. I decided I would give the five hundred dollars to Kyle as a gift. I mean he hadn't asked me for a dime for all the fabric he had purchased making bridal gowns I would probably never wear.

The decision to give Kyle the money made me realize that I needed to call Pierce and make arrangements to meet him and call off the engagement or at least discuss my concerns in depth. I slowly turned the beautiful engagement ring and thought how naked my hand was going to be without it. But no ring could justify how I felt inside. I was looking in my closet for something to wear when the phone rang.

"Hello," I said.

"Praise the Lord, girl," Sheila said.

"Praise the Lord," I responded.

"Well, let's get started. How was the pageant?" Sheila asked.

"It was great. I'm sorry you didn't make it."

"You'll have to tell me about it when we finish our prayer. Got anything special you want to pray for this morning?"

"Yeah, I want to send a special one up for Kyle; he's having some money problems," I sighed.

"Okay, and you know since we're praying for him we should ask the Lord to take that demon spirit out of him," Sheila said.

"Demon spirit?" I quizzed.

"Yeah, Kyle's a homosexual, isn't he?"

"Yeah, but what does that have to do with anything?"

"Well, Nicole girl, you know homosexuality is a demonic spirit," Sheila said.

"It is?"

"Yeah, girl, read the Scriptures," Sheila advised.

"Which ones?" I questioned.

"I don't know any exact one. My minister preached on it a few weeks ago. I'll find out which ones," Sheila said.

"Yes, please do that, Sheila, because I don't think you're right. Christ loves all His children."

Sheila didn't respond; she simply started praying and I couldn't help but think about what she had just said. Her tone had the same tone of hate that Pierce's voice had the evening before in Harlem. Suddenly I was happy that I would see Dr. Huntley in less than an hour.

I didn't wait for Dr. Huntley to ask me how I was doing before I started to tell her about what happened with Pierce and about the accident. I told her how I couldn't believe Pierce had called the man black and how much it hurt me.

"Why did it hurt you, Nicole?"

"Black. I hate that word. Sometimes I think it's worse than the *n* word."

"The *n* word?"

"Yes, nigger."

"You think black is worse than nigger?"

"Sometimes."

"Why, Nicole? Why are you crying, Nicole?"

"It was a beautiful red dress. My first evening gown that was bought especially for me," I said through my tears.

"A red dress?"

"My mother didn't think I should buy a dress that color because of my being so dark-skinned. But my daddy said I looked beautiful in it and I felt beautiful when I tried it on. I really felt special, like I could really win."

"Win? Win what, Nicole?"

"The Miss Conway County pageant. It was my first pageant. During rehearsals, all the white girls were so nice to me. I think that's because they didn't view me as serious competition; didn't think I could win. Until they heard me sing. They all changed. And that night at the pageant it happened."

"What happened? Tell me, Nicole," Dr. Huntley said softly.

"Candance was backstage helping me with my wardrobe and when the evening gown competition was ready to get started I couldn't find my gown. Candance and I looked all over the place. We couldn't find it. All the other girls were all lined up in their beautiful gowns preparing to go onstage for the competition. No one offered to help us find the gown."

"What did you do?"

"I couldn't go out on stage without an evening gown. I just started crying sitting there in my slip. Crying so hard that I ran into the bathroom and that's where I saw it." I paused.

"The dress?"

"Yes."

"Where was it?"

"In the toilet covered with—covered with . . ."

"Covered with what, Nicole?"

"Stuff. Excrement. You know. It was covered with shit!"

"What happened after you found it?"

"Candance came into the bathroom and handed me a note she'd found on my dressing table. The note said take your black ass to the black-assed Miss Black Nigger pageant where your black, blueberry-looking black ass belongs."

"What did you do, Nicole?"

"I started crying again. I couldn't stop until Candance said . . ."

I remembered how much Candance and I always helped each other —how much fun we could have—and how I missed her.

"What did Candance say, Nicole?"

"She said, 'Don't ever let them see you cry. When you cry they win. Don't let them win, Nicole. Please don't let them win.' "

I went on to tell Dr. Huntley how it hadn't stopped there. After the incident my mother was terribly upset but she took her anger out on me. Berated me for trying to force myself into some place I didn't belong. It took both my father and Candance to stop her yelling. I told her how much my mother's words hurt me. How I never forgot that night.

"Did you tell your mother that?"

"No, I didn't."

"Nicole. Your time is up. Are you all right? I have a little extra time," Dr. Huntley said.

"No, I'll be fine," I said as I rubbed my eyes. They were tired from all my tears.

"Nicole, can I ask you something?"

"Yes, Dr. Huntley."

"What color is your mother's skin tone?"

"Light," I said softly. "Very light."

"Do you think that's the root of your problems with your mother?"

"I don't know."

"You don't. Is it a problem for your mother?"

"You'd have to ask her," I said.

"I'm asking you, Nicole."

"You know people can be so cruel. Especially toward children."

"Yes, Nicole, people can be, but what does that have to do with you and your mother?"

"They acted as though I wasn't even there."

"Who, Nicole? Who?"

I was talking like I was in a self-induced trance. "When I was a little girl, my mother would take me to downtown Little Rock to shop. It was our special time together. Just us girls. People always thought she wasn't my mother. Me being so dark and my mother having beautiful honey-colored skin. One day these two ladies kept badgering my mother. Saying it was no way I could be her daughter. When I thought my mother had finally convinced them, they laughed and said my daddy must have had some powerful blueberry genes. My mother joined in their laughter."

"How old were you, Nicole?"

"Six or seven," I said as tears began to roll down my face.

"Nicole, were these women black or white?"

"They were black. Light-skinned black women."

"It's okay to cry here, Nicole," Dr. Huntley said softly. She reached in a tissue box on her desk and pulled out a handful and walked over and sat next to me on the sofa. I couldn't recall her ever coming so close. She gave me the tissue and softly patted my knees and repeated her words. "It's okay to cry here. In my office they can't win," she said.

And then in a move that both shocked and comforted me, Dr. Huntley hugged me tightly until my tears stopped.

I left Dr. Huntley's brownstone feeling a great deal of pressure had been released. How long I had wanted to share that dreadful day with someone who understood. The incident was one I hadn't shared with anyone. Not my mother, father, or even Candance.

With my session behind me, I began to enjoy the day that was sunny but autumn nippy. The leaves were beginning to change colors, painting the city beautifully with warm scarlets and golds. I hopped into a taxi and asked to be let off at a bank near Kyle's apartment. I cashed a check and instructed the teller to give me large bills, which I then slipped inside my pink stationery, on which I'd written Kyle a little note, telling him to keep his head up, that things were going to get better. When I arrived at Kyle's apartment, Grady, the regular doorman, was not on duty, in fact no one was on duty. This was strange, but since I was in a hurry I walked through the security door and caught the elevator up to Kyle's floor. I would slide the money under his door. Just as I stooped down, I heard music blasting from Kyle's apartment and noticed the door slightly ajar. I gently pushed the door open wider and called out Kyle's name. There was no response. "Kyle?" I called out again, this time louder.

"Who is it?" Kyle's voice called back.

"It's Nicole," I said as I walked into the apartment. Kyle wasn't in the living or dining area and something seemed different. It was the smell. As I walked into Kyle's apartment I felt as if I had inhaled enough vodka to bathe in. At least it smelled like vodka; it was definitely some type of alcohol. Suddenly Kyle appeared from the bedroom. He looked a mess in a pajama top and not-so-clean underwear.

"How did you get up here?" Kyle demanded.

"Kyle, what's the matter?" I asked.

"Nothing. Answer my question. How did you get up here?"

"There wasn't anybody at the door," I stumbled.

"I'm sorry, Nicole. I'm not feeling well. That medication has me knocked out all the time. I'm sorry, darling. I didn't mean to yell," Kyle muttered.

"What's that smell?" I asked.

"Oh, it's alcohol. I've been rubbing my back down with it," Kyle said.

"How do you do that?" I inquired.

"Well, not me. I have a guy who does it for me," Kyle said.

"Oh, you've got it like that," I said, trying to remove some of the unanticipated tension in the air.

"Do you have the money?" Kyle asked.

"Yeah, I got it," I said as I searched my purse for the envelope. "Is there anything else you need me to do?"

"No, I'm fine. But since you're here why don't you try on the slip I made for one of your gowns?" Kyle suggested.

"I don't know if I have the time," I said, looking at my watch.

"Oh, come on, girl. Run in the bathroom and try it on," Kyle said.

"Okay," I said.

"Come here, Miss Nicole. What is going on with your hair? It's truly worryin' me. It's doing a Newark hair thang," Kyle joked.

"I'll fix it while I'm in the bathroom."

I went into Kyle's bathroom. As I was trying on the beautiful ivory slip he had made I thought of Kyle in the living room. He didn't look good and that had me worried. I realized I hadn't seen a lot of him in recent weeks, but I didn't make much of it since I had been busy and we did talk on the phone at least three times a week. Before I took off the slip I walked into Kyle's bedroom and used the phone to check my messages. There was a message from Pierce begging me to meet him at a restaurant for lunch so he could explain everything. His voice sounded desperate. I called him back and agreed to meet him at a nearby restaurant when I left Kyle. He sounded relieved and hopeful.

I went back into the bathroom and was changing back into my clothes when I realized I'd left my purse in the living room. I wanted to freshen up my makeup and hair before heading out to meet Pierce; I'd decided I would give him a chance to talk. I opened the bathroom door and asked Kyle to please bring me my purse. It seemed to take him forever. He was walking around like an old man. This back problem was more serious than I'd thought.

When he finally brought it to the bathroom door, I looked into his eyes. There was definitely something wrong. His eyes were weighted down with sorrow. The sheer force of Kyle's regular personality was nowhere to be found. I couldn't burden him with my problems.

I was touching up my makeup when I opened Kyle's vanity cabinet to see if he had some Visine. It looked like Kyle had everything but. As I was about to close the cabinet, two bottles caught my eye. One of the bottles had Valium printed clearly on it, but the name on the bottle was Darius Allen, and then there was a large bottle of white capsules with blue stripes. I couldn't pronounce the name of the medication but this one did have Kyle's name on it. I looked in my purse, pulled out my small writing pad, and wrote down the name on a piece of paper. Pierce would know what it was. Who did I think I was, Christy Love?

As I walked back into the living room, I mentioned to Kyle that I'd run into a friend of his at the pageant.

"Oh yeah, who?" Kyle asked.

"Colin St. Martin," I said.

"Oh, him. How is he doing?"

"Oh, he seems fine. He said he was a model with Zoli," I said.

"Since when?" Kyle asked.

"Oh, I didn't ask him that. He showed me his book," I said, trying to study Kyle's eyes.

"Chile, that book has been seen in more gay bars than in anybody's modeling or booking agency," Kyle said dryly.

"You think so? He is good-looking and he said he'd just booked a national underwear ad," I said.

"An underwear ad? I guess we're moving up if they're letting someone that dark do an underwear ad. But he's an IBMer, so I guess that's understandable," Kyle said. Here was a small glimpse of the old Kyle.

"What's an IBMer?" I asked.

"Itty bitty meat," Kyle smiled.

"Kyle, you're so crazy," I laughed.

"What's the matter with you? Your eyes look like you've been crying," Kyle said.

"Oh, I didn't sleep too well. I'm fine."

I leaned over to give Kyle a kiss and he gently pushed me back.

"I'm fighting a little cold, Nicole. Let's just do cocktail kisses," Kyle said as he playfully blew me a kiss.

"Okay, baby. Get better. I'm meeting Pierce downstairs," I said.

"Tell Doc, I said hey," Kyle said as he shut the large steel door.

I was glad that Pierce had suggested we meet at a Mexican food place located on the ground floor of Kyle's building. The restaurant was packed with the lunch crowd and I spotted Pierce at a small table against the wall.

"Sorry, I'm late," I said.

"Thanks for meeting me. I was afraid you wouldn't show up," Pierce said.

I wasn't listening or looking at Pierce. I was thinking about Kyle.

"Nicole, please look at me. I need to explain."

"What?"

"Nicole. What's the matter? You seem miles away."

"I don't know. Something is up. Pierce, have you ever heard of this medication?" I asked as I handed Pierce the small piece of paper with the name of the mysterious medicine. Pierce's eyes suddenly got big and he reached inside his jacket and put on his glasses.

"Who's taking this?" Pierce asked.

"Kyle, I think. What is it and how do you pronounce it?" I asked.

"Retrovir Caps, 100 mg, zidovudine," Pierce said out loud as he read from the tiny piece of paper.

"Sounds serious. What is it in layman's terms?"

"You sure you want to know this?" Pierce asked.

"Yes," I said impatiently.

"Nicole, it's AZT. Whoever is taking this has AIDS or is, at the very least, HIV positive," Pierce said solemnly.

"Are you sure?" I asked.

"Yes, Nicole, I'm sorry but sure," Pierce said.

"Pierce, I'm sorry but we'll have to talk about this later. I have to go. I promise I will call you later." Any problems Pierce and I had could wait. I had to contact Delaney immediately.

Twenty-one

I love the fall. It stirs a great many fond memories. Vibrant September, golden October, and brilliant November. It was in the fall that I scored my first high school touchdown against North Central. A twenty-three-yard reception between two defenders who were much bigger than I was. It's a feeling I will never forget. It was also in the fall when I first made love to another man, another feeling that I will never forget. And it was in the fall when I discovered the pleasures oral sex brought, not only to my female partner, but to myself as well.

I love fall weather. Cool, crisp nights watching the summer try to hold on until fall's colorful foliage forces its hand and sends it packing. But there was something different about the beginning of this fall that led me to believe this year's would not be the same. They say winter is the season of discontent, but sometimes discontent comes early.

One of my fondest memories of the fall was my initiation into KΛΩ, my college fraternity. I pledged during the time when black fraternities *really* pledged, hazing and all. It was hard to believe it had been close to fifteen years since I and nineteen other *line brothers* crossed the sands into KAΩ, so it was only natural that all twenty of us planned to meet to commemorate this important event in our lives and to enjoy the brotherhood of those who would follow us.

Before heading to Tuscaloosa, I stopped at my parents' home. I'd been so upset by my night in Jersey City with Basil that I'd decided against going to my family reunion. My mama would have been able to detect that something was wrong and wouldn't have let up until I confessed. I still couldn't lie or tell half truths to my mama face to face, so I just called and said I was having problems with a former client. They were disappointed but Jared did show up so I guess he took my place. I cut short a conversation with my parents when they were going on and on about how Jared helped and how all the relatives thought he

was a member of the family. The phone call and my own jealousy
ruined my day. I wondered how Jared felt being at my family reunion
without me. I missed Jared something terrible. He and I still weren't
talking, but I was seriously considering initiating a truce. As it was, I
wasn't talking to much of anybody these days. Basil still hadn't called
me to explain or apologize and I definitely wasn't calling him. (I must
admit, though, one of the reasons I didn't go to the family reunion was
because I was afraid I might miss his phone call.) It looked like Basil
was off to a super year with the Warriors if the sports pages were
correct. He was getting an awful lot of press. Maybe he had visited the
sportswriter after all.

I wasn't talking to Kyle as much either. At first it was because his
phone was out of order but then whenever I did get through, I got his
answering machine or else he was asleep. Kyle seemed to be cooling
out. I hoped he wasn't harboring any hard feelings regarding my representing Basil and sleeping with him. He'd changed his mind at the last
minute about coming to Atlanta for Labor Day weekend saying he had
just picked up two new clients and had a shot at doing some of the
costumes for Nicole's new Broadway show. I worried some that our
lack of communication was due to Kyle's drinking and doing drugs
again. He'd been disappointed when I'd chosen not to go to Los Angeles for the beach party on the Fourth of July weekend. It surprised me
when he'd decided against going to Los Angeles alone.

I stopped at my folks' home before heading back to campus because
I wanted to help with the problems developing with my little brother
Kirby. My parents had decided Kirby was going to spend his first year
of high school at a prep school and had gotten him into the exclusive
Andover Academy in Andover, Massachusetts. They were cashing in
savings bonds they'd had since I was a little boy. Prep school was an
opportunity I would have jumped at, but Kirby wasn't feeling it. Pops
had spoken and so my little brother was on his way East whether he
liked it or not.

My parents had made a deal with him. If he made good grades and
showed more responsibility, then he could choose where he went to
school during his sophomore year. Come home with anything less than
a B average then it was back to prep school or possibly a tougher
military school. I guessed my parents were attempting a more politi-
cally correct method of child rearing with Kirby. Making deals and
talking things out. When I was growing up the only talking that occurred was after I had gotten my ass whipped.

I talked with my little brother the day before he and Pops planned to leave on their long drive to Andover. He was becoming quite a handsome young man, looking more like Pops than even me. Kirby had a basketball player's build and shared my pops's brownish-green eyes that were even more distinguishable because of Kirby's slightly darker skin tone.

"What do you think about this prep school stuff?"

"I ain't got no choice," Kirby said.

"I don't have a choice," I corrected.

"Whatever you say," Kirby retorted.

"It won't be as bad as you think," I said.

"You think so. It's co-ed, you know," Kirby said.

"Oh, you like that, huh?"

"Damn betcha," Kirby said as he playfully threw a boxer punch toward me.

"Cool out, little boy, before I have to lay you out. Come here. Do you know what this is?" I asked Kirby as I showed him a gold condom wrapper.

"Shoot, yeah, it's a rubber. I got one in my wallet," Kirby boasted.

"Do you know what it's for and how to put it on?"

"Come on, Ray-Ray, chill. I know that stuff," he answered bashfully.

"Do you know about AIDS?" I asked.

"Yeah," Kirby said, hanging his head.

"Okay, then make me a promise. You won't put your piece anywhere without one of these on. Deal?"

"Yeah, yeah. I won't, Ray-Ray," he laughed, and playfully punched my shoulders.

"I'm serious, Kirby. Don't play around with this shit. Understood?"

"Yes, big brother. I understand," Kirby said.

I don't know why but I got the feeling my little brother wasn't a virgin. I'd noticed the change in him last Christmas. The boyish charm was gone and was replaced by a cockiness, which was one of the reasons he found himself headed for Andover. From the questions he asked and the posters in his room—Olympic gymnast Dominique Dawes and the little girl from the "Fresh Prince of Bel-Air"—I assumed he was heterosexual. I hoped I was right. I didn't want my little brother going through all the pain and turmoil I had and I didn't think Pops could stomach both his sons not being totally heterosexual. I also realized adolescent heterosexuality was not an indicator of what might happen in the future. My main concern with Kirby going to Andover was that I didn't want him to come back talking and acting like a white boy.

I was happy I'd stopped off to see my little brother before he left home for his first extended stay. Not only for Kirby and myself but my mom as well. She broke out into a loud cry when Pops and Kirby pulled out. I thought maybe she would be happy about having Pops all to herself finally. Mama's quiet tears turned to loud sobs and I held her tightly in my arms until she had gotten everything out. I waited until she'd turned in for the night before I left for campus, turning on the alarm, and locking the door. I'd left her a nice note telling her Christmas was just around the corner and Santa was going to bring her two handsome young men. As I pulled out of the driveway I thought about how it seemed as though it was only yesterday I'd left for college for the first time. I'd begged my parents to let me drive alone and I'd sneaked out during the wee hours of the morning to avoid my mother's tears.

Nothing could have prepared me for what would happen at my fraternity reunion. It was great seeing everyone I had pledged with. All of my line brothers had returned for the reunion, the vast majority with wives and children. Everyone wanted to know why I wasn't married and why I let Sela get away. Luckily there was no hard court press on the marriage question since five of my line brothers were also single.

Everyone met at the fraternity house, reliving memories of the past and creating new ones with the undergrad brothers who now ran the frat. I had grown up so much through my association with ΚΑΩ, and it was still one of my most treasured associations, but things seemed a bit different with the new frat brothers.

All of the major black Greek organizations, both sororities and fraternities, had instituted something called risk-free pledging. In other words it was walk right up, sign up, and you're a frat brother. Gone were the days of nine-week pledge periods, complete with physical and mental hazing. In a lot of ways this was good. Pledging had gotten out of hand all across the country with brutal beatings and accidental deaths touching all the fraternities. The sororities didn't have the deaths but word was out that the ladies were almost as physical as the men. So in a rare agreement, the heads of all the sororities and fraternities got together and decided to implement rules by which the groups would abide.

KAΩ had always been selective in the past, but this was soon to change. People used to say the hardest thing about pledging KAΩ was getting on line. That's the way I thought it should be. Some fraternities accepted guys just to be able to kick their asses during the pledge period—not that I hadn't kicked a little ass during my undergrad years —but risk-free pledging had its own problems. There didn't seem to be the brotherhood that we'd shared. After you went through a pledge period in the old days you really felt like brothers and the fraternity meant a great deal to you because you had worked so hard to become a member. The current pledge period was nonexistent; once you were accepted as a pledge you became a member a few days later. There was a marked difference between the new brothers and the old ones. This new risk-free process was even less rigorous than when guys used to pledge in graduate chapter, which was always looked down upon, because it was a lot easier than pledging in undergrad.

After everybody got together, we started breaking off into groups just like the old days. They weren't exactly cliques but the people who hung out together in undergrad migrated toward those people now. So I ended up with my former roommate Stanley and his wife Lencola and Trent Walters, president of my pledge class, who was surprisingly still single and was much better-looking than I remembered. Matter of fact, Trent had been pretty square-looking as an undergrad—braces and thick glasses. He'd been an ROTC man, always in the books. I had never really thought about Trent's looks when we'd first met pledging. Trent Walters had gone through a major makeover.

We left the frat house and went to the bar at the Hilton Hotel for drinks before heading back to the house for an evening meeting of the alumni and undergrad brothers.

Stanley was a professor at the University of Kansas and the proud father of two little girls. His wife—one of his former students—was a little frumpy-looking, but really nice.

Trent was an architect working for a Chicago design firm. He boasted about living on Chicago's Gold Coast. Stanley and I kidded each other about being the odd couple because Stanley was so meticulous and I was so messy. We reminisced about how we'd come home late at night or early in the morning and raid the icebox, usually eating Captain Crunch, lemon creme cookies, and fried egg sandwiches after a night of drinking KAΩ punch. Stanley asked me if I still talked with Sela and said he'd heard I had come pretty close to marrying a movie star. He had even heard it was Robin Givens. I smiled at the thought of Nicole and how she did look like Robin Givens but only better.

"Ray, the frat's pretty boy with all the pretty girls," Stanley remarked.

"Yeah, Ray was the lady-killer," Trent chipped in.

Boy, if they only knew, I thought, as I accepted their compliments with a guarded smile.

"I knew he was a motherfuckin' faggot. I told y'all," the deep voice said from inside the house. Trent, Stanley, and I walked back into the fraternity house in the middle of a chapter meeting. The brothers were discussing one of the new pledges who was about to become a full member after Sunday's ceremony.

The three of us leaned against the back wall listening to the frats talk about the pledge whom they had set up to find out if he was gay. From what I could gather from the meeting conversation, the current members had been looking for a way to keep the guy, whose name must have been Miller, out of the frat. So they'd convinced one of the guy's line brothers to try to entice the pledge into meeting him for a sexual escapade.

It appeared their plan had worked. The guy'd evidently taken the bait and one of the members laughed and said, "He had fallen to his knees just about to get busy on Terry when we broke in and cold-busted his punk ass."

"You should have seen the look on that motherfucker's face," another member chimed in.

"But do you think national is going to let us keep him out?" a voice quizzed.

"Damn straight. I don't think that punk ass Miller Thomas will even show up around this frat house again. If he does we ruin his faggot ass," the presiding officer stated.

Shocked at the proceedings, I continued to stand against the wall. There had always been rumors about gay members in all the fraternities. They were supposed to be service organizations, but that was just a cover. Sure we did a couple of service projects a year but the majority of the activities centered around the social. I still didn't understand what a person's sexuality had to do with his ability to serve the fraternity, provided he didn't force himself on other members or do anything to embarrass the fraternity. In theory that should be the only question, but deep down I knew better. It just hadn't hit me how homophobic fraternities were and continued to be.

Trent seemed to be annoyed at the ongoing dispute and pulled one of the current members over to find out more information about the situation. I stood close to Trent and listened as the current rush chairman explained that Miller had been accepted as a pledge because he had a 3.88 grade point in Chemical Engineering and was the number-one tennis player on the university tennis team. In addition his father was a judge in New Orleans and a KAΩ alum, making Miller a legacy. We always accepted legacies. It seemed all the guys in the fraternity were crazy about Miller until the rumor got started.

Only a few current members had come to his defense and when they did their own sexuality came under question. Since Miller had already been accepted, they couldn't just kick the guy out. So instead the plan was to blackmail him into quitting before the formal induction service.

My stomach churned. I was thinking about this young guy whom I didn't know and what would have happened to me if people had discovered my doubts about my sexuality before pledging KAΩ. Or, more important, if I had been found out after my affair with Kelvin during my senior year. What would have happened had I defended somebody I didn't know; what shadows would it have cast on my reputation as one of the better-known and better-liked members of KAΩ?

"It sounds like this guy would be great for the chapter. I mean with his father and all. And he's on the tennis team," Trent said.

"Yeah, you're right, frat, but he's a punk. We can't have no punks in KAΩ. After a while they'll be taking over," a guy who identified himself as Dale said.

"Yeah, but if he's the number-one player on the university tennis team then he's very likely to go pro," I said, trying to interject a business perspective.

"I think it's a dead issue. He ain't gonna show his face around here again," one of the ringleaders of the protest said.

It seemed as if Trent's and my arguments were falling on deaf ears. The members seemed to have already made up their minds and since we were not active members of the chapter, our opinions were just that, opinions.

I did take note of Trent's posture toward the case. It seemed he was really bothered by the entire situation and that made me feel good. The more I thought about it, Trent had seemed open-minded and levelheaded for as long as I'd known him. He always had a girlfriend, but he was always so quiet. Could my line brother and fraternity brother be in the silent frat too?

The rest of the weekend went according to plan, at least until the end: beer drinking, barbecue eating, and re-creating the past with men who were like family. But like a family reunion, there were relatives I wasn't as excited about seeing and new relatives I was sorry I ever met. The weekend also made me realize I could still love and be close to Jared and not have to sleep with him. I mean I loved the majority of these guys. Maybe not the way I loved Jared, but I still loved them. It also helped me understand how important my friendships with men were. Saturday night after the football game I got a little full of the spirits and, I guess, emotional. So emotional that I called Jared to tell him how sorry I was for being such an ass wipe and to tell him I had to see him once I got back home. Jared, being Jared, was quite receptive and told me over the phone he'd missed me and looked forward to re-newing our friendship. He warned me not to drink too much and to drive safely back to Atlanta. Right before I hung up there was an awkward silence and then before saying good-bye, I said, "Jared, you know I love you. I mean like a brother."

"Yeah, I know, Ray. That's why I put up with you. 'Cause I love you too. Stay strong," Jared said.

"Talking to one of those sweet Atlanta peaches, frat?" Derrick Hall asked. Derrick was the current president of the fraternity and leader of the gay witch hunt. He was probably also a card-carrying member of the all-body, no-brain club.

"Naw, just talking with a good friend," I said. I wondered if Derrick overheard my conversation and was just being nosy.

"So tell me, Ray. You're not married. From what I've heard you always had the finest girl in the frat," Derrick said.

"Yeah, but things change, Derrick. You'll learn that as you get older," I said coldly.

"Okay, frat. Well, I just wanted to thank you for coming up and for the checks you send. They really help out," he added.

"Sure, no problem, Derrick. Nice talking with you," I said as I looked to see if Trent was in the area.

I thought about how cold I was toward Derrick and how he really didn't have a clue that I was treating him coldly. Nor would he have known why if he'd been aware of my feelings. I thought about the checks I sent in support of the fraternity and the house and how my money was helping to perpetuate this hate. For the first time since I knew about KAΩ I felt embarrassed about being a member of one of the most prestigious organizations for black men.

Sunday arrived and before leaving, Trent and I had breakfast at the Hilton Hotel. We talked about what a wonderful weekend it had been and promised to do a better job of keeping in touch. The evening before somehow managed to end on a good note even after my stoic conversation with Derrick. After seeing KAΩ perform at a jamming step show and singing the fraternity hymn with over one hundred brothers all in perfect pitch, I realized it wasn't KAΩ I was ashamed of, just some of the members. Just as I knew you couldn't diss your entire family because of a few relatives.

While Trent and I ate toast and eggs I asked him what he thought about the "gay issue" within the frat. Trent pulled his coffee mug up to his lips, took a sip, and slowly placed it on the saucer.

"Well, it's like this, Ray. I say to each his own and if homosexuality was wrong then why did God make so many people gay? I mean why would anyone choose some shit like that?" he said as he looked me directly in my eyes as though he were looking right through me.

"Well, I guess you're right," I said as I glanced around the restaurant for our waitress, trying to avoid Trent's eyes.

We decided to stop at the fraternity house one last time before heading out. When we walked in it was like a morgue. Brothers were lying around looking as if somebody had died. Initiation, which was to take place that evening, was a solemn occasion but not this morose.

"What up, frat?" I asked a brother with whom I had chatted over the weekend but whose name escaped me.

"Bad news, frat. Real bad news," the frat brother said.

"What?"

Just as he was getting ready to answer, Derrick walked into the library of the frat house.

"Ain't no reason for you niggers to be all depressed. We didn't do it. Besides being a fag, the boy was weak too," he said as he looked around the room at all the long faces.

"What happened, Derrick?" I asked.

"That guy, Miller. Fool motherfucker tried to kill himself last night. The other fraternities and his girlfriend are saying it's our fault."

"What? What did he do?"

"Slit his wrists," Derrick said with no visible emotion.

"How is he?"

"Don't know. They won't give us any information. His family flew in this morning and I heard his father is coming by the house. That's why we need you older brothers to stay," Derrick said.

"What the fuck for?" I shouted. "To save your asses for being so motherfuckin' stupid?"

"Ray, cool down," Trent said, as he pulled me by the arms.

"I'm cool, frat. I'm getting my ass out of here. It smells like shit in here to me," I said as I walked out the door and to my car. I didn't turn around to see who was calling my name. I just wanted to get back to Atlanta and to make my peace with Jared.

I couldn't believe what had just transpired. I was upset over some guy whom I had never laid eyes on. A young black guy paying for being different. I thought how this could have been me. I recalled how I once considered suicide while living in New York because my secret life had been discovered. I laid my head on the steering wheel of my car and did something I rarely did. I cried and prayed Christ would see fit to give Miller and me another chance.

Part Two

Loss

No Crying,

No Hymn Sanging

Twenty-two

"*It* seems like only yesterday when I got the call."

"The call?" Dr. Huntley quizzed.

"Yes. At first Candance's mother was just making small talk about Candance pushing back her wedding date because of her being in the hospital and all and then she started crying and her husband took the phone away from her. He told me Candance had AIDS."

"What did you do?"

"I dropped the phone. I cried. It was so surreal. I recall going into my bathroom, throwing up and putting on my makeup, and catching a taxi to the hospital. Everything else is a blur."

"So Candance never told you?"

"The words never crossed her lips."

"Are you certain you should be the one who calls Raymond?"

"I at least have to make sure he knows. I don't know what I'll say, but I have to call him."

"Are you up to this?" Dr. Huntley asked as she moved from behind her large desk.

"This isn't about me. Kyle needs his friends for support. Candance only had her parents, Kelvin, and me. All the friends she had and none of them knew until it was over."

"Have you talked with Pierce?"

"Just a few conversations but not about the black thing."

"Are you going to?"

"Yes, I'm going to be completely honest with him about why I feel this way and my true feelings for him. I've always said I wanted people to be honest with me in relationships and I haven't given Pierce the same courtesy."

"I think you're on the right track, Nicole," Dr. Huntley said. She even gave me a soft reassuring smile.

"You think so?"

"Yes, I do. How is your friend, the one who was attacked? Delaney, right?"

"Yes, Delaney. Right now she's dealing with the news about Kyle. Still not talking about the attack."

"Do you think she's going to just let it go?"

"For now . . . but if I know Delaney like I think I do she will confront the issue when she's ready."

"Do you need an extra session this week?"

"I don't know if I'll have the time. Can I call your service?"

"Sure, Nicole. That will be fine."

It was a call I never wanted to make. Despite the confidence I displayed with Dr. Huntley, I was petrified. I mean it took me days to find Raymond's home phone number without asking Kyle for it outright. There were several Raymond Tylers listed in the Atlanta directory. I later realized that his number might be unlisted and I didn't know the name of the firm he was working for, but I knew it was owned by a black female, so I called a couple of my Atlanta sorors who came up with the name. Then I found someone who knew someone inside the firm who could get me Raymond's home number. I didn't want to call him at his office. What would I say? And I still wondered if I was doing the right thing.

Kyle had not verbally confirmed anything, but his actions did. He wasn't taking Delaney's or my calls and left strict instructions with his doorman that no one was to come up to his apartment not even Delaney or me. Besides seeing the pills, I had some other supporting evidence. One of the male dancers in *Jelly's* had expressed his sympathy about Kyle after first confirming that Kyle and I were close friends. When I asked him what he was talking about he simply put his hands to his lips and said, "I'm sorry. You don't know?"

I guess there is a great gay computer service out there disseminating all sorts of information regarding gay men. The sad thing is that all the information and rumors these days have to do with AIDS.

I'd learned a lot through the pain of Candance's death. I wasn't afraid to be around anyone with AIDS, but it seemed that people with AIDS wanted to keep the pain private. In addition to Candance I had lost several male friends from the cast of *Dreamgirls* to the disease, but they were not as close to me as Kyle was and in many cases, they traveled back to their hometown to die. I had never been around someone for a prolonged time during his illness. The disease seemed to hit so quickly. One day they were on stage dancing and pleasing crowds and a few months or sometimes just weeks later a note would appear on a backstage bulletin board with instructions on where to send flowers and donations.

In the weeks that followed my discovery of Kyle's pills I had been asked to sing at an AIDS cabaret benefit and at a program at Spelman honoring Candance early next year. I cried through both phone calls after saying yes.

I called Raymond's number all weekend but I just kept getting his answering machine. I didn't leave a message. It would be heartless to just leave a message. Maybe Raymond would get the wrong idea and think that after all these years I'd changed my mind and decided to give him another chance. I wondered how he would respond to my call and the news. What if he knew? I mean he and Kyle were very close. For all I knew Raymond could be in New York right now at Kyle's apartment taking care of him. They say women are secretive but men can be just as much so.

Late Sunday night, I sipped hot spiced apple tea and stared mindlessly at the phone. I decided to call Raymond one more time before I went to bed. All I would have to do is to hit redial, since his number was the only one I had dialed all day. I'd even missed my morning prayer call with Sheila and instead just prayed in my apartment alone. I was still waiting for those Scriptures she'd promised.

Delaney agreed that I should call Raymond. She said that at least that way we could confirm what we believed to be true. I asked Delaney if she knew anything more and she said, "No, but don't you think Kyle had been acting strange all summer?" I was ashamed to say I hadn't noticed. I looked at my clock and realized that midnight was approaching, so I did something I always do when I'm in doubt. I got on my knees and prayed about five minutes for guidance and direction on what to do. I also explained to the Lord I would dial Raymond's number one more time and if he didn't answer then that would mean he already knew and, if he answered, then that meant I was supposed to tell him.

I got off my knees, walked into my bathroom, flossed and brushed my teeth, and then walked slowly down the hallway to the living room and my phone.

I didn't hit redial, I pushed 4-0-4 and the rest of Raymond's number.

One ring, a second ring, and I prepared for the answering machine to pick up after the third.

"Hello," the deep voice said. I felt my knees lock.

"Raymond?"

"Yes."

"How are you doing?"

"Nicole? Is this Nicole Springer, famous Broadway actress?" he asked.

"You recognized my voice," I said.

"How could I forget your voice? What a pleasant surprise," Raymond said.

We started talking in a desultory way and I determined he didn't know why I was calling. "So when was the last time you talked to Kyle?" I asked.

"Oh, it's been a couple of weeks. Funny you should ask. I just got back home from a fraternity reunion and I thought about Kyle all the way home. He's been so busy with his business and all. You know I'm really proud of him," Raymond said.

I didn't respond. Raymond started his rambling sentences again.

"Nicole, Nicole? Are you still there?"

"Yes. I'm sorry, Raymond."

"So tell me about this new musical you're in. Maybe I can make this opening," Raymond said.

"Well, that's on the back burner right now. I'm still doing *Jelly's*."

"Oh, great. Maybe I'll get a chance to see you the next time I'm in New York," he said.

"Yeah, that will be nice. Raymond, do you know anything about Kyle being sick?"

"Kyle sick? You mean mental—yeah, I've known that . . . for quite some time."

"Raymond, seriously. I think Kyle has AIDS," I said, interrupting Raymond's light-hearted banter.

A period of silence followed. I felt my eyes begin to fill with tears.

"Raymond, are you there?"

"Yeah, Nicole, I'm here. Are you sure? I mean, Kyle would have told me something like this," Raymond said, as his voice trailed off.

I told Raymond about the pills I'd seen in Kyle's apartment and all the strange things that happened during the summer and what my friend from *Jelly's* had said. Raymond shared with me Kyle's not pressing him on a few trips they were supposed to take during the summer and Kyle's not calling him as much, but he'd thought it was because Kyle was so busy. He expressed slight disbelief in what I shared with him because he said Kyle had been in perfect health on Memorial Day, but I think he believed me when we realized Kyle had told us different versions of his back injury. He told Raymond he'd strained a back muscle moving furniture. Kyle was a lot of things, but he wasn't a liar.

Twenty-three

Nicole's phone call left me in a state of shock. A numbness cloaked my body. My first instinct was to call Kyle right away but instead I called Jared, who promised to come right over. While waiting for Jared I managed to finish a half bottle of red wine and drink three Stolis with grapefruit juice. I needed instant courage.

I was well aware of the fact that at some point AIDS would again touch my life. I just didn't know who and when. I myself got tested every six months even while I was celibate. Basil and I always practiced safe sex. As far as I knew, Kyle had been practicing safe sex ever since the mid-eighties. Maybe Nicole was wrong. Yeah, that was it. This was some terrible mistake. I picked up the phone and hit the speed dial button next to Kyle's name.

"Hello," Kyle answered.

I was startled and surprised to hear his voice sounding so clear.

"Kyle, where have you been?" I slurred.

"Ray, what's the matter with you?" Kyle asked.

"Why haven't you returned my calls?" I asked.

"I've been real busy. Chile, I met this man this weekend. Ray, he had a dick big enough for two people," Kyle laughed.

"I hope you had safe sex," I said.

"Of course. I put two rubbers on it," Kyle snickered.

I was waiting for the right time to tell Kyle about Nicole's call but he kept talking about this new man and all the jobs he was getting. This did not sound like a man with AIDS.

"So when was the last time you talked to Nicole?"

"Oh, it's been a while. You know she's busy with the show and planning her wedding. Like I said, we've both been real busy," Kyle said.

I told Kyle about my weekend in Alabama and what happened with the fraternity and the young guy who tried to commit suicide.

"So is this why you're so drunk and sound so sad?" Kyle asked.

"Yeah, I guess so," I lied.

"I don't know why you want to be bothered with those homophobic boys. That's college boy shit. You're a grown man now," Kyle lectured.

Just when I was getting ready to ask Kyle if he had anything he wanted to share with me, I heard a beep on my phone line.

"Hold on, Kyle," I said.

"Naw, I've got to go. I hear Grady buzzing me. Sleep it off, Ray, and call me tomorrow," Kyle said.

"Kyle?"

"Yeah, Ray?"

"I love you."

"Yeah, I know. I love you, too," Kyle said softly.

The beep was my doorman informing me Jared was on his way up. It was now early Monday morning.

Jared's face was covered with a big smile when I opened the door. The smile made my body feel warmer than the vodka and wine combined. I gave him a bear hug and whispered, "I'm sorry for being such a jerk."

"No problem. I knew you'd come around. Pops told me you could be moody," Jared said as he removed his sweater, walked into the kitchen, and opened the icebox. Just like the past months never happened.

"You got any lunch meat?" Jared asked.

"If I do, I wouldn't suggest eating it," I said.

"Old, huh?"

"Real old."

Jared grabbed a beer and I stared at my empty glass on the counter and wondered if I had any more wine in my bedroom bar. I excused myself and found a miniature bottle of chardonnay. This would do it. This glass would give me the final push I needed. I poured the wine into the glass, walked back into the living room, and saw Jared standing near the sliding glass door.

"So, I'm your niggah again?" Jared asked.

"Yeah, you're the man," I said looking around the sofa for the remote control to my CD player. I located it and pushed the power button and out piped Luther Vandross's voice singing "A House Is Not a Home."

Instead of telling Jared about me, I started to tell him about the weekend at AU and Kyle. I asked him what I should do, since Kyle wasn't confessing to anything and there was still a possibility Nicole had her facts confused.

"You should go to New York and find out what's going on," Jared advised.

I expected Jared to ask me if Kyle was gay, but he didn't. He just listened intently as I spoke of my frustrations about not knowing what to do. He also told me I had to overlook my fraternity brothers because they were young and didn't know better.

"We men can be such jerks," Jared said.

"Yes, present company included," I said, pointing to my chest. Jared smiled.

"It's good talking like this, Ray. You know I've missed it," Jared said.

"Yeah, I have too. I don't know why I acted like I did," I said.

"Isn't Nicole that lady you were so in love with?" Jared asked.

"Yeah, and when I heard her voice tonight, I felt like it was just yesterday when things were going so great for us," I said.

"Do you still love her?" Jared asked.

"Yeah, I think so. But I haven't seen her in almost three years and she's engaged. Jared, can I ask you something?"

"Yeah."

"You ever been in love?"

Jared didn't respond right away. It looked like his eyes were filling with water. He looked around the living room, got up, and walked over to the sliding glass door. Then he turned, faced me, and nodded blankly.

"Yeah, I was in love once," Jared said after taking a deep breath.

"You want to talk about it? Will you share it with me?" I asked.

Jared went on to tell me a sad story of love and betrayal. He had been in love with a woman he had known since the ninth grade, Pamela Phillips. He described her as a light-skinned beauty who was from one of Atlanta's "high-colored" families, he laughed. Pamela and Jared had dated for over seven years and were engaged to be married. Their wedding was going to be one of the highlights of the Atlanta summer social season, only Pamela stood Jared up on their wedding day. She left town with Jared's best friend and roommate, Jergen Lassic, whom she later married.

As Jared told the story I could tell how painful this had been. His face was etched with sadness. It appeared to me he'd really loved Pamela and Jergen and that the experience left him scarred. I now realized why my friendship was so important to Jared. I knew also that I had to accept the reality that Jared was heterosexual.

Yeah, I knew of stories where guys in the closet could change a *he* to a *she* and tell a convincing tale of true love. I had done it myself. But I felt Jared's story was true. I could see it in his eyes and hear it in the sound of his voice. This woman had hurt my friend badly. He ended the story by saying the only things that compared to the hurt he felt on his wedding day were when his father left him when he was five years old and when he thought our friendship was over. Again I apologized and grabbed Jared and held him tightly. I took my fingers and traced the small crease between his brow and he smiled fondly. I was close enough that I could feel the warmth of his body and the heat of his breath. But this closeness was not sexual but something more fulfilling than sex could ever be. It was during this moment that I realized Jared had much more to offer me than sex.

Jared decided to spend the night since dawn was now only hours away. I decided not to tempt fate or myself, so I went to get sheets, pillows, and blankets from my linen closet for Jared to sleep on the sofa. Jared and I had, however, slept in the same bed before without incident. I was so touched by Jared's openness and even more so because I had not told him the truth about me. I was going to wait until later in the day when suddenly the vodka impelled me to tell Jared the truth.

"Jared, when I told you about Kyle possibly having AIDS why didn't you ask me if he was gay?"

"Because it doesn't matter to me," Jared said.

"Are you sure?"

"Yeah, Ray. Why, is Kyle gay?"

"Would it matter to you if I was gay or bisexual?"

"Are you?"

Jared's eyes met mine. The silence in the room was thick. A moment of indecision came over me.

"Yeah, Jared, I am," I said slowly.

"Well, that's cool," Jared said. His voice came out as a slow whisper.

"Is that all?" I asked adding bass in my voice. "Cool?"

"What am I supposed to say? That I knew? Well, I didn't. Never thought about it. That I'm gay or bisexual too? Well, I'm not. But I am your friend, your brother, and I love you with everything that's in me. That's all that matters. That's all that will ever matter," Jared said as he looked at me thoughtfully, his voice back to its normal volume.

"Aren't you worried about guilt by association?"

"Guilt?"

"You know."

"Have you molested any little children?"

"No."

"Forced anyone to have sex with you against their will?"

"No."

"Like I said, guilt?"

I stood in the doorway of my bedroom staring at Jared, listening to the power in his voice as he played lawyer. I shivered slightly, as if something calm and miraculous had been whisked through my body. For the first time a man besides my pops or Kyle had told me he loved me and I believed him with everything that was Raymond Winston Tyler, Jr.

I started to walk into my bedroom when Jared yelled out, "Hey, boy?"

"Yeah?" I said as I turned to face Jared's smiling face.

"So is that why I've got to sleep on this hard-ass sofa?"

"You sure you want to sleep in here with me?"

"I've done it before. What's different about tonight?"

"Nothing I guess."

"You guess?"

"Nothing."

"Damn straight. So what up?"

"Come on, boy. There's room for you in here," I said.

I went straight to Mico's desk once I arrived in my office Monday morning.

"Mico, I need to see Gilliam first thing this morning. Can you arrange that?" I asked.

"Sure, Ray. As a matter of fact, Gilliam asked me to put you on her schedule first thing this morning," Mico said.

I walked into my office and stared out the picture window without removing my suit jacket. Over coffee, Jared had convinced me I should at least go to New York to see Kyle and I knew he was right. I had to find out for myself. If Kyle was sick I would know if I saw him in person. We had reached a point in our friendship where Kyle couldn't lie to me face to face and vice versa. I would go to New York and ask him point blank if he had AIDS.

I hit my intercom button and asked Melanie to check on flights into New York or Newark and to get me a hotel for a couple of days in midtown Manhattan. Nicole had mentioned a hotel called the Paramount that was nice and reasonable so I told Melanie to check there first. After noting my requests, Melanie informed me Gilliam was ready to see me.

"Good morning, Raymond. How was your fraternity reunion?" Gilliam asked as I walked into her office.

"It was great, but I realized I'm getting old," I said.

"Don't mention it. My sorority is having a reunion in the spring and all I will say is that my reunion number is higher than yours," she laughed. "Seems like only yesterday I was signing up for *Jack and Jill.*"

"You're a Delta, right Gilliam?"

"Yes, a Delta Sigma Theta for life," she said proudly.

"Gilliam, I have something I need to talk with you about," I said.

"Okay. But don't you want to hear my news first?" Gilliam asked.

"Sure. You're the boss."

"Well, Raymond. I've made no secret about how pleased I am with your work. I mean the way you handled that Henderson case was masterful. His own attorney told me what a jerk he is and said he would be forever in our debt. We both agreed what he did was horrible. . . . And I've told you of my desire to add another partner."

"Yes, Gilliam. I knew you were looking," I said.

"Well, are you interested?" Gilliam asked as she came from behind her desk and positioned herself directly in front of me.

"In being—I mean, being a partner?" I stuttered.

"Yes, Ray. That's what I wanted to talk to you about. I want to make you a full partner in the firm immediately," she said.

"Gilliam, yes . . . of course," I agreed, forgetting for a moment what I'd come in to discuss with her.

"Great. Then let's talk details," Gilliam said as she walked back behind her desk.

"Gilliam, before we talk details, I have something I need to discuss with you. Not great timing, but I need to take some time off immediately. It might just be a couple of days but it could be longer. I have a close friend who might need my assistance and I have to leave for New York today."

"Today?"

"Yes, and then I'll be in a better position to discuss your offer."

At first Gilliam looked a bit alarmed and apprehensive but when I explained about Kyle and the call from Nicole, she offered to give me a week to go to New York to find out what was going on. She said if I needed longer than that we might talk about a short leave of absence. She didn't mention how this might affect my pending partnership.

I couldn't believe this was happening. Here I was in the midst of what should be one of the happiest days in my career and I wasn't excited. All I could think of was Kyle and New York City.

Jared, who was now a deputy director for the Clinton for President campaign in Georgia, gave me a ride to the airport and assured me everything was going to be just fine. I gave him keys to my condo, car, and mailbox and he promised to look in on things every other day while I was away. He was really excited at the news of Gilliam's offer and said, "When you get back we'll celebrate Kyle's good health and your new station in life."

"You think Kyle is going to be all right?"

"Of course, he will be all right and if there are problems, we'll deal with them."

I was relieved I was leaving for New York with Jared solidly in my corner. It really didn't matter to me anymore that he was heterosexual because I felt now we would have a much stronger relationship— purely platonic, but stronger. I'd always thought most straight men believed every gay man wanted to go to bed with them after a confession. I didn't get the feeling Jared felt that way at all. In fact he seemed even more at ease, but it was still just less than twenty-four hours. I knew Jared still had lingering questions about my sexuality. That morning before we left for work, I asked Jared if there was anything he wanted to know. At first he said, "No," but then he blurted out, "Ray, you don't let them . . ." He paused.

"Let them what?" I asked.

"You know," Jared said as he moved his index finger in and out of a circle he formed with his free hand.

"What are you asking me? Do I let them poke me?"

"Yeah, but you don't have to answer that," he responded shyly.

"Does it matter?"

"No!"

"You sure?"

"I'm sure."

I will never understand the curiosity straight folks have with who is doing who.

During the ride to the airport I told Jared what had happened between Nicole and myself and about the confession at the hospital. I wondered out loud why it took tragedy to get me to tell the truth to people I loved.

Just as Jared was getting ready to drop me off at the airport, he took his huge hands and gave me a powerful slap on my thighs. "Now don't worry, buddy. I'm only a phone call away if you or Kyle need anything. Stay strong," Jared said in a low, reassuring voice.

"I know, buddy. I know," I repeated as I grabbed my garment bag from the backseat and headed toward the terminal gate. Before I entered the automatic doors I looked back and saw Jared waving, his killer smile in full effect.

I arrived at Newark Airport and took a taxi to the Paramount Hotel on Forty-sixth between Eighth and Broadway right across the street from JR's, a bar I used to meet Nicole at while we were dating. From the street the bar looked crowded and lively. The Paramount was a European-style hotel with a beautiful art deco lobby and small, but stylish guest rooms. All the bellmen and desk clerks looked like New York models instead of hotel workers, dressed sharply in black suits with white cotton T-shirts.

I quickly checked into my room, dialed Kyle's number, and got the answering machine. The answering machine bleeped out Kyle's voice and the command: "You know what to do." I didn't leave a message. I looked into my briefcase and got the keys to my old apartment, which I had brought just in case there were any problems.

Although I was excited about seeing Kyle, I was also a bit nervous, so I passed on the taxi the doorman offered and decided to take the subway instead. Being on a New York subway would loosen me up or at least take my mind off what I was preparing to face.

The city looked cold and naked against a dark sky. I walked past JR's and headed toward the Forty-second Street subway station. I could hear the subway sizzling underneath the busy streets. As I walked the sounds and scents of New York triggered so many images, manic moments Kyle and I had shared in this part of the city, moments that were now mere memories.

I could smell warm pizza toppings and burned dough and I watched men scurry in and out of the adult bookstores that lined Eighth Avenue. I smiled to myself at the recollection of Kyle and myself going into some of these same bookstores after the bars closed. I was a bit surprised that business still seemed to be booming in the age of AIDS.

The Number 1 train quivered to a stop at the busy station at Ninety-sixth and Broadway and I stepped out into a murky autumn evening on the Upper West Side. I'd made this stop so many times on the way to my high-rise apartment that still had my name on the lease. I walked into the building and it seemed as though nothing had changed. The lobby was sparkling clean and Grady was still at the door protecting the entry from unwanted guests.

"Grady," I said as I smiled and gently embraced a man who had guarded me for years.

"Mr. Tyler. What a surprise. How have you been? It's great seeing you," he said as he patted me on my shoulders.

"I've been great. I'm living in Atlanta now. It's really great seeing you," I said.

"You here to see Mr. Benton?"

"Yes. How is he doing?" I asked, making it appear I already knew what Grady had to know.

"Not too good, Mr. Tyler. His mother came in today, but she just left about thirty minutes ago," Grady said as he shook his head in dismay and gently brushed his thick gray mustache with his fingers.

"Grady, do me a favor. Don't buzz Kyle. I've still got my key. I want to surprise him."

"I don't know, Mr. Tyler. Mr. Benton left specific instructions not to let anyone up, including those pretty ladies who used to come and visit him," Grady said.

"Come on, Grady," I said, and I gently placed a ten-dollar bill into the palm of his hand.

Grady looked at me, smiled, and looked absently around his station and the lobby as if he didn't see me as I walked past his station and toward the elevators.

I walked slowly down the hallway to Kyle's door. I slipped my key in the door to see if it still fit. I turned the key very slowly so I wouldn't startle Kyle. I realized he didn't have the safety latch on, so I slowly cracked the door and listened for signs of movement. The apartment seemed still. I then closed the door, took a deep breath, and rang the doorbell. I pushed the bell for about five minutes without response. I placed the key back in the door and opened it wide and this time stepped inside the apartment. The door made a loud creaking sound.

"Ma? You back already?" Kyle called from the bedroom.

"No, Kyle, it's me, Ray," I yelled as I closed the door and looked around the apartment.

"Bitch, what are you doing here?" Kyle yelled back.

I walked into Kyle's bedroom where he was sitting up in his bed supported by many pillows.

"I heard you needed me," I said as I looked at Kyle's shocked face.

"So who told you?" he asked mournfully.

"Nicole."

"Why can't that damn diva mind her own business?" Kyle said as he looked toward the window.

"Well, I think she loves you, like I do," I said. I felt tears filling my eyes as I looked at my dear friend. He seemed so frail and lifeless. His normally flawless brown face looked distressed. His forehead was covered with worry lines. The only thing that looked vaguely familiar was his eyes. This couldn't be the same person I had seen in May in D.C. I felt my heart plunge to just above my toes. A shiver of fear ran down my spine. I hadn't prepared myself for Kyle looking so bad.

"First rule. No tears . . . no hymn sanging," Kyle said lightheartedly. "If you're gonna cry then you have to leave here."

"So what are you trying to tell me? That I have to grow up?"

"Yep, I think that's it. Ole Kyle ain't going to be around to teach you the ropes anymore."

"Who am I going to grow old with?"

"There will be other people in your life. You'll make new friends, but I'll always be around."

I walked over to Kyle's bed and sat on the edge of it, just staring at him. I was silent, trying to absorb Kyle's body and what he was saying. The dim light from one lamp was all that alleviated the darkness in Kyle's cluttered bedroom. I firmly put my hands on the blankets covering his legs and they felt like bones through the fabric. Kyle just looked at me.

"So, what do you need me to do?"

"Well, there's not much you can do. My mom came today, but I'm glad you're here. How long are you here for?" When he spoke, his voice was soft and low.

"As long as you need me," I said soberly.

"Okay. Just as long as you know the rules. I don't need anybody to feel sorry for me. I'm ready whenever He is," Kyle said as he looked upward and positioned himself against the headboard and pillows. He sounded like a general getting ready to go into battle. "So tell me, what's going on in Atlanta?" Kyle asked. "Do you want a drink? Probably need one right about now, huh?"

"No, I'm fine."

I told Kyle about Gilliam's offer and tried to convince him how excited I was. I also told him the great love of my life was not going to be because he was straight. Kyle said that was okay and that I needed a good friend like Jared. He asked me about Basil and then said, "No, I don't want to hear about that asshole." I told him I agreed with him. I was going to go back to celibacy and concentrate on my career. Kyle just looked at me and shook his head and smiled. He told me his mother was going to stay with him for a couple of days. He said she was holding up well and he hoped they wouldn't drive each other crazy. He told me I was more than welcome to stay with him, but I told him I already checked into a hotel.

"Chile, that's one thing I can say about you. You're forever grand," Kyle chuckled.

Kyle went on to explain he had known of his condition for about three years. He'd found out he was HIV positive when he had checked into rehab. Kyle kept talking, then closed his eyes for a few minutes, then opened them, and started talking as though nothing was different. Just two friends talking about old times.

"Kyle, why didn't you tell me sooner?"

Kyle raised his eyes and stared at me for a moment. "I blocked it out. Long story short, I didn't want to spend the rest of my life dying."

He then shut his eyes and tilted his head toward the ceiling, making it clear he saw no reason for further conversation. He was engaged in a battle to survive and part of that battle, the most important part, was always to preserve his strength.

I got up from the bed and moved closer to Kyle. I gently kissed his forehead and touched his hair, which felt baby soft. I went over to the nightstand and turned out the lamp. As I walked out of the bedroom

Kyle suddenly called out, "Ray, please put on my Vanessa Williams CD when you leave. Put on 'Save the Best for Last' . . . track six."

I nodded my head soberly. I located the CD, placed it in the carousel, pushed the play button, and walked out of the darkened apartment.

I sped past Grady with just a wave and walked out into a much colder night. As I stood on the corner of Ninety-sixth and Broadway hailing a taxi, I felt tears rolling down my face, but the cool, brisk wind quickly dried them on my skin. No tears and no hymn sanging.

Twenty-four

"*Nicole?*" his deep baritone voice said. How I loved his voice.

"Raymond?" I asked.

"Yes, Nicole, it's me," he said.

"Where are you?"

"I'm in New York. I'm staying at the Paramount Hotel," he said.

"Oh, the Paramount. So you decided to stay there?" I said trying to make polite conversation before the news.

"Well, I wanted to thank you for calling me and letting me know about Kyle."

"Did you talk to him?"

"Yes, I saw him last night."

"You saw him? How is he?"

"You were right, Nicole. Kyle is very sick," Raymond said in a mournful tone.

I sat on my bed and clutched my robe. I didn't know what to say. I hoped this was a bad dream and I would awaken soon. Suddenly my thoughts went back to the day I got the call from Candance's mother.

"Nicole? Are you still there?" Raymond asked.

"Yes, Ray. I'm sorry. I was praying I was wrong," I said.

"Yes, I was too. That's why I came up," he said.

Raymond went on to explain Kyle had some type of cancer and his mother was with him. He said he'd talked with Kyle's mother and she said the doctor's prognosis was anywhere from three months to a year. My eyes filled with tears and I began to weep openly as I thought about not having Kyle around and the pain he was going through. Why hadn't he told me? Raymond tried to console me over the phone by saying, "It's okay, Nicole . . . go ahead and cry." Raymond said Kyle didn't want anyone feeling sorry for him and he didn't want any tears so Raymond wanted me to get them all out before I saw Kyle.

I asked Raymond when Delaney and I could see Kyle. He said he would be on his way to Kyle's apartment when we hung up and he would call me from there. I thanked him and told him I'd wait for his call. Just before I hung up Raymond said my name as he had so many times. "Nicole, it's great hearing your voice and I'll be forever in your debt for calling me. I hope I'll see you real soon."

When I hung up the phone I looked toward the ceiling and said out loud, "Why, Lord? Please, not again."

I walked slowly around my apartment wondering what to do next. I needed to call Delaney and let her know about Kyle. I was walking toward my bathroom to wash my face when my phone rang. It was Pierce.

"Are you still not talking to me?" Pierce asked.

"Hello, Pierce. I know we need to talk but I've just been so upset about Kyle," I said.

"So your suspicions were correct?"

"Yes, I'm afraid so. I just got a call from Raymond. He spoke with Kyle last night," I said.

There was a brief silence.

"Pierce, are you still there?"

"Yes, Nicole. Raymond—isn't that your ex?"

"Yes, Raymond is the guy I used to see."

"You're not going to see him are you?"

"What? I'm sure I'll see him."

"Are you excited about seeing him?"

"Pierce, please. Right now my only concern is Kyle."

"Well, let me know if there is anything I can do."

"I will, Pierce. I will call you the first chance I get. We will talk. We have to."

"Okay, Nicole, I'll wait for your call."

"Okay."

"Nicole?"

"Yes?"

"I'm really sorry about all this," Pierce said sadly.

"I know, Pierce. I know. Thank you."

I hung up and called Delaney before I took my shower. I figured if I started crying again I could do it in the shower with the rush of the warm water.

"Hello."

"Delaney, this is Nicole, darling. I was right," I said.

"About Kyle?" she asked.

"Yes," I said.

"Then he really is sick?"

"Yeah, Delaney. Raymond just called me and broke the news on what I already suspected," I said as I started to look in my dresser for a book of poetry I was going to give to Kyle.

"Raymond? How does he know for sure?" Delaney questioned.

"He's here in New York. He saw Kyle last night," I said.

"I knew something was up. I mean all of sudden Kyle was so busy. I mean he's always busy but at least before he was able to make time for us," Delaney said.

I shared with Delaney what Raymond had told me about Kyle's not wanting any sympathy. He wanted things to stay the same.

"Stay the same?" Delaney exclaimed. "How in the fuck can things stay the same?"

"Delaney, calm down," I said. "I know you're upset, but you've got to calm down."

"I'm sorry, girl. You know I think Kyle tried to tell me this before Memorial Day."

"What do you mean?"

"Well, he was talking about all the big gay events. Washington, D.C., for Memorial Day, L.A. for the Fourth, and so on, and he said this was going to be his last Dreamboy tour. I thought he meant he was going to stop hanging out so much," Delaney lamented.

While Delaney was talking I tried to think if Kyle had given me any signals when I suddenly caught a glimpse of the wedding slip I had hanging on my closet door. It hit me why Kyle was in such a hurry to make my wedding gown and my eyes filled with tears again. My tears turned into sobs and Delaney begged me to stop crying because she had already put on her makeup and she didn't want to join me. Delaney told me she had an audition in about an hour but she would come by my apartment when she finished and not to make a move without her.

"Delaney, please be on time. I don't think I'll be able to sit around this apartment waiting," I said.

"Do you think I should cancel my audition?"

"No, Kyle wouldn't want you to do that."

"You're sure?"

"Yes, I think I'm right about this."

"If I see where I'm running behind I'll call," Delaney said.

"Where is your audition?"

"On the Lower East side," Delaney said.

"Who is it with?"

"Some singer I've never heard of."

"Delaney, please be safe," I said.

"Don't worry about me. I'll be fine. We need to be worried about Kyle right now."

"I know but I just want to be sure you'll be safe."

"I will be."

"Delaney?"

"Yes, Nicole?"

"Are you sure you're all right?"

"Yes, girl. Why do you ask?"

"Well, I just keep worrying about you."

"Because of the rape?"

I paused for a second. This was the first time Delaney had used the word rape.

"Yes, the rape, Delaney. You should make sure your agent checks these people out," I said.

"My agent always does that," Delaney defended.

"Did you tell him what happened?"

"No, it's none of his business."

"It is, Delaney. I just don't think you're dealing with this."

"I'm dealing with it slowly."

"Well, you know I'm here for you."

"Yes, darling, I do, but right now we've got Kyle to worry about."

"I know. Bye, Delaney."

"I'll see you later, darling."

After hanging up the phone, I got on my knees and started to pray for Kyle. I had to believe that prayer changed things.

I took a shower and ordered coffee and pumpkin muffins from the neighborhood deli. As I sipped the hot brew I skimmed through a copy of *Essence* magazine and pulled a Maya Angelou book of poetry from my bookshelf. This would calm me down while I waited for my phone calls and Delaney.

I had started my magical journey with Maya's words when the phone rang.

"Hello," I said.

"Nicole?"

"Raymond?"

"Yeah, just wanted to get back with you. I'm up at Kyle's. He wants to know if you would come and take his mom to get something to eat and take her out for a while?"

"Sure," I said quickly. "What time?"

"What time is convenient for you?"

"Let me put on some clothes and I'll be right over," I said.

"Okay. We'll look forward to seeing you," he said.

"I'll see you guys soon," I said as I clicked off the phone.

I looked in my closet and pulled out a flowered vest, black-pleated slacks, and a crimson silk camisole edged with lace and laid them across my bed. After putting on my makeup, I brushed my hair, pulled it up in a bun, then suddenly let it out, allowing it to fall to my shoulders. Before leaving my apartment, I placed a call to Dr. Huntley's office to arrange an appointment. I had a feeling I would need to see her after leaving Kyle's. I also called Delaney's service and left a message telling her that I couldn't wait, and to meet me at Kyle's.

The afternoon was sunny and very fall-like. I asked the taxi driver to go through Central Park so I could view fall's beautiful colors prancing like a jazz dance troupe throughout the park. As we sped through the park to the West Side, I laughed out loud when I thought of how Kyle always said, "Go head, girl, and catch your chariot over to the rich East Side." I'd never really stopped to think how much I treasured Kyle's friendship. He'd taught me so much.

Right after Candance's death and my breakup with Raymond, I didn't want to have anything to do with black men, especially black, gay or bisexual men. I was angry at what they were capable of. The dishonesty, the outward perfection that caused women to fall for them without knowing the whole truth. I assumed such actions had to be part of a calculated plan, like a conspiracy against black women. There were so few black men out there and I really felt all the sharp ones had chosen to be gay so they wouldn't have to compete with the men women sometimes chose . . . the ones who abused women but who really had it going on when it came to lovemaking. I was angry for all my young sisters coming after me who would have to learn the lessons I'd learned the hard way. I didn't like seeing a good-looking, smart black man only to have to think about the fact that he might choose Kyle over me. Once Kyle and I became close, we'd see a good-looking guy and I would look at him and whisper, "Would he prefer you or me?" Kyle helped me understand that these moves were not calculated. He would get upset with me every time I asked, "Why did he have to *choose* to be gay?" Through Kyle, I was starting to have a better understanding of gay black men and some of the struggles they had to deal with day to day. With Kyle I was able to ask questions and get honest answers that increased my understanding when it came to homosexuality and bisexuality, questions that prior to my moving to New York it would have never occurred to me to ask. I didn't know any gay people in Arkansas except for a couple of hairdressers I met through my pageant experiences and they actually lived in Memphis.

I rushed through the lobby of Kyle's building and up to his floor. I took a deep breath and then rang the bell. When Ray opened the door I was momentarily stunned. He was a more powerful presence than I'd remembered.

"Nicole. How are you?" Raymond said as he took my hands and led me into Kyle's apartment. He gave me a quick kiss on the lips. It wasn't a romantic kiss, but a glad-to-see-you kiss.

"Raymond. How are you?"

"I've been better. You look beautiful," he said flashing his bright, glacier-white teeth. A brightness that was second only to his green eyes. Eyes I felt were looking right through me. I just stood inside the foyer, stone-like, looking at Raymond and how handsome he was. We were standing there like two kids on their first date trying to decide whether or not to go for the first kiss. I was getting ready to inquire about Kyle and his mother when I heard Kyle call from the bedroom.

"Is that Diva Detective?" he yelled.

"Yes, Kyle, it's me. Do you want me to come back there?"

"No, darling, I'm on my way out," Kyle said.

I was getting ready to ask Raymond how long he was going to stay when out walked Kyle's mother, an attractive, small-boned woman with a peach-colored complexion.

"You must be the Broadway star diva Kyle's always talking about," she said as she came over, gave me a hug, and brushed her cheek against mine.

"What has Kyle been telling you, Ms. Benton? I'm so glad to finally meet you."

"Call me Peaches, darling. Peaches Gant. I never married Kyle's daddy," she said.

"Oh, I'm sorry," I said, bringing my hands to my mouth as to cover up my mistake.

"Don't be sorry, darling. I'm not. He was a piss-poor sorry-ass man. I'm not the least bit sorry. The best thing he ever gave me was the sperm that created Kyle," she laughed.

Now I knew where Kyle got his quick wit and sense of humor.

"Where would you like to go eat?"

"Don't matter to me. Just so long as it ain't fancy and no Indian food. Can't stand the stuff," Peaches said.

"How about soul food?"

"Oh yeah, I'm sure Peaches would like Sylvia's," Raymond interjected.

"Or I was also thinking about Copeland's," I said quickly, trying to ignore Raymond's suggestion. I hoped he didn't think he was going too.

"Where's Copeland's?" he asked.

I turned to face him, "Oh, it's uptown off Broadway."

I was doing just fine until I looked in the corner and saw Kyle's dressmaker's dummy wearing the wedding gown he had made for me. It looked like he'd finished it. My eyes were welling up when Kyle walked into the living room. He looked frail. I couldn't believe how much weight he had lost. He was wearing baggy corduroy pants and an ivory-colored turtleneck.

"Hey, Diva Detective. You couldn't think of a better way to get this nigger up here?" he joked as he walked slowly over to me and gave me a gentle embrace. It was like hugging his bones.

"Hey, baby," I said as I pulled him closer to me and whispered, "Don't embarrass me, bitch," with clenched teeth and frozen smile.

"Where is that other tramp?" Kyle asked.

"Oh, she had an audition. I left her a message to meet me up here," I said.

"Good, I want her to meet my mother," Kyle said.

I took a seat on the sofa and watched Raymond, Kyle, and Peaches interact warmly. Raymond had his large arms covering both Kyle and his mother. He was dressed wonderfully as usual. Starched white shirt and pleated trousers that fitted his body like a banana peel fit a banana.

Kyle seemed happy and I was glad he was not mad at me. I picked up the portable phone and dialed my number to see if I had any messages. There was a message from Dr. Huntley saying she had an opening and for me to call to arrange an appointment.

"So are you two joining us?" I asked, looking at Kyle and Raymond.

"Are we, Kyle?" Raymond asked.

"No, let the ladies go out. I mean the real ladies," Kyle giggled.

"Kyle, you're so crazy," I said.

"Ain't he a pistol?" Peaches piped in.

"Well, I guess maybe the next time," Raymond said, looking directly into my eyes. He was making me nervous. It was time to dash.

"Well, Peaches, you need a jacket. The wind is picking up," I said.

"Please, don't let her have more than two cocktails," Kyle said.

"Mind your own business," Peaches said.

"Well, you guys have fun. Raymond, it's great seeing you," I said.

"Same here, Nicole. Same here," he smiled.

I gave Kyle a hug and a kiss, but I just looked at Raymond. The first kiss was enough for one day. I gave him a wan smile and led Peaches out of the door and to our lunch date.

Over lunch I learned that Princess was her birth name, but she had been called Peaches for as long as she could remember. Peaches spent the majority of our lunch talking about Kyle. How smart he was as a little boy and how beautiful he was as a baby. She shared with me some things I knew about Kyle and some I didn't. How Kyle helped to support her and his ailing grandfather, something Kyle never mentioned. Not once during our entire conversation did she refer to the fact that Kyle was gay or dying from AIDS. There is nothing like a mother's love, I thought, as Peaches glowed while she talked about her son and my friend.

When I asked her where she got her nickname, she replied, "In south Jersey, everybody who wasn't dark skinned was called red and my grandmother didn't want people calling her grands red, so she started calling me Peaches because of my skin color and my cheeks. She said they looked like cling peaches."

I invited Peaches to go to the theater with me but she declined, saying she needed to give Ray a rest since Kyle could wear a normal person down.

As we were walking out of the restaurant I turned to Peaches and asked, "Peaches, how did you feel when you found out Kyle was gay?"

"What do you mean?"

"Well, were you upset?"

"No, I wasn't upset. I guess I always knew he was. . . . Well, people in my family would call him sweet or even sissy, but Kyle was always so confident of himself that he didn't let it bother him so neither did I."

"So it never bothered you?"

"How could it? He was my child. I was just glad he wasn't out blowing up things and stealing from people. If you're lucky enough to have your own children, you'll understand what I mean," Peaches said.

"So how are you holding up with this?"

"Oh, I'll be okay. Right now I'm just worrying about my baby boy," Peaches said softly. The taxi dropped Peaches off at the apartment and then sped down the West Side Highway to the theater. I'd had such a good time over lunch that I was now running about a half-hour late. I called Pierce and asked him to meet me at B. Smith's after the show.

Pierce was already seated at a booth near the door when I got there and he broke out into a huge grin and waved to get my attention. I was headed toward the booth when I suddenly paused and looked up at the bar. This was where I'd met Raymond. When I looked at the bar I saw attractive couples engaged in lively conversation enjoying the evening. Everything looked the same. The bartender was dressed in a white formal shirt with black bow tie. Ladies were sitting on bar stools as their men stood and gazed lovingly into their eyes, some with cigarettes in their hands and others with cocktail and wine glasses. I wondered what they were talking about. Were they married couples, just dating, or meeting for the first time? I suddenly longed for those times years ago, when Candance was alive and we were both so in love.

"Nicole, over here," Pierce called out breaking my moment.

"Hi, Pierce," I said as I gave him a quick brush on his chapped lips.

"What do you want to drink?"

"Just some hot tea."

"How is Kyle?" Pierce asked.

"It's hard to tell. He was all covered up," I said, recalling Kyle in the oversized turtleneck.

"So what are we going to do?" Pierce asked.

"About what?"

"Well, about us. That is why you called me, right?"

"Yes."

"Okay. Well, I've told you how sorry I am. You know I'm not a racist," Pierce said.

"Yes, Pierce, I think I know that, but your actions hurt me. That man could have been my father. As a matter of fact he reminded me of my father," I said as I sipped the hot tea.

"Well, Nicole, you've said things that could be considered racist. I think it just proves we're human," Pierce said as he picked at the salmon on his plate.

"What are you talking about?"

"Do you remember the time you bought your camcorder?"

"Yes."

"What did you tell me about the price?"

"What are you talking about?" I asked, wondering what point Pierce was trying to make.

"Remember you said, 'I got a great deal on it. I was able to 'jew' the guy down almost three hundred dollars.' Do you remember that?"

I didn't answer. So this was the point—that maybe both Pierce and I sheltered racist attitudes. I hadn't thought anything about the statement—I'd made it often, not only to Pierce but to other friends.

"Yes, Pierce, I do recall saying that. You're right, it was wrong for me to say something like that. Why didn't you correct me then?"

"Well, I knew you didn't mean any harm. Just like what I said in anger to the man in Harlem," Pierce said.

"Well, I know I took your statement more personally than maybe I should have. I never told you how my little brother used to tease me because I was so dark," I said.

"No you never did. Why?"

"I don't know."

"But I love your color. I think it's beautiful. Your beautiful skin color was the first thing I noticed," Pierce said.

"Is that why you think you're in love with me?"

"*Think* I'm in love, Nicole? I'm certain I'm in love with you," Pierce said in a very stern voice.

"Pierce, the race thing we could work out. We could even work out the religious part," I said as I picked up a bread stick from the basket sitting on the table.

"So what's the problem?"

Well, it was now or never. I had to tell Pierce how I felt, but I didn't want to hurt him. I must find a way to do it gingerly. I hated this feeling. Pierce motioned to the waiter to bring him another drink. Maybe I should order some wine.

"Can I have a glass of white wine?"

"Sure," the waiter said. "Is the house wine okay?"

"Yes."

"So, Nicole, what is the problem?" Pierce repeated.

"Pierce, I'm having second thoughts and before we go any further, I need to be sure," I announced.

"What's the matter, Nicole?"

The waiter brought my wine and I took a long gulp. I drank it as if it was strawberry Kool-Aid.

"I love you, Pierce, but I'm just not certain I love you enough. Maybe we need to take a break."

Pierce didn't say a word, he just slowly sipped his drink. I felt miserable; I hated the feeling of hurting someone just as much as I did being hurt.

"Is it because of what I said?" Pierce said as he gazed at me sternly.

"No, Pierce, I'm just finally being honest with myself."

"Well, let's talk about this. What can we do to change things?"

"Change things?"

"Yes, what can we do to change your feelings?"

"Do you think that's possible?"

"If we work at it."

"You don't think we've been working at it?"

"Not really."

"I don't know, Pierce. Maybe if we take a break . . ."

"A break?"

"Yes. I have a feeling Kyle is going to need me."

"But I need you too," Pierce said.

I looked at Pierce after his statement. There was something uncharacteristically insecure in the tone of his voice.

"Pierce, have you ever thought that maybe you're in love with me because of who you think I am?"

"What do you mean?"

"I know this sounds so typical, but maybe I'm some kind of fantasy for you."

"A fantasy?"

"Am I, Pierce?"

"Yes, you're beautiful. You'd be a fantasy for any man."

"Well, I don't want to be a fantasy for anyone. Pierce, there are many times when I don't feel beautiful or successful."

"Why?"

"Sometimes I think you want me to be somebody I can't be. Like all the Diahann Carroll references?"

"I thought you'd be flattered."

"Flattered. What if I said you looked like Kevin Costner?"

"I don't look anything like him."

"My point exactly. I'm not Diahann Carroll."

"I know that, Nicole. I'm in love with you not Diahann Carroll."

"Pierce, I wish I could say I'm in love with you. This is not easy for me."

His eyebrows met in the middle of his face and he stared at me without smiling and said, "Easy for you? Do you know how much I've invested in you?"

"Invested in me! What are you talking about, Pierce?"

"You know exactly what I'm talking about. Do you think I pulled strings and invested in a project that I may never make a single cent off because I didn't love you?"

I took the final gulp from my wineglass. Suddenly my head started to spin. Pierce's words and the rush of wine caused a sudden headache. Pierce looked aimlessly out of the window and then reached into his coat jacket and pulled out a cigar. He knew how much I disliked cigars. He looked around the table for matches and when he didn't see any he signaled for the waiter.

"Can I get some matches?"

"Sir, this is a nonsmoking establishment. You can't smoke in here," the waiter said.

"Fuck," Pierce said as he placed the cigar back into his jacket.

"Maybe you should take this back," I said as I slowly slipped the engagement ring off my finger and slid it to the middle of the table.

"No," Pierce said loudly. "I bought it for you. Keep it, Nicole."

"No, Pierce I think you should have it. Maybe I took it under the wrong circumstances," I said. I was starting to feel sick.

"Yeah, that way all the men out there will know you're available," Pierce said in a tone similar to the one he'd used when he'd made the investment statement. I guessed I was right; Pierce did view me as an investment or possession.

We sat in silence for about ten minutes, me back to sipping my now cold tea and Pierce absently playing with the spoon from the coffee he'd ordered but not touched. I decided that it was time for me to leave and started to gather up my things.

"Pierce, maybe we should take some time and then try to talk about this. I'm sorry but I'm not feeling well and I don't think we're going to get anywhere tonight."

Pierce didn't respond. When I got up from the table and made it clear that I was ready to go, Pierce said in a very short tone, "I'll hail you a cab."

"You don't have to do that," I said as I picked up my purse and moved toward the door. On Eighth Avenue as I held my hand up in the air to hail a taxi, an attractive, conservatively dressed black man came up to me and said, "Sister, I've been standing out here for ten minutes trying to hail a taxi. Will you help me? I'm up here visiting from Baton Rouge."

"Sure," I said, and just as quickly as the words came out of my mouth a taxi stopped; the man stepped in front of me and jumped into the taxi. Before he closed the door he looked at me and said, "Thanks a lot, miss, New York is so hard on a brother."

I smiled and hailed another taxi. One pulled up right behind the cab that was just driving off. As I got into the backseat, I remembered what the visitor had said and thought New York was hard on a sister too.

Twenty-five

Kyle had good days and bad days. There were times when I thought he'd live forever. He once joked, "I'm not leaving here until Diana Ross has another hit record." But slowly, as the weeks went by, it became obvious he would need more help. It was becoming clear that he wouldn't live forever. I wanted to spend twenty-four hours a day with Kyle, but he would have no part of it. He told me constantly to go out and enjoy New York City, but how could I, with my best friend confined to his bed and cluttered apartment?

Kyle's mother returned home, but she called every day to check on him. When she asked me how he was doing it was hard to give her an answer because Kyle never once complained. We spent our days indulging in nostalgia and talking about the future. Kyle had just a few goals. He said he wanted to live until his thirty-fifth birthday, which was December 28. So we'd begun making plans for a big Christmas and birthday bash.

Kyle's nightstand was filled with catalogs from department stores where he had charge accounts and he spent days ordering gifts for all of his family and friends whom he kept in contact with. He had a spiral notebook with the addresses and sizes of all his friends and relatives, the limits on his charge accounts, and stars by the accounts that included insurance that would pay the bills once he died. He was always trying to get me to order something for myself, but I couldn't. It just didn't seem right. So he ordered a lot of nice things for Janelle, Christopher, Nicole, and her friend Delaney. While Kyle was taking naps, I would try and keep up with clients and prospects over the phone. Gilliam was still paying me full salary so I tried to stay on top of things by phone or fax and made myself available whenever she had questions or needed clarification with sports jargon.

Nicole came over to Kyle's almost every other day, usually when I was back at my hotel making phone calls, changing clothes or working out. The exercise became a necessary release for the stress of caring for my friend. It was nice seeing Nicole so often. She was even more beautiful than I remembered. Her skin looked as smooth as a glass of chocolate milk, her abundant black hair pulled back to show off her beautiful oval face, her delicate ears and luminous brown eyes. The first time she saw me, Nicole's manner was very restrained and formal. She seemed preoccupied with something every time we were in a room together, so I didn't suggest the two of us getting together although the thought crossed my mind whenever I saw her. Besides, she was engaged to some guy and this was not the time to further confuse my life.

Nicole's friend Delaney was also very attractive, but she too seemed distant toward me. She didn't appear interested in my conversation. Had Nicole told her something unfavorable about me? Of course she had. But maybe I was taking Delaney's coolness the wrong way. I mean they were worried about Kyle just as much as I was. They both came and told him stories about what was going on in show business and brought over different music videos that hadn't been released yet for Kyle to look at. Most times when the two of them came over I felt left out so I would take long walks near Central Park or run errands, but whenever I came back into the apartment it seemed like a party had been going on.

Kyle had a knack for making ladies love him. I wasn't at a point in my life where I was comfortable with women knowing my sexuality just for the sake of knowing or conversation. I felt some women treated gay men differently from straight men, as if they were girlfriends, which I guess could be considered an honor since most women I knew treasured their girlfriends. But this was not the type of relationship I desired with most women. Janelle was the only woman with whom I'd developed such a comfort level, but there were even times I had to put her in check. We had come to a point where I was comfortable discussing my male dates or listening to her advice when it came to men. But I could never envision a day where I would feel the same way with Nicole.

I was still staying at the Paramount and the manager had moved me into a junior suite, which was a little bit larger than my prior cramped quarters. I just hoped American Express would continue to extend credit. I realized I should start to look for a sublet or consider moving in with Kyle. Maybe Nicole knew of something through her theater friends.

I spoke to Jared almost every day. He provided a great deal of support even though he was so far away. At the end of every conversation he said, "If you and Kyle need anything, just call and I'll be on the next flight."

Gilliam was supportive too. When I got to New York and realized the severity of Kyle's condition, I called and offered my resignation. Gilliam wouldn't hear of it and told me we'd discuss the partnership whenever I was back in the office full time. Gilliam said my daily phone calls and keeping up with my clients via phone and fax weren't causing any major problems and that she'd hired a law student to assist with research. She didn't flinch when I told her Kyle had AIDS; if she did I couldn't tell by her voice.

I don't know what I expected when I told people about Kyle's condition. I thought maybe they would inquire about his sexuality and mine as well. But this was not about me or what people thought of me. I guess maybe the heterosexual community had finally realized that this was not only a white gay man's disease. But I still felt the African-American community had a long way to go in the areas of education and support of minority AIDS patients. Kyle often mentioned that there were very few support groups run by African-Americans. I thought of all the black churches in New York City and wondered if they had support groups for their members afflicted with this dread disease.

All the support Kyle received outside of family and friends came from the white gay community. The Gay Men's Health Crisis called weekly to check to see if Kyle needed anything and gave Kyle free tickets to Broadway shows when he was up to it. Since I had been in New York we had seen *Five Guys Named Moe* and *Two Trains Running*. I thought it was kind of funny that they always gave Kyle tickets to black shows, but that's what he wanted to see anyway. Besides, why look a gift horse in the mouth? I wanted to see either the show Nicole was in, or *Miss Saigon*, but Kyle had seen them both. I was really waiting for a personal invitation from Nicole for *Jelly's Last Jam*.

There were times when I enjoyed being back in New York, but I became sad when I thought of New York without Kyle. He was always encouraging me to go out and have fun . . . to go down to the Village or call some of my old friends, but I protested. I was not in New York to socialize. So my life revolved around going between the Paramount and Kyle's and the local establishments in my old neighborhood.

My days with Kyle were as different as the colorful leaves that painted Manhattan. I sometimes stopped at the McDonald's and got a couple of Egg McMuffins and coffee. Kyle's appetite wasn't that good but I think he enjoyed the thought of just wishing out loud for different foods, knowing that between Nicole and myself, he would get it. It didn't matter if he only took one bite. Most days though, we just sat in his bedroom and talked. Kyle shared stories that were alternately uproarious and heartbreaking. He'd managed to have an active sex life up until the end of August, so he had funny stories about his conquests. He assured me all of his rendezvous were safe-sex encounters. Sometimes Kyle talked about his childhood, about how close he and his mother were. One day he spent alot of time remembering the day his father left.

"Do you think about him, Kyle?" I asked after the story.

"Sometimes," Kyle said lightly.

"When was the last time you saw or heard from him?"

"When I was nine. He came to my birthday party."

"Is he still alive?"

"I think so. I really don't know."

"Did you ever think about trying to get in touch with him?"

"No!" Kyle said sharply.

Kyle and I began to talk about more pleasant things, like the prospect of Janelle and Christopher coming up and the big Christmas birthday party we were planning when suddenly Kyle looked at me with big weary eyes and said, "Ray, do you think you could find him?"

"Find who?" I asked.

"My father. Do you think you can help me find him?" Kyle repeated.

"Is that what you want?"

"Why do you think I asked? You know you're one dumb bitch," Kyle said, trying not to appear serious.

"If that's what you want, then consider it done," I said confidently, knowing deep down I didn't have a clue what to do next.

When I got back to the hotel that evening, I became depressed. How was I going to find Kyle's father? The only information Kyle had was his full name, where he was born, and the last place he had lived. I

started to call Kyle's mother to see if she had any information that
could assist my search, but I thought I should clear it with Kyle first.
Instead, I went to the hotel gym, worked out, and then came up to my
suite to take a hot shower. I was looking over the room service menu
when the phone rang.

"Hello."

"Ray? What's going on, dude?"

"Jared. You the man. It's great hearing your voice," I said.

"What? I've been calling you every day. You didn't think I'd call?"
Jared asked.

"No, that's not it. I just need to talk," I said quietly.

"Well, talk," Jared said.

I told Jared about Kyle's request and how I didn't know what to do.
He assured me Kyle would be thankful for anything I did but I
shouldn't put pressure on myself. Jared went on to tell me that he'd
sent via overnight delivery the mail he'd picked up from my home and
office and told me some guy named Trent called. He had told Jared to
tell me that Miller was doing okay and to give him a call some time.

"Who is Miller?" Jared asked.

"Oh, that's the kid I was telling you about with my fraternity," I
said.

"Oh yes, another guy called while I was there, but he didn't want to
leave a message. In fact he was really rude," Jared said.

"Oh, I wonder who that could be?" I asked, knowing full well it was
Basil.

"Ray. I've got a plan. I'll help you find Kyle's father," Jared said.

"What? How are you going to do that?" I questioned.

"Oh, I have plenty of connections through the Clinton staff and the
congressman's office. What's his name?" Jared asked.

I gave Jared the information Kyle had shared with me. Jared asked if
it was okay if he called Kyle if he had any more questions and I assured
him Kyle would love to talk with him. While I listened to Jared talk
about the places he planned to check, I thought about how I wished
Jared could meet Kyle. But that would be impossible. Kyle was really
self-conscious about his current physical appearance and allowed only
close friends and family to see him.

When Jared was getting ready to say good night, he suggested I go
out and get something to eat.

"Leave that hotel and go out and have yourself a nice dinner," Jared
said.

"Yeah, I think you're right," I said.

"Ray?"

"Yes."

"Can I ask you something?" There was a serious tone in his voice and question.

"Sure, Jared. No more secrets," I said.

"You're okay, right? I mean you've been tested?"

"Yes, Jared, I'm fine. Just a little bit tired right now, but I'm going to follow your advice and get out of this room."

"Can I ask you something else?" Jared's tone remained serious.

"Sure, Jared. What?"

"I want to meet Kyle," Jared said.

"You want to meet Kyle?"

"Yes. I'll fly to New York when you say it's okay," Jared said. "You've talked about him so much and he really sounds like a special person. I'd like the chance to meet him."

"I don't know, Jared. Kyle's not seeing a lot of people. It's basically just been family and a few close friends," I said.

"Will you ask him?"

I paused, pondering Jared's question.

"Ray?"

"Yeah, I'm still here."

"So, what do you think?"

"I think it's a great idea. I'll ask him."

"Great! I've got to come up to D.C., for a meeting and I could fly to New York first."

"Okay, I'll let you know after I've talked with Kyle."

"So you promise me you'll go out and get something to eat and I'll talk with you tomorrow," Jared said.

"I will, my brother. Stay strong."

When I hung up the phone, I stood in the middle of the hotel bedroom and just smiled to myself. Then I took my arms and folded them around my chest as if I was giving myself a hug. Jared's questions and concern about Kyle were just the warm embrace I needed tonight.

I was on my way to the Village when I jumped into the taxi, but when we came to the corner of Forty-sixth and Broadway I suddenly changed my mind and instructed the cab driver to take me to Kyle's instead. I wanted to see how he felt about meeting Jared and I wanted to share the news about Jared's offer to search for his father.

I arrived at Kyle's and took the stairs instead of the elevator. I reached his apartment a little bit out of breath. I rang the buzzer a couple of times, out of courtesy, and then slipped my key in the lock and went in.

"Kyle," I called out. "It's me."

"Ray?" I heard Kyle call from the bedroom. "Don't come in here," he said faintly. But it was too late. I walked into Kyle's bedroom and I saw the anxious look on his face and Kyle's ailing body hooked up to a machine. He didn't have on a shirt and his frail body was covered with large, purplish black spots. It was the first time I was face to face with AIDS and it looked horrible to me.

Kyle quickly reached for his robe, trying to cover himself up. "Get out of here!" he yelled. "What the fuck are you doing back here?"

"Kyle. I'm sorry," I said as I walked toward him. He was sitting on the edge of the bed with the machine close by.

"What's this, Kyle? What's going on?"

"It's a part of my treatment," he said shyly. "I didn't want you to see me like this."

"Like what, Kyle?"

"Like this, Ray. Look at me!"

"You look fine, buddy," I lied, my body numb from the shock of the sores covering Kyle's body. I reached and helped him put on his robe and moved the contraption away from his bed. I looked at the bottle at the top of the strange-looking device and saw the word *chemotherapy*.

"Kyle, why didn't you let me help you with this treatment?"

"I can do it myself. I can do it myself!" Kyle yelled. "I don't need you for every damn thing. Why don't you carry your yellow ass back to Atlanta?" he screamed.

I looked at Kyle and then I turned to face the window. If tears were forming in my eyes he must not see them. I could see our faint reflections in the window as a light drizzle was now falling from the gray sky. I bit down hard on my lips and looked outside at the streets, watching car headlights slice through the darkness. I silently counted five red cars from the window and then I turned and faced Kyle.

"Are you okay now? Are you glad you got that out?"

Kyle was positioned upright in his bed now with his robe and spread covering him up.

"Yes, I'm okay. Are you?" Kyle asked softly.

"I'm fine. I've got something I want to ask you."

"What?"

"You feel like some company?"

"Company? Who? Not any of those kids from the bar."

"Jared. He's coming up to New York on business and he wants to meet you. He thinks he can find your father," I said.

"You sure he wants to meet me?" Kyle asked.

"Yes, I think he needs to talk with you to help with the search," I lied.

"Let me think about it. It will probably be okay," Kyle said.

"Kyle?"

"Yes, Raymond."

"Can I ask you something?"

"Sure, baby boy."

Baby boy. He hadn't called me that in years.

"Are you scared, Kyle?" I asked in as calm a voice as I could manage.

"No, baby. I'm not scared. I'm just tired," Kyle said.

Kyle slowly shifted his body on the bed and lay there with his vulnerable brown eyes open and very still, looking at me with a gentle smile. A moment later he was asleep.

I walked into the living room and gazed out of the window. I could see storm clouds building in the gray sky and I prayed a powerful rain would fall. Since I couldn't cry, maybe the sky would.

Twenty-six

*A*lmost every other day I received a package from Victoria's Secret or Bloomingdale's, courtesy of Kyle's generosity. I didn't feel quite right accepting the gifts, but Delaney said it made him feel good so I didn't say anything. If I didn't really love the gifts so much I probably would have given the stuff to a homeless shelter, so to make myself feel a little better about my good fortune I packed up a box of old clothes and donated them to the Salvation Army.

Delaney and I spent as much time with Kyle as he or Raymond would allow. He was watching over Kyle like a high-priced bodyguard.

Whenever we talked, it was about Kyle, because I didn't dare delve into his private life. I wondered if he was dating somebody in Atlanta and, if so, how he—or she—felt about his being away. I overheard Ray and Kyle mention a guy named Jared, so I assumed that's whom he was seeing. Knowing Raymond, I thought he probably had a woman on the side also.

Raymond was always polite but distant to Delaney and me; he always smiled with his usual courtesy and gave me a soap-opera-type kiss on the cheek.

Delaney didn't talk a lot about Kyle's illness. I presumed this was the first time someone close to her had been this sick. She didn't have much to say about Raymond either. When I asked her what she thought of him, she replied, "He's okay if you like that butch, pretty-boy type." I hadn't talked with Pierce since the night I tried to give him back the ring. I didn't want to admit it, but I missed the attention. Since Pierce wasn't around, Delaney and I spent more time together. We got our nails done, caught a movie matinee, and spent days shopping in midtown. At one sample sale we each ended up buying Kyle pajamas, mine were white linen and Delaney's navy blue silk with white trimming. We'd rushed over to the apartment with our presents and were each clamoring for him to try ours on first when he calmly asked us to wait in the living room. When he called us back we found him wearing the top to the pajamas I bought and the bottom to Delaney's pair. We all had a good laugh.

Whenever I went to Kyle's I'd say a silent prayer as I entered the building and try to think of happy times. Kyle had a rule about no sad time, and definitely no tears. This was hard for me, because I seemed to cry all the time. I cried when I was happy, when I was sad, and sometimes when I realized how blessed I was. So, whenever I felt tears coming on I quickly excused myself and went to another room until the sadness passed.

When Candance died, I didn't know a lot about AIDS. It hit her so hard and quick that there was little time for me to get AIDS educated. But with Kyle, I tried to find out as much as I could about the type of cancer he had and its treatment. I was always persistent about Kyle taking his medications. I also noticed the different attitudes people had about the disease. When Candance died I received a lot of sympathy and compassion from my family and close friends. But when I shared Kyle's illness with the same close friends and family, namely my mother, the sympathy wasn't there once they found out he was gay. The assumption seemed to be that he was getting what he deserved. No one deserved this.

I tried on occasion to talk with Kyle about giving his life to the Lord, but he only bristled and said, "I've got that under control. I have a prayer cloth from Reverend Ike," he'd joke. Sometimes he let me read Bible scriptures to him, but mostly he wanted to hear inspirational poems by Maya Angelou or Langston Hughes. I ordered him a subscription of the *Daily Word* and he thanked me, but I doubt if he ever read it.

His mother, Peaches, seemed to be religious. She often quoted Scripture whenever she got a little tipsy, which was quite often. I think she drank a lot to cover up her pain and to give the appearance of being strong and in control. Whenever she came to New York she encouraged me to read the Bible to Kyle and when he protested she said, "Then read it to me, Nicole, read it to me."

I questioned Kyle about whether or not he'd practiced safe sex—I couldn't recall him every having a shortage of suitors, even though he never seemed serious about any of them—and he assured me he had for years. I knew other gay men and it seemed they too had short-term relationships but so did a lot of the black women I knew. Gay men were always breaking up with someone and starting new relationships right away. I guess it was even more difficult for them than it was for black women to find permanent mates. And the specter of AIDS probably didn't help any.

It was a bright fall day and there was a slight chill in the air, but all of the Upper West Side was bathed in a clear soft sunlight. I stopped at a bakery to get a couple of muffins and cookies for Kyle before heading to his apartment.

I was pleased Grady was no longer lying to me and was allowing me to go right up to Kyle's apartment. Whenever I came to the door I took a deep breath because I never knew who was going to answer the door. Today it was Raymond.

"Raymond. How is Kyle? How are you doing?" I asked as we performed our normal fake smile and cheek kiss. Or was he faking it? Maybe I was just being a bitch. I would never classify Raymond as a fake. Maybe awkward was a better word to describe our greeting.

"Oh, he's doing okay. How are you?"

"I'm fine," I responded as I headed toward Kyle's bedroom, avoiding Ray's eyes.

"Hey, Miss Thingamajig. Come on in here," Kyle said. He was sitting up in bed and sewing something.

"How are you doing, baby?" I asked as I kissed Kyle on his forehead.

"I'm doing good. What's the 4-1-1 and where is Delaney?" he asked.

"She has an audition, but she will be up later," I said.

"Did you talk to Ray?"

"Oh, we spoke," I said quietly.

"Chile. What is wrong with you two? Y'all act like you don't even know each other," Kyle chided.

"Oh no, it's not like that. It's just when I come up here, I come to see you. Oh, I have some news for you," I said, trying to change the subject.

"What?" Kyle asked with excitement in his voice.

"I broke up with Pierce," I said.

"You did what? When, chirl?"

"Early in the week. But he won't take the ring back," I added.

"Chile, then don't push him. That big rock will make a nice little necklace," Kyle said.

"No, I'm going to give it back to him," I said.

"Miss Thang, don't be no fool. Keep the ring. You've earned it, darling." Kyle said. "Are you doing okay?"

"I'm doing fine."

"Kyle?" Raymond said as he walked into the room. He startled me.

"Yeah, Ray?"

"I'm going to the store. Do you need anything?"

"Naw, I'm fine," Kyle said.

"Nicole, can I get you something?" Raymond asked.

"No, Raymond, thanks for asking," I said politely.

"Okay. How long are you going to be here?" Raymond asked.

Before I could answer Kyle giggled and said, "I, at least, plan to be here until you get back."

"I'm glad, Kyle, but I was talking to the beautiful lady," Raymond said, flashing that killer smile.

I didn't say anything, I just stared at him. He had on a bleached-out sweatshirt and torn jeans. I didn't ever recall him being so unkempt.

"Well, Miss Nicole, answer the man," Kyle said, looking at me.

"Oh, Ray, I'll be here when you get back," I said.

"Okay. Great," he said, and turned toward the doorway.

"Raymond," I called out.

"Yes, Nicole?" He lowered his voice in a seductive tone.

"Well, I was wondering . . . I mean, would you like to come see the show the next time I go on? I mean, I could get you tickets," I said.

He raised his eyebrows and stared at me for a moment. The silence in the room was loud. I could hear my heart beating fast. What was he waiting for? I was getting ready to take back the invitation when he finally spoke.

"Sure, Nicole. I would love that," he said. His smile was warm and reassuring, as if he realized how hard it was for me to invite him to the play. I wondered if he recalled my inviting him to *Dreamgirls* so many years ago?

As Raymond walked out of the room, Kyle looked at me, smiled, leaned over, and whispered in my ears, "You go, girl."

I was slightly startled when I walked out of the stage door and almost bumped into Raymond. I was busy putting my scarf in place around my jacket collar when he called out my name. "Raymond," I said, looking directly at him with a surprised look. His face was relaxed and friendly. "What are you doing here?"

"Well, I needed to talk with you about Kyle's party. Do you have plans? Could we maybe go and have a late supper?" he asked.

"Sure. I don't have plans. I was just going to catch a taxi home. How is JR's?"

"Sounds great," Raymond said as he helped me tuck in my scarf. I felt his hands gently touch the back of my neck. Some of the female cast members stopped in their tracks as they came out of the theater and saw me with him.

"Did you see the show?" I asked as we started walking toward Eighth Avenue and JR's.

"No, I just walked up here from the hotel. I want to wait to see you in it," he smiled.

As we walked silently down the busy streets, I took in the sounds of the city. The night air felt cool on my face, but my body was warm and tingling.

Raymond pushed open the huge walnut door with one hand and a waitress promptly greeted us and offered a table in the corner near the jukebox.

"So what do you feel like?" Raymond asked.

"Well, I'm not really hungry. I think I'll just have some fries and a salad," I said, looking over the mini daily menu that was on the table.

"It's been a long time since I've been in this place," Raymond said as he looked around the restaurant.

"Yeah. It's always been one of my favorite places."

The waitress came over and took our drink orders. Raymond got up and walked over to the nearby jukebox. He was dressed neatly, in black pants and a creamy beige polo sweater. This was the type of attire I was used to seeing him in. He reached into his pocket, dropped some coins in the box, pushed several buttons, and then returned to his seat facing me. Smiling, he said, "It's good seeing you, Nicole. You're still one of the most beautiful women I've ever laid my eyes on."

"Thanks, Raymond. It's good seeing you. Kyle is very lucky to have a friend like you." I blushed.

"No, I'm the lucky one."

"So how are you really handling it?" I quizzed.

"It's hard to say. I don't think it's really hit me. Besides it's not about me and how I feel. This is about Kyle and how he feels," Raymond said as he circled his fingers around the top of the water glass. I noticed a thin gold chain gleaming alongside his gold watch. "I'm trying to do everything possible to make his life happy," he added.

After ordering our food, we began to talk about the party. Raymond, always very orderly, went over the things he had in mind. He wanted to make sure all Kyle's family members could make it and told me he was hoping his friend could find Kyle's father. We decided to have the party in the game room in Kyle's building. Ray wanted to have it at the Paramount Hotel, but since Kyle's energy level changed from day to day, we agreed it would be better to have it at the apartment building. He asked me if there was anyone special that I want to invite and when I said no, he asked me about the person I was engaged to.

"Oh, didn't Kyle tell you? I've broken that off," I said, suppressing a smile.

"Oh, I'm sorry to hear that," Raymond said.

"I think maybe it's for the best," I responded. We both let it drop.

Our food was served and Raymond folded the napkin he was using to jot down notes. I realized talking with Raymond seemed like old times.

"So who are *you* dating, Raymond?"

"Oh, I'm not dating anyone," he said quickly.

I was disappointed because I wanted to know if he was going to mention a man's or a woman's name. He talked about his family and how close he and his father had become and said that his little brother was away at prep school right outside of Boston. Raymond said he wasn't going home for Thanksgiving and he was thinking about having his little brother meet him in New York. He said he really wanted me to meet Kirby and maybe I could join them for a night on the town.

I told him I would love to meet his brother, but I would have to check my schedule since Renee was talking about taking off a couple of weeks around then. The rumor mill at the show had Renee starring in an independent film, which was being shot in Jamaica, but she hadn't mentioned it to me. Whatever the reason, I was happy because it looked like I was going to be performing more during the holiday season. I told Raymond about the cabaret show that some of my friends were doing for AIDS and he appeared really excited.

"Then I'll have quite a few chances to hear that wonderful voice," he said.

I didn't respond as I toyed with the pyramid of french fries facing me. I thought what a wonderful man Raymond was, with the one big exception. No woman would ever have him completely. I wanted to ask Raymond where he was in his personal life. We hadn't talked in depth since I'd called him in Birmingham years before. In a letter I wrote him after Candance's death I told him I was interested in a relationship with him only if he could assure me he would never be involved with another man as long as he lived. And I demanded the truth along with a firm commitment. His lack of response told me he couldn't make that type of promise.

"I guess Kyle's illness puts a kink in your perfect-world theory," I said after we had both given ample attention to our food.

"Yes, it does," Raymond said, looking straight at me. There seemed to be a sadness in his eyes as his facial expression softened.

"I keep hoping I'll pick up the paper and they will have found a cure," he said. "This has got to end."

"Yes, I know how you feel. I've lost a lot of friends since Candance. None as close as Candance, until now."

Raymond asked how Candance's parents were doing and I told him they were involved in a couple of AIDS charities. He also expressed his surprise that Kyle and I had become such good friends. He said he was selfishly happy about it because he was always able to hear how great I was doing through Kyle. I started to tell him I felt the same way but I didn't. Instead I asked him if he ever heard from Kelvin, Candance's husband.

"No, I haven't talked to him since Candance died," he said mournfully. Then he added he'd heard Kelvin remarried.

"He what?" I shouted.

"Nicole, calm down. I didn't mean to upset you," Raymond said.

"How could he?" I asked. "Does this woman know about Candance?"

"I just heard about it, Nicole. I'm not even certain it's true. Maybe they were talking about Candance. It could have been old information. Doesn't he keep in contact with her parents?"

"No. Candance's mother wanted to, but her father was definitely opposed to it," I said.

"Nicole, why the reaction?" Raymond asked with a careful voice.

"Oh, I just get upset every time I think about men like Kelvin and . . ." I paused and took a sip of my coffee. A long sip.

"And men like me?" Raymond questioned as though he knew what I was going to say.

"That's not what I said."

"But that's how you feel. Right, Nicole?"

"Let's change the subject," I said.

"It's not going to change the way you feel, Nicole," Raymond said firmly.

"At times I don't know how I feel. You hurt me a great deal, Raymond. It still lingers with me," I said softly.

"I know, Nicole, and I'm sorry. If there was any way I could change what happened I would, but it has helped me. I know it sounds crazy after hurting you so, but I learned so much about myself and how to treat others," he said.

"How?" I asked blankly.

Raymond told me how the situation with Candance, Kelvin, and me taught him always to tell the truth up front in relationships. He said it had prevented some relationships with women he was interested in dating but some women really seemed to appreciate the truth. He laughed and said they weren't necessarily interested in going to bed, but they respected him for his honesty. He added that the look on my face in the hospital so many years ago had never left his mind; it was what had made him realize what pain his secrets had caused. He vowed to change, so no woman he was with would ever have to pay the price Candance had. I wanted to ask him if he was saying Kelvin was HIV positive, but I didn't. I still believed men both gay and straight shared a fierce loyalty to each other.

Raymond ended his confession by saying he prayed that one day we could have a new relationship, one based on truth. When I heard him say the word prayer, I asked him if he went to church in Atlanta. He said he'd recently gone with his boss Gilliam, and he mentioned how much I would enjoy the church and meeting her.

As Raymond prepared to pay the check he reached over and touched my hand, and while stroking it, looked into my eyes and smiled. His bushy eyebrows met in the middle of his face and he continued to stare at me. "Nicole," he said, "if there was any way I could rewrite our history and the pain I caused you I would do it in a heartbeat. Do you know that?"

"Yes, Raymond, I do." For the first time I think I understood the pain our breakup had caused him.

We walked out of the restaurant and across the street to his hotel. He had the doorman hail me a taxi. As we stood in front of the hotel Raymond leaned over and delicately kissed me on the lips. It still wasn't a romantic kiss, just more of a heartfelt thank-you.

Twenty-seven

*A*n obedient fog parted, allowing a blue sky to preside over an early Saturday morning coolness. It was a beautiful day, so I decided to walk to Kyle's apartment instead of my usual taxi or subway ride. The long peaceful walk up Eighth Avenue and then over to Broadway was one of the things I missed about New York. I stopped and looked in the windows of shops and read headlines from the newsstands along the stretch that led to the Upper West Side.

While I was looking into a store window a frail black man walked up beside me and smiled. His face looked familiar but I didn't know where I knew him from.

"Raymond? You're Raymond Tyler, aren't you?"

"Yes," I responded, noticing his badly blotched face. The blotches looked like the ones Kyle hoped I hadn't noticed on him.

"Lester Davis. I met you at the Nickel Bar years ago. Remember I'm from Greenwood, Mississippi? I went to Ole Miss and I used to tease you about Alabama."

"Yes, Lester, of course. I didn't recognize you right away," I said before it was too late. It was at times like this I wished for a trap door.

"Yes, I've lost a little weight and, yes, I have AIDS."

"Oh, Lester, I'm sorry to hear that."

"Thank you, but I'm cool with it. How is Kyle doing? I hear he's sick too."

"I'm on my way to his apartment right now. He's hanging in there. You went to NYU Film School, didn't you?"

"Yes. Matter of fact I'm in the process of making a short film on my last days," he said with pride.

"Are you going back to Mississippi?"

"No, my parents aren't dealing with this very well. Maybe they will see the film."

I just stood there looking at Lester hoping the right words would roll from my mouth.

"Well, Raymond, it's good seeing you. Please give Kyle my best."

"I will, Lester. You stay strong," I said as I reached over and hugged him tightly. I watched dumbfounded as he walked away from the store window and disappeared from sight. Suddenly the handsome face of a healthy Lester from so many years before flashed in my mind.

The past week had been a busy and trying one. I had surprised Nicole by showing up unexpectedly one night at the theater and talked her into going for a late supper under the guise of planning Kyle's Christmas/birthday party. It was an enjoyable dinner and it was wonderful just being in her company. I found out she was no longer engaged but she didn't go into great details. The dinner with Nicole also made me realize more clearly the pain our breakup caused her. I knew there must be some anger lingering. I tried to point out that her letter left little room for me to try and salvage our relationship. Her request that I promise to never sleep with another man was something I knew deep down I could never live up to. It wasn't the being faithful that was hard to commit to, but denying my desire for men would have been impossible.

Yes, I might have tried if we were married, because I would have honored my vows. I just don't think she understood fully the situation I found myself in. I loved her deeply, and I think a part of me still loves her, but my desires for men weren't, and aren't going to disappear. I had to face the truth of my desires just as people like Lester and Kyle faced their illness. I think, in the long run, removing myself from her life was the best thing I could have done.

During my time of self-doubt, I believed Nicole deserved someone who could love her without reservation. I knew it was hard for black women to find that type of love, especially if they were doing something with their lives, like Nicole. Maybe that's why she had turned to a white guy. I was seeing more and more attractive black women dating white men and I wondered if men like myself were the cause? I also wondered why successful and most times attractive black gay men in search of long-term relationships turned to white men.

Did these women not understand the pressure black men, gay or straight, were under constantly on a day-to-day basis? Maybe white men didn't bring extra baggage into relationships. I mean, why should they? White men had been given all the power in this society, and when they weren't, they took it. A black man trying to do the same thing was considered a major threat and was dealt with accordingly. Black gay men also encountered the fear of rejection from their own community, if not from their immediate family then certainly from the African-American family as a whole.

Kyle had said earlier in the week that now when he did certain things he did them as though it was the last time . . . the last time he would trick the phone company with one of his rubber checks, go to a certain restaurant for a favorite food, go to a club, or hear a particular song. All of this was really just Kyle getting his life in order, and as hard as it was for me, I assisted him. He asked me to administer his estate, which much to my surprise was quite substantial. Being practical was never one of Kyle's traits, or so I had thought. He had six life insurance policies ranging in value from ten thousand dollars to ninety-nine thousand. When I asked him why he didn't just get one policy equaling the amount of all six combined, he explained how most insurance companies made you take the AIDS test if you were a single male and requested insurance in excess of one hundred thousand dollars. So he said he signed up with every insurance company that accepted him when he looked healthy. Kyle had wanted to make sure his mother was well taken care of. One policy was earmarked specifically for a special charity that he said he would explain later.

Kyle also took the time to write personal notes to several people he had been involved with sexually, informing them of his illness and strongly suggesting they get tested. One thing I didn't do, but wanted to, was ask Kyle if he had any idea whom he got the disease from. Kyle led an active sex life, but I knew you could catch this disease with just one encounter. Even though I thought Kyle might be willing to speculate, the question was insensitive. It would be hard anyway to go back and try and relive those years of free love that existed in New York in the early eighties.

Kyle talked about the loneliness the disease brought to him and how people with AIDS were often deserted by their friends. He had been involved with a group called Body Positive for the past two years. He said the sad thing was that so many of these men were alone when they left the meeting and he felt blessed by the fact he had Nicole, Delaney, me, and a mother who offered unconditional love. I was surprised, when I waited in the lobby for Kyle after a meeting, to see so many healthy-looking men come out of the room. I guess I thought they would all look sickly and thin. It was during these times I realized how little I knew about the differences in being HIV positive and having full-blown AIDS.

One of the things that distressed Kyle most was how he was treated by other black gays once the rumors of his illness spread. He talked of the feelings of isolation he felt when he went to the Village and to the bars, all places where he'd spent some of the most enjoyable times of his life. He shared with me his experiences on his visit home about a year ago while he was still healthy, to break the news to his mother. He said at first Peaches thought he was playing a cruel joke, but when she realized he wasn't she'd broken out into uncontrollable sobbing. It was the first time I saw tears form in Kyle's eyes, but they never fell. Kyle was strong that way, never letting anybody know how he really felt. He said outside of his mother, and maybe the Body Positive group, no one else knew. No one but him and God.

There wasn't going to be a funeral for Kyle Alexander Benton. He made me promise I would prevent it. He said he knew his mother wanted one and she would get pressure from other family members, but he was adamant about being cremated right away. "If you must do something, throw a party and talk about the good times," he said. Kyle went on to tell me they would give me a lot of grief but I had to be strong and put my foot down. "I don't want anyone to see me like this, Ray. This is the only promise you must keep. Don't let them do it," Kyle said. I suggested a closed casket and Kyle gave me a firm no, and made me promise again that I would have him cremated.

"You know how we black folks act at funerals and I ain't having it!"

When Kyle started to talk about wills and what he wanted to happen when he died, I told him new cures were coming out every day and he might just outlive us all. Kyle replied, "Yes, if I believed in magic, which I don't."

It was hard to enjoy New York and the magical place it could be in the fall with all the people and activities. I missed Atlanta and the people at work and, of course, I missed Jared. He told me about all the college football games he was going to and how much fun he was having working for the Clinton campaign. He called the night of the election telling me what a wonderful victory party they had given and how he might be in line for a position in Washington. I thought that would be cool if I was living in New York, but not if I returned to

Atlanta. He told me not to make any plans for the week of January 17 because we were going to Washington, D.C., to party with the new Administration. I shared with him the pain and joy Kyle and I had as Kyle got up from his bed to go cast his vote for Bill Clinton. I had mailed my absentee ballot in weeks before. When Kyle came out of the voting booth he looked at me, grimaced, pretended to smile, and said, "Well, that's the last white man I'm going to vote for for president. Maybe in my next life I can vote for a black man or woman."

Kyle was up and sewing like a madman when I walked into the apartment. He was dressed in a bright red turtleneck sweater and jeans. Kyle always wore turtleneck sweaters when he went out to cover up the sores the Kaposis sarcoma cancer caused around his neck. Kyle said his biggest fear was that the cancer would spread to his face. He still took the time to give himself a weekly facial—every appearance was a personal appearance. So I'd ordered turtlenecks in several different colors for Kyle to wear to all the activities we planned.

"What's up, Ray?" Kyle asked cheerfully as I walked in and gave him a hug and a kiss on the forehead. I walked into the kitchen following the smell of coffee and called back to Kyle, "Nothing. What are you working on?"

"Nicole's backup wedding gown," he said as he pulled some pins from his mouth.

"But she told me she broke off her engagement," I said.

"Yes, she broke off that one. But the diva is going to get married one day," Kyle said confidently.

"Oh, you sound certain of that," I said.

"Oh yes. Once I get assigned to my angel troop up in heaven. I'm going to send somebody for her," Kyle said calmly.

"What about me?" I asked, trying to keep the mood lighthearted.

"Oh, I'll send somebody for you. What do you what me to send? A man or a woman?" Kyle quizzed as he formed a deliberate smile.

I didn't answer right away and Kyle put down the fabric and just looked at me with a puzzled look. Then he stood up, put his hands on his hips, and sighed. "Well, Mr. Tyler. What's it going to be? A man or a woman?"

I smiled at Kyle's question.

"Send me somebody who loves me," I answered quietly. "Just make sure they love me."

Saturday was a good day for Kyle. His mother was coming back from Jersey later that evening and he was feeling well enough to go out. We decided to go to the Village, something I hadn't done since returning to New York. As we walked out of Kyle's apartment, Grady gave us both a big grin as he got a taxi for us. "It's good to see you up and about, Mr. Benton," he said.

"Thanks, Grady. I won't forget you at Christmas," Kyle said.

The taxi sped through the city. It was like old times, with Kyle and me in the backseat, excited at the prospect of what an evening in the Village might bring. I asked Kyle if he felt like walking a little and when he said yes, I instructed the driver to let us off on Christopher and Bleecker.

The Village was packed with people filling the sidewalks, eating in small cafés, and doing all the things that made the Village a place like no other. On this Saturday night there wasn't a hint that this community had been devastated by AIDS. From the goings-on in the bars and the people on the streets, you could see sex and romance were still alive and well in the Village. The moon was nearly full and hung over the Village like a Christmas tree bulb. It was still very much a magical place where people of different colors, genders, and backgrounds could feel at home. Tranquil and safe.

Kyle and I started to walk toward Keller's and the Pier, but Kyle said he felt like something hot and sweet. At first I was certain he was talking about a man, but he quickly corrected me and informed me he was talking about hot cocoa and dessert. I smiled at my misunderstanding. He wanted to go to a place on Hudson Street that specialized in different types of coffees and rich and fattening desserts.

I had never been to Café Sha Sha. When you walked in, the place reminded you of an old-fashioned bakery, with a double-decker case full of beautiful cakes and pies. A hostess led us up a small flight of stairs to a covered patio in the back. The place was packed with mostly gay white male couples, and the music of K.D. Lang surged from strategically placed speakers. Kyle and I ordered hot chocolate and German chocolate cake.

While we waited for our treats, Kyle relaxed in his chair and looked at me, smiling. "Isn't this nice?" he said.

"Yeah, this is a nice place. How did you find it?"

"Oh, a guy I was dating used to bring me here," Kyle said.

"So, you were mellowing out in your old age," I teased.

"Oh, he was a much older guy who couldn't stand the bars, so I would get him to bring me down here, and after a nice long conversation, I would put him in a taxi and dash over to Keller's or Two Potato."

Thoughts of the old Kyle made me smile. "Kyle, would this be easier if you were in love?" I asked him.

"I am in love. In love with you, JJ, Nicole, Delaney, Christopher," Kyle said lightly.

"Yeah, I know, but somebody special?"

"Ray, I don't have any qualms about how I've lived my life. I had a grand time. I learned early on that the kids are too fickle to trust your feelings with, so I've relied on friends for my emotional support."

"Yeah, I guess you're right," I moaned.

"You know I'm right," Kyle said.

As we sipped our hot chocolate we talked about the difficulty of relationships among black gay men as well as the problems black women have. Kyle agreed with me that the day-to-day stresses we faced rolled over into our relationships, making their survival difficult. "We don't have any models to follow," Kyle said.

We laughed and remarked about JJ being the only one of us who was happy in a strong and positive relationship.

"Who would have thought that gutter girl would end up the lucky one?" Kyle laughed.

"When is JJ coming up?" I asked.

"I don't think she is. She's scared," Kyle said.

"Scared of what?"

"Of this," Kyle said as he pulled down his sweater to reveal one of the purplish lesions.

"You think so?"

"I know so," Kyle said.

"Don't worry, she will show up."

"She calls me late at night all the time but she always ends up crying and hanging up. If she doesn't come, I'll understand. I know JJ loves me."

I told Kyle I was thinking that perhaps I should move back up to New York. And I talked about Gilliam and all the fun I had working with college football players.

"Then why leave?" Kyle asked.

"Well, I want to be here with you," I said.

"I'm glad, Ray. But you can't give up your life for me. I might be gone tonight or years from now. I know you love me. You don't have to be up here to show that love," Kyle said.

"Yeah, I know, but aren't you glad we've got this time together?" I asked.

"Sure. Lord knows I could have very easily been killed by some crazy-assed trade. At least this way we get to say good-bye," Kyle said in a low rich voice.

I blinked and smiled in agreement. The waiter brought the check and two mints wrapped in green foil. Kyle quickly grabbed the check and reached for his wallet.

"I'll get this, Kyle," I said, reaching across the table for the check.

"No, Ray. Let me get it. I'm not broke. Besides I get a discount here," Kyle said.

"A discount?"

Kyle showed me a card that allowed him discounts at the majority of restaurants and stores in the Village. It was given to people with AIDS who registered with the Gay Men's Health Crisis. I asked Kyle if he was ready to call it a night and he said, "No, I want to go to Keller's."

Kyle and I started our walk toward Kelly's. It was one of the few places that was still intact from my New York days. Kyle and I had often talked of how we really missed the Nickel Bar. "If it weren't for the Nickel Bar, you and I would have never met," I said.

"Oh, we would have met," Kyle said.

"You sound sure of that."

"Yeah. I believe things happen for a reason. I think you and I knew each other in a different life," Kyle said.

"You for real?" I asked.

"Yes, and I'm sure we'll meet again in the next world," Kyle said with certainty.

"So you think there is an afterlife?"

"Of course. It's a thin line that separates this life from the next," Kyle said.

"So do you believe in heaven?"

"Of course. That's where I'm going," Kyle said. "But there may be a few more stops before we end up there."

"What do you think it's going to be like?"

"I don't know but I think it will be something like birth," Kyle said.

"How?"

"I don't think you'll remember it. Do you remember being born?"

"No."

"But I think heaven will be so much better than this place."

"So you think everybody's going there?"

"Everybody that believes, my friend," Kyle said. "Everybody that believes."

Twenty-eight

I couldn't wait until Christmas to give Kyle the special gift I planned. I was so excited about it, I decided to give it to him early. I would just have to get him something else for Christmas. Kyle was a big Vanessa Williams fan, and I knew Vanessa from her Miss America days. She was in the pageant a few years after I competed and I introduced myself to her backstage the year she won. I must admit the twinge of jealousy I felt when she became Miss America. I came so close but I don't think America was ready for a dark-skinned winner so I got over it. We started our friendship after the *Penthouse* magazine incident when she moved to New York City. I wrote her a note expressing my support and she called me days later. I called her whenever I was on the West Coast once she married and moved to Los Angeles.

I was so happy for her tremendous comeback. I never doubted for a minute that she would be a big success. I was upset at the way the Miss America people treated her. In the end it was Vanessa who got the last laugh.

Vanessa was in New York often, hosting a television show for a national cable network. I called her and told her about Kyle and his illness and what a big fan he was and she was happy to help out. Vanessa was in the process of working on her tour, therefore she wasn't certain she would be in New York over the holidays, however, she wanted to help in any way she could.

She originally agreed to come up and surprise Kyle but when that fell through, Vanessa and I came up with the idea of a personalized video with all of Vanessa's music videos and a special message to Kyle at the beginning and at the end. Vanessa went through a lot to pull this off. When I saw the finished product I cried.

She wrote Kyle a little note, enclosed an autographed picture, and then had the tape delivered to my apartment. When I finished viewing the video, I took it over to Delaney's and she started crying too. We pulled ourselves together and headed to Kyle's.

When we reached Kyle's apartment he was sitting in the living room reading. His mother was in the kitchen cooking something that smelled wonderful.

"Hey, baby," I said as I leaned over and kissed Kyle on the forehead.

"Hey, boy," Delaney said as she did the same thing.

"Hey, girls," Kyle said. "You see Mrs. Mother in the kitchen?" he asked.

"Yeah, when did you get back, Peaches?" I asked as I walked into the small kitchen to give her a hug and kiss. She was wearing a full apron and laboring over a hot skillet. She had a cigarette in one hand and a glass of wine close to the stove.

"Hey, Miss Nicole. How you been?" Peaches asked.

"I've been fine. I'm glad you're back," I said. "What you cooking?"

"Fried pork chops. You knew I couldn't stay away too long. Take off your coat. These chops will be done in a few," Peaches said. "I think I'll make some gravy and smother them. I should make some skillet cornbread too."

I walked out of the kitchen and Delaney walked in to give her hellos to Peaches. I went back into the living room, removed my coat, and sat down next to Kyle.

"So how are you really doing?" I asked Kyle.

"Oh, I'm okay. Raymond and I went to the Village last night, so I'm a little tired," Kyle said.

"Where is Raymond?" I asked.

"He went to rent a car. His friend Jared is coming in town this afternoon and Ray is going to pick him up," Kyle said.

"Jared?" I quizzed.

"Yes, that's Ray's friend who's looking for my daddy," Kyle said.

"I don't know why you want to find that no good motherfucker," Peaches yelled from the kitchen.

"Mind your own business, Mrs. Mother," Kyle yelled back.

Suddenly Kyle started coughing and I panicked. I started patting him on his back, making sure I didn't hit him hard.

"Are you all right, Kyle? Do you need some water?" I asked as I jumped up and ran into the kitchen for some water.

"What's the matter?" Delaney asked as she reached for a glass to pour some water for Kyle.

"I don't know," I said.

I rushed back into the living room but Kyle had stopped coughing. "Here, Kyle. Drink this," I said as I put the glass close to his chapped lips.

Kyle drank the water and then looked at me and smiled. "Thanks, Nicole. Get that worried look off your face. I'm not going yet."

Kyle had shared with me once when we were talking about his disease that the cancer was starting to spread throughout his body. His doctor told him there was a possibility that he might choke to death. Anytime he coughed or had trouble breathing I got scared. That was the first thing that went through my mind when he started his coughing attacks.

"So you sure you're okay?" I asked.

"I'm fine, baby," Kyle said as he gently patted my legs. "What's Peaches cooking in there?"

"Pork chops," Delaney said.

"Is she making gravy?" Kyle asked.

"Yes, and it looks great," Delaney said.

"Chirl, when I was growing up, Peaches had me thinking gravy came on everything. When I went away to college I was wondering what happened to the gravy. If we don't get her out of that kitchen with all that grease, we are all going to die from heart attacks," Kyle joked. "Ma?" Kyle called out.

"Yes, baby?" Peaches said as she walked from the kitchen wiping her hands with the apron she was wearing.

"Will you make me some cherry Jell-O?" Kyle asked.

"Sure. I'll run down to the store and get some," Peaches said.

"I'll go," I offered.

"Naw, baby, I need to get out of here anyway," Peaches said.

"Ma, with peaches. Make the Jell-O with peaches. Okay?"

"Okay, baby, with peaches."

Peaches walked back to the kitchen and Kyle turned and gave me a bright smile.

"I've got a surprise for you," I smiled.

"What?" Kyle asked.

"Well, let me put it in the VCR. Delaney, call Peaches into the bedroom," I said. "Tell her to wait before going to the store. I want her to see this."

I went into Kyle's bedroom, put the tape in the VCR, and cleared off the bed. Kyle's nightstand was covered with bottles of pills and empty glasses. I picked up some of the glasses and walked back to the living room. "Are y'all ready?" I asked.

"Let me take out the last chop," Peaches said.

"Oh, this tastes so good," Delaney said as she took a bite of the pork chop. I never recalled her eating anything fried before.

"Put that on a plate and bring it into the bedroom," I said.

"Hold your horses. We're coming," Peaches said.

Kyle was slowly walking into his bedroom and I started to help him but he resisted. He didn't like folks thinking of him as an invalid.

"This better be good. Making me get up from my spot," Kyle said with an agitated tone.

"It will be," I assured him.

"You're going to love this," Delaney said as she walked into the bedroom with a paper plate with pork chops and potato salad piled high.

Peaches took off her apron and was in the bathroom brushing her hair in place.

"Come on, Peaches," I called out.

I stood by the television as though I was Vanna White getting ready to turn letters. I was smiling and feeling excited from the tip of my toes to the top of my head. Delaney and Peaches situated themselves on the bed with Kyle, placing their food and drinks on the nightstand I had just cleared off.

"Okay, you ready?"

"Yes, girl. Work your show," Kyle said.

I pushed the play button and moved to the side to watch Kyle's face when Vanessa appeared on the screen, looking beautiful and talking directly to Kyle. Kyle let out the most exhilarating laughter I've ever heard. He started hitting his fist in the pillows and looking over at his mother and Delaney, yelling, "You go, Miss Vanessa. You go, girl. Work!"

He moved to each of Vanessa's videos and got up from the bed and started dancing when the *Work to Do* video came on. At the end of the video when Vanessa came back on talking to Kyle, she had changed into a beautiful royal blue mini-dress. Kyle bounced up and down in pure glee. When the tape was finished he came over and gave me one of the tightest hugs I ever recalled.

"Thank you, baby. This is the best present I've ever gotten," he said.

"Thank Delaney, too. She had a lot to do with it," I said.

"Not really. It was all Nicole's doing. I'm not close, personal friends with Lady Vanessa," Delaney said.

"She's being modest, Kyle. Delaney got a friend of hers to do Vanessa's makeup at the last moment and she got the tapes edited," I said.

"Come on over here, Miss Girl," Kyle said as he motioned toward Delaney.

The three of us were standing in the room hugging. Peaches had gotten up with tears in her eyes and raced to the bathroom.

"What's this? A group hug?" an unfamiliar deep baritone voice said.

The three of us broke our circle and turned to face a tall, attractive black man standing in the doorway of Kyle's bedroom. We all looked at each other with puzzled looks. Had somebody broken into Kyle's apartment?

"Hi, I'm Jared Stovall, Ray's friend," he said. "Ray's on his way up. He gave me the key. I hope I didn't startle you," he said apologetically.

"Hi, Jared. I've been looking forward to meeting you," Kyle said. "Ray said you were good-looking, but damn, Jared, he didn't say you were fine. You got it going on," Kyle said.

Jared blushed and flashed a smile of perfect teeth. For a moment I stared, because he looked familiar, but I couldn't place him. Raymond had good taste in men, too.

"Hi, Jared. I'm Nicole Springer and this is Delaney Morris."

"Hi, Nicole and Delaney. My gosh, you two are beautiful," Jared said as he extended his hands.

He was trying to be gentle but his enormous hands, with neatly clipped nails, were so big that my small hands felt as if they were cracking.

"I used to be beautiful too," Kyle joked.

"You still look great," Jared said.

Boy, was he a charmer. Delaney nodded toward me and walked over to the window.

"Be still, my heart," Kyle said as he playfully acted as if he was going to faint.

"I see you've met Jared," Raymond said as he walked into Kyle's bedroom.

"Yes, we've met and we're all moving to Atlanta," Kyle said.

"So how long you here for, Jared?" I asked.

"Just overnight. I have to be in D.C. in the morning," he said.

"Well, sorry we can't stay but we've got to dash," I said.

"Oh, come on, Nicole. Do you have to leave?" Raymond asked.

"Yes, I'm afraid so. Got to get to the theater," I said.

"Oh, I didn't know you had a show on Sunday," Raymond said.

"No, this is a rehearsal for the other show I was telling you about. The benefit."

"Oh," he said.

"Maybe I'll see you on your next visit to New York," I said to Jared.

"I'd like that," Jared said. His big hush puppy brown eyes were soft and shining. Raymond's eyes gazed fiercely at me and then he looked at Jared. Nothing in his neutral expression gave me any indication what he might be thinking. Did he want my approval of his boyfriend?

"You know you look familiar," I said.

"Who me?" Raymond joked.

"No, not you. Jared. Where did you go to school?"

"Morris Brown. Class of '83," he said.

"Oh, maybe that's where. Spelman '82," I said.

Jared looked at me, smiled and nodded, then walked over to Kyle's bed to talk with him. Peaches walked into the room and let out a loud squeal. "Where did these two fine bucks come from?" she asked.

"Cool your pussy down, Mrs. Mother. They are here to see me," Kyle said.

"Hey, Raymond Junior," Peaches said as she gave Raymond a hug.

"Hey, Ma," Ray said. Ray introduced Jared to Peaches as I looked for my bag and the rest of my belongings. I walked into the living room and Delaney was sitting on the sofa flipping through a copy of Jet magazine.

"I've got a question for you, Nic."

"What?"

"Why are all the Jet beauties from Oakland?" Delaney asked as she laid down the magazine on the coffee table.

"Girl, you are some kinda crazy," I laughed.

"You know I'm not lying. Every one of those bitches are from Oakland or some place like that."

"You ready, girl?" I asked.

"I'm ready," Delaney said as she got up and grabbed her bag.

I could hear the voices in Kyle's room laughing and Vanessa's music in the background. I called out a final good-bye but no one responded. I stopped in the kitchen, put a piece of Peaches's skillet cornbread in a napkin, and placed it in my bag. Delaney looked at me and smiled as we headed out of the door and down the hallway.

Twenty-nine

In less than twenty-four hours, Jared Stovall charmed New York City, or at least Kyle and Peaches. He came in town the weekend before Thanksgiving to meet Kyle for the first time and get additional information for his search for Kyle's father. I planned to take Jared to a show and nice restaurant, but instead we ended up spending the time at Kyle's. When Kyle and I suggested taking Jared to some of New York's nightspots, he declined, saying there would be time for that later.

It was magical seeing Kyle and Jared talk and act as though they had been friends for life. Peaches was constantly putting plates of food in Jared's hands and spending a great deal of time flirting with him. She commented to Kyle, "I'm glad to see that you guys don't have all the fine boys."

Kyle replied, "Turn your dimmer down, darling. The shine is hurting my eyes."

When I took Jared back to the airport, I asked him how he got to be so smart and he replied with a big smile, "I read a lot."

Before he got on the plane I told him how special he was and he said, "You and Kyle are the special ones."

Jared promised Kyle that with the additional information about his father, Jared would hopefully have some good news by the first or second week in December. Peaches encouraged him not to put himself out to find the asshole.

I don't know what Nicole thought of Jared. She and Delaney didn't hang around, but Jared commented on how beautiful they both were. He said he remembered Nicole from his college days.

Thanksgiving turned out to be different and quite special for me in many respects. First it was going to be one of Kirby's last Thanksgivings while he was still alive or at least able to walk. My little brother took the train down to New York and showed up at Penn Station with baggy jeans hanging from his narrow hips, an earring, and mini dreads covered by a Malcolm X hat. I was certain Mom and Pops would kill him for Christmas.

It was our first Thanksgiving not spent with Mom and Pops. We called them and told them how we were going to spend our day feeding the homeless at Nicole's church. They said how much they missed us, but that they were proud of how we'd planned our holiday. I didn't tell them about the hairstyle or the earring.

Nicole and Delaney fell in love with Kirby instantly. My little brother was quite the ladies' man. He and Kyle hit it off too, and I was proud that Kirby didn't appear uncomfortable around him; Kyle's physical condition had deteriorated and teenagers were sometimes squeamish around sick people. Kirby told Kyle all about prep school and how he was going to go to a black college when he graduated. He hadn't even shared that with me. Kyle kept repeating, "Kirby is such a little man," with that glint in his eyes usually reserved for good-looking men.

I was glad Nicole had suggested we assist with dinner at her church. It made me realize how blessed I truly was. After spending most of the afternoon at church, we all came back to Kyle's, where Peaches had prepared a feast. Some of Kyle's cousins came to New York and I couldn't believe how we all fit into the one-bedroom apartment, and we all had a good time.

Kyle's three male cousins and Peaches were engaged in a lively game of bid whist. Almost every minute someone would yell out, "Take this, motherfucker. Looks like we're going to Boston."

While enjoying watching the game, I noticed Nicole walk into the kitchen and I followed her. She was at the sink removing dishes from the counter and she smiled as I walked in. We both broke out in laughter as we heard Peaches scream at the top of her lungs; "Now who's going to Boston, you country-assed motherfucker? Who taught your sorry ass how to play bid? I thought you went to college."

"Sounds like Peaches just won a hand," Nicole said.

"Yep, I think so," I said.

Nicole looked especially elegant Thanksgiving Day in black stretch pants and a turtleneck topped with a mauve jacket. Her hair was pulled into a thick ponytail held together tightly by a gold barrette. I've always been a sucker for a girl with a ponytail.

I offered to help Nicole with the dishes and she quickly accepted my offer. She washed and I dried. We were about halfway finished when she looked up at me and said, "Your little brother is wonderful and quite handsome."

"Well, get a good look at him, because this might be the last time you see him like that," I joked.

"Why?" Nicole asked with a puzzled expression.

"Oh, I'm just kidding. I was just thinking what Mom is going to do when she sees him Christmas."

"The earring?" Nicole asked.

"And the dreads," I said.

"I think they look cute on him," Nicole smiled.

"Good, then write him a letter of endorsement. It might help his sentence," I laughed.

"You think she's going to be that upset?"

"At first, but then she'll get over it. My mom has gotten over a lot more," I said.

"I'd like to meet your mom one day," Nicole said.

"I'd like that too. I know you two would hit it off," I said.

"Your friend Jared seemed nice," Nicole said. There was something different in her voice.

"Yeah, Jared is one of a kind," I said. I wondered if Nicole thought Jared was gay and was *my friend.* There was a brief period of silence with the exception of the sound of Nicole's hands going in and out of the sudsy sink and then, "This has been nice," Nicole said as tears came into her eyes. She blinked hard to force them back.

"Why the tears? Are you all right?" I asked, reaching out and grabbing her by her narrow shoulders.

"I'm all right. I mean the whole day has just been wonderful. First at church and then here with Kyle and his family. Isn't this what Thanksgiving is supposed to be about?" Nicole asked.

"Yes, Nicole. Days like today are what it's all about. Family and good friends," I said.

"I think this is what the Lord had planned," she said, managing a small, but endearing smile.

Later that evening, Nicole and Delaney took Kirby and Peaches to the movies. I wanted to go, but since Kyle didn't feel well, saying he had eaten too much, I stayed at the apartment and played cards with him and his cousins.

Hours later the ladies returned with Kirby and we headed to mid-town via the subway. Kirby seemed to be having the time of his young life, his face covered with an indelible smile.

"So you're having fun, huh?"

"Yeah Ray-Ray. This has been a lot of fun! Nicole and Delaney were so nice to me. They are so pretty," Kirby said.

"So you like them?"

"Yeah. Don't you? They are so dope!"

"Dope?"

"Yeah, you know, cool, fly. Dope!"

"Oh yeah. What about Kyle and Peaches?" I asked.

"They're real nice too. Especially Peaches. She had us cracking up," Kirby laughed.

The train arrived at our stop and when we walked from the subway station I realized a light snow had begun. The New York night fell silent under the graceful force of the cold and clean snow. I was savoring the magical snowflakes falling on my warm face and Kirby was playfully sticking his tongue out catching them when he suddenly turned to me and asked, "Ray-Ray, Kyle has AIDS, right?"

"Yes, Kirby, Kyle has AIDS."

"How did he get it? Is Kyle soft?"

"What do you mean soft?"

"You know soft, sissy, a fag," Kirby said as he levitated his glove-covered hand side to side.

"Don't use those words Kirby." I was startled and my voice was measured and tight.

"What words?"

"Fag or sissy. They're demeaning. Kyle is my friend and that's all that matters. You got a problem with it?"

"Naw, Ray-Ray, I'm sorry," Kirby said. A frightened look crossed his face.

I turned and positioned my body directly in front of Kirby and reached out and grabbed him by his thin shoulders. He was shaking and I didn't know if it was the cold weather or my amplified voice.

"Kirby, I'm sorry. I didn't mean to scare you. I just don't want you to use words like fag. Think before you just make assumptions or label someone. AIDS can strike anybody. Get that fag shit out of your vocabulary. Do you understand?"

"Yeah but why, Ray?"

" 'Cause I said so," I said sounding very much like my pops.

"Dope," Kirby replied.

"Kirby."

"Yes."

"Don't forget what I told you about using a condom. Promise."

"Don't worry, I promise."

As we entered the hotel I realized I had to talk to my little brother in more detail about my sexuality before the world had a chance to turn him into a hopeless homophobe. I just prayed it wasn't too late.

That night back at the hotel after Kirby fell asleep, I did something rare. I got out of the bed, got on my knees, and silently prayed for a miracle for Kyle and thanked God for my own blessings. I also prayed for guidance on what to do about my little brother and for his safe return to school. When I got up from my knees I realized that I needed to call my parents before my talk with my little brother.

When my pops picked up the phone I asked him to tell Mama to get on the other end and told them I had something serious to talk about. When I didn't elaborate there was a long silence over the phone lines and then my pops in his majestic voice inquired, "You don't have that disease, son. Please tell us that's not it, son."

"No, Pops. I assure you, I don't have AIDS."

I heard my mother breathe a sigh of relief. "How is Kyle?" she asked.

"Good and bad days. He's hanging in there."

"Tell him I'm praying for him," Mama said.

"Yeah tell him to hang in there," my pops interjected.

"I'll make sure I tell him first thing," I said.

"What was it you needed to talk to us about?" my mother asked.

"I think it's really a conversation we should have in person. Don't worry. I probably just wanted to hear your voices."

They told me to make sure Kirby got back to school safely and to keep them posted on Kyle's condition.

Before hanging up, I said, "I love ya."

"We love you too," my mother said.

My pops responded, "Back at ya, son. Back at you."

Jared shipped my laptop computer up to New York and I started working on some of the items I'd left behind in Atlanta while Kyle slept or went to his doctors' appointments. Sometimes I went with him, but most of the time a service provided by GMHC picked Kyle up and returned him safely.

The time after Thanksgiving was strange. Kyle didn't look like Kyle anymore and he spent more and more time in his bedroom in bed. Still, he didn't complain about pain. Occasionally he asked for help in getting his pillows in order or changing his sheets after nights of cold sweats. His voice was becoming weak and breathy.

One afternoon after watching a movie, Kyle started talking about his illness. He said when he first found out he was HIV positive he went into denial. He refused to see doctors or take any medications. He felt good. He was certain the doctors had made a mistake. "I figured they got my results mixed up with one of the other addicts at the clinic," he said. "I kept telling myself no way . . . no how."

Kyle explained to me that the loss of his voice meant the cancer was spreading to his voice box. When I asked him if it hurt he shook his head.

"What do you miss the most, Kyle?" I asked late one evening.

Kyle started laughing and said, "I miss not being able to take a shower with a man or for that matter taking a shower by myself."

"Do you think they will ever find a cure for this?" I asked.

"Yes, one day, but it will be too late for many of us," Kyle said.

Kyle told me how angry it made him that black people only started talking about AIDS once Magic Johnson and Arthur Ashe became infected. "What about all the black gay men and black women that have died? Aren't they important too? We are their brothers and sisters too," Kyle said. "Aren't we, Ray?"

"Yeah, Kyle, you're right," I said.

"Damn straight I'm right! Ray, promise me something," Kyle said softly.

"Sure, Kyle, what?"

"Don't let this happen to you. You like to use your dick. Give up this shit. Find a woman," Kyle said in a serious and mournful tone.

"Come on, Kyle. It was you who got on me about my confused life. What happened to your gay pride?" I joked, trying to get him into a light mood.

"I used all my pride being black," he said. Kyle's face was expressionless. I listened to his words and searched the room as though I was going to get some clue as to how to respond when Kyle started talking to himself.

"Ray forget about what I just said. Be true to yourself and just be safe."

"I will, Kyle. I'll always be safe."

"Some mornings when I wake up and the sun is shining brightly on my face I smile. I smile because for just a moment I think my life and body are the way they used to be. And when it hits me that I'm sick, I get so fucking mad at black gay men for loving me when I was young, healthy, and beautiful and then turning their backs on me now when I need them the most. But most of all I get mad at myself," Kyle said. His voice was filled with an eruption of betrayal, hurt, and anger." Kyle glanced away as a pained look settled onto his face. There were moments of excruciating silence. I didn't want to say or ask something stupid, but then Kyle's special brand of humor kicked in.

"You know what they say?" Kyle voiced.

"What?" I asked.

"Life's a dick. You suck it, fuck it, and then you die," he said with a hoarse laugh.

I shook my head soberly.

Thirty

"*Nicole*, I have some bad news,"
Kyle said sadly.

"What, Kyle? What's the matter?" I asked nervously.

"You better sit down," he instructed.

I took a seat on the clothes-covered chair next to Kyle's bed and looked into his eyes. I gently stroked his hands when he began to talk. My heart was beating so wildly I thought it would burst inside me like a water-filled balloon.

"I didn't want to have to tell you this, but I have to tell someone," he said.

"Come on, Kyle. It will be all right. Just tell me what's wrong."

"You promise not to tell anyone. Not even my mother or Raymond?"

"I promise."

"All my credit cards are over the limit," Kyle said, looking away from my eyes.

Was I hearing him right? "What did you say, Kyle?"

"I don't know what I'm going to do. Every one of them," Kyle said. His voice suddenly filled with laughter.

"Kyle, stop messing with me," I said as I hit him playfully.

"Chirl, you should have seen your face," Kyle said.

"Kyle, that's not funny. You scared me to death," I said.

"What happened to your sense of humor?" Kyle asked.

"Where is your keeper?"

"Who? Raymond or Peaches?"

"Both."

"They went shopping for a Christmas tree," Kyle said.

"So I guess your big problem will put an end to your Christmas shopping," I said.

"Well, I've finished. Oh, please mail these cards and letters when you leave," Kyle said as he handed me a stack of cards and two legal-sized envelopes. I dropped them into my bag, which was sitting beside the bed.

"Okay. Have you talked to Delaney?"

"Oh, she called this morning. She and Jody are coming by later," Kyle said.

"Do you know Jody?" I inquired about a girlfriend of Delaney's who was visiting from California.

"I've heard Delaney talk about her, but I haven't met her yet," Kyle said.

"I haven't met her either, but I've been busy with two shows and the cabaret," I said.

"Has she said anything about reporting that asshole or a least filing a lawsuit against him?" Kyle asked.

"No, she spends her time at the Rape Counseling Center. Whenever I try to bring it up she bristles," I said.

"I think I'm going to ask Raymond to help," Kyle said.

"How?"

"Well, his firm deals with entertainers; maybe they've had a case like this. I just don't want to see the jerk get away without even a slap on the wrist," Kyle said.

"Yeah, you're right. Sometimes I forget Raymond's a lawyer."

"How is the new musical?"

"I'll know in a couple of hours. We're having the final read through before we go into tryout rehearsals. The director said we would even have the music."

"Before you go, will you put some fresh water in here? It's time for me to take these horse pills," Kyle said as he handed me a pitcher from his nightstand.

I went into the kitchen, washed out the pitcher, and filled it with water from Kyle's filtering system. This was one of the few times in recent months Kyle's apartment was so quiet and empty. Since I'd found out about Kyle's illness I'd tried to get over at least every other day. Members of Kyle's family and those of his friends he allowed to see him always kept the apartment bustling. And it seemed like Raymond never left the apartment.

Watching Raymond take care of Kyle made me realize what a special man he was. It was as though he'd put his entire life on hold for his friend. I'd heard a lot of horror stories about people with AIDS being deserted by family and friends.

Kyle's mother was devoted also. She took the bus back and forth between Jersey and the city to take care of her son. Peaches might love her cocktails, but she didn't let them interfere with Kyle's care. She always managed a brave front around Kyle and Raymond, but one night when Kyle was asleep and Raymond went out for a walk, Peaches broke down and cried in front of Delaney and me. She said she never thought she would have to bury one of her children. "Do you know how hard that's going to be? When you girls have children I hope you'll never have to go through something like this." Delaney and I just gave her a hug because we had no idea what to say.

Raymond and his friend Jared were feverishly trying to locate Kyle's father for Christmas. I was praying for their success because I got the impression this was really important to Kyle. Peaches wasn't excited about it but she realized it was what Kyle wanted.

I walked back into Kyle's bedroom with the pitcher and he was sitting up in the bed laughing loudly and clapping his hands.

"What's so funny? What are you looking at?" I asked as I poured Kyle a glass of water and sat the pitcher on the water-stained wood.

"Chirl, sit and look at this. This is a mess. I had that child," Kyle said.

"Who?" I asked, looking at the television where Kyle was pointing.

"Him. The guy on this show. Look at him actin' all butch," Kyle said.

Kyle was watching a television show called "Studs." I had seen it a couple of times but I never really paid that much attention to it. The guy Kyle was talking about was an attractive-looking, brown-skinned man. The three women on the show were going on and on about how fine and romantic he was on their dates. Kyle wasn't saying anything; he just stared at the television with a wide grin on his face. I didn't quite understand the format of the show, but at the end the guy Kyle knew and a very attractive girl won a weekend date to San Francisco.

"That's the last place she should want to take him," Kyle said.

"Is he gay?" I asked.

"Is Rockfeller Center lit up like a Christmas tree? Does Robin Givens have the best weave in the world?" Kyle asked. "I slept with him a couple of times when he was in New York on business."

"So I guess the answer is yes."

"You got it, girl!"

"Oh, this is so depressing," I sighed.

"What?"

"That's why I'm so scared to start dating again. I would never have thought that guy was gay," I said. "What am I gonna do, Kyle?"

"Don't worry, darling. When I get up there. I'll send you somebody," Kyle smiled as he pointed toward the ceiling.

"Make sure he's all man," I said.

"Do you want him black, white, or high yellow?" Kyle asked.

"At this point I just want somebody who loves me," I said.

"He might already be down here. I may not have to do that much work," Kyle said.

"Who are you talking about?"

"Just mind your business. I'll do the work, but in the meantime I'll give you one of your Christmas presents early. Go over there and look in the bottom drawer and pull out that shoe box," Kyle said.

"What is it?"

"Just go over there and get it," Kyle said. "It's been used but it's still in working order."

I went over and pulled out the box from Kyle's drawer. When I opened the box I let out a loud squeal. It was a vibrator.

"Kyle, you are sick!" I yelled.

"Chirl, you better get a grip. That thing got me through a lot of cold winter nights and this is going to be a cold one," he laughed.

I put the box back in the drawer and slammed it shut.

"So you got it like that? You'll be wishing you had taken it. Don't worry I won't tell anyone."

"Kyle. You know that's not me," I protested.

"Oh, I forgot, Miss Black Kathie Lee Gifford."

"Kyle, you're a mess. But I love you," I said.

"And I love you too," Kyle said.

"Kyle, can I ask you a favor?" I said in a serious tone.

"Sure, Nicole. Why so serious?"

"Well, I want you to pray with me. You know Jesus is still in the blessing business," I said.

"I know you mean well, Nicole, but I'm straight with Jesus. But if it will make you feel better you can pray, but no songs and you can't tell anyone," Kyle said.

I fell to my knees and took Kyle's hand and started praying out loud. Asking God to come down and ease Kyle's pain and to take this dreadful disease from his body. I was praying so fast, words poured from my mouth like water from a rushing shower head. My body became warm and soaking wet after praying. My clothing felt sticky against my skin as I got up from my knees and looked into Kyle's eyes. There was a blank expression on his face.

"Are you all right?" he asked.

"I'm fine. No, I'm blessed," I said.

"Nicole, something you said earlier is bothering me," Kyle said.

"What, baby? What did I say?"

"When I said I was going to send you somebody. You asked me to make sure he was all man. Do you think Raymond and I aren't all man? Do you think gay men are less than whole?" Kyle asked in a very serious manner.

"No, Kyle, I don't think that." I smiled, trying to conceal my discomfort.

"Think about it, Nicole. I know you don't mean any harm but I've had the feeling for a long time that although you love gay men, you're still harboring ill feelings. It's not uncommon for straight women to feel that way, but I think you ought to be aware of it," Kyle said.

I could tell he was very serious about this and I felt tears forming in my eyes. *Was* I homophobic? "Kyle, I'm sorry. I don't consider you any less of a man. I'm actually hurt you feel that way," I said.

"Like I said I don't think you say or feel a certain way to hurt me. And I'm not accusing you, so don't get hurt. But women ought to think about the men who really hurt them. It's not gay men who lie, cheat, beat them, and leave them alone with kids to fend for themselves. Well, sometimes these confused gay men do. But when you think about it, heterosexual men beat women down daily. Especially black women."

"You have a point there. How long have you felt this way, Kyle?"

"I realize that you and I became friends because you wanted to keep in touch with Raymond and that was okay. I know you loved him dearly, Nicole, and he hurt you. But have you ever thought about the pain he goes through daily? I'm comfortable with being gay. Raymond's not and may never be."

I slowly moved my hands over Kyle's quilt, studying the beautiful patchwork. I started to bite the ends of my hair, which I did when I was nervous. I was listening to his words but I couldn't look into his eyes. His words hurt, but it is true that the truth hurts sometimes. I remained silent, trying to absorb what Kyle was saying.

"Nicole! Look at me!" Kyle said sharply.

"What!" I said, looking at Kyle's eyes for the first time since the conversation took this dramatic turn.

"You realize Raymond loved you, don't you?"

"Did he? Does he?"

"Yes, Nicole, he does. Please, darling, if I don't leave you with anything else let me leave you with the fact that no man black or white chooses to be gay. That goes for women too. There is nothing gay about this life."

"I'm learning that, Kyle. Please be patient with me," I pleaded.

"I don't have much time, darling. I don't want to leave you here not knowing the truth. I know you've come to love me and I love you. I didn't always feel this way."

"You didn't?"

"Chirl, like I said I realized why you were so hot to be my friend. I figured I could meet some men through you and get some business. But I fell in love with you. You really are a special lady and I realize how Raymond fell in love with you."

"Oh, Kyle, that's so sweet," I said.

"It's the truth," he said as he gently rubbed my hands and smiled. "Now don't get mushy and I really don't want to see any black puddles on your face."

I spent another hour with Kyle. For a brief time we were both silent. I was thinking about our conversation; I don't really know where Kyle was. But slowly, in the comfort of the dimly lit bedroom, Kyle began to talk. He started in a whisper but when he got excited, he broke into giggles and then his voice cracked. He seemed to be speaking under stress. I asked him if he wanted some more water or tea, but he insisted he was fine. Our conversation ventured to religion. Kyle explained to me he had a personal relationship with Christ and he was certain he was going to be with Him. He told me that as a little boy, he'd realized that he was different and that that difference was being gay. He felt Christ was the only one who understood him and loved him just the way he was.

Kyle said he got AIDS not because he was gay or promiscuous, but because Christ knew he could handle it. That maybe Christ needed him.

His face lit up when he talked about seeing all his family and friends once he got to heaven. "I'll look Candance up," Kyle said. "But it might take some time. She'll probably be as far away from the sissies in heaven as possible," he laughed.

"Kyle, don't say that."

"I'm just kidding, chile."

"You don't think AIDS is God's work?" I asked.

"Chile, no. AIDS is some of man's shit. But I think when we come into the world, it's already established when we're going to leave. My time is just almost up," Kyle said matter-of-factly. "I'm just happy it will be a peaceful exit."

"What's it gonna take to find a cure?" I questioned.

"When they realize everyone's life is worth saving. The men, the women, and the babies. When they realize gay men do more than hair and sew dresses," Kyle said.

"You think people still think it's a gay disease?"

"Oh yeah. They have to believe that. It makes them feel safe."

"You know I've learned a lot this afternoon, Kyle. I really must look seriously at some of my religious teaching."

"Good, because if I hear God created Adam and Eve not Adam and Steve one more time I'm going to croak. Who thought of that stupid ass shit? Who the fuck is Steve anyway? I ain't even trying to hear that shit. I'm looking for Leroy or Tyrone," Kyle laughed as he snapped his fingers in the air.

"I don't know, baby. I never thought how silly it sounds."

"You better start *thinking*, girl. You didn't think Pierce would turn out like he did. I won't be around to school you."

"It sounds to me like you have a better relationship with God than a lot of people I know, including myself," I said.

"I think God just gets mad with us when we get down here and try to be something we're not. I really think that pisses Him off."

"I think you're right, Kyle. I think you're right."

I looked at my watch and realized I had fifteen minutes to get to rehearsal. I grabbed my jacket, gave Kyle a big hug and a kiss on the lips. He held my hands so tightly I had to gently pull them away.

"I've got to go. I'm running late, but I'll see you tomorrow," I said.

"Okay, baby. Tomorrow. I love you, Nicole," Kyle said. When I looked at Kyle there was a disheartened look on his face and melancholy in the sound of his voice.

"I love you too, Kyle. Are you sure you're all right?"

"Yes, I'm fine. Get on out of here," Kyle said as he waved his hand in the air.

"You know we ought to go to see the Christmas tree at Rockefeller Center," I said.

"Okay. Maybe tomorrow."

I blew Kyle a kiss as I rushed out of his bedroom and bumped right into Raymond's hard body.

"What's the rush?" he asked.

"I'm in a hurry. Where's Peaches?"

"Downstairs talking to Grady," Raymond said.

"How's my boyfriend?"

"Who, me?" Raymond asked with a big smile.

"No, not you. Kirby," I smiled.

"Oh, that's how it is. Knucklehead's fine. He hasn't stopped talking about you," Raymond said.

"That's sweet. I've got to run. Go in there and take care of him. He's kinda down. Spent the whole afternoon reading me. But I needed it," I said as I pulled open the door.

"What did you do?"

"Kyle will tell you."

"Nicole," Raymond called out.

"Yes."

"Thank you," he said softly.

"Thanks for what?" I asked.

"For being you," he said.

I smiled and leaned forward and gave him a soft kiss on the lips. He tasted wonderful.

"Why were you surprised, Nicole?"

"I just didn't realized he felt that way. I didn't realize that I was that way," I said softly.

"Where do you think that comes from?"

"Well, it would be easy to blame it on Raymond, but he's just one person and I have to take some of the blame."

"How so?"

"Well, maybe I didn't make it clear. I pursued Raymond and he responded. It's not like he sought me out just to hurt me. I guess I always thought gay men were like . . ."

"Like what, Nicole?"

"Like sissies. Wanting to be women."

"Why?"

"It's the image I was given growing up. What I saw on television. What was said in church. The stereotypes."

"How do you feel now?"

"I'm not sure."

"Not sure?"

"Yes. A part of me still gets upset to think that there's a large pool of smart, good-looking black men who will never be available to me."

"So are you saying you want a black man?"

"I think that's what I've always wanted."

"Then explain your long relationship with Pierce."

"How can you not respond to a man who treats you as nice as he treated me—at least for the most part—no matter what the color," I said.

"Then color really doesn't matter?" Dr. Huntley asked.

"In a perfect world, no. But here, I'm sorry to say it does."

Dr. Huntley gave me a supportive half smile and leaned closer to her desk.

"Maybe there was a time when I thought dating a white man would be different. Better."

"Why did you think that?"

"Well, right after I broke up with Raymond, I went out a couple of times with two different black guys. Both of them were big trouble."

"How so?"

"Well, the first one used very abusive language all the time and I just felt the next thing was going to be some type of physical action. He used to always tell me that I was beautiful, but dumb. Those aren't the words he used, but that was the message. The other one always made a point of staring at white- and light-skinned women after I shared with him how I felt about the color of my skin."

"You thought a white man would be different?"

"Yes. When Pierce came around trying to be a friend and treating me so differently from anyone else, I just thought it was my fairy tale coming true."

"So that's why you dated him for so long?"

"In a lot of ways, yes. I felt like I was living in a fairy tale. The nice restaurants, the limos. I guess it didn't matter that I wasn't truly in love."

"How do you feel about that now?"

"Well, I'm realizing life's not a fairy tale. That I have prejudices that I must face and remove from my life. That I'm not in some beauty pageant. That I can't expect to live *in* a perfect world if my own attitudes are so imperfect."

"Do you believe there will ever be a perfect world?"

"Not here. But Kyle said something I will always remember."

Dr. Huntley tipped her head forward gently. A movement for me to tell her what he'd said.

"He said God only gets mad at us when we come to earth and pretend to be something we're not. I think he's so right."

Dr. Huntley smiled her reassuring smile. I smiled back.

"You're making a lot of progress, Nicole. A lot of progress," Dr. Huntley said as she stood up from her chair.

"I think I'm just beginning."

Thirty-one

They say you can learn things about yourself when facing adversity. Some of the things I was learning about myself didn't sit too well with me. I guess I could blame my parents, but that wouldn't be quite fair. My parents always taught Kirby and me we were just as good as anybody and, because we were black males, in many cases we had to be better. I took that to heart. This became crystal clear to me one day when Kyle wanted to rent the movie *Paris Is Burning*, a movie about black drag queens, over my most vehement objections.

In a lot of ways I thought I was better than drag queens even though we both slept with members of the same sex. In fact, there were times when I felt superior toward gay guys who were overly effeminate or passive in bed. I also knew I was not alone in my thinking; I thought about men like Kelvin, Basil, and Quinn. We all had what could be called homophobia within the homosexual community. When I went out to the bars I was polite, but with chilly overtones, when drag queens or fem guys approached me. I smiled and then gave them that don't-even-think-about-it look. I thought back to Sherrod's client, Charles Marshall, and how my support of Basil's actions was desperately wrong. My feelings toward Marshall were based on his appearance and mannerisms, and my ill feelings were just as damaging as Basil's fists. No matter what Basil or I thought about Marshall's advances, he didn't deserve Basil's beating or my contempt. I realized that I must come face to face with those feelings and fears so that I could overcome them. I questioned what type of example I was setting for my little brother; I remembered his use of the words *soft* and *fag*. Hopefully, it wasn't too late to stop his cycle of malice and misunderstanding.

The feeling of superiority was not exclusive to "masculine" black gay men. For years, my light skin and green eyes gave me a certain edge in the black community. My education separated me even further. Black Ivy Leaguers were compared to those with degrees from schools of less prestige. I chose Alabama over Alabama State or Morehouse because of my misplaced perception that the white school was better. I knew black Ivy League law school graduates who turned up their noses at students who received their law degrees from schools like Howard and Texas Southern.

I thought if I ever could create a perfect world, I would want everyone to be equal. A world where the only rule would be respect, respect for each individual to live life the way he or she saw fit. A world where the only hate was directed toward hate. Remove the world's isms, and the ills would soon take leave. People would be judged as individuals and not in groups. Groups caused fears.

The mere fact that God created different types of people, like drag queens, made their lives just as important as mine. Their pain, though different, was still pain. Now the black gay community was facing another separation . . . those with HIV and AIDS and those free of both.

As I watched the movie, I began to feel the pain this separatism caused. I was moved by the struggle the characters faced daily simply because they were different. The truth was, we were all different. Different right down to our DNA. I thought of the Scripture that stated we are all equal in the sight of Christ. How I wished we lived by that. I guess any change starts with oneself and I made a promise to myself, that day, watching a film I didn't want to see, that I would never ever again think I was better than anyone.

I was on my second cup of hot coffee and eating a piece of Oreo cheesecake, which was serving as breakfast in my hotel suite. Reading the sports pages of the *New York Times*, I saw a picture of Basil and the announcement of the All-Pro football team. I guess he was having the season he dreamed of. The picture in the paper made me think back to the summer and the sex. Before I became lost in memories, I grabbed my phone book, quickly found Basil's number, and dialed it.

"Hello," Basil said after only one ring.

"I guess congratulations are in order," I said.

"Is this who I think it is?" Basil asked.

"Yeah, it's me. I guess you thought I'd never call," I said.

"I've called you a couple of times but I didn't leave a message," Basil said. "So how is Atlanta?"

"I wouldn't know. Haven't been there for months," I said.

"What, you moved? Where are you living now?"

"New York City."

"No shit, Sherlock," Basil said. "So you're following me," Basil said with his familiar cockiness.

"Not even," I retorted.

"So when will I get the chance to see you?"

"I don't know. You're the big superstar, Mr. All-Pro," I said.

"I told you I was going to make it," Basil boasted, "So, did you see many of my games on television?"

"Every one of them. So how many yards did you end up with?"

"Over one thousand, eleven hundred thirty-three; second in the league."

"That's great, Basil," I said. "I'm really happy for you."

"Are you really?"

"Of course I am."

"So you're not mad at me?"

"Do you care?"

"Of course I care."

"No, not anymore."

Basil and I agreed to meet that evening. I didn't tell him why I was in New York and he didn't apologize for the night in the closet. Right after I hung up the phone it rang and Jared was on the other end.

"I found him," Jared said.

"You found Kyle's father?"

"Yes. He's in Tallahassee, Florida. That's the good news," Jared said.

"So what's the catch?"

"He doesn't sound that excited about seeing Kyle and especially not Kyle's mother."

"You're kidding, right?"

"I wish I were, Ray. I even offered to pay for the ticket. He said he would call me back later this afternoon, but from my conversation with him I don't expect much," Jared said.

"Motherfuck!" I said as I hit my fist against the telephone stand. "I don't believe this shit."

"Well, I can give you the number and you can give it a try," Jared offered.

"Okay. Give it to me. Do you have Kyle's number?"

"Yes. If I hear anything I'll call you there."

Jared advised me to wait until later that afternoon before making the call to Kyle's father. And we both agreed it didn't make any sense to tell Kyle until we were certain we could deliver.

After I hung up with Jared I called Kyle to let him know I was on my way up.

"Is there anything you need?" I asked.

"Stop and get a video please, Ray," Kyle said.

"So what's the feature film today?" I asked.

"See if they have *Dark Victory* with Bette Davis," Kyle said. "If they don't have that get *The Women*."

"Is that it?"

"Oh yeah, please stop at the drugstore on the corner and pick up my prescriptions," Kyle said.

"Got it. I'll see you in about an hour."

Although it was cold I decided to walk to the video store near Lincoln Center. It was so cold you could see your breath in front of you even if your mouth was closed. The winter air carried the familiar scents and sounds of the season. Christmas music and the smell of Christmas trees filled the air and wreaths were on every corner. I hadn't bought a single gift or informed my parents I wouldn't be home for Christmas. Having missed Thanksgiving and the family reunion, I knew this news was not going to sit well with my folks and they were curious about what I wanted to talk about with them.

I got the film Kyle had requested and picked up *Daughters of the Dust* for the afternoon feature. I also picked up Stephanie Mills's Christmas CD to help get Kyle and me in the holiday mood.

The second week in December we'd had a scare when Kyle's doctor put him in the hospital for a couple of days to run some additional tests and to give him something to protect him from some other diseases, like pneumonia. I'd spent the night walking up and down the ammonia-scented halls; everything was sterile, fluorescent, and clean. Kyle didn't like hospitals and neither did I, so I was really happy when his doctor released him after the two-night stay. Nicole called but she didn't come to the hospital, which I understood since it was the same hospital Candance died in.

I left the record store and walked up to the Seventy-second Street subway station. Before heading down into the station, I looked at the busy shops along Seventy-second Street and thought about the Nickel Bar, where Kyle and I had met. I started to walk up the street to where the bar had been to pay homage to the Nickel but I knew Kyle was waiting and decided to do it later. I caught the express train and was at the Ninety-sixth Street stop before I could get settled into a seat. I got Kyle's prescriptions and headed upstairs to the apartment.

The smell of soul food and the strains of Smokey Robinson's "Baby, Baby Don't Cry" greeted me. I caught Peaches slow dancing with the broom in the living room like she was in a massive ballroom in full gown.

"Hey, Peaches. You in the Christmas spirit yet?"

"Hey, baby. I'm getting there," she said as she stopped her waltz.

"What you cooking?"

"Greens and neckbones and sweet potato casserole."

"Neckbones smelled like hamhocks to me," I said.

"You like hamhocks, baby? Why didn't you tell me? I'll cook you some tomorrow," Peaches said.

"Great! How is he doing?" I asked as I gave Peaches a kiss on her forehead.

She grabbed me by the waist and whispered, "He's in sort of a strange mood. Delaney and Jody are in there with him."

I walked into Kyle's room and Delaney and a petite woman were in the bed with Kyle looking at magazines. The three of them were laughing. It was the most exhilarating laughter I'd heard in his room in a long time.

"What's so funny?" I asked as the three of them looked up from the magazines.

"Ray. You bring the movies?" Kyle asked. I didn't answer Kyle but instead held the videos in full view.

"Hello, Raymond," Delaney said. "This is my friend, Jody Brown."

"Hi, Raymond, nice to meet you," Jody said as she lifted herself from the bed and extended her small hand.

"Hi, Delaney. Nice meeting you, Jody. How long you here for?"

"I'm leaving Christmas Eve," she said.

"Where are you from?"

"San Diego," she said.

"Is it snowing outside?" Kyle asked.

"Naw," I said.

"Well, we better go and let you get some rest," Delaney said as she searched for her shoes under the bed.

"Don't rush on my account," I said.

"No, Jody and I are meeting Nicole for lunch," Delaney said.

"Tell her I said hello," I said.

"I will," Delaney said as she leaned over and kissed Kyle on the forehead.

"Nice meeting you, Ray. Kyle, I'll see you before I leave," Jody said as she kissed Kyle on the cheek.

Delaney and Jody said good-bye to me as they put on their jackets and headed out of the bedroom. I could hear them talking to Peaches in the living room.

"I didn't mean to run your company off," I said to Kyle.

"You didn't run them off. They were getting ready to leave anyway," Kyle said.

"I don't think Delaney likes me," I said.

"Oh, she's just scoping you out. I think she likes you. She has a lot on her mind, though. You remember what I told you about that guy who attacked her?" Kyle said.

"Oh yeah. Whatever became of that?"

"Nothing," Kyle said.

Suddenly an odd look crossed Kyle's face and he called out Delaney's name. A few seconds later Delaney walked back into Kyle's bedroom.

"Did you call me?" Delaney asked.

"Yes, darling. Come here and sit down," Kyle said as he patted a spot on his bed close to him. Delaney complied.

"I've been doing some thinking. We really need to take care of that asshole," Kyle said.

"What asshole?" Delaney asked.

"The motherfucker who ate your pussy without your permission, chile. Don't play dumb."

"Kyle, please. You're embarrassing me," Delaney protested.

"Well, you know Ray knows. You know I tell him everything," Kyle said. A passive look rested on Delaney's face.

"Delaney, there is no reason to be embarrassed," I offered.

"Yes, that's right. But you can't ignore it, darling. I was thinking maybe Ray can help you out since he does have a lot of free time. It will get him out of my hair for a while," Kyle said.

"Help. How?"

"Sue the motherfucker. Since you won't go to the police."

"I still think we should report it," I said.

"But it's been so long. They won't believe me. Besides, what about my career?" Delaney asked.

"Delaney, if he thinks he can do it to you and get away with it he'll do it again. Let's get him where it's bound to hurt. In his wallet," I said.

"You think we can do that?"

"What you told Nicole and Kyle happened, right?"

"Yes, Raymond, it happened. Almost like it was yesterday," Delaney said.

"Then let's do something about it. I will give you a call a little later. We'll go over your statement. I'll also talk to my boss and maybe she has some connections to the management at his record label," I said.

"See, baby, it's going to be fine," Kyle said.

"You think so?" Delaney asked.

"Yes," Kyle assured.

"First thing you need to do is file the police report," I told her.

"Okay. What else?"

"Were there any witnesses?"

"Not to my knowledge. But I saw a janitor when I walked out. I also called 9-1-1 but I left before they sent someone," Delaney said.

"That may be more help than you think. Write down any details you remember. But first go and file the report," I said.

"I will. Thank you, Raymond. Thanks, Kyle," Delaney said as she leaned over and kissed Kyle on the lips.

"Well, don't thank me yet. Let's just see what we can do," I said.

For the first time Delaney gave me a warm, sincere smile as she left the room.

"Thanks, Ray," Kyle said.

"For what? I want to help. Maybe this will make up for my defense of you-know-who," I said.

"Yes, I think it would," Kyle said.

"Look what I got," I said, removing the Stephanie Mills CD from the bag.

"Oh, look at Miss Stephanie's haircut. I like it," Kyle said. "I heard she does a fierce version of Donny Hathaway's 'This Christmas.' "

"Yeah, I heard it on the radio. It does kick," I said as I examined the back of the disc.

Kyle suddenly whispered and motioned for me to come closer to him.

"Are they still out there?" he mouthed.

"Who?"

"Delaney and Jody," Kyle whispered.

"I think I heard the door shut. Why are we whispering?"

"I think Delaney and Jody are family," Kyle said.

"What do you mean?" I asked.

"You dumb motherfucker. I think they're bumping pussies," Kyle said.

"You mean they're dykes?"

Kyle nodded his head with a big smile.

"Naw. They are beautiful. As Kirby would say, dope. They couldn't be lesbians," I said.

"So pretty women can't be gay?"

"You know what I mean."

"Whatever, whatever. I'm almost certain. I think Delaney has been trying to tell me for months. You should see the two of them. There's a serious sexual thing going on," Kyle said.

"No shit. Does Nicole know?"

"Not hardly. You know I love Miss Thingamajig to death, but she is so dense when it comes to shit like that," Kyle said.

"Ain't that just the shit. I never would have guessed Delaney was gay. So I see you can't always tell about women either," I said.

I wondered how Nicole would react if she knew Delaney was gay. That is, if she was, in fact, gay. I knew Kyle had a tendency to think everybody was gay to some extent, but that was usually with men. He used to kid Janelle all the time about being lesbian.

I was also checking my own reaction to Kyle's news. First, his use of the word dyke and my thinking that because Delaney was so beautiful, she couldn't possibly be gay. If I followed my thinking to its conclusion, I guess all lesbians had to look like diesel truck drivers. There again went life's stereotypes.

I don't know why Kyle wanted to see a sad movie. I had never seen *Dark Victory* and this certainly wasn't the time. I'd had a similar reaction when we watched the movie *Beaches*. Kyle teased me by saying they were only movies and they were supposed to make you sad. When

I realized where the movie was going, I jumped off the bed and went into the kitchen to talk with Peaches. I told her about Jared finding Kyle's father. She rolled her eyes and shook her head in disgust.

"You don't like him just a little bit?" I teased.

"Low-down motherfucker. J. D. Benton ain't shit. Ain't never been, won't ever be," Peaches said. "What you wanna bet he don't show up?"

Just as I was getting ready to answer, Kyle called out from the bedroom. "Ray, I'm lonely," he yelled. "Come put in this *Daughters* video."

I looked at Peaches, gave her a grimace, and went into the bedroom. I popped in the film and got in the bed with Kyle. I figured I could handle this one. Right before it started, Kyle looked at me and asked, "Do you want my fuck films?"

"What?"

"My boy movies. They are in the closet in a shoe box. I've collected some good ones. All with black, big-dick men," Kyle said. "Oh and I forgot, my magazine collection too. They will help you on those lonely nights in Atlanta."

"What do you want me to do with them?"

"You can keep them or burn them. I just don't want Peaches to see them. She's liberal but she might faint if she sees them." Kyle laughed out loud at the thought of Peaches viewing his porn collection. "Now don't forget all your assignments." Kyle said

"What are you talking about?"

"Don't act so stupid, child," Kyle said. "When it's over call Dr. Brooks first. Make sure the porn collection is gone. Now I'm telling you Peaches is going to want to do this funeral, but you've got to stand firm and have me cremated right away," Kyle said in an even tone.

"Kyle, why are we talking about this? You're getting better. You might outlive us all," I said.

"Not with thirty-two T cells, baby," Kyle said as if he were giving his LSAT score.

"Kyle. What happened to all the boys you used to date?"

"You know trade. I found a perfect way to get rid of them once I got tired of them," Kyle said.

"How?"

"I just loaned them money. It got rid of them every time."

Kyle and I were silent as we enjoyed *Daughters of the Dust*. Just as the film was finishing its rewind, the phone rang. Peaches called from the kitchen to say it was for me.

"Ray." It was Jared.

"Yeah, what's up?"

"Mr. J. D. Benton called. He'll be in New York this evening. His flight arrives at seven-ten at Kennedy. I told him you would probably send a car for him," Jared said.

"Consider it done. Jared?"

"Yes?"

"You're the best."

"I know," Jared said as I hung up the phone. My heart was racing and Kyle was looking at me with a hurry-up-and-tell-me look.

"So what's up?" Kyle asked.

"Are you ready for this?"

"Ready for what?" Kyle asked.

"Jared located your father. He'll be here this evening," I said.

Kyle was silent. He look toward the window, then at me, and he smiled faintly and nodded.

"Well, I better go in there and warn Peaches," I said. When I reached the doorway Kyle called out my name.

"Ray," he said.

"Yeah, buddy."

"Thanks."

I smiled.

The hours before the arrival of J. D. Benton seemed to take longer than a winter night descending into dawn. I could tell Kyle was nervous and Peaches was now drinking her vodka straight. Kyle asked me to wash the white pajamas Nicole bought him so he could have them on when his father arrived.

I offered to take Peaches to the movies or to a play so Kyle could have the time alone, but Peaches said she wasn't having it.

Kyle and I sat in the bedroom just talking about days gone by. I told him about my wanting to go see what type of business now occupied the Nickel Bar's infamous spot. Kyle laughed and said that was a great idea. Kyle asked me if I'd talked with Janelle and if she and Christopher were going to make his birthday party. I assured him I would call once I got back to the hotel to make sure she was coming.

"Are you excited about seeing your father?" I asked.

"I'm kinda nervous," Kyle said.

"Oh, it will be fine," I assured.

"Ray?"

"Yes, Kyle," I said.

"Have I told you how lucky I am to have you as a friend for all these years?" Kyle said softly.

"I'm the lucky one," I said.

"Not many people like me have friends like you," Kyle said.

I didn't say anything because I felt tears coming on. I started to imagine happy times . . . Kyle and I dancing wildly in the Nickel Bar to Chaka Khan's "I'm Every Woman" and then to Whitney Houston's new version following right after, the sounds beating faster than my heart after a hundred-yard dash. We danced as though we didn't have a care in the world. As though everything was the way it used to be before AIDS infiltrated the planet.

I snapped out of my daydream as I heard the buzzer from downstairs sound and I looked over at Kyle. A single tear was sliding down his cheek. He quickly wiped at it with the back of his palm and glanced away.

I got up from the bed and walked to the front door to greet Kyle's father. Peaches was sitting at Kyle's sewing machine with a glass in one hand and a cigarette in the other. She looked at me and shook her head as I opened the door.

"Come on in, Mr. Benton. I'm a close friend of your son. My name is Raymond Tyler, Jr.," I said as I extended my hand toward Kyle's father. Kyle didn't look exactly like him, but I could tell from his smile that he was indeed Kyle's father.

"J. D. Benton. It's a pleasure to meet you, young man," J.D. said.

J. D. Benton was an athletically lean man of medium height. His paper sack brown face was shaped like a pear and his pepper-colored hair was thinning at the top. Thick eyebrows hovered over his enormous eyes. J.D. looked at Peaches and smiled. "It's good seeing you, girl. Looks like you're taking care of yourself," J.D. said.

"Wish I could say the same about you," Peaches mumbled.

J.D. looked at me and said, "Some things never change, young man."

I took J.D.'s thin black garment bag and placed it in the closet. I told him he could stay in my hotel room and I would write down the directions and leave a key. When he asked where I was going to stay, I told him I was staying with a friend in Jersey City. I was thinking about Basil awaiting my visit to his villa.

"You sure, young man? I could stay here and sleep on the floor," J.D. said.

"Oh no, you won't," Peaches chirped.

"No, don't worry, Mr. Benton. I've already made the arrangements," I said.

"Call me J.D.," he said.

"Okay, J.D. You ready to see your son?"

"Yeah. You got anything to drink?"

"Sure. I should warn you Kyle's had a tough time. He's worried about how he looks," I said as I gave J.D. a beer.

J.D. took a long swig of the beer, let out a loud belch, looked at me and said, "Let's go."

I led J.D. into Kyle's room. Kyle was looking up at the ceiling in the still room. He seemed comfortable in his solitude.

"Kyle," I said softly. "I've got somebody here to see you."

"How you doin', son?" J.D. said as he walked close to Kyle's bed. Kyle didn't react to his father's greeting.

"I'll leave you two alone," I said.

Kyle looked at me and smiled as he formed the okay sign with his hand. I smiled back and said, "Let's walk up to the Nickel Bar tomorrow. You think you'll be up to that?"

"Yeah, that would be nice. Maybe tomorrow. Yeah, tomorrow, baby boy," Kyle said softly.

I gently shut the door. This was the first time I recalled the door being shut tightly in a long time. I felt Kyle and his father deserved the privacy. I made sure Peaches was all right and I darted out into the cold December darkness.

Daybreak came. I awakened from a restless sleep and slid from under Basil's down blanket out onto the icy, cold hardwood floor and looked around the room for my clothing. The night before with Basil had been a lazy, soothing night, perfect for a one on one. Basil was happy to see me when I arrived. He told me how sorry he was about what happened with Dyanna. I was so hungry to sleep next to a warm body that I readily accepted the apology. My need to be caressed far outweighed my pride. I couldn't think of a better body than Basil's.

I didn't tell Basil about Kyle's illness. I just told him I was exploring some business options in New York. Basil, as self-assured as ever, was convinced I was considering moving to New York to be close to him.

Basil and I polished off a bottle of wine and listened to Marvin Gaye's "What's Going On" CD all night. We didn't have sex, even though Basil's sex was erect the entire night. We held each other, kissed, and brushed each other's hair with the palm of our hands. I explained to Basil I had something on my mind and much to my surprise, he was very understanding. "But you owe me," he said.

Basil emerged smiling from the shower and gave me two towels. After my shower, he brought up coffee and toast and offered to give me a ride back into the city. He said he didn't have to be at the stadium until after lunch. I was anxious to get to Kyle's and make sure Peaches and J.D. hadn't killed each other.

Basil looked handsome in a brick-red cotton sweater and jeans. He was very talkative as we rode in his shiny black Porsche through the Holland tunnel back into the city. Basil blew his horn every two minutes to drivers who either recognized him or got in his way. As we got into town, Basil stopped talking and started adjusting the radio. It was a bright dreamy day. The peacock blue sky stretched out to eternity and a heatless winter sun was shining bright. As I listened to Christmas music from the radio, I thought maybe I could get in some shopping when Kyle and I made our sojourn to the Nickel Bar. There were several stores along Columbus Avenue where I could get gifts for Pops, Mom, and Kirby. "You want to go on a trip with me?" Basil asked, interrupting my shopping plans.

"A trip? Where?"

"The Black Ski Summit in January after the Pro Bowl," Basil said. "Dyanna has a job and can't go."

"So I'm second choice. Where and when?"

"I don't know the exact date but it's in Vail."

"As in Colorado?"

"Yes."

"Can't do it," I said quickly.

"Why?" Basil asked.

"Don't you know about the boycott?"

"What boycott?"

"They passed an anti-gay law up there and a lot of people are boy-cotting the state," I explained.

"Aw, Ray, that's white folks shit. Gay white boys don't give a shit about us," Basil said.

"Well, I don't disagree with you on that, but I don't think it's right. If they think they can do it to gays, then it will be blacks and Jews next —or should I say again? You know history sometimes repeats itself," I said.

"So you won't go?"

"I won't go to Vail, but I'd go to someplace like Vermont with you."

"Vermont?"

"Yeah, I hear it's beautiful there. We should try it."

"I've already paid my money. Maybe I'll ask another one of my bitches," Basil said.

"Suit yourself. I've told you 'bout that shit. You really should check yourself, man. Bitches, faggots? You're better than that."

"Where is your hotel?" Basil asked, obviously slightly disturbed.

"Forty-Sixth right off Eighth Avenue," I instructed. Then I thought maybe I should head straight up to Kyle's just in case his father was still at my hotel room. I could stop at the hotel and offer him a ride, but Basil's car was a two-seater.

"On second thought, take me up to Ninety-sixth and Broadway," I said.

"You want to make a friendly wager?" Basil asked.

"A wager? on what?"

"The Sugar Bowl. Mighty Miami is playing countryassed Alabama," Basil said. I was so involved with Kyle's care that I forgot that Alabama was having a great football season.

"Let's talk about it later, but sure I'll bet something."

"I know what I want if I win," Basil smiled.

"Niggah, please," I said as Basil sped up the West Side Highway.

"Who lives up there?" Basil asked.

"Kyle," I said.

"How is he doing? You two still tight?"

I was silent for a couple of streetlights.

"Yes, we're still tight. Basil, there's something I should have told you. Kyle is sick," I said.

"Sick? What do you mean?"

"You know," I said.

"It's not what I think, is it, Ray?"

"If you're thinking AIDS, then yes," I said soberly.

"Man, that's fucked up. So that's why you're in the city," Basil said as he maneuvered through the busy city traffic. When we reached a stoplight he gently tapped his head against the steering wheel.

"Yes. That's why I'm here."

"How are you holding up?"

"I'm hanging," I said.

"Is there anything I can do?" Basil asked.

"No, not right now. But thanks for asking," I said as I rubbed the palm of my hand across Basil's hard thighs. Basil flashed his bright smile and asked me to call him later that evening to pay up. I smiled and promised at least to call him later. I informed him that I might need a place to stay.

When I walked into Kyle's apartment I immediately sensed something was wrong. Peaches and J.D. were huddled on the sofa consoling one another.

"Ray," Peaches said in a weak trembling voice. "Something is wrong with Kyle. He won't wake up."

"I just came out of his room. I think it's over," J.D. said.

I stopped in the center of the living room, gazed at the dressmaker's dummy and the clear day outside the window. This was the moment I had dreaded since coming to New York. This couldn't be happening I thought. This is a dream. Time, which had been our faceless companion for months, was ready for departure.

"Ray, will you go in there and wake him up?" Peaches said.

I didn't answer. I just walked into Kyle's bedroom and saw him resting peacefully.

"Kyle," I called out. The room was silent. I moved close to the bed where Kyle was resting. I touched his face and it was icy cold. I reached under the blankets and pulled out Kyle's limp arms, feeling for a pulse. Nothing. A dry sweat crept across my face. Kyle was dead.

I bit my lips and walked over to the window and silently counted five black cars and then slowly moved back to Kyle's bed. No change. The inside of my stomach churned. I wanted to gather him in my arms and rock him back to life. I wanted to tell him everything would be all right, but instead I kissed his forehead and gently ran my hands across his face and closed eyes. I walked back into the living room where Peaches and J.D. were still huddled together. They looked up at me with imploring, anxious eyes.

"It's over," I announced. "Kyle's gone home," I said as I clenched my fingers into tight fists. Peaches screamed like an actress in a bad horror movie. Tears flowed down her face and she shook her head in disbelief. She was in a great deal of pain, but so was I. I gave Peaches a firm hug but she suddenly bolted from my embrace and raced into Kyle's room. J.D. started behind her but I quickly grabbed him and said, "Let her have some time alone with him." J.D. nodded and looked into my eyes. With his voice choked with sadness he said, "Tell me about my son."

"There isn't enough time right now. I have so much work to do."

Part Three

Love

When You

Least Expect It

Thirty-two

My heart should be used to this. My heart does not stop for death but it hurts. It was death that pulled Raymond and me apart. It was death that brought us back together. Back together in something more powerful than what we shared before. A friendship based on love, mutual respect, and honesty. A friendship of the heart.

Though I thought I was prepared, Kyle's death shocked me. I knew his health was fading fast but I thought he would make it to Christmas and his birthday. When Raymond called I went into shock and then uncontrollable tears. Delaney came over and the tears started again the moment I opened the door and saw her standing there. We cried in each other arms before leaving for Kyle's apartment.

We didn't have a chance to see Kyle before they took him to the crematorium. He was cremated in the twilight of the day he died. Raymond, in a very organized manner, was taking care of everything, rapidly. He was sitting at Kyle's sewing machine with a list, marking off tasks as he completed them or assigned them to one of Kyle's family members or friends. He took Kyle's loose-leaf phone book and gave Delaney and me pages of Kyle's friends to call and inform them of Kyle's death. This was not a pleasant task. Most of the phone calls were short; Kyle's friends would thank us for calling and ask if there was going to be a funeral. Raymond also took on the task of peacemaker. Kyle's family started to come in from Jersey, all demanding a funeral and a look at Kyle's will. He informed them there wouldn't be a funeral, but he was going ahead with the plans for the party and they could pay their respects there. He would read the will after the party.

I learned Kyle's father had come to town and visited Kyle before his death, but he'd left shortly after Kyle died because he and Peaches were at each other's throats. Kyle's father blamed Peaches for Kyle being gay and therefore for his death by what he considered a gay disease. Peaches threatened to kill him. Despite his father's ignorance I was glad Kyle got to see him before he died. When Delaney and I saw Peaches we gave her a collective hug. She started sobbing hysterically and then suddenly collapsed. Raymond picked her up gently and placed her limp body in Kyle's bed. Delaney prepared cold compresses and laid them on her head and sat at the edge of the bed for hours. Raymond went in to relieve Delaney and I think they even exchanged a smile.

I was finding it difficult to spend time in Kyle's bedroom. I was somewhat relieved when Delaney volunteered to look after Peaches. I kept thinking about my last conversation with Kyle. Had I been a good friend to him? Did my disappointment over my breakup with Raymond and Candance's death cloud my feelings toward all gay men, including Kyle?

I hoped Kyle really knew how much I loved him. I loved him for who he was, for what he taught me about myself and the feelings I was too afraid to acknowledge. More importantly he made me realize that many are born male, but it took more than what you did in the bedroom to be a man. Kyle Alexander Benton was a man in the real sense of the word.

Instead of having the party on Kyle's birthday, we held it on Christmas Day. It was not the type of Christmas I'd planned. About thirty of Kyle's friends came by and Janelle came up from North Carolina with her little boy, Christopher. Janelle looked a lot different. She appeared slimmer than I recalled and she was a lot nicer to me. We actually exchanged pleasant conversation about her son and her graduate studies. I suppose marriage and living in the South were agreeing with her. When I'd first met Janelle, I didn't like her at all and I think the feeling was mutual. She was constantly making fun of my beauty pageant experiences by asking questions as though she was really interested. I could tell she was just patronizing me by her tone and the way she looked at Kyle. Kyle later confirmed my suspicions, but explained that she didn't mean any harm. "She's just a fag hag," he said. When I asked Kyle if I was a fag hag he just laughed and said, "Not yet. It takes years of training and you haven't even been to a gay bar yet." I came to realize fag hag was a term of endearment.

The party was really nice. Raymond opened it with a prayer and then explained Kyle's desire that we all celebrate his life, not mourn his passing. He stressed that Kyle didn't want any tears, so everybody agreed that if they felt tears coming on they would leave the room.

Several people did leave the room after telling their stories, mostly funny, about Kyle and what he meant to their lives. I shared a story about how Kyle always acted fearful whenever we got on an elevator with white people. Kyle would clutch his chest and playfully tremble in fear and, of course, they looked at him strangely. "I want them to know how we feel when they act that way toward us," Kyle had told me the first time he did it. Everybody in the room laughed and said in unison, "That's Kyle." Delaney told a story of how Kyle fell out of love quickly when the guy he was seeing said "those three words." "I asked Kyle why he was afraid of 'I love you' but he explained that those weren't the three words he meant. 'What words then?' I asked. 'Lay a Way,' Kyle said." The room rocked with laughter.

I left the room and stepped out to the hallway when Raymond began talking about the first time he'd met Kyle and how much he learned from Kyle about living in New York City. I didn't come back into the room until I heard a female voice talking. I didn't think I could handle seeing the pain on Raymond's face.

A couple of days after the party, Raymond showed up at my house with two huge boxes. He said Kyle made him promise he would make sure I got them. I opened the boxes and broke into tears when I saw two beautiful completed wedding dresses. Raymond put his arms around me and held me tightly until the tears stopped.

Raymond was still maintaining his strong and confident manner. Not once did I see him cry or anything remotely resembling a tear in his eyes. I did notice that every time I was around him he had a drink in his hand. When I asked him if I could help him pack up Kyle's apartment he assured me he had everything under control. A few days after Christmas he rented a van and took Peaches' and Kyle's belongings to New Jersey. He promised to keep in touch.

The new year was showing signs of promise. Raymond had moved from the hotel and had told me he was house-sitting at a friend's place in Jersey City. He said he just couldn't bring himself to stay in his old apartment. When I'd offered to let him stay at my place, he'd politely declined, though he'd promised to stay New Year's Eve. I told him my sofa was a sleeper.

When Raymond came back to New York on New Year's Eve, he

called me the minute he got in. He'd got Peaches settled but said he was worried about her drinking. I convinced him to go to the New Year's Watch Service with me and we came back to my apartment afterward. On the carpet-covered floor of my apartment, we sat cross-legged and drank a bottle of champagne and talked. It was during our talk that I realized the pain Kyle's death was causing him. His green eyes went from misty to angry within moments as he talked about Kyle's last days.

"You are okay, Raymond?"

"If you mean, am I still HIV negative then the answer is yes. I'm not certain I'm all right."

"You'll be just fine," I assured Raymond.

"How did you handle it, Nicole?"

"Handle it?"

"Candance's death. I mean, how do you deal with losing your best friend."

"I prayed a lot. I cried, and I'm going to tell you something I haven't told anyone."

A puzzled look crossed Raymond's face.

"I got professional help," I said.

"Professional help?"

"Yes, Raymond. I've been seeing a therapist for over three years and believe me it has helped a great deal."

Raymond looked at me thoughtfully, but didn't respond to my confession.

I wanted to ask him about his life in Atlanta and his friend Jared, but the late hour and the champagne was taking its toll.

I was going to offer him my bed and I was going to sleep on the couch, but we started talking again and I felt relaxed with him so close by. He came into my bedroom displaying his muscular body, naked to the waist and wearing only boxer shorts below. I didn't remember him wearing boxer underwear. When he got into bed he pulled me close to him and I didn't resist. The feel of his body, his scent, was familiar and comforting. During a time when I should have been comforting him, Raymond was protecting me. We slept that night with our bodies glued together. Not a sexual glue, but a close, tender embrace. This was the type of night we both needed.

The next morning I made a big breakfast of toast, grits, and eggs, but Raymond just picked at his food. I was certain he had lost weight since Kyle's death. He said he had a few more things to take care of and then he was heading back to Atlanta. He thanked me for the previous evening and said, "Nicole, you know I will always love you. I hope one day very soon you find a man who deserves you." He then gave me a sweet, simple kiss. "I hope this is the beginning of a beautiful friendship," he said.

"More beautiful than you'll ever know," I said.

"Thank you for everything," Raymond said.

"Raymond, can I ask you something?"

"Sure, Nicole, sure."

"Why do you think you're gay or bisexual?"

Raymond pursed his lips together and looked around the small kitchen. He began tapping his fingers in a cadence on the kitchen counter. "I don't really know the answer to that. All I know is it feels right for me. A part of me. It's just who I am. Do you understand?"

"I'm trying."

"Well, you know what goes on inside your head when it comes to sex or being attracted to someone. Even if that someone isn't right for you?"

"I'm not sure I understand what you're saying or asking," I said.

"All I can say is my sexuality is something that I didn't choose. I don't control the signals it sends me. What I can control is acting on those signals. Sometimes being alive and the person Christ wanted me to be means acting on those signals. Is that a little better?"

"I think so. I shouldn't have asked. I'm sorry."

"I'm glad you asked. I wish I could explain it better. There are times when I wish there was a way we could really look inside each other's hearts and minds. I think then and only then could we understand another person's dilemmas and pain."

"I think I understand what you're saying."

When Raymond left New York City I began to feel very lonely. The emptiness in my life was immense. Dr. Huntley was on vacation out of the country so I turned to prayer, silent and private prayer. Delaney was busy with an industrial show and was talking about moving to San Diego. When I asked her why, she said she was getting burned out with New York City and its problems. She had finally filed a police report and Raymond was assisting her in a lawsuit against the bastard. Delaney said she felt a great deal of relief when Papa Kee was arrested. Raymond was also able to determine that a janitor had witnessed the whole incident and told me that it was likely the guy would have to do some time and still have to pay for Delaney's pain and suffering. Delaney mentioned using the money to open a dance school near a housing project in San Diego. I suggested she open a school in New York and she said Dance Theater of Harlem more than fit the needs here. She also mentioned Jody hated New York.

I didn't know a lot about Jody. She seemed nice, but I was so busy with *Jelly's* and *To Tell the Truth* that I didn't get the chance to spend a lot of time with her. I must admit I was getting a tad bit jealous of all the time she and Delaney were spending together.

I decided with the new year that I was going to take control of my career and only pursue the recording opportunities. I gave my two-week notice to *Jelly's* and was almost certain I wouldn't sign a contract with *Truth*. The script and music were horrible. They were still doing rewrites but I didn't think anything was going to save this brewing fiasco. They were talking about not trying the show out of town and just opening on Broadway, which in most cases always spelled trouble. One evening after rehearsal, I went to JR's for drinks with Timothy and found out he was feeling the same way I was about the play. He said, "This musical is so bad it will probably close after the first song."

In the midst of caring for Kyle and going back and forth between two shows, I had lost track of what was happening in my home state. But Governor Clinton had won the presidency and I received a call from the inaugural committee asking me to perform at one of the balls. The member of the committee who called was a big fan of mine from my Miss Arkansas days and promised to give me a prime spot with a lot of national coverage. It was an offer I couldn't refuse. And since I had missed Christmas with my mother I figured this would be a good time to bring her East. I was going to have her meet me in Washington, D.C., and then we'd take the train back to Manhattan together. I was really excited when she accepted. This solved two problems. I wouldn't have to worry about an escort and it would give my mother and me a chance to spend some time together.

I had just finished my final set at the Arkansas Ball in Washington, D.C.'s beautiful Convention Center. It was a wonderful experience. The President came to the ball and the crowd was warm and receptive to my singing. It was a moment I will never forget. It was a great night to be an Arkansan. The most powerful man in the free world was from my small home state. All the major networks covered the event and I was interviewed by C-SPAN. Several Hollywood types came up to me between sets, gave me cards, and asked me to give them a call. I knew the men might just be flirting but I took each card and made mental notes to myself as to my gut impression of the validity of their offers. I mean, I had to be realistic, I was out of work.

I wore an ivory gown drenched in bugle beads Kyle had made a couple of years back. I dedicated "If I Could" to Kyle; it took all I had to finish the song without crying. Kyle and I first heard the song when we went to the Essence Awards and Regina Belle sang it in a tribute to Nancy Wilson. I went out the next day and bought the sheet music.

I was on my way outside to find the limo driver the committee had provided when I heard someone call my name. The voice was deep and melodic.

"Nicole?"

I turned and I was face to face with Jared, Raymond's friend from Atlanta.

"Jared, right?"

"Yes. How are you doing?" he asked.

"I'm fine. You're not from Arkansas, are you?" I asked.

"No, but I worked on the campaign and I saw in one of the programs that you were performing here," he said with a bright smile.

"Is Raymond here? I invited him," I said.

"No. I tried to talk him into coming but he's still having a tough time," Jared said.

"I know he is, though he won't admit it," I said.

"You're a wonderful singer. I stayed for both sets," he said.

"You did?"

"Yes. This is the place to be and when I heard you sing I realized why."

"You're too kind."

"Where are you going after this?"

"I'm heading to my hotel," I said. "I was looking for my driver."

"What hotel are you staying at?" Jared asked.

"The Four Seasons in Georgetown, and you?"

"The Omni in Georgetown," he said.

I wondered why he was interested in where I was staying.

"Well, it's nice seeing you, Jared. Please give Ray my best," I said as I started to exit the packed Convention Center.

"Nicole," Jared said.

"Yes."

"Could I interest you in a late dinner or some coffee?"

"Dinner?"

"Yes, unless you have some other plans," he said shyly.

I hesitated briefly. I didn't have plans except to go back to my hotel and read. My mother had canceled her trip because her arthritis had flared up and she didn't feel up to flying. I'd tried to talk Delaney into coming with me, but she was still in rehearsal for the industrial. Jared was looking quite handsome in his black tux.

"Sure, Jared, I'd like to get something to eat," I said.

"Great!" he smiled.

"What's your last name?" I asked.

"It's Stovall," he said.

"Oh, Jared Stovall."

"No, Jared Taylor Stovall," he beamed.

"So where to?"

"Do you want to go to the hotel and change? I mean you look great but I do have a car," he said.

"Oh, sure, that would be nice. Let me tell my driver."

After locating my driver, I followed Jared to the front of the center where he gave the valet a ticket. Moments later we were driving through the crowded city. The city was swimming in moonlight on this cold January night. White cotton clouds filled the darkened sky. Jared appeared a bit nervous as he slipped into the busy traffic entering Georgetown.

We talked about how excited we both were at the prospects of a Clinton presidency. Jared told me about his interest in politics and some funny stories from the campaign. Our conversation moved briefly to Kyle with Jared telling me how glad he was that he got to meet Kyle before he died. He then said he was trying to keep close tabs on Ray since his return to Atlanta. Jared appeared warm and sensitive.

Jared suggested one of the several restaurants close to my hotel. I changed into a black sweater dress and put on my leather coat and boots. A warm sweatsuit would have been nice, but I didn't know what type of restaurant we were going to. Jared parked his car at the hotel and we walked to the restaurant.

Georgetown had a carnival-type atmosphere with street vendors and people everywhere. Car horns were blowing in impatience and celebration. Everybody spoke to one another as they passed on the cobblestone streets. After an hour's wait, Jared and I settled into a booth in the packed restaurant. Jared ordered Mexican coffee and chicken wings. I liked the way he took control.

The restaurant had a small-town flavor even though it wasn't small. It was an old Victorian-type house, with excess atmosphere. A very romantic mood presided over the restaurant from the decorations to the many couples staring into each other's eyes. There were fresh flowers on every table and in every booth with framed poster art and celebrity pictures on the walls. Beautiful mahogany bookshelves lined with leatherbound books completed the decor.

"So how long have you and Ray been friends?"

"Almost four years," he said. "But let's talk about you."

"Me?" I wondered why he was interested in me.

"Yes. You know I'm going to tell you something that's going to shock you," Jared said.

What was he going to tell me . . . that he was gay? I already knew that.

"What?" I asked.

"I've been a secret admirer of yours since you won Miss Morehouse. You lived in Height Hall and you're an AKA," he said.

"How do you know all that? Did Ray tell you?"

"No. Did you forget I went to Morris Brown?"

"Oh, I'm sorry I forgot."

"No problem. I always thought that you were one of the most beautiful women on the yard," he said.

"You're sweet to say that," I said. "Why didn't you ever say something to me?"

"I wasn't exactly in your social class. I was just a local boy going to college because of work study and a Pell Grant. I even used to bus tables at Spelman's dining hall. You were always with this other pretty sister."

"Oh, that was my best friend, Candance. And what do you mean my social class? If it wasn't for grants and beauty pageants I never would have had the chance to go to Spelman."

"I was pretty surprised to see you when I walked into Kyle's. I never would have made the connection that you were the Nicole that broke Ray's heart," he said.

"So that's what he told you?"

"Well, that's the impression I got," he said.

"So that's when you came in," I said.

"Excuse me?" Jared said with a puzzled look on his face.

"I mean, is that when you and Ray became lovers?" I said.

Jared broke out into a loud laughter. He was laughing so hard he almost fell out of the booth. "Ray and I lovers? Nicole, don't get me wrong, I love Ray to death, but like a brother. We're not lovers," he said.

"Oh, I'm sorry. I just thought—" I said, feeling a little bit embarrassed.

"Oh, that's funny. Wait until I tell Ray," he said.

"So do you have a lover?" I asked.

"A lover like in male lover?" Jared asked.

"Yes."

"Nicole, I don't know how to break this to you, but I'm not gay or bisexual," Jared said.

"You're not?"

"No. I hope that doesn't halt our friendship," he said.

"Oh no. I'm sorry. I just thought . . ."

"No problem."

I looked into Jared's eyes to see if I could detect deception. Why would he lie about his sexuality? Kyle and Ray taught me you couldn't always take a man at his word on this or a lot of other things for that matter when it came to dealing with women. But Jared seemed different and he was so nice that I really believed it didn't matter. The sincerity in his voice was real and I wanted to know more. He shared with me a story about a lady he'd dated while in college and told me how after their breakup he'd concentrated heavily on his career. He said there'd been other women but nothing major.

As he talked, a delicious warmth filled my body. Jared was very interesting and when he paused and smiled I felt his smile was inviting me into his world. He exuded an aura of strength and confidence. When he talked there was passion in his eyes, along with a boy's natural softness. He talked about his mother and sisters and how he was renovating an old house in the west end area of Atlanta near the AU center.

In a lot of ways Jared reminded me of Raymond. Since Candance's death and my relationship with Raymond, I'd never considered the fact that men could be close friends without it being sexual. It was very clear that Jared cared a great deal about Raymond—it was apparent during the few minutes I met him in New York and in the way in which they talked about each other—but I guess it was ridiculous to think all

Raymond's friends would be gay or to think men couldn't have relationships similar to the ones women shared.

Jared and I became so involved in conversation, we didn't realize how late it was. The restaurant had extended its normal hours and remained open all night. When I stopped looking directly into Jared's eyes and glanced out the window I saw that morning had come.

Thirty-three

"I want to be happy. I just don't think it's possible."

"Why, Raymond?"

"You know why," I said.

"Is it because of your confusion over your sexuality?" Dr. Paul asked.

"I'm just afraid of dying like Kyle. Alone, without someone special loving me," I said.

"But from what you've told me Kyle had a lot of friends. Nicole, Delaney, and you."

"Yes, but you know what I'm saying. We were Kyle's family. I'm talking about romantic love. As wonderful as Kyle was I don't think he ever had the romantic type of love we dreamed of as children."

"So that's very important to you?" she asked.

"Yes. Is there something wrong with that?"

Dr. Paul didn't answer. She looked at her watch and laid down her yellow legal pad, which meant my hour, or fifty minutes in reality, was up. I raised myself from the flowered sofa, picked the throw pillow up from the floor, and returned it to its original place.

"So, same time tomorrow, Doc?"

"Yes. Are you still having a difficult time sleeping?"

"No, but I'm still taking the medication."

"What about the lights?"

"I'm still leaving them on," I said.

"Well, let's talk about that tomorrow," Dr. Paul suggested.

I walked out of Dr. Paul's office into the small waiting area. I avoided eye contact with a slightly overweight white lady with dirty brown hair who was sitting there. I didn't know if you should make eye contact in a psychiatrist's office. Perhaps she was like me and didn't want anyone to know she was seeing a therapist.

I quickly left the building, entered the parking deck, and walked directly to my car. Today was another gray day in Atlanta and that didn't do anything to help my mood. After returning to Atlanta from New York, I'd drifted into a deep depression, terminal melancholy, not caring very much about anything. The only work I had done was to get a hefty settlement for Delaney from her assailant—even though he received only a slap on the hands from the courts. I hadn't returned to work and nothing seemed to lift me from my depressed state. Not Jared, my pops, or my mother, who had driven down two weekends in a row to try and take care of me. She'd made all my favorite foods, which I'd only picked at. She had even made banana pudding filled with strawberries, something I loved. During her visits my mom didn't press me on what I needed to discuss with her and Pops.

A couple of days before Jared left for Washington, D.C., I decided to follow Nicole's advice and seek professional help. I didn't tell a single soul. I called a doctor's referral service and explained the problems I was experiencing and the type of doctor I wanted. The service then gave me a list of possibilities and tried to match me up with a doctor.

My first choice was a black gay male doctor but the service stated they didn't have a doctor listed with those qualifications. Why was I not surprised? So I opted for a white, female doctor. This was because I was convinced that a white male doctor wouldn't understand my problems, a black non-gay male doctor certainly wouldn't, and a black female doctor would probably be judgmental. The first name on the list was a Dr. Jessica Paul. Her address indicated that she was close by.

Dr. Jessica Paul was an attractive woman, in her early forties, with ash blond hair, ocean blue eyes, and light brown freckles usually covered by thick glasses. I felt comfortable with her from our first meeting. She had a soothing quality, but she didn't give me any answers. She always said, "Well, what do you think?" There were times when I wanted to shout, bitch, that's what I'm paying you ninety-five dollars an hour for. But I resisted. I saw Dr. Paul every morning at ten o'clock. I then came home, turned the television on, and gazed at it throughout the day. How I missed Kyle. How I hated my life.

Jared seemed to think I would eventually snap out of this mood. He thought it was pretty normal considering the fact I had just watched my best friend die. But where was my grief? I still hadn't dropped a tear since Kyle died. I just went about the business of doing what he'd asked me to do. Most times my body felt numb but somehow I managed to keep moving.

Nicole was a big help. I'd spent New Year's Eve with her and even spent the night in her bed with her warm and wonderful body next to mine. I felt her protecting me and it felt nice. Not a sexual nice, but a friendship warmth that I'd thought was possible only from another man. I seriously considered moving back to New York, but there would be so many memories of Kyle. It took everything I had to pack up and clean the apartment where both Kyle and I had spent so many nights. Peaches helped, but almost every thirty minutes she would come across something that caused her to break down and cry.

I tried to keep in contact with her for weeks after Kyle's death but it was difficult because every time she heard my voice she started wailing over the phone. Instead of making me feel better, she forced me into a deeper depression. But I couldn't tell anyone but Dr. Paul. I had to be strong or at least put on a strong front. It was what I was expected to do. I had to be a man. I had to stay strong!

"So do you think I can be cured?"

"Cured from what, Raymond?"

"You know. Being attracted to men," I said.

"Is that what you want?"

"It would make life simpler," I mumbled.

"How?" Dr. Paul quizzed.

"Maybe it would make me feel better about myself."

"How do you feel about yourself, Raymond?"

"I know I'm a good person. But why can't I adjust to my sexuality? Why can't I make a decision to be with a man or a woman?"

Dr. Paul remained silent. She glanced at a picture on her shelf. I assumed it was her husband and child.

"Did I tell you that years ago my father recommended I see a doctor to get cured?"

"What did you do?"

"Nothing. Just went on living my life the way I had been taught. Never facing who I really was."

"That being?"

"I don't know yet. I think maybe Kyle knew."

No response. She just wrote on her legal pad. When she stopped writing she gazed into my eyes, waiting for me to start talking again.

"You know I really, really love Nicole and I think she still loves me. But it wouldn't be fair to her."

"How does she feel about that?"

"She wants a man who would love her completely. She doesn't want to have to compete with another person, especially another man. She deserves that. I mean when I'm with her I feel like I can be faithful to her. But the moment I see a good-looking man that sexually arouses me, I know I can't totally commit to a woman or at least be faithful."

"What about the guy you mentioned before? Basil?"

"Basil, he's a total fuck-up. More confused than me. Did I tell you he's talking about getting married? Yep, he's going to marry this actress who doesn't have a clue he loves dick more than she does."

"How do you feel about that?"

"I know I have to get him out of my system. I can't be involved with another married man. I want someone for me. Someone committed to me like I would be to them. If I fall in love with Basil it will mean nothing but trouble. Didn't I tell you about Quinn?"

"Quinn?"

"The married guy I fell in love with while I was dating Nicole."

"What does he have to do with Basil?"

"Married. The married thing."

"Oh."

"So that's why I'm trying to decide what to do with Basil. Breaking up with Quinn was painful."

"Sounds like you've already made your decision."

"Yes, sometimes I think I have, but whenever I'm in the same room with him, it's hard. I mean the boy has it going on sexually. He's awfully hard to resist."

"So it's sexual?"

"Well, he has his good points. He was supportive after Kyle died by letting me stay at his condo while he went skiing. As supportive as Basil could be. He can be rather self-absorbed. But I guess we all suffer from that time to time. Right? He's into his sports and cars and laying as many women as possible. I guess it helps him keep his manhood intact."

"It sounds like that's important to you too," Dr. Paul said.

"What do you mean?"

"Well, is that the reason you have problems with your attraction to men?"

"Oh no. I have problems with men because they lie, they won't commit to a long-term relationship, and you never know if they are sleeping around with other guys."

"Sounds like the same things women say," Dr. Paul said as she looked at her watch and placed the legal pad on her nearby desk.

"Yeah, ain't that the shit," I said as I lifted myself from the sofa.

Another day. I wasn't feeling much better. My phone rang constantly and I had so much mail the mailman brought it up to my apartment because my mailbox was stuffed. I was looking forward to seeing Dr. Paul.

Dr. Paul's question lingered. I had to think about it.

"When was the first time you became aware of your sexuality? With a man or a woman?"

"With a girl. It was in the seventh grade. The first time I slow-danced with a girl. Rose Burns. A beautiful girl. I remember how my heart would race whenever I saw her when we changed classes. Changing classes . . . that was a big deal in the seventh grade. I practiced slow dancing for months with myself in front of a mirror. One . . . two . . . back . . . one . . . two. My mother and father demonstrated the steps. They laughed and kissed. They were having fun dancing. It seemed as if they forgot I was standing there watching." I paused and laughed out loud at my youthful memories.

"The dance came and I was scared shitless. I had on a new gold Ban-Lon shirt with matching socks, new penny loafers, and half a bottle of my pops's Old Spice aftershave. I watched the ninth-grader boys and girls slow-dance with each other with such ease. Many of them were doing more slow grinding than dancing. When I finally saw Rose alone I darted over and asked her to dance. I expected her to say no but she smiled and said yes. I even remember the song."

"What was the song, Raymond?"

" 'Stay in My Corner' by the Dells. We were dancing in a corner and I just wanted to hold her forever. She smelled good and she was so soft. My heart was beating so fast. She didn't even notice when I went two . . . two instead of one . . . two."

"And when did you realize you were attracted to men?"

"I never slow-dance with men. But that's not what you asked me. The first time Kelvin pressed his sex against mine and I responded. At first I freaked but it felt so good. Like something I had never felt. My heart racing and sweat covering my forehead. He smelled good. His body hard. Like the dance with Rose, my body responded. It was so wired but so wonderful. Whitney Houston's 'You Give Good Love' was playing on the radio. They were true words of what was about to happen."

"Did it surprise you when your body responded to Kelvin?"

"Shocked the shit out of me."

"Why?"

"It just did. So many gay men say they knew ever since they were little boys. I swear it had never crossed my mind."

"That can happen," Dr. Paul said.

"I'm glad to hear you say that, Doc. I wish you could tell that to my pops and Kyle."

Dr. Paul smiled.

"I don't know why but I went to a bar last night."

"A bar? What kind of bar?"

"Oh, a black gay bar. I wanted to see if it felt different."

"Different?"

"Yeah, like to see if I belonged."

"And did you?"

"Don't know. It was just the way I remembered. A packed bar full of good-looking black men. Everybody trying to reject you before you reject them. Noses so high the clouds of smoke are covering them. Men drinking away their sorrows or simply drinking to get the courage to talk to someone."

"Did you drink?"

"No, I drank cranberry juice."

"That's good. You shouldn't drink with the medication I prescribed."

"I don't think I'm going to drink again until I fall in love."

Dr. Paul brushed her hair back from her face, put her pen toward the corner of her mouth, and gave me an okay, go-on look.

"I met a guy last night. Good-looking, but a liar."

"Why do you say that?"

"After I told him I used to live in New York and went to Columbia Law School he told me he had just been accepted to law school."

"So what was wrong with that?" Dr. Paul asked.

"He said he had been accepted to Princeton Law School. When I asked him if he was certain he said yes. When I informed him Princeton didn't have a law school he walked off without a good-bye."

"How did that make you feel?"

"It just goes to prove my point. Everybody's trying to outdo each other. Even to the point of lying about it."

"Do you think that's a black gay problem?"

"Not really. I mean straight men lie too. But they lie about other things."

"How do you mean?"

"Well, I think black men in general lie or embellish their standard of living to impress women and about their escapades with other women. They lie to each other about a multitude of things."

"That's a broad generalization. Do you think it only applies to black men?"

"That's all I know. White men don't interest me."

"Why is that?"

"First, I don't find them sexually attractive. Second, they don't have any problems. I mean why should they? They control everything."

"Don't you think that sounds racist?" Dr. Paul said as she raised her eyebrows.

"Yes. I mean I used to have a lot of white friends when I was in high school and college, but I think white gay men have made me feel the way I do. I've seen good-looking white men but I'm just not attracted to them. Maybe I won't allow myself to be attracted to them. I want to make sure I'm not contributing to a master-Mandingo mentality. I mean the first time I realized there was a difference was when I tried to go to a white gay bar. They wanted five pieces of ID from me and ten from the darker-skinned black man I entered with."

"Why do you think that happened?"

"I guess they're trying to make themselves feel better than someone else and guess who gets to be on the bottom of the totem pole? Black gay men. I really get upset when I see black gay men chasing white guys and talking white. That's why I'm worried about my little brother at prep school."

"How so?"

"You know, I'm not worried about him being gay but about him talking and acting white. Plus I'm still worried about the comment he made when he met Kyle. I know a lot of that talk comes from peer pressure."

"From what you've told me that doesn't sound like a problem. Your little brother sounds pretty independent."

"Thank God for that!"

"Let's talk a little more about your feelings toward white men."

"Why? They aren't strong feelings either way."

"What do you mean?"

"Well, maybe I didn't make myself clear. It's not like I see white men and go shit, there goes another white man trying to oppress me. When I meet them one on one and view them as individuals I usually get along with them really well. It's the group as a whole that I have a problem with."

"Explain."

"Well, if I meet somebody white who does something to bug me then I put them in the group."

"The group."

"Yes, I guess the same applies with anybody. Like the black guy at the bar. When he did something to upset me I put him in the group."

"Do you think that's right?"

"No, but everybody does it."

My phone rang, but I didn't answer it. I turned up the answering machine to see who was calling. After the beep went off I heard Jared's voice say: "Ray, Raymond Junior, if you're there, pick up, pick up. Come on, Ray, pick up."

I sat on the edge of my bed staring at the red light flashing on the machine as Jared continued.

"If you don't answer this phone, I'm getting in my car and coming over there. Don't forget I've got a key."

I quickly leaped from the bed and grabbed the phone before it was too late.

"Jared, I'm here," I said.

"Still screening your calls?" he asked.

"Yeah."

"How are you doing?"

"Okay."

"You don't sound okay. Do you feel like a visit from your best friend?"

"Not today. I hope you understand?"

"I do, but it doesn't make it easy," Jared said.

"I know."

"Ray."

"Yes."

"You know I'm here if you need me, don't you?"

"Yeah, I know that."

"Ray."

"Yeah."

"I love you."

"I know."

I hung up the phone without a good-bye. I wanted to cry, but instead I took my medication and fell asleep.

"I think Jared has a crush on Nicole."

"How do you feel about that?"

"Haven't really thought about it," I said.

"Are you sure?"

"Well, I know it's over between Nicole and myself and Jared is a great guy, but I do feel a pang of jealousy. I mean sometimes I look at Jared and think he's living the life I should be living."

"How?"

"Well, he's so perfect. Good-looking, nice, truthful, and heterosexual."

"So that makes him perfect?"

"In the eyes of society and women like Nicole."

"How does Nicole feel about Jared?"

"I don't think she knows. I don't think Jared realizes that I know. I mean he's been real supportive of me but he asks me questions about Nicole and when he mentions her name his face lights up."

"Have you asked him about how he feels about her?"

"No, not yet. He told me he had a crush on her when they were in college, but I think Nicole might hurt him and that wouldn't be good."

"How so?"

"I think Nicole's into white men and Jared is far from white."

"Are you clear on your feelings about Jared?"

"Yes, I think so. I love him but it isn't romantic love like I once thought. There is no denying his good looks, sex appeal, but I get so much more from him by just being friends. Like brothers. Besides he's straight! The envy I have is a good thing."

"How so?"

"Well, it's not like I begrudge him for being straight. I mean I think at times he wouldn't mind having my life. At least the part about being raised by both parents and never really having to want for anything. I know things were tough for him growing up. My relationship with my father was not always the best, but he was always there. He gave a lot of tough love but he's always been there when I needed him."

"Do you still try to please your father?"

"Yes. I guess I always will. I think he deserves that."

"Is that why you want to change your feelings about men?"

"No, because I think if I found the right man, my father would be cool about it. I think . . . I don't know . . . I mean it's probably how a father feels about his daughter when she becomes sexually active. I mean they know they're doing it but they don't want to see it. My father knows that I like men but I don't think he wants to see me being affectionate with a man in his presence. I think it's okay as long as I don't throw it in his face."

"Is that okay with you?"

"Yes. I mean I owe him that."

"What about your mother?"

"You know I'm ashamed to say I've never really thought about how she feels. She always been very supportive of me, no matter what. My mother is pretty soft-spoken and she pretty much goes along with Pops."

"What do you owe yourself?"

I didn't answer. Instead I looked at my watch, got up, and left the room.

"Why do you feel guilty about Kyle?"

"Well, I wasn't there at the end. I was over in Jersey City hugged up with Basil. I didn't get to say good-bye."

"Think about all you did for him."

"He would have done the same for me."

"What else could you have done?"

"I don't know. I keep looking for him to show up. To call."

"Why?"

"I want to say good-bye."

"That's understandable."

"Sometimes I get angry at him."

"Angry. Why?"

"For not fighting harder. For giving up."

"Do you think he didn't fight?"

"At times."

"Is that the only reason?"

"When he was living, I'd get angry at him for falling into the trap."

"The trap?"

"Yes. The endless circle of looking for love and affection in all the wrong places with the wrong people."

"I'm not sure I understand you."

"Well, Kyle, like a lot of gay men, probably equated good sex with love and acceptance."

"Have you ever done that?"

"Sure."

"When?"

"With Basil. There are times when I'm with him I feel better about myself."

"How so?"

"Maybe because as a professional football player he epitomizes manhood. At least in the eyes of many."

"In your eyes too?"

"At times, but I know his secrets. In a way I know him better than he knows himself."

"Did I tell you about the empty bottle?"

"The empty bottle?"

I got up from the sofa and gently separated the mini-blinds. I saw office buildings across the parking lot. It looked like it was going to be a sunny day. Maybe if I told her it might ease the guilt.

"Raymond. What empty bottle?" Dr. Paul asked, interrupting my thoughts.

"When I was cleaning up Kyle's apartment I found an empty bottle of medication."

"Yes."

"Well, it was the bottle I had picked up for him the day before he died. I looked at the date to be certain. It was all gone. I knew there had to be at least fifty pills in that bottle."

"Do you think Kyle killed himself?"

"No!" I screamed.

"Why?"

"He would have told me."

"Would you have supported that decision?"

"I don't know. He never complained about pain but I know he was hurting. I would have talked him out of it. I mean that would have prevented him from going to heaven. With suicide you can't ask for forgiveness. Kyle deserves to be in heaven," I said softly.

"Maybe that's why he didn't tell you. There could also be other explanations."

"Like what?"

"I don't know but maybe Kyle poured out the medication or maybe his mother did. You did say she helped you clean up his things."

"Yeah . . . Yeah. I never thought about that. Maybe Peaches poured it out."

"Have you asked her?"

"I haven't talked to her since the end of January. I'm feeling stronger now. Maybe I can talk to her now."

"Are you still sleeping with the light on?"

"Yes."

"What are you afraid of?"

"I don't know."

"Are you afraid of Kyle?"

"No!"

"Are you sure?"

"Why would I be afraid of Kyle?"

"Maybe because you think you let him down."

"You think I let him down?"

"Have you cried yet, Raymond?"

"No. Not yet."

Thirty-four

"*I'm* just so afraid to fall in love again."

"Why, Nicole?"

"I just don't think I could stand the thought of losing someone else important in my life."

"So you're going to spend the rest of your life avoiding involvement?"

"I don't know," I said.

"Nicole, this guy Jared does sound different. I mean I was only around him for a few minutes but from what you tell me," Delaney said.

"He is different. But I'm just not certain he doesn't have homosexual feelings that he hasn't acknowledged."

"Why?"

"Well, for one thing he and Raymond are close. So close as a matter of fact that the only way I know how Ray's doing is from my conversations with Jared."

"Do you think he's honest?"

"Yes."

"Have you asked him if he's gay or bisexual?"

"Yes."

"And what did he say?"

"He said he was certain he's heterosexual."

"I rest my case," Delaney said.

"Yeah, you're right. I'm glad Raymond and Jared are so close."

"Are you?"

"Yes. Men can have relationships like us. Right?"

"Yes, Miss Girl."

"But you know I think I'm scared because I believe in what goes around comes around. And you know how I hurt Pierce."

"So what does that mean?"

"It means it's my time to get hurt."

"Nicole, one day you and Pierce might become friends. From what you've told me both of you had a lot of shit going on. I think you hurt each other."

"I hope you're right."

"So go for Jared," Delaney suggested.

"But Jared lives in Atlanta," I said.

"And? Isn't LaFace Records down there?"

"Yes, but I can do most of my recording up here. I'm not going to sacrifice my career for a man."

"Then why are we talking about this?"

"Come on, girl. You're supposed to help me."

"How do you feel about Raymond and what does he think about you and Jared dating?"

"I don't think he knows. He knows we met in D.C. But I don't think he's aware we talk every day. But Raymond and I are cool. We love each other but we realize it will never work."

"You're not interested in Jared because he reminds you of Raymond, are you?"

"No. Granted they are a lot alike but they're different too. Jared came up the hard way like I did. He didn't have things handed to him on a silver platter. He's devoted to his mother and sisters."

"Don't you think that will create a problem?"

"What do you mean?"

"You know how black mothers are about their sons. They can be a real mess," Delaney said.

"Jared said his mother is looking forward to meeting me."

"I hope he's right. Are you sexually attracted to him?"

"Yes, girl, oh yes, girl. When I'm around him I feel a strong sexual desire. But he's always respectful of me."

"Well, you know what Kyle would say. Test drive it before you buy," Delaney laughed.

"What if this is the one? Maybe I should wait until I'm married."

"Well, he knows you're not a virgin, doesn't he, Black Kathie Lee Gifford?"

"Stop teasing me."

"He isn't a virgin, is he?"

"No, child, I don't think so. Let's stop talking about me. What about you? When are you going to find a man?"

"Who said I was looking for one?"

"You want to get married and have children, don't you?"

"I want children. I don't know about the husband."

"So what about San Diego?"

"Well, I'm going out there at the end of March to check out a space Jody found for the school."

"Does she like me?"

"Who?"

"Jody."

"Why do you ask that?"

"I don't know. I just got a funny feeling she didn't like me. I was so preoccupied with Kyle and all I didn't get to talk to you about it. In a way, she reminds me of JJ and she didn't like me at first either."

"Well, I'm not that big a fan of Janelle's myself," Delaney said.

"Why?"

"Because she didn't come up and see Kyle until it was too late. I think that really must have hurt him."

"You know how some people are around death. I guess I'm getting used to it," I defended.

"That's no excuse. Kyle was her friend. Then again, I don't know her at all. But back to your question. Jody never gave me any indication she didn't like you. Stop tripping, girl."

"I'm not. You know I've been thinking about seeing a therapist."

"A therapist. For what?"

"Well, just about what we've been talking about. I don't want to lose a chance at happiness but I couldn't stand to make a fool of myself again. I really feel confused."

"Nicole, you don't need a therapist. I'll be your therapist. Between me and Miss Jesus you should be covered," Delaney said.

"Why don't you like Shelia?"

"It's not that I don't like her. It's just her holier-than-thou attitude that's gets me. If she doesn't like gay people then she better not go to heaven."

"I don't think she doesn't like gay people. She's just trying to live by the Word."

"So Jesus Christ doesn't like gay people?"

"No, you know that's not what I'm saying. People just interpret the Bible differently," I said.

"Yes, a Bible that was written by men. Well, I think it's more than different. It's wrong."

"Delaney, I've got a confession," I blurted out.

"A confession? What, girl?"

"Well, you know what I said about seeing a therapist?"

"Yes."

"Well, I've been seeing a doctor up in Harlem ever since Candance died."

"No kidding. I'm sorry I made a joke before. Why didn't you tell me?"

"I was ashamed. You're only the second person I've told. You know how people are about things like that. My mother and Shelia would suggest that praying would solve everything and at times it does. But I needed additional help."

"Did it help?"

"It's still helping."

"So you're still going?"

"Yes."

"Nicole, if it's helping you to deal with some of your issues then I think it's great. I hope I didn't do anything that made you feel uncomfortable telling me," Delaney said.

"No, you didn't. It was just one of those secrets I was keeping to myself. Besides you've had your own share of problems."

"I'm glad you shared this with me, Nicole. There are times when I've thought about it."

"You have?"

"Yes."

"So how are you doing?"

"I'm fine."

"Even though that jerk got off so easy?"

"Oh, he didn't get off that easy. His career is over and my checking account is full," Delaney laughed.

"You know sometimes you remind me of Kyle."

"What are you talking about?"

"How you guys cover up pain with laughter."

"You got a better suggestion?"

"Did you ever really deal with the anger of being violated like that?"

"I deal with it every day."

"You do?"

"Yes, Nicole, I do."

"You want to talk about it?"

"About what?"

"How do you deal with it?"

"When it first happened, I thought about it every second, then minute. As days passed my thoughts about it became less frequent. Like now I think about it once a month. In time it will be less than that."

"Well, you know I'm here for you and Dr. Huntley is great. So let me know if you want to see her or if you want me to get a recommendation from her."

"I know and I will."

"Can I get a hug?"

"Sure, girl," Delaney said as she pulled me close to her and softly kissed my forehead.

Dr. Huntley was back!

"I guess my admission to Delaney means I'm starting to feel better about myself."

"I never felt you were ashamed of getting help through a difficult period in your life. A lot of people do, Nicole," Dr. Huntley said.

"But not a lot of black people," I protested.

"Who do you think make up the majority of my patients?"

"Black people?"

"Yes, black people," Dr. Huntley said as she put the top back on her pen.

A late February snow surprised the city. The busy streets were washed by the melting snow and the air smelled cool and fresh. I was leaving an audition for some background singing when I bumped into an old friend of mine. Dyanna Watson and I had met on several auditions. We shared a casual friendship similar to what I had with some of my castmates. She was now living in California where she was doing a soap opera.

"Nicole," Dyanna said, "it's great seeing you."

"You too, girl," I said as I hugged her or rather hugged her beautiful black mink coat.

"I heard you left *Jelly's*," Dyanna said.

"Yes, I did."

"Why, girl? That's a great show. I would kill to be in it," she said.

"Well, I still may do the national tour. I wanted to spend more time on my recording career. Are you trying to move back here?"

"Yes, chile. I'm getting married," she said as she held out her hand adorned with a beautiful diamond ring.

"Who's the lucky man?"

"Basil Henderson. He plays for the New Jersey Warriors," she said proudly.

"Is that football or basketball?"

"Football, honey," Dyanna said.

"When's the big day?"

"In June sometime, though we might elope."

"That's wonderful!"

"I heard you were engaged."

"Oh, that's over," I said.

"I'm sorry," Dyanna said.

"Oh, don't be sorry. It was the right thing to do," I said.

"Nicole, give me your address. If we have a big wedding, I want to make sure I invite you."

"Oh here, I have a card with all the information. Are you auditioning for the jingle?"

"Oh no, chile. I'm not that good of a singer. You know I'm a dancer who sings. I do white Broadway folks singing. That's why I'd never make it in *Jelly's*," she said.

"I don't know. You know we have the Hunnies," I said.

"Yes, child, but those divas can sing too," she said.

"Well, it's great seeing you, Dyanna. Let's get together sometime. I'd love to meet your fiancé."

"Yes, that would be nice. Call me."

It seemed as though everybody I knew was getting married if they weren't already. Not only my New York friends but also my Spelman sisters and the white girls I grew up with in Arkansas. I saw a lot of them in Washington, D.C., and they all acted so surprised to find that I wasn't married. I told them I was married to my career.

"It wasn't really love. Not that kind of love. But it was something I thought I wanted and needed."

"And how did he feel?"

"I think he loved me but I think we both overlooked some very major issues."

"What do you mean?"

"The religion and the fact we both had some racist views we were afraid to acknowledge until they reared their ugly heads. Maybe both of us were living fantasies," I said.

"What about Raymond?"

"What about him?"

"Did you love him?"

"Jared, I've told you I loved him. I still love Raymond, but as a friend," I said.

"You're not upset are you?"

"No. I just thought we'd gotten all that cleared up. How is he doing anyway?"

"Much better. He's still handling Kyle's estate and he's talking about going back to work," Jared said.

"I'm happy to hear that."

"So when am I going to see you?"

"Well, planes are still running between Atlanta and New York," I joked.

"Don't say that. I'll be on the next plane," Jared said.

"I might be in Atlanta the first part of April. I'm going to be meeting with a songwriter and I've got some stuff to do with a scholarship fund Candance's parents are setting up," I said.

"That will be great. You can meet my mother, see the place I'm redoing, and let me cook you the best meal you've ever had."

"That would be nice," I said. "Oh, did I thank you for the cards and flowers?"

"Yes, you did," Jared said.

"You've got to stop doing this every day."

"Why?"

"It's expensive."

"I think you're worth it," Jared said, his deep voice sounding softer.

"You're really special. Thank you," I said.

"After waiting all these years. I can't do enough," Jared said.

"You're really sweet, Jared, and I thank you."

"So are you."

"Are you going to take the position at HUD?"

"No. I really want to stay here. I'm thinking about running for the City Council," Jared said.

"What's going to stop you?"

"Raymond," Jared said.

"How so?"

"Well, I'm going to need him to run the campaign. I just want to make sure he's all right," Jared said with concern.

"He isn't drinking heavily, is he?"

"He's not drinking at all. Told me he wasn't going to drink again until he falls in love," Jared said.

"You really look after him. He's lucky to have a friend like you," I said.

"We are both lucky," Jared said.

"Do you ever worry about him getting AIDS?"

"No more so than I would worry about anybody else I know," Jared said.

"How did you get so smart?" I asked.

"I live every day like it's the first one and I try to learn something new each day," Jared responded smoothly.

"Praise the Lord, Nicole," Shelia said.

"Praise Him. How are you doing this morning?" I asked.

"I'm blessed," Shelia said.

"Well, do you want to start?"

"Do you have anything special you want to pray for?"

"For guidance and strength," I said.

Shelia had started praying over the phone lines when my eyes caught a glimpse of a picture of Kyle, Delaney, and myself. I thought about Kyle and wondered what he was doing and if he was really in heaven. How I missed him. Not only because he made me laugh but I missed his friendship as well.

"Nicole, are you ready?"

"Yes, Shelia, but before I get started I want to ask you something," I said.

"Sure, Nicole. What?"

"Do you think gay people go to heaven?"

"Sinners can't get into the kingdom, Nicole. You know that," Shelia said.

"But what about adultery and other sins?"

"If sinners ask for forgiveness they can enter the kingdom," Shelia said.

"But not homosexuals?"

"What are you getting at, Nicole?" Shelia asked.

"It's just that I have a lot of gay friends and I'm really having problems with what I see as your problem with gay people," I said.

"I just think they need to give up the wicked life," Shelia defended.

"Don't you think Christ made them gay?"

"Oh no! That's Satan, Nicole. You know that's Satan's work," Shelia said.

"Do you love the Lord, Shelia? I mean really love Him?"

"Child, yes. You know that. Why would you ask me that?"

"Have you heard 'How can you love me who you have not seen and not love your brother who you can see?' "

"I still have a right to how I feel," Shelia said boldly.

"Well, I don't agree. I think the biggest sin is not believing. I'm going to hang up before I get upset and say something I'll regret. Have a blessed day."

After I hung up the phone I yelled something meant for Shelia. Bitch!

"Why didn't you call her a bitch?"

"To be honest, I hate the word and it wouldn't be nice," I said.

"Do you have to be nice all the time, Nicole?" Delaney asked.

"I used to think so, but that's beginning to change," I said.

"I'm really proud of you, Nicole. Kyle would be too. That doctor must really be helping you," Delaney said.

"I don't know what got into me. I guess not saying anything made me just as guilty as Shelia," I said.

"So are you still going to keep her as a prayer partner?"

"I don't know. I have to think about it. It's not that I want everybody to agree with me. It's just the way she speaks of gay people with such disdain."

"Most black people feel like that," Delaney said.

"I wonder why?"

"They just don't understand," Delaney said.

"Do you think it's because so many black men are in the closet?"

"Don't forget the women," Delaney said.

"Oh, I'd forgotten about that."

"Have you told Jared about Dr. Huntley or your problems with Shelia?"

"I've mentioned the problem with Shelia and he's in total agreement with me. I haven't told him about Doc Huntley. But I'm going to very soon."

"How do you think he's going to respond?"

"I think it will be fine. It has to be. If I want complete honesty from him, then I've got to give him the same thing."

"Well, you've got a valid point," Delaney said. "Where are you getting all this spunk from?"

"What do you mean?"

"Well, girl, since you've met this Jared guy you've been right up there in people's faces. No longer a little Barbie doll. You better warn Jared he's getting a pussy plus package."

"Girl, you're crazy."

"And it looks like it's rubbing off on you," Delaney said.

"Let's just say I'm still a work in progress."

Thirty-five

"I'm starting to feel much better."

"That's great, Raymond. I feel like we're making progress."

"I'm still sleeping with the lights on," I said.

"Why do you think you're still doing that?"

"I don't know. You tell me."

Dr. Paul didn't respond.

"I think Nicole and Jared are about ready to have a relationship."

"How do you feel about that?"

"I don't know. A part of me is happy but a part wishes it was me."

"So have you told Jared and Nicole that?"

"He hasn't asked and I haven't really talked with Nicole. Jared walks around like he's walking on eggshells. I know he's looking out for me." I suddenly smiled.

"What are you smiling at, Raymond?"

"The other night Jared said one of the nicest things anyone has ever said to me."

"What did he say?"

"Well, I was down in the dumps. What else is new, huh? You know Basil is getting married and he wants to continue our relationship, but I can't do that. So I'm really feeling sorry for myself while Jared is trying to contain his excitement about Nicole. Anyhow he looks at me with those big puppy-like eyes of his and says; 'One day you're going to find somebody who will love you as much as you love them. And I'll be happy and sad. Happy because you deserve it. Sad because it won't be me. Raymond, if I was the least bit gay or had the inclination to be bisexual, all your problems would be solved. It would be a love of the century. Do you understand what I'm saying?' "

"What did you say to him?"

"I asked him if he had ever been with a male."

"What did he say?"

"He laughed and said, 'Naw, you can't fake the funk.' But wasn't that nice for him to say, Dr. Paul?"

"Yes, it was. How did it make you feel?"

"Very special."

"Don't you think you're special?"

"Sometimes," I mumbled.

"Just sometimes?"

"When I'm around my family sometimes. Always with Kyle and Jared or Nicole."

"We haven't talked about Nicole or women. Are you still attracted to women sexually?"

"Yes. Do you think that's going to change?"

"Do you?"

"You're the doctor," I answered in an annoyed tone.

"Where is that anger coming from?"

"I get sick and tired of people thinking you can't really be attracted to both sexes. Why would I lie to you? I'm paying you to tell the truth," I snapped.

"I don't think you're dealing with your feelings. What do you like about women?"

"I love their softness. The warmth of their bodies. On the outside and inside. The taste of their bodies. The way they believe in fairy tales. Their honesty."

"What about men?"

I smiled. "Their bodies. No matter what size. Their ability to be soft when they think nobody's looking. Strength. Their power."

"So you find different things in each sex?"

"Yes."

"That's understandable."

"Is it wrong?"

"What do you think?"

"I'm beginning to feel that's the way it is for me."

"What don't you like about women?"

"The guilt I feel sometimes when I don't tell them the truth."

"With men?"

"The fact that they rarely tell the truth when dealing with another person's feelings."

Dr. Paul looked at her watch and laid down her legal pad.

"Well, I think we can cut back to twice a week. How do you feel about that?"

"That's cool. I've got to handle some problems with Kyle's estate. I'm going to my office to talk with Gilliam about coming back to work. I think I'm almost ready to face the real world."

"I think you're ready."

"I hope you're right, Doc. I hope you're right."

If I was going to rejoin the real world I had to start at home. That night I decided to sleep with the lights out. I started to have a drink, but I remembered my promise and I stopped myself. I didn't even take my medication. I drank a cup of hot chocolate, read a few days of a *Daily Word* Nicole was sending me, and got on my knees and prayed. I filled my CD player with music and climbed into my bed in the dark.

It must have been very late or early morning when I woke up because there wasn't any music playing. My bedroom was still in darkness and I was wide awake. Pitch black and silent. I was sitting up in the bed but I couldn't move. Suddenly I felt a gentle invisible hand shielding me and directing my body back to my regular sleeping position. A vast presence came close to me, comforting me. There was an undeniable sense that somebody was in my bedroom. And then a peacefulness covered me like a homemade quilt. I fell back to sleep.

The next morning I leaped from my bed determined to jump-start my life. I made coffee and then cooked eggs and bacon. I made a couple of phone calls to Jared and Melanie and then I started to go through my mail, which had been unopened since I'd returned. I knew my credit must be shot to hell. The envelope marked **American Express** was thicker than a deck of playing cards. Not a good sign. A nice note from Delaney thanking me again. More bills and Christmas cards and a large manila envelope that fell to the carpet. When I reached down to pick it up I immediately recognized the handwriting. It was Kyle's. I ripped it open so fast that I tore the corners of the letter.

Dear Raymond,

Well, my friend, sometimes shit happens when you least expect it. I guess the fact that you're reading this letter means I'm gone. That is unless I screwed things up. Isn't this great drama? You know me, I wasn't going to let AIDS and death upstage me.

I'm writing this letter on a cold December evening. You just left for the hotel for some much needed rest. I'm sitting in my chair, looking out the window, and enjoying this beautiful winter night. I always loved the winter. The promise of passion that snow brings. I've enjoyed some passionate winter nights in my life so I think I want to leave with the winter.

I'm writing because words are tough these days and I wanted to thank you for being the best friend a faggot could have. Now don't flinch. I know how you hate the word, but it loses its power when you use it to describe yourself. How long have we proud African-Americans been calling each other niggers?

Seriously, this journey called life would have been a dull trip without you. Of all the big-dick boys I've met in bars too countless to mention, none have compared to my meeting you and I never saw your dick.

You know so many people go through life without ever knowing true friendship. We spend our lives trying to find someone to love us, or to love what we want them to think we are. But true friends accept you for you and that my friend is a joy. A joy I would have never known had I not met you. Don't you feel sorry for the people who never experience the joy of true friendship? Friendship turned out to be the one thing in the gay lifestyle that I could depend on. Lord knows I couldn't depend on trade.

The last two months, though filled with great physical pain, have been among the best in my life. Spending my final days looking into your beautiful eyes and seeing the warmth and love sparkling like tiny diamonds against a black velvet sky. It was worth waking up for each day. I know I've given you a hard time about slinging both ways, but you have to be true to Raymond. Don't ever let anyone put you in a box. Save some secrets for yourself.

You know one of the truly sad things about AIDS is the loneliness. There were times I sat in this chair and felt a loneliness so overwhelming that it made me scared. I was scared until the night you turned the key to my apartment. I was never afraid of the disease. Some people might say I earned it. I did in fact spend my life as a dick receptionist. But I wouldn't change a thing about my life. I was scared I'd never get the chance to tell you what your love and friendship meant to me. Now our love and friendship don't have to end because I'm gone. It now becomes an affair of the heart. I always wondered what people meant by that saying.

I know I've asked you for a lot of favors and you've always delivered. I have two more things I would like for you to do. First, check in on Peaches every now and again. I know she's a piece of work, but she was my mother during this journey and she was a good one. She loved me from the moment I came out of the tunnel and I know she loves you too. So please call her on her birthday and Mother's Day. Make sure she doesn't spend the money in one place and please don't let her spend it on a man.

I want you to take the money from the Chicago Mass Insurance policy and start a foundation that will provide support and little gifts and cards on a regular basis to minority AIDS patients. I don't care if they are men or women, gay, bisexual, or straight. Let the only criteria be that they don't have a Peaches, Nicole, Delaney, or a Raymond Winston Tyler, Jr., in their life. Hopefully you'll live to see the day when there won't be a need for the foundation or the need to specify color.

Now back to you. I want you to live your life the way you feel most comfortable. Please know that Christ made you from His own image. If it's good enough for Him then why worry about mere mortals. Cherish the friendships you have with Jared, Nicole, and JJ. I hope that you and Delaney will become friends. She's a wonderful chile.

Now this is not good-bye. Like I said true friendship never ends. Who knows I might be back quicker than you think. I read the other day where Vanessa Williams is pregnant again, so if she has a little boy it might be me; same thing applies if it's a little girl. You know Vanessa and I are very close. Maybe I'll come back as a rich white lady and we will meet in a plush deluxe bar and start all over.

You know I'm leaving because it's time. Maybe God needs me to deal with all the kids taking over heaven. Don't worry I'll get it right before your arrival . . .

Thank you, my sweet prince, for the friendship, the love, and giving my life meaning, memories, and magic. Now give some back to yourself. Get back to life. It's over, Raymond, you can cry now but please no hymn sanging. Stay strong, my brother.

Love always,
Kyle

I laid down the letter on my kitchen counter and tears started to pour from my eyes like hot lava from an erupting volcano. So many tears that they were blinding me. The tears were joined by loud sobs. Sobs so loud that the crystal silence of early morning was broken. My sobs stopped but the tears that made no sounds continued. It seemed impossible that I could have contained my grief for so long. I went to my bathroom to wash my tearstained face and when I looked into the mirror, I broke out in boisterous laughter. That Kyle, I thought, leave it to him to have the last word.

Kyle's letter provided me the inspiration I needed to make the trip home to Birmingham for *the conversation* with my parents. The two-hour drive seemed shorter than usual and in no time I was pulling up the driveway of my parents' home. When I got out of my car I could see the reflection of the television in the sliding glass door to the family room, so I knew my pops was home. Mama never watched the big-screen television alone. I tapped lightly on the sliding glass door and suddenly my pops pulled back the curtains and let out a broad smile when he saw my face.

"Marlee, come here. You'll never guess who's begging outside our door," my pops joked.

"Hey, Pops," I said as I walked through the door and shared a half hug and a couple of pats on the back with my father.

"How ya doing, son? What are you doing here? Is everything all right?"

"Yeah, Pops, I'm okay. Which question do you want me to answer first?"

"Ray Junior, what are you doing home?" my mother asked as she appeared in the family room from the long hallway.

"Can't I just come home to see my folks?"

"Of course," my mother said. "Have you eaten? I got some cold baked ham. Do you want me to make you a sandwich?"

"Naw, Ma, I stopped and got a sandwich right before I left."

"So come on, sit down," my pops said as he took a seat in his regular chair near the phone table covered with newspapers and magazines. "The Andy Griffith Show" was playing on the television. I remembered that this had been one of my father's favorite shows. Whenever I walked into my parents' home it was like walking back into my childhood. A happy time. I took a seat on the deep comfortable sofa close to my father's chair, laid my car keys on the thick glass-top table, and started to rub my hands nervously. I could have used a drink. I heard my mother rambling around in the kitchen. As I listened to pots and pans rattling, I studied my father's handsome brown face and noticed that he had put on a little weight. The extra weight hung noticeably around his waist.

"Do you want a drink?" my father asked.

"Yeah. No," I said.

My father suddenly turned his attention from the television and looked at me.

"Are you all right, son?"

"Yes, Pops, but we need to talk."

"Fine. Come on, let's go downstairs to my office. We'll have some privacy there."

"I want Mama in this too," I said.

My father gave me a curious look and then called my mother from the kitchen. She walked briskly from the kitchen wiping her hands with the hem of her dress bringing to mind Peaches coming from the kitchen at Kyle's. The memory of Peaches and Kyle brought a sudden sadness to me. A sadness that must have covered my face because my mother said, "What's the matter, baby. Something is wrong."

"No, Ma, everything will be fine. We just all need to talk."

"Is this a kitchen table or dining room table conversation?" my father joked.

"Family room. Let's just stay right here," I said.

"Fine," my mother said as she took a seat next to me on the sofa.

"How is Kirby?" I asked.

"Kirby is fine. He getting used to school. But what do you need to talk to us about?" my father said.

"Is this the conversation you called us about?" my mother asked.

"Yes, Ma."

My mother smiled back. How I loved her smile and the powdery clean smell that she always brought into a room in this house full of men. Her big sable brown eyes were soft and shining. Both of my parents gazed at me, waiting for me to speak. A short silence ensued until I finally spoke. I started by telling my parents how much the death of Kyle had affected me in both positive and negative ways. My parents listened intently as I shared with them some of my experiences during Kyle's demise and how for the first time I was ready to live my life on my own terms.

"What do you mean on your own terms?" my father asked.

"Well, Pops, it's not like I'm talking about major changes. I just want you and Ma to accept me just as I am."

"What do you mean, Ray-Ray? We've always done that," my mother said.

"I know, Ma, but . . ."

"But what?" Pops demanded.

"Well, even though you guys know about my sexuality, we never really talk about it. It's almost like you'd like to forget about it, but it's a part of me."

"We've talked about this, Raymond. What was that talk I had with you in New York about? We love you but do you have to push this stuff in our face?" Pops said.

"Stuff? Do you think this is stuff? And how do you think I'm pushing it in your face?"

"Both of you calm down," my mother said.

"I'm calm. I just don't know what he's talking about. What does he want from us?" my father asked my mother as if I wasn't there.

I went on to tell them about Kirby's comment in New York about Kyle and how I was worried about his attitudes about gay people and maybe if he knew about me then it would help him to be more understanding.

"But why do you have to tell him now?" Pops asked. "He has enough problems."

"When, Pops?"

My father rubbed his chin and looked toward my mother, who sat quietly on the sofa. When I looked at her she bit her lip and glanced away. A hushed tension dominated the room. I informed my parents that I was seeing a doctor trying to work out some of my own ambivalence about my sexuality. That I might want them to sit in on some therapy sessions in the future and maybe include Kirby. I told them if I was ever going to have a true love in my life I needed to know that I could count on their support, support regardless of whether I ultimately chose a man or a woman. I told them how I was afraid of their reaction if I ever brought a man home as a partner and I shared with my father the jealousy I sometimes felt when I saw him and Jared together. I told him that I sometimes thought he wished Jared was his son and that I was afraid that he loved Kirby more because he was straight. He shook his head in dismay.

My parents said they had no problem participating with my therapy. Then my father looked at me and said, "How can we deal with this, Ray-Ray, when you haven't? When you came back home from New York you acted the same way you had all your life." His voice vibrated with pain and anger. His statement was painfully true.

"I know, Pops," I said. "I'm still learning."

He nodded sympathetically and his face became relaxed and somewhat friendly. I suddenly felt my mother's arms around my neck and she pulled me close to her and gently rocked me as if I were a small child. Tears started to stream down my face and I felt my father standing over me.

"Son, I know you're in a lot of pain, losing your friend and all. But like your mother and I have always said, you're our son and we love you. We love you just the way you are."

"That's right, Ray-Ray. You know we love you. But I think we should all talk with Kirby together when he comes home this summer. I don't want any friction between my boys," she said.

"That's cool, Mom."

"Yes, I agree with that. Everything will be fine. We will see this doctor of yours and we'll figure out how to handle this with Kirby," my father said.

I smiled in silent admiration at my pops calmness. His cool confidence controlled the room.

"Is there anything else?" Pops asked.

"Not right now," I said.

My mother gave me a strong hug and kissed my forehead before she walked into the kitchen. Pops gently tapped my knee and released the mute button. Bernard Shaw's voice coming from the television was the only sound in the room for about fifteen minutes.

I finally got up from the sofa, went into the kitchen, and was greeted by my mother's smile and a thick ham and cheese sandwich.

"So how are you feeling about all this?" I asked my mother.

"Just as long as you don't get that dreadful disease, I'm fine," she said. She then fixed a sandwich for my father and took it and a cold beer into the family room. When she came back to the kitchen I looked at her and said, "Ma, the dreadful disease is called AIDS. You can say it."

"I know. I hope neither one of my sons get AIDS."

I silently shook my head in agreement and she then looked at me and said, "Of course, you're spending the night. I'm going in here and put clean sheets on your bed."

I smiled in agreement. It suddenly felt good to be home again.

Thirty-six

It's an experience so wonderful, yet every time it happens to me I wish it would be the last time. Falling in love. A heart longing to love. Learning to separate old fears from a new love. My heart was speaking to me and this time I was listening. I was falling in love with Jared Taylor Stovall and I was pretty certain he was falling in love with me.

Since that night in Washington, D.C., it became easy, incredibly easy to think of Jared and nothing else. I talked to him at least three times daily and every day I received a card or some little memento from Jared via the mail, FTD, or Federal Express.

Jared had made several trips to New York and I'd traveled to Atlanta once. Each time he came to New York he checked into a hotel even though we spent almost every second together. There was no pressure for sex although it was evident he was interested. So was I. The first time he kissed me, my whole body began to tingle and the more he kissed me the more delightful the sensation became. His kiss was more sexually exciting than any kiss I'd ever experienced with anyone before.

We spent a lot of time talking and reading out loud passages from books and poems we each loved. The only disagreement we had was over a television show. One week Jared arrived on Thursday and came straight to my apartment. I was watching "A Different World" and Jared took the remote control and turned to "Martin." I quickly grabbed it back and switched back to "A Different World." The back and forth went on the entire half-hour and we both missed our favorite show. We started laughing, gave up the contest, and let the remote control slide under the bed.

Jared came into town one Friday when I was meeting my girlfriend Dyanna Watson at Honeysuckle's for drinks. She wanted me to meet her fiancé and to give me some information on an independent film project she was involved in. I had given Jared the address of the place that morning before he left Atlanta. I got to the restaurant first. Dyanna and her beau showed up minutes later.

Dyanna's fiancé, Basil Henderson, was quite a looker. He was tall and well built with sensuous gray eyes and a melt-your-heart smile. He was a real sweetheart and somewhat of a flirt. Not the sickening kind, just the sweet, make-you-feel-good kinda flirt. The three of us were having a great time. Dyanna was talking about their upcoming wedding and the film project that needed my type once shooting started in New York. Since I was only selecting music for my demo I was looking for something to fill my days.

Jared showed up with bags in tow. He gave me a quick kiss, greeted Dyanna with a light peck, but when he and Basil were introduced the chill was unmistakable. Jared looked faintly surprised. Something was going on and the first thing that came to my mind was how Raymond reacted to certain men. Oh no, I thought, this couldn't be happening again. I was barely listening to Dyanna I was so busy watching the non-conversation going on between Basil and Jared. While Dyanna and I talked Jared and Basil barely spoke. When they did it was in monosyllables and half-finished sentences that made no sense. When they weren't talking they were giving each other condescending looks and rolling eyes the way I've seen women do to each other. I had never seen Jared act like this and I couldn't wait to get him out of the club to find out what was going on. Before I could think of an excuse to leave, Basil went to the men's room and when he came back his beeper went off. He excused himself and when he returned he instructed Dyanna it was time to leave.

Dyanna and I agreed to get together later the next week. The minute they left the club I turned to Jared and asked, "What was that about?"

"How well do you know Dyanna?"

"Not that well. We met on a couple of auditions."

"So that's the first time I guess you've met him?"

"Who, Basil? Yes, but I understand he's some big-time football player."

"He is."

"Do you know him, Jared? You were awfully cold."

"I don't really know him. He's a friend of Ray's. At least he used to be."

"What kind of friend?" I asked as I noticed the concern on Jared's face.

"Well, I don't know the full extent, but I get the impression from Ray that it was more than friendship," Jared said.

"You mean he's gay?"

"I think so. Ray didn't go into a lot of detail. But I think there was something there."

"Is that the guy Ray was going to see in Jersey City?"

"I think that's where he lives. He was in Atlanta for a while also."

"I knew there was something going on. I was worried for a moment."

"Worried about what?"

"I was afraid my bubble was getting ready to burst. Kyle always warned me to watch for tension between men. He said straight men didn't act like women do."

"So you're saying we were acting like women. Hold up. I just don't like him because he's always been an asshole around me and I think he's trying to dog Ray."

"Well, he is fine. How do you know he's dogging Ray?"

"Fine? What? Lady, don't start tripping. I just think he's a dog," Jared said as he pretended to be jealous.

"You think I should tell Dyanna what you said?"

"Maybe she already knows."

"I don't think so."

"Well, it doesn't look to me like you're that close," Jared observed. "Maybe you should stay out of it."

I thought about what Jared said and then I tried to put myself in Dyanna's place. Matter of fact, a few years ago I was in her position. Would I have wanted my friends to tell me? I knew Candance would have, but what about a casual friend? Maybe she would think I was trying to take her man or something. Plus, Jared might have had a point—maybe Dyanna already knew—or maybe he was simply mistaken about Basil.

I would talk it over with Delaney and see what she thought before I made a decision. I was becoming a little bit less concerned about Jared's involvement in the Basil-Dyanna situation when he didn't appear preoccupied with it during the rest of the weekend. I knew he was concerned about Raymond and even Dyanna, but I didn't want to compete with either of them for Jared's attention. That would have not been a good sign; instead he lavished all his attention on me.

———

"I think you should stay out of it, Nicole."

"Do you really think so? She's going to marry this guy in a couple of months."

"Then that's her business. What are you becoming, the heterosexual liaison for Queer Nation?"

"What's Queer Nation?"

"A gay group that takes it upon themselves to tell the world who's gay and whose not."

"You think that's what I'm doing?"

"First of all, it ain't your business. And this guy sounds like he's big and powerful. He just might kick your natural ass for running your mouth."

"But what about Dyanna?"

"What about her? I'm telling you, Nicole, she may already know. She could be a lesbian and it's a cover marriage."

"A cover marriage? What's that?"

"Bitch, I swear. What do you know? Are we turning back into a mindless Barbie doll?"

"Dyanna's not gay," I defended.

"How do you know?"

"You've seen her; she's beautiful."

"And?"

"Well, she doesn't look or act gay."

"Chile, just because she ain't asked you to let her eat your pussy don't mean she can't be gay."

"But what if she isn't? Doesn't she have a right to know that the man she's marrying is bisexual or gay?"

"The truth always comes out in the end. But you don't have to be the truth patrol."

"Well, I guess . . ."

There was a long pause and then Delaney's voice changed to a more serious tone.

"Nicole, what are you doing?"

"Talking to you."

"I mean this evening."

"Just looking at some music. Why?"

"I have something I need to talk to you about. I've been meaning to do it for some time and I guess there's no better time than now," Delaney said.

"Well, talk."

"No, I don't want to say what I have to say over the phone. I think I need to do this in person."

"This sounds serious."

"Well, that will depend on how you take it."

"Don't do this to me, Delaney. Now you have me all nervous."

"Don't be nervous. I'll be over there in an hour."

Delaney hung up and I stood in the kitchen looking at the phone. What did she want to talk with me about?

I was listening to a Kathleen Battle CD when my doorman buzzed me and told me Delaney was on her way upstairs.

When I opened the door, Delaney forced a smile but I could see the concern on her face. She was wearing a bulky red sweater and a short black skirt. Her hair was in a ponytail that was wrapped up like a wreath. I looked at Delaney's stomach. Maybe she was pregnant.

"Hey, girl. You want some wine?"

"What kind?"

"I think it's Chablis."

"Sure that would be nice," Delaney said as she went in and sat on the sofa.

"I love those boots," I said as I admired Delaney's shining black army boots.

"Thanks, girl."

"Do you want me to change the music?" I yelled from the kitchen as I searched for wineglasses.

"Oh no, I love this music. It's very appropriate."

"It is?"

I found the glasses, poured the wine, and placed the glasses on a tray. I looked in the icebox and pulled out some dip. I smelled it to see if it was still good as I reached in the cabinet and took out some chips. I poured them into a bowl, brought them into the living room, and sat them between Delaney and myself. Delaney's face looked pensive.

"So what's the big news?" I said casually.

"Well," Delaney started. "You know I love you, Nicole, and how much I treasure your friendship."

"Yes, I know that, Delaney. What's the matter?"

"Well, I would have told you sooner but I didn't know how you would take it."

"Delaney, you didn't run into that dreadful guy, did you? He's not threatening you, is he?"

"No, it's not that. Please let me finish!" Delaney said.

"Okay, I'm sorry."

"I just hope you'll be my friend after I tell you this and if you aren't I will understand."

I didn't say a word. I just looked into Delaney's eyes searching for the cause of the pain in them. Tears came into her eyes and she blinked hard to force them back.

"Nicole, I'm gay. I've been gay all my life. I know I should have told you but I didn't think you could handle it."

I was flabbergasted. Delaney went on to reveal she and Jody were more than friends. Jody was her lover and that was why she was moving to San Diego. She said she wasn't coming on to me but she really loved me as a friend. My friendship was important to her. I wanted to tell Delaney every thing was all right, that I was still her friend and I understood, but the avalanche of words poured out of her so uncontrollably that it would have been cruel to stop her. When she finally stopped talking, her eyes filled with tears, and I gently pulled her close to me and patted her back. "Is that it?" I asked.

She looked up at me and shyly nodded.

"You're sure this isn't because of that attack?"

"No, Nicole, it's just who I am. You have any problems with that?"

"No, Delaney, I don't. I'm just blessed you're my friend."

Exposing your true self to a friend is a wrenching experience that most people will never endure. Most people aren't that honest. While Delaney's confession took me by surprise I tried to be supportive. I couldn't help but think back on Raymond's confession and the pain that covered his face. I saw the same pain in Delaney's face. But I don't think it was a pain that came from being gay, it was more the pain of not feeling comfortable enough to reveal their true selves at the beginning of a relationship.

I had never had a female gay friend, at least not to my knowledge. But I loved Delaney and I didn't see how her sexuality would create a problem. She explained to me that she didn't hate men. Delaney said that she still found herself attracted to men but she was committed to her relationship with Jody. She said it was a man who had helped her to discover her sexuality. Delaney said in her wild days, a guy she was dating got her to go along with a three-way with another girl he was seeing on the side. She said at first she said no but he kept asking her to try it at least once. Delaney said the woman was beautiful and when they made love it felt like the most natural thing in the world to her.

She told me she left the guy and started an affair with the older woman before moving to New York. While she was explaining her introduction to her sexual discovery, I was wondering why men liked the idea of two women having sex. Was it power or just an erotic allure?

After Delaney finished her disclosure she asked me if I had any questions I wanted to ask. I told her I understood. That night before going to bed, I searched for and found a copy of *Essence* magazine that dealt with the issues of black gay women coming out and with bisexuality. I just wanted to make sure I had told the truth.

I wondered why I was so calm when Delaney told me and why I was so accepting of her being gay when I was furious about Raymond's being gay? Was it less threatening to me for a woman to be gay? I was a bit upset Delaney waited so long to tell me. Did she doubt our friendship? Was it something about me that made people hold back when it came to their sexuality? Did they think I couldn't deal with it? I suppose they might have been right—past tense, I hoped.

Thirty-seven

"I always viewed my father as some immortal."

"Why is that, Raymond?"

"When I was growing up I thought he could do anything. That he was perfect. I couldn't imagine life without him. When I grew up I always wanted to please him no matter what."

"But it sounds like your father is proud of you and he accepts your sexuality," Dr. Paul said.

"Maybe he accepted it before I did. I guess I was trying to appear perfect in his sight."

"Perfect."

"Yes, I had so many advantages in life thanks to him and my mother. What's that saying—to much is given, much is expected. I was trying to give it all to them. To me being attracted to men ruined the perfection."

"Why?"

"Maybe because it was how other people viewed it. I never felt disgust for gay people but I felt sorry for them."

"Why?"

"Because of the way people treated them. I felt they would never have love."

"How do you feel now?"

"Well, everything has changed for me. But now the hardest part is staying true to myself."

"True to yourself?"

"Yes, by remembering that perfection is something we all strive for, but never attain."

"Does that bother you?"

"Less and less every day."

"Tell me a little about your relationship with your mother."

"It's always been great, but I never gave her a chance to voice her feelings about my life. In a lot of ways I've treated her just like my father does."

"How so?"

"That she will always be there—giving her unconditional love and support," I said.

"Do you think your parents will accept a male lover in your life?"

"I think so after our talk. It still may be a little difficult at first, but I don't think we have to worry about that."

"Why not?"

"Well, I don't think I'll be taking Basil home. He wouldn't go in that role anyway."

"What role?"

"As a boyfriend."

"So the trip home and the letter from Kyle seem to be helping you."

"Yes, I think they are. I didn't say all I wanted to say to my parents but I think when we meet with them, I'll be able to say the rest."

"The rest?"

"Yes—to tell my father he can't be immortal in my eyes anymore. That he has to be human."

"And your mother?"

"I just want her to say how she really feels."

"Does that frighten you."

"No."

"Why not?"

"Whenever I really want to know how love feels, I think about my mother, taking care of me, never judging, just taking me as I am."

"I think talking to your parents was a giant step, Raymond," Dr. Paul said as she got up from her chair.

"Yes, I think you're right. Now if I can just keep walking. I have to keep walking. Forward. Right, Doc?"

Dr. Paul didn't smile, she just nodded ever so slightly.

A problem with one of Kyle's insurance policies finally forced me back to work, but after my conversation with my parents and a couple more sessions with Dr. Paul I was ready. Chicago Mass Insurance Company didn't want to pay benefits on Kyle's policy because there wasn't an autopsy following his death. They were contending Kyle knew of his condition when he purchased the policy. I was going to make them prove that. I thought it was ironic the only policy we had trouble with was the one Kyle had earmarked for his foundation.

After several conference calls with the Chicago Mass legal staff I decided I could only get my desired results if I went to Chicago and bartered with them in person. Gilliam gave me names of a couple of lawyers in Chicago who handled insurance companies in case I needed help. This would be the first time in my career I would be negotiating with an insurance company directly. In Basil's and Delaney's cases both insurance companies were happy to pay to avoid legal action and embarrassment to their clients.

Gilliam and I agreed I would come back to work at the firm full time in June. This would give me time to handle Chicago Mass and set up Kyle's foundation, which was still without a name. Nicole and Jared had both agreed to be on the Board of Directors, so I knew I could count on them for support in establishing the foundation. I had also spoken with Janelle a couple of times and she was excited about the foundation and shared with me a letter she'd received from Kyle. I cried as she read hers and she cried when I read mine.

The calendar said spring but a winter mist lingered over Chicago. I left Atlanta without an overcoat. If I stayed longer than overnight I would have to buy one.

I took a cab to the Chicago Mass building on Michigan Avenue. When I arrived I discovered their legal staff was located in a separate office building. The receptionist offered directions and told me it was close enough to walk. When I exited the building there was no hint of what was about to happen. I was standing at a stoplight waiting for the Don't Walk sign to change and hoping I wouldn't get lost or be late for my meeting when I heard a very familiar voice say, "I don't believe it. Raymond Tyler, Jr."

I looked around to see who was calling my name on my first visit to Chicago. I blinked when I turned and realized I was standing right next to my frat brother Trent Walters.

"Trent. What are you doing here?"

"I live here, frat. Did you forget? What are you doing here?"

"Taking care of some legal business," I said as we exchanged the secret KAΩ handshake at the busy intersection.

"Where is your business? How long are you going to be here?"

"Over on North LaSalle—125 North LaSalle," I said.

"Well, ain't that just the shit. That's where my office is located. I'll show you where it is."

Trent and I walked through the busy city and talked about the last time we had seen each other. I thanked him for calling and leaving the information on Miller.

"No problem. I called you a couple of times after that," Trent said as he gently leaned his body into me directing me through the busy Chicago sidewalks.

"Yeah. I got the messages. I was in New York for an extended stay. Sorry I didn't get back with you."

"No problem. Were you in New York on business?"

"Yes, sort of."

"You didn't say how long you're going to be here."

"Well, my meeting this morning will determine that. I may be going back this afternoon. I have a room reserved at a hotel on Michigan Avenue though, just in case I have to stay overnight."

"My condo is near Michigan Avenue. You have to let me take you to dinner no matter what happens with your meeting. I won't take no for an answer," Trent said. He looked distinguished in a black cashmere overcoat, opened at the top revealing a beautiful blue and yellow tie. His dark brown skin was clean-shaven and his cinnamon eyes sparkled under well-shaped brows.

"Sure we can have dinner. Give me your office number and I'll call you when I'm done."

"Great! If you finish early maybe we can even have lunch together," Trent said as he pulled a business card from his wallet. As Trent handed me the card he guided me into a huge office building.

"This is the building. What floor?"

"I'm going to the twenty-second floor."

"I'm on thirty-three. Come up or call when you finish."

"I will."

"It's great seeing you, Ray. I look forward to dinner," Trent said as he flashed a charming smile.

"It's great seeing you, Trent. I'll talk with you later," I said as I saw the number twenty-two light up on the elevator board.

I realized Trent was right when the taxi cab driver said three dollars in an annoyed tone. I could have walked. Trent's condo was in a huge old building that looked like a church from the outside. I walked into the lobby and punched in Trent's name on the automated keyboard. Trent's voice came over the intercom instructing me to come to 2317. Inside of the lobby were several small shops and a large grocery store directly across from the elevators. I took the elevator up to the twenty-third floor and walked down the carpeted hallway. When Trent opened the door an inviting aroma of food greeted me.

"Come on in, Ray. Glad you could make it. Have any trouble finding the place?"

"No, I took a taxi."

"Oh shit, frat. You could have walked. It looks like a beautiful night outside."

"Yes, it is, but it's chilly."

"That's 'cause you're used to that Southern spring weather."

"What's that I smell? I thought we were going out," I said as I looked around Trent's beautifully decorated living and dining area. His condo was filled with the accoutrements of success. There was a large picture window in the living room looking out over a lighted Lake Michigan.

"I decided to cook. I'm making stuffed pork chops," Trent said as he took my jacket and placed it in a nearby hall closet.

"You didn't have to go through all that trouble, frat. I was going to treat you."

"You can do that when I come to Atlanta. What can I get you to drink?"

"You got any club soda?"

"Club soda? What's up, frat? This isn't the Raymond Tyler I know."

"I'm just taking a break from the stuff," I said as I walked over to Trent's wall unit and looked at his pictures. "Who is this?" I asked, eyeing a picture of Trent in military gear with a little boy.

"That's Trent Junior," he said proudly.

"I didn't know you had kids. I forgot you were in ROTC."

"Just Trent Junior, and yeah, I served in the Marines right after college. Had to pay Uncle Sam back."

"How old is Trent Junior?"

"He's five years old. Lives in Montgomery with his mother."

"Whose his mother?"

"Kisa Lewis. I dated her at Alabama. She was a Delta."

"Oh yeah. Real pretty lady."

"She still is quite beautiful," Trent said as he brought me a sparkling liquid in a frosted glass.

"I hope this water is okay," Trent said. He was also carrying a large wine goblet filled with burgundy wine.

"Nice place. I see you're living large."

"I do okay. I'm sure you're doing okay in hot Lanta."

"Yeah, I do okay."

"Have a seat, Ray. You're not in a hurry, are you?"

"No," I said as I sat down on the large pit sofa sectional. Trent took a seat on an ottoman facing me.

"So how did your meeting go?"

"It could have gone a little better. It looks like I'll be here at least another day."

"Great. Then you can take me out tomorrow. I'll even get a chance to show you my city," Trent said as he smiled with clear honest eyes.

"So you like living in Chicago?"

"I love it!"

Trent got up, walked over to his stereo system, and placed some CD's in a carousel that popped out. Seconds later the voices of After Seven filled the room.

"I have that CD. Those guys live in Atlanta," I said.

"Yeah, that's right. Seems like all the top music acts are moving there."

"Yeah, I think so. . . . The food smells great, Trent."

"I hope you'll like it," Trent said as he hopped up and went to the kitchen to check on dinner. He was wearing baggy jeans and a kelly green sweater.

"How big is your place?"

"Two bedrooms plus den. I'll show you around after dinner."

The food was great. Trent had prepared broccoli and corn on the cob to go along with the pork chops. While eating, Trent and I talked about college days and the recent reunion. Trent's voice filled with anger as we relived the incident with Miller and the fraternity.

"Man, I'm thinking about sending the money I normally send to those jerks to the United Negro College Fund," Trent said.

"That's not a bad idea," I said.

"Do you ever hear from Sela?"

"Through my mother. They keep in touch. I was just home a couple of weeks ago. Sela's happily married and has two little girls, Taylor and McClain."

"Interesting names for little girls," Trent said.

"Power names."

"I guess so. Come on, let's go into the den," Trent said as he led me from the living area. "You sure I can't get you an afterdinner drink?"

"Not until I fall in love," I said.

"What?" Trent asked with a sheepish smile.

"Oh, don't pay me any mind. I decided I wasn't going to drink until I fall in love again."

"What brought that on?"

"Long story."

"Any prospects?"

"No. Not yet."

We walked into Trent's den and were greeted by a fireplace glowing with a freshly laid fire. A single log burned, suddenly slumped, and then released a spiral of red sparks.

"This is nice, Trent. A fire in April."

"Only in Chicago."

Trent's and my conversation ventured from black college football players turning on their white universities after failed pro-football attempts to the Sugar Bowl game. When we talked Trent looked me directly in the eyes and I could have sworn he was inching closer to me on the small leather sofa in his den. There was definitely a tension in the air, but a nice one.

I shared with Trent the loss of Kyle and how I had been with him in his final days. While I was talking about Kyle my eyes welled up. I stopped talking and glanced away. Trent touched my arm with silent understanding and I bit my lower lip and smiled.

"Can I ask you something, Ray?" Trent's voice was thick with mystery.

"Sure, Trent," I said.

"Was Kyle your lover?"

Trent's question paralyzed me momentarily. My heart began to pound and my underarms became wet despite my antiperspirant.

"Why do you ask, Trent?"

"You don't have to answer, Ray."

"I'll answer."

"I'm just curious. I mean when you talk about him there is a lot of love in your voice and eyes," he said. His own voice was full of concern.

"I did love Kyle. But we weren't lovers. We were just friends. No, we were more than friends. We were like brothers."

"Oh."

A few minutes passed in silence.

"Did you want to ask me if I ever had a male lover?"

"If you want to tell me," Trent said. His face looked startled at my question.

"Yes, Trent. I have had a male lover. And you?"

"No," Trent said quickly. There was another brief silence in the room, Trent and I eyeing each other with suspension.

"But it's not because I haven't desired one. I spent so much time in the military and I haven't met the right guy yet," Trent said as I looked at him with a disbelieving stare. The stare was not because I couldn't believe Trent was gay, it was because of the honesty in his voice when he spoke.

"So I guess you've been to bed with a man before?"

"Yes."

"When did you realize that you were gay? Or are you bisexual?"

"Well, I don't sleep with women anymore, so I guess you would classify me as gay."

"So when did you know?" I asked.

"Know what?"

"That you were gay?"

"You want to know the truth?"

"Yes, the truth would be nice."

"When I first saw you," Trent said softly. "The first time I saw Raymond Winston Tyler, Jr., at a rush party, Friday, October 1. That's when I knew for certain."

"Good answer," I said, managing to keep a thin smile instead of a broad grin. "Very good answer, Trent."

I completed my business with Chicago Mass in three days. I got them to agree to pay 50 percent of the policy. In a way they were right, Kyle did know of his condition when he took out the policy, but he lived two days past the time period the policy required. I established a good rapport with the lawyer from Chicago Mass and she and I were able to reach a compromise. I was anxious to get the foundation started—to help the people Kyle wanted to assist.

Although I finished in a short period of time, I stayed in Chicago for an additional week. I was having a wonderful time with Trent. He was an exceptional host, even getting tickets to sold-out shows and concerts. One night we stayed in and watched a taped replay of the Sugar

Bowl with our beloved Alabama football team beating Miami, Basil's alma mater. I was happy with the fact that Trent seemed to enjoy sports as much as I did. Who else besides me would have a taped collection of college football games and the U.S. Open tennis championships as prized possessions?

I had moved out of the hotel the morning after Trent's confession and moved into his condo. We didn't have sex the entire week but I felt as if I had. Sleeping with Trent's body so close to mine every night filled me with a delectable warmth. We both agreed to wait until we knew what was going on before engaging in sex. Neither one of us wanted meaningless sex no matter how passionate. I told Trent I wanted to make love and not just fuck. Trent looked at me, formed a deliberate smile, and said, "Don't worry, I don't fuck for fucking sake. Our lovemaking will be stupendous!"

Trent took off every day at noon while I was in Chicago and we spent the afternoons walking down Michigan Avenue absorbed in conversation. I wasn't surprised by how much we had in common. A couple of evenings we bundled up and walked along Lake Michigan, stopping to stare at the glowing neon of the city.

During one of these walks I learned how deeply religious Trent was and I promised to take him to First Birth when he visited Atlanta. He said he became comfortable with his sexuality after years of praying for Christ to take it away. "I became comfortable with myself when I understood God knew and understood that everybody else was secondary."

I told him how I prayed a similar prayer many times and how I felt deserted when my prayers went unanswered.

Trent wasn't *out* at work but he said when people tried to set him up he always declined. He also told me everybody important to him knew, with the exception of his son. "I'll tell him the moment I'm certain he will understand." I shared with Trent the reason for my recent visit home and he said he was proud of me. That it was a great start toward self-acceptance.

The week I was with Trent I felt nervous, excited, and exhilarated all at the same time. Trent seemed anxious to please and our days were filled with laughter, serious talks, and a lot of hugging and kissing. With Trent I felt I could say anything, that I was talking with somebody who understood and who had known me for a great deal of my adult life. So many times, I thought, we look for love in all the wrong places.

I talked a lot about Kyle, Jared, and Nicole. He said he was looking forward to meeting the two of them and wished he had known Kyle. I didn't mention Basil directly or with any special significance.

Trent told me about a couple of brief affairs he had been involved in, including one while he was in the Marines. During one of our early morning confessions we learned both our first sexual experiences with a man had been with the same person, Kelvin Ellis. At first I was a bit put off, but since they were only together a couple of times after I left for Columbia, I cooled out. It wasn't Trent's fault, and Kelvin and I weren't lovers at the time. Trent and I agreed to always be honest with our feelings no matter what the situation.

"We won't agree on everything, Raymond; if we did, one of us would be unnecessary," Trent said.

When it was time to leave, Trent and I both became sad. Trent promised to come to Atlanta the very next weekend and we promised to call each other every day. I tried to dissuade Trent from taking me to the airport but he insisted, saying, "After all the years of wanting to be close to you, I'm not going to waste another minute."

"I can't believe you never said anything before now, Trent. If not when we were in college, then at the reunion. Look at all the time we've missed," I said during the ride to the airport.

"The timing was never right. That is until now," he smiled.

In a time when my life had locked up and shut down, Trent Carlton Walters had secretly owned the key for more than a decade.

"What if it doesn't work out?"

"Do you think it won't?"

"I don't know. I'm excited and yet I'm very scared."

"That's normal. Does it bother you that Trent's a man?"

"What do you mean?"

"Well, would you be feeling these apprehensions if it was a woman?"

"I think so. It would be the same with any relationship. I don't want to hurt Trent. He says he's already in love with me. I can't handle being hurt again myself."

"And how do you feel about him?"

"Well, I care about him. I could even fall in love with him. But there is Basil."

"You haven't talked about him in a while."

"Yes, I know, but he's been calling since I got back. I'm going to see him later this week. A part of me feels that with Basil it's just sex and I have made up my mind that I'm not going to deal with him once he's married."

"Oh. Why wait until he's married?"

"Good point. But can I do that?"

"What do you think?"

"I don't know. . . . Did I tell you what Trent said?"

"About?"

"Well, we're both virgins in a certain way," I laughed. "Neither one of us has given up the booty—but he's willing to try for me."

"Why is that funny?"

"Well, I don't know if he expects the same thing from me."

"Will that be a problem?"

"Might be. From what I can tell Trent does not have a starter-kit dick. If you get my drift."

Dr. Paul tried to prevent a smile.

"Is that just a barrier you're putting up, Raymond?"

"No, I'm serious."

"Is Basil going to be a barrier?"

"He could be. He has spoiled me sexually. But I know I'd never allow myself to fall in love with him."

"Why?"

"Trouble with a big T."

Dr. Paul placed her pen over her thin lips and lowered her eyes.

"Nicole is in town. She's working on a demo. I think she's in love with Jared."

"How does he feel about her?"

"Oh, he's long gone. Come to find out he had a crush on Nicole when he was engaged to that other girl. I think it's interesting Nicole and I both had secret admirers in college we knew nothing about."

"Interesting," Dr. Paul repeated.

"Yes. Nicole and I had lunch the other day. She wants me to talk Basil into telling Dyanna the truth," I said as I stood up to stretch and peek out of Dr. Paul's window.

"How do you feel about that?"

"About what?"

"Basil and Dyanna."

"I told Nicole I would talk to him, but I don't hold much hope that it's going to do any good."

"Why?"

"Basil's pretty set in his ways. He's all about the cover. He once said to me the best way to camouflage your sexuality was to play professional sports. You've got to admit there is more affection and butt patting on the football fields and locker rooms than in many married bedrooms in America."

Dr. Paul let out a quick laugh and then quickly regained her composure. She was in a great mood today. It was one of the first times I ever recalled her showing so much of herself.

"So you must agree with me."

Dr. Paul didn't respond. She reached into her jacket pocket and pulled out a handkerchief and wiped her mouth. When she pulled it out I suddenly smelled a familiar perfume.

"So is my time up, Doc?"

"You have a few more minutes."

"Well, I'm going to see how I feel after Trent's visit. I mean he really thinks we can make it if we are honest with each other. I told him I was still attracted to women. As a matter of fact, Sherrod called me the other day to invite me to dinner."

"Are you going?"

"Yes."

"Why?"

"Well, I think I might enjoy her company. I want to prove to myself I can be attracted to a person no matter what their physical wrapping looks like."

"Person or woman?"

"Both."

"Is Trent attractive?"

"I don't know if most people would call him attractive. He is in a basic sorta way. A soft masculine handsome. Not as good-looking as Basil. He's kinda like Jared. He wears Ivy League–type glasses and he just had braces removed about a year ago. But he has a nice body, especially his butt, and we've already talked about the dick. Dick—I can't believe I'm using that word in here. I think Sherrod is attractive in her own way too. I love the way she carries herself. I love her spirit."

"Does it bother you that Trent isn't as handsome as Basil?"

"No, it's a bonus. It allows me to take the emphasis off physical attributes. But I did learn something from my relationships with Nicole and Sela." I paused and looked at Dr. Paul, who was putting down her legal pad.

"That being?"

"If you love someone deeply, the truth gets in the way of fantasies."

"Explain?"

"Well, I'd always dreamed of getting married and having two kids. A boy and girl. I remember when Kirby was born and how my mother would allow me to hold him. I loved it. I couldn't wait to get married and have my own kids. I almost talked my first girlfriend Sela into marrying me right after high school."

"High school?"

"Yes. We had sex for the first time on the night of my senior prom. A couple of weeks later Sela was convinced she was pregnant. So I told her we should get married."

"Was she pregnant?"

"No, but I think all girls worry about that after their first time."

"So it wasn't your first time?"

"Fuck no. I'd been boning since ninth grade," I said with a broad smile.

"What's that smile about, Raymond?"

"I told Sela it was my first time."

Thirty-eight

"**More** Than Friends. That's a great name, Jared."

"Yeah, boy. That's a great name, More Than Friends," Raymond said.

"Glad to be of service," Jared said.

"I'll get started on the incorporation papers right away," Raymond said as he put his black leather folder in his briefcase. "So we all agree on the organization?"

"It sounds good to me," I said.

"I'm cool," Jared said.

"Nicole, you let Delaney know what we've decided. I'll get in contact with Janelle," Raymond said.

"I can do that."

"Well, I've got to run. I've got a meeting in Stone Mountain," Jared said as he scooted out of the booth next to me. "Will you make sure Nicole gets back to the house, Ray?"

"Sure, no problem," Raymond said.

"You sure I can leave you two alone?" Jared joked. At least I thought he was joking.

"I don't know. Raymond's looking really good in that blue suit," I said.

"Come on, you guys, stop teasing," Raymond said.

"How does spaghetti sound, babe?" Jared asked, looking at me with that twinkle in his eyes. He was looking quite handsome himself in a khaki-colored suit and ocean-blue shirt.

"That sounds great. I'll make a salad," I said as I gave Jared a quick kiss on the lips.

"Okay, I'll see you guys later," he said as he hurried out of the midtown Atlanta restaurant.

"Would you like some more coffee?" Raymond asked.

"Sure."

Raymond motioned the waiter by holding up his coffee cup in my direction.

I sat at the booth facing Raymond, slowly twirling my empty coffee cup. This was the first time we had been alone since Jared and I began seriously dating. We'd talked on the phone several times but this was the first time we were alone.

The three of us had gotten together to discuss the formation of Kyle's foundation. Raymond was going to serve as chairman and Jared vice chair. They decided I would be best for treasurer and fund-raising and Delaney would be secretary. We didn't know how much time Janelle would have to spend with the foundation, so we put her on the Board of Directors.

Raymond had big plans for the More Than Friends Foundation. Ultimately he wanted it to rival the Gay Men's Health Crisis. Initial plans were to provide support services to minority AIDS patients in the way of gifts, cards, books, and financial help with prescriptions and transportation for family members, but the full scope of what Raymond had in mind would take years.

The waiter refilled my coffee cup and I smiled as Raymond thanked him. "You really look happy, Raymond."

"I'm doing okay. Life is much better."

"I'm happy for you," I said.

"Looks like you and Jared are doing okay."

"Yes. Jared is really something special. I guess I should thank you again."

"For what? I didn't do anything."

"Well, I wouldn't have met Jared had it not been for you."

"Maybe you should thank Kyle for that. Besides, you and Jared would have met eventually."

"Kyle," I laughed. "He said he was going to send me someone. At first I thought he was talking about you."

"Oh you did. Well I think he's been busy up there," Raymond said as he lifted his head toward the ceiling of the flower-filled restaurant.

"Yeah, I bet he is."

"I should thank you," Raymond said.

"For what?"

"Suggesting I see a doctor. It's really helping."

"I'm glad. But we owe each other a lot. Your helping with Delaney."

"I was glad to do it. I'm pleased things turned out the way they did," Raymond said.

"Yes, so am I. Thanks again."

"So is she doing okay? They say scars from something like that can last a lifetime."

"Delaney's fine. I'm sure Jody helps a lot."

"That's good. How are things going over at LaFace?"

"Aw, okay. The producers I'm working with are still looking for music for the album. But it might be a while since the people in artist development are busy with a new thirteen-year-old singer they are having big problems with."

"Problems? What—he can't sing?"

"No, that's not it, he has a magnificent voice. They're just giving him a Michael Jackson How to Appear Masculine crash course," I said.

"Oh, so it's like that."

"Did that sound tacky?"

"No, not really. I understand what you're saying."

"Ray, can I ask you something?"

"Sure."

"Are you sure Jared isn't gay or bisexual?"

Raymond looked at me with charmed amusement. "Have you asked him?"

"I've asked every man I've dated since you."

"Nicole, I don't profess to know everything about Jared Stovall, but there is one thing I do know and that is Jared is not a liar."

"Thank you, Raymond. Thank you very much."

I decided to take a long relaxing bath before Jared got home. I took my portable CD player into the bathroom, put in a Winans CD, added a double measure of bath oil to the flowing hot water, turned it off, and then eased into the steaming tub.

This was the second night I stayed at Jared's large west end house. Jared bought the house in a foreclosure sale and was in the process of remodeling a major part of the house on his own with the help of Ray and myself. I actually helped paint half of a bedroom.

The house was a large four bedroom about ten minutes from the Atlanta University Center. It was sparsely decorated with a distinctly IKEA flavor. Ray and I teased Jared that we were going to give him an interior decorator as a birthday present.

I was enjoying my return to Atlanta and was not really looking forward to getting back to New York, but my agent had scheduled several soap opera auditions and I'd promised Delaney I would help her pack for her move to San Diego.

It was great spending time with Jared in his own environment and being able to see him in mine when he came with me to the studio to listen to tapes of music submitted by several songwriters.

I slid down into the tub, allowing the suds to cover my breasts, leaned back, and closed my eyes to daydream when I heard Jared's voice.

"Nicole? You in there?"

"Yes, sir. Don't come in here," I yelled.

"I promise not to look." Jared giggled.

"Jared!"

"How long are you gonna be? Should I start the spaghetti?"

"Give me ten more minutes. I've already finished the salad and don't you touch it."

"Okay, but hurry up, I want to take a shower before dinner."

I got out of the tub, dried off, put on a light lip gloss, sprayed my face with mineral water, and dabbed a touch of perfume behind my ears and between my breasts. I slipped on a navy blue teddy and put on a Spelman sweatshirt and jeans. Some of Jared's rooms were still filled with dust and work materials. It was not the type of place you could sit around in an evening gown, but it would soon be.

"How ya doing, big boy?" I said as I gave Jared a kiss. As I tried to pull away he pulled me back and our lips blended together in a long, passionate kiss.

"You must have had a great day," I said as our lips finally parted.

"I always have great days when I know I'm going to see you."

"Well, get in there and clean that dusty butt. I'm hungry."

"Five minutes."

I walked into the huge dining room and saw that Jared had set two place settings at one end of the long table. There were two candlesticks and a light wind blew through the open window. I started to close the windows but the breeze and the sounds of people and birds chirping added a nice ambiance.

As I walked back toward the kitchen to get the salad and wineglasses, I passed the bathroom where Jared had left the door open—he was stepping out of the shower. It was the first time I saw Jared's body and it was beautiful. I stood quietly and secretly watched Jared towel-dry his muscular frame. I thought how nice it would be to be in his arms holding his nude body and allowing him to hold mine, but we were still holding off with sex. We both wanted to have a solid relationship before we took that step and we were going to have an AIDS test together. I was glad Jared had made the suggestion of the tests.

I waited until Jared moved toward the sink before I crept to the kitchen unnoticed.

"You like what you see?" Jared yelled from the bathroom.

"What are you talking about?"

"Nicole!"

"Oh, I didn't mean to look."

"Yeah, right."

Jared came from his bedroom in a sleeveless black undershirt and tight-fitting blue jeans. We walked toward the table to share a nice quiet dinner and as I prepared to sit, Jared gently pulled my chair out, something he always did. Then he lit the two candles facing the two of us. Music was playing in the background and moonlit shadows bounced through the windows onto the bare walls and the corner of the table.

"So how does it taste?" Jared asked.

"Great. I didn't know you could cook so well."

"There are a lot of things I can do well," Jared said with a sexy smile.

"How's the salad?"

"Pretty good considering a Spelman, AKA, BAP made it."

"That's not nice. I've told you 'bout that BAP stuff."

"You know I'm messing with you. It's great, baby."

"So, can you take me to the airport in the morning?"

"Are you sure you've got to leave? I miss you already."

"Yeah, baby, but I'll see you in Little Rock in a couple of weeks. And if you miss me really badly you can always call Delta Airlines."

"I'm really excited about the foundation. I'm glad you and Ray asked me to join in."

"I think it's going to do a lot of good. It seems to have given Ray a new lease on life."

"Yeah, that and Trent," Jared said as he poured more wine into my glass.

"Trent?"

"Yeah, Ray's friend. At least I think he may be. It's somebody he's known since he was a freshman in college. One of his fraternity brothers."

"So that's why he's so happy."

"Yeah, I think that's one of the reasons."

"Jared, can I ask you something?"

"Sure, babe."

"What did you think when Ray told you he liked men?"

"At first I was a little taken aback but I didn't let him know. I wanted to be supportive because I could tell he was in a lot of pain about it. But the next morning I knew it would only make our relationship stronger."

"What do you mean?"

"Because there wouldn't be any secrets between us. One of the reasons I'm so crazy about Raymond is because I feel I can be myself around him. We talk about things other than women and sports. I never had a relationship like that with another man. I would trust Raymond with my life," Jared said as he lifted the wineglass to his lips. There was a softness and a sweet, caring look in Jared's eyes.

"So you don't feel like you could have that with other men or a woman?"

"Yeah, I guess I could, but they wouldn't be Raymond. I think most heterosexual men, not all, but most are threatened by gay men because of their own insecurities and in general they don't realize they can get and learn some valuable things from a relationship with a man that doesn't involve physical pleasure. Gay men don't look at all men in a sexual way, just like all men don't look at every woman sexually. I know I can have that from a woman. My mother and sisters have a lot to do with that. How did you feel about Delaney's confession?"

"Oh, I was surprised, but it doesn't bother me."

"Are you sure?"

"Yes. I love Delaney and I know she's not interested in me."

"Well, the same thing can be said about my relationship with Raymond. You see, women may be more comfortable with a female friend being gay because society won't and doesn't frown at your closeness. For the most part society doesn't think of relationships between women in sexual terms. Men think women are for their sexual pleasures alone. There may be a lot of men keeping sexual secrets from women, but I'm sure there are just as many women with the same secrets."

"You make a good point. How did you get so smart?"

"I'm blessed with a smart mother."

"Your mother is a sweet lady."

"She thinks the world of you. She keeps asking me when we're going to get married."

"Married?"

"Yes. Why the shocked tone?"

"Oh, I didn't mean to sound shocked. But you know we've known each other less than six months."

"Don't panic, Nicole. I'm not asking you to marry me. But there is something I should tell you."

"What?" I asked in a very high-strung tone. There was a jittery silence that seemed to last a millennium.

"Well, I don't know how strongly you feel about me, but I do know you care and I only have control over how I feel. I have only told one other woman this besides my mother and she didn't deserve it," Jared paused and playfully swung at the candlelight.

I didn't say anything, not wanting to interrupt his thoughts. I looked at him, smiled, and arched my eyebrows in an *is that it?* movement. Jared took a deep breath and started to tell me how much he cared for me, how beautiful I was, and how he would spend every second with me. I became mesmerized by the rhythm and cadence of his voice. I was so moved that I began to cry.

"I love you, Nicole," Jared said.

"I don't deserve somebody like you," I said.

"What do you mean?"

"I don't know, Jared. You think I'm so beautiful and wonderful but I'm not," I said softly.

"Why don't you think you're beautiful and wonderful?"

"Look at me. Look at my skin color," I said, looking into Jared's eyes.

"What about your skin color?"

"I'm so black," I said for the first time vocalizing on my secret shame.

"Nicole, please. Your skin is beautiful. Don't tell me you believe I couldn't love you because of that. It's beautiful. Please give me more credit than that," Jared said.

My eyes filled with tears and I felt goose bumps cover my arms. I didn't say a word as Jared came close to me and accepted my tearful embrace. I felt my body come erotically alive under his touch. He lifted my face to his lips and he kissed me powerfully and passionately for at least thirty minutes. Without a break.

"I can't believe I've been able to keep so much shit in a studio apartment," Delaney said as she sat on a trunk trying to keep it shut.

"You do have a lot of stuff, girl."

"Yes, and I've got more stuff in storage."

"So you're not taking everything?"

"No. You never know when this bitch of a city will call me back," Delaney said as she released the barrette from her hair.

"So you sure you want to do this?"

"Do what?"

"Move to San Diego. Are you going to be able to find work?"

"Well, you know about the dance studio and who knows, maybe I'll try out for the Fly Girls, Lord knows they can use some more black faces. Can you believe there's only one sistah dancing with those bitches?"

"Are you sure?"

"Yes, Miss Honey."

"I can't believe I'm going to be here all alone," I said as I walked to the window and looked out on Columbus Avenue.

"Well, come on and go with me, Nic—but I don't think Jared is going to let you stay up here that long."

"What do you mean?"

"Nicole. That guy is in love with you and I hope you won't be no fool and let him get away. He's a good brother and I hope you don't fuck him around."

"I'm not going to do that. I just have to be sure."

"Sure about what?"

"That this is really the one. The real thing."

"Well, don't wait too long. Atlanta is filled with pretty women and I don't think he's going to wait forever. Have you told your mother?"

"I told her I was bringing somebody home for her to meet."

"What did she say?"

"I hope he's not white," I said.

"Your mother sounds like a pistol. I hope I get the chance to meet her," Delaney laughed.

"Well, come to Little Rock with me."

"Little Rock? Naw, honey. You two come to San Diego or Seattle," Delaney suggested.

"What else do you have to do before you leave?"

"I've got to make a few stops to pay some bills. Why?"

"Just asking."

"So how long do you think you're gonna stay in New York, Nic."

"I don't know. The only calls I'm getting regarding work are calls from temp agencies wanting me to do legal word processing."

"What about the *Jelly's* national tour?"

"I'm still waiting to hear."

"Don't worry they will call."

"I hope you're right. Do you want to go downstairs and get some Chinese?"

"Yeah, that sounds good. Let me brush my hair and try to find my purse in all this mess," Delaney said as she walked toward her bathroom.

The day was perfect. The incessant sounds of spring filled the air. The sun above was bright and it generated heat that hit my face as we walked out of Delaney's apartment. I was trying to stay focused on happy times and trying not to think about Delaney's leaving and the fact that I would once again be without a close female friend in the city.

Delaney was a lot like Kyle when it came to good-byes. She said we shouldn't think about it. There was always the phone and the planes. It was at times like these when I realized how we can take friendships and people we care about for granted.

Delaney and I were seated on the patio at our favorite Chinese restaurant. We had finished two glasses of plum wine before our food was served. I looked at Delaney as she brushed a wisp of hair back into place with her fingers and pulled chopsticks from their wrapping. I knew this would be one of the last times we would have to talk before she left and the plum wine gave me the kind of courage I had been missing.

"How does it feel?"

"What?"

"Having sex with another woman?"

"Well, it's not just sex, Nicole. It's making love and it's wonderful. It's just the best," Delaney said as her face seemed to light up.

"Really?"

"Yes, Nicole. The first time it happened it was the most sensual thing I'd ever experienced. It felt so natural to me."

"Do you think you'll ever be with a man?"

"It's hard to say, but I doubt it. He would have to be a special type of man," Delaney said as she lifted the chopsticks from the plate to her pink-colored lips.

"What? Good-looking? Great in bed?"

"No. I think he would have to be sensitive and responsive to my needs. I'm not interested in a man on some macho trip who is not concerned about my needs. He has to be in touch with his feminine side. That's one thing I love about being with a woman. We're naturally sensitive and we know how to please one another."

"Do you think all men have a feminine side?"

"Yes, doesn't Jared?"

"I guess if you call being sensitive a feminine trait."

"There's nothing wrong with it, Nicole. Don't worry."

"Oh, I'm not worried."

"Good."

"Do you think you chose to be gay, Delaney?"

"Let's just say we chose each other. How long have you been wanting to ask me these questions, Miss Lady?"

"Ever since you told me."

"I thought so."

"Do you mind me asking?"

"Nicole, no. Have you ever thought about being with another woman?"

"Darling, no!" I said quickly. Delaney raised her eyebrows as she sipped tea from the tiny white cup.

"That was a quick no, Nicole. It's not for everybody but it's not gross or something really bad either."

"I know, or I should say, I believe you. I love men too much to even consider it. Did I tell you I saw Jared nude. He has a great body."

"Oh no, Miss Honey, now don't change the subject. I know you're not gay or remotely interested in being with a woman. When I first met you I realized you were one of those women who thought any man in his right mind would want to have some of your pussy."

"What do you mean?"

"Not in an arrogant, diva bitch sort of way. Moreso in a Southern beauty type of way. You were brought up to think little girls belong with little boys. That's why I think gay and bisexual men are attracted to you."

"I don't understand."

"You're so feminine, darling. You let a man be a man. You don't challenge them. Have you ever been satisfied sexually?"

"You mean have I had an orgasm?"

"Yes, but that's not the whole deal."

"Well, I did enjoy the one time with Raymond. He's a master at oral sex. My first boyfriend was okay and Pierce was pretty good."

"Well, make sure Jared is interested in pleasing you. Don't be in that I'm a woman and he's a man type of shit. Take home boy's head and lead it to the correct place."

"Delaney."

"Nicole," Delaney said, mocking my expression.

"Jared is sensitive. I think if we ever have sex it will be good."

"Good? Girl, you better want better than good. Now I'm not saying only a woman can take you to the moon. But sex a lot of times is more mental than it is physical and I just am more mentally in tune with women."

"Oh."

"Got any more questions, my deep-thinking sistah?"

"Not right now but if I do I'll write them down and you can mail the answers back to me," I laughed.

"So should I send pictures or draw diagrams?" Delaney smiled.

"I don't think so. That won't be necessary."

Thirty-nine

"**You've** got to be kidding, right?"

"No, I'm not. Why won't you be in my wedding?"

"Basil, first of all I don't think you should be getting married and I wouldn't feel right standing there right before God and Dyanna knowing what I know. Besides, with all your teammates you shouldn't have any problems finding men to be in your wedding."

"I know that, but Dyanna has nine bridesmaids and she really likes you. Come on, Ray, do it for me."

"Basil, I'm not unmoved by your plight. I simply can't accommodate it."

"Why are you being such an asshole?"

"Why I got to be an asshole? I've been meaning to talk to you about this wedding anyway," I said as I came from the kitchen and sat on a bar stool next to Basil.

"What about it?"

"Are you really in love with Dyanna? Do you understand we can't be fuck buddies once you get married?"

"Fuck buddies? So that's what we are?" Basil asked.

"You want me to be honest? Yes, that's the way I see it. We're sexually attracted to each other but I don't think we're friends. I'm looking for something more."

"Like what?"

"Somebody to spend time with, Basil. Someone to talk to when I need a friend."

"I thought we were friends. Why don't you find a lady like Dyanna?"

"What are you talking about?"

"You're still attracted to females, aren't you?"

"Yes, but I'm also about telling the truth."

"I got a question for you."

"What?"

"What does a man with a twelve-inch cock drink?" Basil smiled.

Without thinking I asked, "What?"

"I drink Rolling Rocks. You got another one?"

"Yes, asshole, but this has to be the last one. I've got to pick somebody up from the airport," I said as I laughed and walked back into the kitchen.

"Who are you picking up?"

"A friend."

"What type of friend?"

"Mind your own business, Basil," I said as I gave him another beer.

"So that's why you're trying to get rid of me. You found some other nigger," Basil said as he unzipped the jacket of his green and purple warm-up suit. When he did this I no longer needed to imagine his exemplary body.

"Tell me why you're getting married."

"Well, I love Dyanna," Basil said as he took a swig of beer.

"Are you sure?"

"Why can't I be sure?"

"Well, I'm just picturing you in some of the positions we've been in," I said with a sly smile.

"Fuck you, motherfucker. I better not ever hear anything about that shit," Basil said.

"I ain't gonna tell nobody. But a friend of mine knows Dyanna. She also knows you're bisexual. She wants me to talk you out of it before she tells Dyanna."

"Who?"

"I'm not saying who but you should really think about Dyanna. What if she finds out?"

"She won't find out. Dyanna's too busy being a BAP. Her father and mother love me. I fuck her real good a couple times a week, eat her pussy every now and then, and she's happy."

"Well, I don't know if I can keep my friend from telling Dyanna," I said as I anxiously looked at my watch. I realized it was getting very close to when Trent's flight would arrive at Hartsfield, and I wanted to meet him at the gate.

"Who is this bitch?"

"Why does she have to be a bitch, Basil?"

"Whoever she is she better mind her fucking business. I'm the wrong one to fuck with," Basil said as he gave me a contemptuous stare.

"Stop calling her a bitch!"

"Well, that's what she is. I know who it is. It's that Nicole bitch your boyfriend was with. That's who it is. She is a bitch and that black bitch better stay out of my life," Basil said as he got up from the bar stool. His face was contorted with anger.

"You still didn't answer my question. Why does she have to be a bitch? Nicole is more lady than anybody you know."

"She's a fucking black bitch," Basil yelled.

"What does that make your mama?" I asked angrily and without thinking. A look of disgust and exasperation swept across Basil's face. I looked deep into his angry eyes and wished I had suppressed my last remark.

"Motherfucker," Basil howled at the top of his lungs as he rushed toward me and jerked me quickly by the collar of my sweatshirt. I felt the material ripping from my back. At first I was shocked at how quickly he grabbed me and I was caught offguard, but I quickly pushed him against the wall and shouted, "You fucking sonofabitch, don't pull on me. I ain't one of your bitches."

Basil pushed me back and balled up his fist.

"So what you gonna do, Basil? You gonna hit me like you hit Charles. Well, hit me, motherfucker, but be prepared for what's gonna follow and I ain't talking about your checkbook, fucker. I don't need your money," I said as I clenched my fists readying myself to lay his ass out if he hit me.

"So you're gonna hit me over some bitch?"

"Don't use that word in my house again. Do what you're gonna do and get your ass out," I said.

"Why are we fighting over this shit, Ray?"

"You're the one that started it," I said, evoking a memory of two little boys fighting over a girl or marbles in an elementary school play yard.

"If you don't want to see me anymore then just say that. Don't use my marriage to Dyanna as an excuse. You and that woman should leave me and Dyanna alone."

"I will, but I can't speak for Nicole," I said as I relaxed my fighting stance. Basil was looking down at the carpet and then he raised his eyes and gazed at me for a moment.

"So this is it. If I marry Dyanna that's it for you and me?"

"Yes," I said firmly.

"Why?"

"Because this is more than sex, Basil. You can't use me for your sexual needs. I can no longer use you. I want and deserve more and so do you. But you've got to understand that relationships between men are not just about sex."

Basil turned, taking in my entire condo in one, long sweeping glance. When he was facing me again his sensual gray eyes were filled with water. He moved closer to me, dropped to his knees, jerked down my warm-ups, and pulled my limp sex to his lips. I quickly pulled back the minute I felt his cold lips touch my sex. I wanted to give in and enjoy sex with Basil one more time but Trent's face immediately came to mind and my indecisiveness was gone in an instant.

"No, Basil, we can't do this," I said as I moved away and pulled up my warm-ups.

"Come on, Ray," Basil pleaded.

"I can't, Basil. Please get up."

Basil lifted himself and stood very close to me. His body seemed to be generating steam. I wanted to grasp him and hold him but I knew my sleeping sex would soon awaken. I couldn't confuse the issue. This had to be over. There was a long, tense silence broken by the ringing phone. I picked it up on the second ring.

"Hello."

"I'm here! Where are you?" Trent said cheerfully.

"I'm on my way. I lost track of time."

"I'll be in front of the United terminal. I can't wait to see you."

"Me too," I said softly. I hung up the phone, looked at Basil, and said, "I have to leave."

Basil picked up his wallet and the Atlanta Braves hat that was resting on the bar. He slipped his wallet inside his jock and placed the hat on his head without a word. A pained look settled onto his face and he walked out of my place—and most likely out of my life.

I wasn't going to let my fight with Basil spoil Trent's visit. He seemed so excited to be in Atlanta and in my company, but I continued to think about the fight with Basil at least once every hour.

Trent was in the living room listening to music while I was in my office trying to catch up on work. Every thirty minutes my phone would ring and as soon as I picked it up I would get a dial tone. I assumed the annoying calls were from Basil.

After a couple of hours Trent walked into my den, leaned over the chair, and started massaging my shoulders. His hands were strong and felt great.

"Is there anything I can do to help?"

"To help?"

"Yes, I want to spend some time with my man," he said.

"I'll be finished in a few. What do you want for dinner?"

"You," Trent laughed.

I turned around and we eyed each other smiling since we both knew what Trent's response suggested. We still hadn't made love with each other. Would this be the night?

"Seriously, Trent. What do you want to do, order in or go out?"

"Let's order a pizza and just stay in."

"Okay. Look in the cabinet over the kitchen sink. There are a bunch of carry-out menus that deliver in the area. Pick out what you want and give them a call," I said. Trent smiled and planted a deep kiss on my lips and then walked into the living area.

When Trent left the room I thought about how lucky I was to have him in my life. I wasn't going to let Basil ruin this for me. For the first time I had a chance at a relationship with a man who knew what he wanted without confusion. Trent made it perfectly clear that he was a gay man who wanted to spend his life with me.

I recalled all the men I had been involved with in the past and how those relationships always involved other people, mainly unsuspecting women and men I would never know. There would be moments when I felt I was in love with Trent, I mean really in love, and then times when I would be uncertain about how our relationship could withstand the distance, not to mention how our wallets would hold up. My own wallet hadn't recovered from Kyle's illness. We were both doing well in our careers. Gilliam and I had decided to wait until the beginning of the year but I would be made a full partner and Trent had been recently promoted to full associate at his firm in Chicago.

I closed up my notebook and walked into the living area where Trent was lying in the middle of the floor reading a copy of *Architectural Digest* and listening to Arrested Development.

"Come down here with me," Trent said. "I have something I want to show you."

I kicked off my loafers and dived onto the floor next to Trent.

"Look at this house. Isn't it the shit?" Trent asked as he pointed to a beautiful house in the magazine.

"Yes, Trent, that's a great house."

"This is the kind of house I want to build for you and me one day. A house just like in the magazines and in the movies," he said as he gave me a small peck on the forehead.

"You think that's possible?"

"What? Me building the house or us being together?"

"Us being together. I mean you live in Chicago and I'm living here. How long can we do this?"

"Well, I hope one day we can live in the same city."

"Yes, but which one?"

"I don't know. I love Chicago and I'm doing great with my career but I know I want to be with you."

"I know but I'm about to make partner and that's here in Atlanta."

"Would you move to Chicago?"

"Would you move to Atlanta?"

"I asked first," Trent said.

Just as I was getting ready to answer or a least put on my lawyer hat the phone rang.

"Hello."

"Ray, this is Basil. I need to talk to you."

"Talk, but be quick."

"Why? Is your niggah over there?"

"Good-bye, Basil."

"Come on, Ray, I said I need to talk with you."

"I can't really talk now," I said.

"Why? Are you in bed fucking?"

"I'm sorry, I have to go," I said as I laid the receiver back into the cradle. Five seconds later the phone rang again.

"Don't you ever hang up the phone in my face, motherfucker," Basil shouted.

"You got your face on the phone?"

"What? Hell no! I've got my ears to it."

"Good! This is for your ears," I said as I slammed down the phone and unplugged it from the wall.

Trent was watching me and he jumped up from the floor and came close to me.

"Are you all right?"

"I'm fine. Come here, Trent, and sit down. We've got to talk. On second thought let's go out on the patio."

Trent and I walked onto the patio. It was a beautiful night in Atlanta, windless, in the eighties. A perfect summer night. I began to tell Trent about my relationship with Basil and the fight that had occurred this afternoon. I informed him that I wasn't in love with Basil but there was an attachment. Trent's face was pinched with curiosity as I explained how I'd met Basil years before and then later the previous year. I told Trent that Basil was getting married but that wasn't the reason the association was over.

"Are you sure how you feel about him, Ray?"

"Yes, I am. I'm not in love with him but he was there during some difficult times," I said.

"How do you feel about him getting married?"

"What do you mean?"

"I mean, how do you feel?"

"I feel sorry for the young lady."

"Why?"

"Because she doesn't have a clue."

"Isn't that usually the way it is?"

"Yes, but it doesn't make it right."

"I agree," Trent said.

"So you got any more questions?"

"You'll always shoot straight with me. Honesty, right?"

"Yes, Trent. I will always be honest with you."

"So you don't want to be with Basil?"

"I don't want to be with Basil. I'm with the person I want to be with."

I looked at Trent's brown profile illuminated by the streetlights below and asked him what he was thinking.

"I just want you to be sure. I've waited too long for this."

"If we're being honest, then we have to face the fact that male-to-male relationships are tough enough and we have all the distance separating us."

"If you want this to work, Raymond . . . it can. I don't know if it means my moving here or your moving to Chicago. What I need to know before I leave this week is that you want this to work. It's not about you wanting to spend your life with a male or female. It's about whether or not you want to spend your life with me. Plain and simple."

"But isn't this too fast?"

"How can everything you've ever dreamed of happen too fast?"

I felt a chill go through me. I didn't answer Trent. I just looked at the stars overhead and began to let myself fantasize a future with Trent and Trent alone.

We didn't talk much that night. We ordered pizza. Trent drank beer. I drank cranberry juice. Trent went to bed early and I plugged in the phone and called Jared to let him know that everything was going great. He said he had something important he wanted to talk to me about but it could wait until tomorrow. He told me to give Trent his regards and he would send one up for us when he prayed before going to bed.

I walked into the bedroom and the only light in the dark room was coming from the television and Trent's bright eyes. He was watching a "Mary Tyler Moore Show" rerun. He gave me an ardent smile as I dropped my pants, pulled off my shirt, and climbed between the clean sheets covered lightly with baby powder—a trick of seduction Kyle had taught me. When I slipped into the bed, Trent immediately edged close to me. I pulled him closer to my body and drifted into a peaceful sleep.

"I was asked to be in two weddings last week."

"Two?"

"I don't know if I'll be in either. I definitely won't be in Basil's and Jared's isn't official."

"Jared?"

"Well, he came over a couple of days ago and asked me how I felt about him asking Nicole to marry him. I must admit I was a bit surprised."

"How do you feel about it?"

"You know it's a strange feeling. A part of me is happy that two wonderful people have found each other and then there is the part that secretly holds on to the hope that it could have been me. I shared that with Jared and though he was a bit surprised he said he understood."

"Surprised?"

"Well, he said he knew that I was happy with Trent and he didn't know I still harbored those types of feelings for Nicole. I explained to him I would always love Nicole but I knew he was the best thing in the world for her. It wasn't necessarily my feelings about Nicole either; perhaps it had more to do with the fact that their getting married meant giving up my fantasy of the life I wanted to lead. I also confessed as to how I used to think about being in love with him, romantically."

"What did he say?"

"Said he was flattered. Flattered. Can you believe he was flattered?"

I went on to tell Dr. Paul I'd suggested Jared propose to Nicole when he went home with her. I told him about a place where Nicole used to tell me she wanted to get married. Jared said he had a special way he wanted to propose but he was still working it out. I told him I supported him a thousand percent.

After we talked about Jared and Nicole, I started to talk about Basil and Trent. How I was certain it was over with Basil but how I felt sorry for him and how I was dealing with my feelings about Trent.

"Why do you feel sorry for Basil?"

"Because he's like I was in a lot of ways."

"How, Raymond?"

"I think he feels he's trapped. Because he's a black man, a pro football star, and he feels that he must conform to what society expects of him. It's like living in a prison. Trust me I know."

"Do you feel like you're still living in a prison, Raymond?"

"No, I think I'm on parole."

"How so?"

"Well, I've been given a chance with someone wonderful like Trent. My parents and I are going to phase three."

"Phase three?"

"Yes, I realized when I talked with my parents that we're going to have to do things in stages. My coming out to my father about four years ago was the first step, talking about it honestly was step two, and the three of us seeking professional help will be another step."

"Sounds good to me."

"Trent also gave me a choice to make."

"A choice?"

"Well, my birthday is in a couple of weeks and Trent has to be in Seattle on business. He suggested I meet him in Seattle to celebrate. He said he only wants me to come if I'm ready to pursue a relationship totally and only with him. He said if things work out we could go back and forth for a year and then decide who's going to move."

"How are you going to decide that?"

"I suggested we play a five-set tennis match. The loser would have to move to the winner's city."

"What did Trent say?"

"He knows I'm a better tennis player than him. He's better at bowling and basketball but he said he wasn't getting in a macho pissing contest with me," I laughed.

"You know you smile a lot when you talk about Trent?"

"I do?"

"Yes, you sure do."

"I wonder what that means. I guess I'm happy whenever he crosses my mind, which is often. I'm going to think about it and pray for direction on what to do. I may end up spending my birthday alone because I don't want to hurt Trent in any way. He is such a great person and he does deserve someone who will love him the way I think he's capable of loving."

"So are you ready to start with the every other week schedule?"

"Yes, Dr. Paul. I know I've got some important decisions to make but my life is looking hopeful. Still a little confused, but hopeful. I often think of Kyle and I think he would be proud of me coming face to face with who I really am. I don't think of him being gone, I think of all the wonderful times we had. I'm smiling a lot these days."

"Well, call my office when you want to start a new schedule," Dr. Paul said as she laid down her legal pad.

"Dr. Paul, can I ask you one last thing?"

"Sure, Raymond."

"When do you give up on old dreams?"

"You'll know."

The weeks leading up to my birthday passed quickly and I still hadn't decided what to do. I was busy catching up at work and when I talked to Trent the first thing in the morning and late at night I thought for certain I was going to Seattle. Trent liked to start his day by calling me and the two of us would share a brief prayer before our conversation and wish each other a blessed and successful day.

My mother called a few days before my birthday and wanted to know how I was doing and if I was going to come home to celebrate. She told me that Kirby was home and doing much better and that he and Pops wanted me to come home so that the four of us could go out to dinner. My mother suggested that this could be a good time to talk with Kirby. When she said that I felt good inside.

I told my mother I might be in Seattle and when she asked if it was business, I didn't lie. For the first time I told her about a man in my life, Trent, and how wonderful he was. After I got through talking about Trent there was a brief silence and I asked my mother if she was all right.

"Oh, I'm fine, baby. This Trent guy sounds very special and important to you."

"He's becoming that way, Mom. Can you believe I've known him since I was a freshman in college? He's from Montgomery. Did I already tell you that? Mom, are you sure you're all right?"

"Yes, Ray-Ray. But I have to be honest and tell you I'm still praying that you'll find some nice young lady and make me a grandmother," she said softly.

"Even after my last visit home? Didn't I make myself clear?"

"Yes, and I think I understand."

"Because I love you so much, Mama, I wish I could tell you it was going to happen. But I'm learning sometimes you have to give up old dreams to be happy today. That's what I'm doing, Ma, I'm letting go of the old dreams and you have to do that too."

"Yes, baby, I hear you. I don't want to give up my dreams of being a grandmother but you know I just want you to be happy. For the first time in a long time you sound happy."

"Yes, I'm very happy and your dreams may come true. I get the feeling Kirby will help you out with that dream."

"Yeah, that's what I'm afraid of. Maybe I should change my dreams and prayers," Mama laughed. It was a warm, reassuring laugh.

"Mama will you and Pops be supportive of Trent and me?"

"Supportive?"

"Yes. Can I bring him home? Will you accept him?"

"If he's as great as you say he is I don't see why not."

"What about Pops?"

"He handles it better than I do sometimes but I'm getting help."

"Getting help?"

"Well, I did some research after you came home and I called this group called PFLAG."

"PFLAG. What's that?"

"Parents and Friends of Lesbians and Gays, I think."

"Did it help?"

"Yes, it did. It cleared up a lot of questions I had. I think all my misunderstandings came from my fear of the unknown."

"Ma, I love you. I love you for loving me so hard and never giving up on me. A lot of people like me never have the type of love I get from you and Pops."

"I love you too, baby, and I know your father does. We're very proud of you for the way you supported Kyle and the way you're facing up to the things you don't understand. Now if you go to Seattle then you have to come home as soon as you get back. We have a few surprises for you."

"Okay, Ma, I will. Tell Pops and Knucklehead I love them."

"I will."

When I hung up the phone from the conversation with my mother I knew what I was going to do.

Forty

The summer I was waiting for all my life happened. It seemed just when I was preparing to give up on straight black men and fairy tale endings, a shining ebony prince, namely Jared Stovall, flew into Little Rock.

Jared joined me for my family reunion and to visit the place where I grew up. The first evening he was there my mother asked him to say grace before dinner. Jared prayed with such a fervent tone that it took me by surprise. I felt a certain kind of power emanating from his voice, so much so that I shivered slightly as if something cool and wondrous had blown through my body. Jared held my hand tightly. It was during this prayer I realized power was in the eyes of the beholder. This wasn't the first time Jared had prayed with me—he had become my prayer partner after my split with Shelia—but this was different. His prayer was so powerful that both my mother and aunt were in tears before he finished.

It was love at first sight for Jared and my mother. In fact, every one of my family members was drawn to his warm personality. After dinner, as Jared and I were preparing to go to our downtown hotel, my mother grabbed my hands and pulled me to her bedroom and said, "Don't be no fool and let him get away, girl. Marry that man today." It was advice given in a warm and friendly tone like we were good, good, girlfriends. I smiled and told my mother if Jared ever asked I would certainly take her advice into consideration. She pulled me close to her bosom and whispered she loved me and was glad I was home. She also suggested we go to the cemetery and visit Daddy before I returned to New York.

Jared had reserved a junior suite at the Excelsior Hotel in downtown Little Rock. The beautifully decorated suite included a large canopy bed and a view of the moonlit Arkansas River. Jared insisted the suite include a VCR. When I asked him why, he said it was a surprise.

After a nice romantic walk through downtown Little Rock, Jared and I retired to the suite where a bottle of chilled champagne was waiting on the small dining table.

"I've got a special copy of *Boomerang*," Jared said.

"*Boomerang?* I thought you'd already seen it," I said.

"I did but this is a special copy a friend made for me. It has a different ending."

"A different ending?"

"Come on, get up here with me. You'll see what I'm talking about."

I climbed into the bed with Jared and began to watch the movie. I had seen it before so I decided I would critique Robin's and Halle's performances. Jared removed his shirt and I lay against his chest. I felt its warmth when I laid my head against him and the strength of his arms when he held me close. I looked up at him and enjoyed the sweetness of his smile and he said, "Don't watch me, watch the movie." I wondered what was so important about *Boomerang*.

When the movie ended I was thinking maybe I missed something as the credits rolled when suddenly Jared appeared on the screen dressed like Eddie Murphy in the final scene.

"Nicole," Jared began from the screen, "Eddie had to learn the hard way but I realized I found the woman of my dreams the first time I kissed you."

Jared pulled away from the bed and pushed the pause button, leaving his face on the screen, and slowly got dowr on his knees. IIe was shaking and goose bumps covered his naked shoulders.

"How did yov do that?" asked

"I'll explain later," Jared said.

"Come on, Jared, tell me. I didn't know you knew Eddie and Halle."

"Nicole, please be quiet. I'm nervous enough," Jared pleaded.

"Okay. I'm sorry."

"Nicole, I know this is really fast but it's something I'm certain of . . . absolutely certain about. When I first saw you at Spelman so many years ago, I thought you were one of the most beautiful women I had ever seen. When I saw you again in New York, the same thing rang true. To find out you're even more beautiful on the inside is a miracle. No, it's a blessing." I felt my eyes filling with tears as I hung on each word. Jared's words blended together and wrapped themselves around me like the overture of a Broadway musical, the warmth and rhythm of his voice filling the suite. Jared took a deep breath and then continued as he reached under the bed and pulled out a small black box.

"Well, in case you don't know where this is leading or what I'm trying to say, I guess I'll just spit it out. Nicole Marie Springer, I would be honored if you would consider becoming my wife."

My heart was pounding like a war drum; everything I had ever longed for was coming together in a way I could not have dreamed of a short time ago.

"Jared, I'm shocked. I mean I love you but this is so sudden," I said.

"I know, baby. But I'm willing to wait until you're ready. Just say you'll wear this until you're ready," Jared said as he opened the tiny black box revealing a sparkling diamond engagement ring.

"Oh, this is beautiful, Jared. It really is."

"Will you wear it, Nicole? Will you make me the happiest man on this earth?"

"I don't know, Jared."

"Do you love me, Nicole?"

"Yes, Jared. I know that," I said.

"Then trust your feelings, baby. Pray for direction," Jared said. "Please know, Nicole Springer, that I promise to always give you the things that I can give for free. Something we can always give to each other until the end of time."

"What's that, Jared?" I smiled.

"Honesty and love. I promise to always be honest with you, no matter what."

"Honesty?"

"Yes, honesty."

This was too perfect, I thought. He was promising me something I always dreamed a man would offer me. I looked into Jared's eyes and down at the ring. It seemed as though his large body was shaking as he remained on his knees. He took his hand and gently touched my face. No man's touch had ever made me feel so warm and breathless at the same time. I reached for the ring and touched the surface of the diamond.

"It will look a lot better on your finger," Jared said.

"You think so?"

"Let's see," Jared said as he placed the ring on my finger. It looked beautiful.

Jared went on to say he was willing to have a long engagement so I could be certain, but he knew his feelings for me would only grow stronger. He wanted to ask my mother for my hand in marriage before he left. He said he supported whatever I wanted to do in regard to my career and he was willing to move to New York.

Later in the evening I lay against Jared's warm body staring at the ring and listening to Will Downing's seductive voice piped from the tiny radio as Jared stroked his fingers through my hair. I turned toward Jared and positioned my body so my lips could be close to his and then I kissed him. Jared responded warmly and his lips and tongue suddenly left my lips and started to explore my neck, my chin, and finally my thinly covered breasts. At first I resisted but it felt so good and then something inside me let go and my body seemed to melt against Jared's. Jared slowly slipped off my silk undergarments and I felt no shame, only pleasure as he stripped down to his underwear. He pulled me close to his chest and I kissed him softly. I could feel his heart pounding beneath my lips. He looked at me and said, "Are you sure you want to do this? I love you, Nicole, and I'll love you even if you make me wait."

"Do you have protection?"

"Yes," Jared smiled and jumped out of the bed and dashed into the bathroom. When he came out he proudly held up two gold-wrapped condoms.

I wasn't sure I was ready to go all the way but I wanted to make sure he was prepared.

Jared started to kiss my lips and breasts as he slowly moved his tongue down my stomach as though it was a paintbrush painting a straight line to my navel. He tenderly pushed my thighs apart and kissed me until I almost passed out from pleasure.

Moans of our sexual delight filled the hotel suite as our bodies passionately entwined. Jared was a skillful lover and each nerve ending of my body responded to his touch. He gently fitted his body into mine, every curve and every muscle, as we drifted from the bed to the carpeted floor. Jared made love to my body with a combination of strength and tenderness. How I had missed the ecstasy of a man's body connected with mine. Hours later, naked and adrift in the memories of our lovemaking, Jared smiled with clear and honest eyes. His body was still warm and his erect sex indicated he was ready for more.

"So when are you going to answer my question or have you already give me my answer?"

"What do you think?" I smiled.

Forty-one

When I was a little boy learning the map of the United States, Seattle, Washington, seemed like the end of the world. How could I have known this beautiful city would be the beginning of my perfect world?

The five-hour United flight seemed to take forever. All during the trip my thoughts swirled like a cotton candy machine at a busy state fair. I was thinking about Trent and what this trip would mean to the both of us.

I didn't read any of the books I brought on the plane or look at the work from the office. My stomach was free of food but stuffed with nervous energy. I was so deep in thought the charm-free flight attendants didn't phase me.

As the plane was landing, I looked out the window and saw a beautiful summer day. Somehow I thought it would be raining. After I got off the plane and entered the gate area I immediately saw Trent—his face radiating a warm and enticing smile. He moved swiftly toward me, gave me a firm hug, and whispered, "I didn't think you were going to show up. Happy birthday, boy!"

"Trent, thank you. It's great seeing you. How are your meetings going?"

"Great! Did you bring a ton of luggage?"

"No, just this garment bag and my overnight kit," I said as I admired Trent's brown body in white baggy shorts and a purple muscle T-shirt. I could suddenly smell the cologne Trent transferred to my body with his hug.

"So what do you want to do first? This is your treat," Trent said.

"What hotel are we staying at? I need to call and let Jared know where I'm staying," I said as we walked through the automatic doors and into the clean warm fragrance of the stunning summer day.

"We're staying at the Westin. We can drop your stuff off and then maybe go to the Space Needle."

"The Space Needle. Do they have a bar there?"

"Yeah. It's at the top. You worried they won't have cranberry juice?"

"No, I think today is the day I give up the cranberry juice for a while. I think I'd like a nice glass of champagne."

Trent stopped at the door of the rental car and gazed at me. He bit his lower lip and then glanced away. When he turned to face me I saw a single tear in the corner of his eye. "Did I hear you right? Did you say you want a glass of champagne?" Trent asked with a nervous giggle.

"Yes, you heard me right. Let's go get a bottle of the most expensive champagne they have. Forget about the hotel. It will wait."

Trent didn't answer he just smiled broadly and jumped into the rental car.

"No matter how much I love you, Trent, the odds are against us," I said as I sipped my second glass of champagne.

"The odds were against us being successful in our chosen careers. They were against us reaching age thirty. We are black men and we've been defying the odds all our life, Raymond."

"Yeah, but how long can we keep beating them? There will be so much against us," I said as I looked into his soulful eyes.

"Then why should we be against each other? We could be like the song."

"What song?"

" 'You and Me Against the World,' " Trent smiled.

As I watched Trent drink from the slender glass flute, a great love for him and life swept through me and I wondered how I'd survived for so many years without it. Trent was absolutely convinced our relationship could last forever. For the first time I had the chance to enter a relationship with no secrets. A relationship with someone who was already deeply in love with me and who knew me fairly well. A relationship based on truth and honesty. No man had ever spoken to me of love in such a positive and confident manner as Trent did. This was about love —and not based on sex.

"So where do we start?"

"First thing we have to promise to always be honest with each other and to tell the truth no matter what," Trent said.

"I agree. Does that mean when I'm attracted to a woman or another man?"

"Yes, though I think after we've consummated our relationship you won't have the desire to stray," Trent said confidently.

"What else?"

"We have to keep it exciting. Never take each other for granted. I want to romance you to the end of time."

"What about our families? Your son? And my desire to have my own children?"

"I'm sure Trent Junior is going to love you like I do. My mother won't be a problem and neither will my father once he gets to know you. If you really want your own children, we'll work it out."

"So, we'll always be honest with each other and always tell the truth, no matter what. I like that. What if you meet some other guy you're attracted too?"

"Ray, I see fine men in Chicago on every block every day and that's what they are . . . fine men. I don't think you understand how much I love you. How having you in my life is what I've wanted for a long time. I'm not some fickle queen who just wants to sleep with you or be with you because of how you look or what you do. I know you and I know what kind of man you are. I know what I want."

I was falling in love not only with Trent, but with Seattle. We drove through sprawling mosaic neighborhoods and down perfectly paved streets with perfectly placed trees lining them. A summer mist lingered over the city. It wasn't a humid mist but more of a warm, supportive one.

"You know one year from now we might consider moving here," I said.

"Get outta here," Trent yelled. "I was just thinking the same thing."

We rushed to the hotel room because Trent said we had to hurry for a surprise he planned. Once we got to the oversized room illuminated with brilliant colors and with a wonderful view of the city, Trent quickly went into the shower. I thought about joining him there, but it might have spoiled his surprise and besides we'd agreed to wait for sex. We just hadn't said how long.

I smiled when I saw Trent's open suitcase sitting on the bed. Right on top was several pairs of new underwear. All types from the jockey boxer to silk bikini briefs. I could tell they were new because the price tags were still on them. My garment bag was filled with the same things. Trent came out of the shower with just a towel wrapped around his body and came over and gave me a kiss.

"Come on, you're wet," I protested.

"Come here," Trent said, pulling me close to him and guiding my hands to his solid buttocks.

"Aren't you glad you came?"

"Came? Did I come? I mean you feel good but not that good," I joked.

"Get in there and take your shower," Trent said.

We enjoyed a pleasurable seafood dinner in the hotel and then went to a jazz bar also located in the hotel. The dimly lit room featured a black female singer with a marvelous voice. I thought about Jared and Nicole in Little Rock as the singer unspooled beautifully arranged ballads like scenes from vivid technicolor dreams. When she finished her song she asked for the house lights to be brought up.

"Is there a Raymond Winston Tyler, Jr., in the house?" she asked.

I glanced at Trent and he had a cat-who-ate-the-canary grin on his face.

I nodded my head toward the singer and she came over and sat on my lap and began to sing "Happy Birthday" to me, encouraging the other patrons to join in as the waiters brought out a huge birthday cake. I was totally surprised. I had forgotten that it was my birthday. I looked at Trent and smiled.

I came out of the shower and walked into the room and saw Trent's half nude body gleaming in the soft evening light as he stood by the open window. Music from the portable radio saturated the room.

"So were you surprised?" Trent asked as he kissed me gently.

"Yes, babe, I was surprised."

"You're welcome. Come here," Trent said.

"Where?"

"Here," Trent said as he opened his arms.

I walked toward Trent and into his arms. His body smelled of scented hotel soap. Tiny beads of sweat covered his chest.

"I want you to do something with me," Trent said.

"Do something?"

"Yes."

"What?"

"Slow-dance with me."

"Slow-dance?"

"Yes, slow-dance," Trent said with a smile.

He switched the tiny knob on the radio until the room was filled with Stevie Wonder's "You and I." We looked at each other and smiled. We held each other tightly and began to sway against each other with Stevie's voice dictating our moves. It was such a special feeling. An indescribable tenderness. We pressed our noses against each other's and then broke out in laughter.

"What are you thinking about?"

"If they could only see us now," Trent laughed.

"Who?"

"The brothers of KAΩ."

"You're crazy."

"Ray, were you serious about us moving here?"

"Yeah. If we still feel the same way a year from now, I don't see why not. You think you can find work up here?"

"If I can't, I'll start my own firm. Besides I'm going to be busy building our house. Remember? Like in the movies?"

"Oh yeah. I could probably still work with Gilliam and open up a Northwest branch and I could always teach. Plus I have More Than Friends work."

"Oh, I brought some plans for Kyle's hospice that we talked about. That's a part of your surprise."

"Let's look at them in the morning. I'm tired. I must have jet lag."

"Lie down. Let me give you a massage and roll some tension off you," Trent said.

"Oh the old massage trick. Now, Trent, I thought you'd be more creative than that," I laughed.

"Come on, boy, lie down."

I lay on the bed and Trent started to deeply massage my shoulders, arms, and even my fingers. Minutes later I felt his tongue kiss the back of my neck and I turned over and kissed his lips. It was then I realized my sex was full and vertical.

Trent gazed at it and gently touched the top of it and looked at me and smiled.

"Trent. I'm sorry. We said we were going to wait."

"Ray. It doesn't matter if we do it now or a year from now. We're going to do it and it will be tremendous," he beamed.

I lay back on the king-size bed loaded with goose-down pillows as Trent started to kiss my entire body. Starting with my lips he went slowly and it appeared he was memorizing every part of me. When he finished, he pulled his taut nude body alongside mine and I held him firmly in my arms. It was as if we had always known each other. It was so right, so perfect. Trent looked into my eyes and said, "Raymond, tell me a story."

"A story? What type of story?"

"Make one up. Make it up just for me," Trent smiled.

"Any particulars?"

"Just a happy ending," he said.

This was an unconventional request but I didn't fret. If Trent wanted a story then I would give him a story.

"Once upon a time in a place called Perfect . . ."

Minutes later I looked down and Trent was sleeping like a baby, quietly snoring but still sleeping like a baby. I pulled his body closer to mine and clicked off the nearby lamp. Even though the room was pitch black I felt as though I was falling asleep under the sun.

Forty-two

New York was cold. An immaculate snow carpet covered the majority of the sidewalks. But after six months in freezer-cold Chicago, New York and all its people brought a warmth to my heart. I was happy to be back if just for a few days.

I was only a few blocks from Dr. Huntley's office. I decided to take the subway because I didn't trust New York cabbies in weather like this. I didn't trust them in normal weather either. I had returned to New York after a successful run of *Jelly's* in Chicago. So much had happened in six months. I would need my full fifty minutes with Dr. Huntley. She greeted me after only one ring.

"Nicole, come on in. It's great seeing you," Dr. Huntley said with her warm smile.

"Dr. Huntley it's great seeing you. It's been a long time," I said.

"Come on in. Let me take your coat."

Dr. Huntley took my coat and slipped it into a closet door behind her desk. I had never noticed the door in all the years I'd been seeing her. It's amazing the things you notice when your life is in order.

"Would you like some hot tea? It's cold out there."

"Sure, I'd love some. But this weather is warm compared to Chicago."

Dr. Huntley walked over to a small buffet area and poured two cups of tea.

"Chicago. I love that city. Tell me about the tour," she said as she looked in the cabinet.

"Oh, it was great. A wonderful experience. But I'm ready to let *Jelly's* go and face some new roles."

"So you've already got something lined up?" Dr. Huntley asked as she placed some hot tea on the small table directly in front of me.

"Yes, my most important role," I smiled as I sipped some of the sweet-tasting tea.

Dr. Huntley's thick eyebrows arched in a quizzical fashion.

"My role as a wife. Have you forgotten? I'm getting married in about six months."

"Oh no. You sound excited."

"Oh, I am Dr. Huntley. But I'm kinda sad too."

"Sad? Why?"

"Well, I'm sorry to say this might be my last visit with you. I think I'm ready to face the real world alone. I mean with Jared."

"Well, Nicole, that's what therapy is about. One day you no longer need it. I'm happy for you."

"So where do I start?"

"Start?"

"Yes, so much has happened. Well, first the bad news. Jared's not perfect," I laughed.

"He's not?"

"No, he leaves a trail of clothes everywhere. Underwear and all. I think his mother and sisters spoiled him. But besides that he's perfect."

"So things are going great."

"Yes. We both have a lot of frequent-flyer miles between Chicago and Atlanta."

"So you've set a date?"

"June 26. In Little Rock at the Old State House. I'm so happy I could just cry."

"Well, it shows on your face."

I played briefly with the yarn on a pillow from Dr. Huntley's sofa. I was thinking about seeing Jared in a couple of days. The thought made me smile. I told Dr. Huntley about my plans to go to Atlanta and spend some time with Jared and then go to Little Rock to start final wedding plans.

"How are things with you and your mother?" Dr. Huntley asked.

"Well, things are better. They're not great but we're getting there. She loves Jared and I think she's happy for me. But there still is an underlying friction on certain things."

"Certain things?"

"Yes. I tried to explain to her how I felt insecure about my skin color and how she contributed to that during my childhood."

"What did she say?"

"She listened. But I just don't think she got it. My mother is one of those ladies who thinks our generation complains too much. That we want everything perfect."

"Do you?"

"Do I what?"

"Want everything perfect."

"Yes, I think I do. Did I tell you about my brother?"

"You mentioned something in our last session. How is he doing?"

"Much better. Mom and I sent him to rehab. He's back in Arkansas living with relatives."

"So did your mother and you agree on that?"

"Yes, we did. In a way caring for my brother brought us closer together."

"So you're happy?"

"I want to be happy. Totally happy. I'm closer to that than I've ever been."

"Is Jared the reason?"

"Just one of the reasons. A major one though."

"So you're not going to see a doctor in Atlanta?"

"No, I made it through six months in Chicago with prayer and just feeling stronger about things. I talked it over with Jared and he supports whatever decision I make. He was very understanding about me waiting to tell him about you and our sessions."

"So he didn't have any problems with it?"

"None whatsoever."

"You've come a long way since your first visit, Nicole. I'm quite proud of you," Dr. Huntley said.

"Yes I have. I have my days. Like it's only a couple of weeks before it's a year."

"A year?"

"Yes, a year since Kyle died. I'm sure I'll be sad on that date. But Ray and all of us are getting together."

"What are you going to do?"

"We're getting together for a dinner party and just celebrating Kyle's life. To be supportive of each other "

"That sounds like fun. So you and Raymond are still close?"

"Yes. I saw a lot of him and Trent in Chicago."

"Trent?"

"Yes, that's Raymond's lover. He's a wonderful guy and he and Raymond seem so happy. I learned a lot from them."

"How so?"

"Well, I'm still learning. But being around Trent and Raymond, I was able to see a different kind of love. Two men deeply in love with each other. A relationship based on love and respect. The same thing Jared and I have."

"So you're more understanding of gay relationships?"

"Yes. I've got some great teachers. I'm going to spend a week with Delaney and Jody in March. So I'll be learning even more."

"Are you looking forward to that?"

"Yes. I'm excited about seeing Delaney and getting to know Jody better."

"Is Jared going with you?"

"I don't think so. He's going to Seattle with Raymond. Did I mention Raymond and Trent are thinking about moving there at the end of the summer. After the wedding."

"So Jared and Raymond are still close?"

"Yes, extremely."

"Are you okay with that?"

"Yes. There is a lot of love between the two of them. A different kind of love."

"Different?"

"Yes, different from Trent and Ray's love. But it's important to the both of them and I love seeing them together. It reminds me of Candance and myself."

"You have made a lot of progress, Nicole."

"Yes, I have. Did I tell you Ray's going to be the best man in the wedding?"

"No."

"Yes. I'm very happy about that. We joked about a month ago that we always figured we'd be together on my wedding day. Never in a million years like this. You know life is wonderful and funny," I said.

"Funny?"

"Yes, funny. I laugh when I think of my daddy, Kyle, and Candance up in heaven looking down and just getting a kick out of the chain of events."

"You think they're happy?"

"I know they are. I just want to do them proud."

"And what about yourself?"

"I'm proud. I'm in love and my life is really just beginning "

"Is your religion still important to you?"

"Oh yes. But I have everything in perspective. In a lot of ways it's better."

"How so?"

"Well, it's actually something my mother said."

"What did she say?"

"She said when you go to church, you go there for Christ. You don't look to the minister or members for that. You look behind the pulpit for Christ. It's a personal internal thing."

"You look very content, Nicole."

"I am. I just keep remembering what Kyle said to me one of the last times I saw him."

"Refresh my memory."

"God only gets mad at us when we come down here and pretend to be something we're not. That really pisses Him off."

"Nicole. You're laughing but I think I see tears."

"You do. But the tears are tears of joy."

"Why?"

"I'm finally living a life that wouldn't piss God or His newest angel off. I'm listening to my heart again."

Session's over.

About the Author

E. Lynn Harris is a former computer sales executive with IBM and an honors graduate of the University of Arkansas-Fayetteville. In 1991, Mr. Harris made a career change which resulted in the best-selling novel *Invisible Life*. *Just as I Am* is his second novel. An avid U of A Razorback sports fan, Lynn resides in Atlanta, Georgia, at work on his first nonfiction effort.